Large Print Fiction Mel
Meltzer, Brad.
The house of secrets

WITHDRAWN

GRAND CENTRAL
PUBLISHING

LARGE
PRINT

ALSO BY BRAD MELTZER

<u>Novels</u>
The Tenth Justice
Dead Even
The First Counsel
The Millionaires
The Zero Game
The Book of Fate
The Book of Lies
The Inner Circle
The Fifth Assassin
The President's Shadow

<u>Nonfiction</u>
Heroes for My Son
Heroes for My Daughter
History Decoded
I Am Amelia Earhart
I Am Abraham Lincoln
I Am Rosa Parks
I Am Albert Einstein
I Am Jackie Robinson
I Am Lucille Ball
I Am Helen Keller
I Am Martin Luther King, Jr.

ALSO BY TOD GOLDBERG

Gangsterland

THE HOUSE OF SECRETS

BRAD MELTZER
AND
TOD GOLDBERG

GRAND CENTRAL
PUBLISHING

LARGE PRINT

SALINE DISTRICT LIBRARY
555 N. Maple Rd
Saline, MI 481

JUN - - 2016

This book is a work of fiction. Names, characters, places, and incidents are the product of the authors' imagination or are used fictitiously. Any resemblance to actual events, locales, or persons, living or dead, is coincidental.

Copyright © 2016 by Forty-four Steps, Inc.

Cover design by Jeff Miller/Faceout Studios
Cover image of father and daughter © Joana Kruse/Arcangel Images
Cover copyright © 2016 by Hachette Book Group, Inc.

Hachette Book Group supports the right to free expression and the value of copyright. The purpose of copyright is to encourage writers and artists to produce the creative works that enrich our culture.

The scanning, uploading, and distribution of this book without permission is a theft of the authors' intellectual property. If you would like to use material from the book (other than for review purposes), please contact permissions@hbgusa.com. Thank you for your support of the authors' rights.

Grand Central Publishing
Hachette Book Group
1290 Avenue of the Americas
New York, NY 10104
grandcentralpublishing.com
twitter.com/grandcentralpub

First Edition: June 2016

Grand Central Publishing is a division of Hachette Book Group, Inc.
The Grand Central Publishing name and logo is a trademark of Hachette Book Group, Inc.

The publisher is not responsible for websites (or their content) that are not owned by the publisher.

The Hachette Speakers Bureau provides a wide range of authors for speaking events. To find out more, go to www.hachettespeakersbureau.com or call (866) 376-6591.

Library of Congress Control Number: 2016934287

ISBNs: 978-1-4555-5949-7 (hardcover), 978-1-4555-6615-0 (large print), 978-1-4555-5950-3 (ebook)

Printed in the United States of America

RRD-C

10 9 8 7 6 5 4 3 2 1

SALINE DISTRICT LIBRARY
555 N. Maple R.
Saline, MI 481

For Cori,
my werewolf
—BM

For Wendy
—TG

Acknowledgments

FIRST, FROM TOD:

My profound thanks to: My brother Lee Goldberg, who takes late-night phone calls and answers 2 a.m. emails on all manner of criminal issues, never mind putting this whole thing together; my agents Jennie Dunham and Judi Farkas, for their continued sage advice and wise counsel; Dr. Juliet McMullin, for a timely conversation on anthropology and an extensive reading list; Agam Patel, my ever patient coconspirator at UCR, for carrying the load on the days I was busy disposing of bodies; Mark Haskell Smith for, as usual, telling me what I needed to hear on precisely the days I needed to hear it; the faculty and students of the Low Residency MFA at UCR for their continued inspiration and, occasionally, a little help with a sentence or two. And, finally, I am indebted to Brad Meltzer, the best writing partner a boy could hope to have...and the most patient one too.

NOW HERE'S BRAD:

I thought we'd kill each other. I mean it. Everyone advised me to work with someone who wrote in a similar style: *You're a thriller writer; find another thriller writer*. Instead, I found the brilliant Tod Goldberg. So my first thank-you must go to him. Tod is a master of character. I love twisting the plot. In my head, I envisioned us as a literary Peanut Butter Cup. Together, we'd either mesh perfectly, or, as I mentioned, murder. So here's what I now know for sure: Wherever your life takes you, spend more time with people who can do things you can't. (Now that I think about it, I took the same approach in finding my wife.) Thank you, Tod, for being a true partner and dear friend. You amazed me on every page. Plus, I love the fact that no one laughed at our jokes as hard as we did.

As always, I thank my own beautiful werewolf, Cori, who always forces me to dig deeper, in every sense. I love you for believing in Hazel. Jonas, Lila, and Theo, this book is a lesson in family.

I am lost without you in mine. Thank you for letting me tell you the best stories. Jill Kneerim, my friend and agent, embraced me from Chapter 1, while friend and agent Jennifer Rudolph Walsh at WME helped us bring this book to reality; special thank-yous to Hope Denekamp, Lucy Cleland, Ike Williams, and all our friends at the Kneerim & Williams Agency.

Thanks to my sis, Bari, who understands what only a brother and sister can share. Also to Bobby, Ami, Adam, Gilda, and Will, for always cheering.

As always, our Hall of Justice was filled with Super Friends who pore over our pages: Noah Kuttler sits at the head of the table. Every time. Ethan Kline brainstorms from multiple countries. Then Dale Flam, Matt Kuttler, Chris Weiss, and Judd Winick help refine, refine, refine.

Every book, there's one person who steps up in such a profound way it impacts the entire production. For me, it was Lee Goldberg, who said these five magic words to me, "You should meet my brother." Lee, I'm so appreciative of your kindness and trust. And yes, you were right. The plot for this book was inspired by a trip into the treasure vault at the National Archives, so thank you to my dear friend, Archivist of the United States David S. Ferriero, for inviting me inside. Also at the National Archives (if you haven't been, go visit),

Matt Fulgham, Miriam Kleiman, Trevor Plante, and Morgan Zinsmeister are the kindest people around.

Extra thanks to Dr. Jeffery A. Lieberman for the brain and memory research. He shared so much scholarship and I'm sure we messed it up. Dr. Ronald K. Wright and Dr. Lee Benjamin for always helping me maim and kill; our family on *Decoded* and *Lost History*, and at HISTORY and H2, including Nancy Dubuc, Paul Cabana, Mike Stiller, and Russ McCarroll. Without you, Jack Nash would never come to life; and the rest of my own inner circle, who save me every day: Jo Ayn Glanzer, Jason Sherry, Marie Grunbeck, Chris Eliopoulos, Nick Marell, Staci Schecter, Jim & Julie Day, Denise Jaeger, Katriela Knight, and Brad Desnoyer.

The books *George Washington and Benedict Arnold: A Tale of Two Patriots* by Dave R. Palmer and *Benedict Arnold: A Traitor in Our Midst* by Barry K. Wilson were greatly informing to this process; Rob Weisbach for being the first; and of course, my family and friends, whose names, as always, inhabit these pages.

I also want to thank everyone at Grand Central Publishing: Michael Pietsch, Brian McLendon, Matthew Ballast, Caitlin Mulrooney-Lyski, Andy Dodds, Julie Paulauski, Tracy Dowd, Karen Torres,

Beth de Guzman, Lindsey Rose, Andrew Duncan, Liz Connor, the kindest and hardest-working sales force in show business, Bob Castillo, Mari Okuda, Thomas Whatley, and all my treasured friends there who always, always push for us. I've said it before, and I'll never stop saying it: They're the true reason this book is in your hands. I need to say a special thank-you and a sad farewell to editor Mitch Hoffman, who may have left the building but will never leave our family. Finally, I want to thank Jamie Raab. Every book, she understands me like no one else. She is our fearless leader and strongest champion. I am forever grateful that she's in my life. Thank you, Jamie, for your faith.

THE HOUSE OF SECRETS

Prologue

J ack Nash decides, at midnight on a Wednesday in the dead of summer in Los Angeles, that his daughter Hazel is ready for The Story.

He was six years old when his father first told him The Story. That's Hazel's age now—exactly six—and she's wide awake, forever asking *why* and *what*: Why does she need to go to sleep? What are dreams? Why do people die? What happens *after* people die?

"You'll know when it happens," Jack tells her.

Six is the appropriate age, Jack thinks.

Five years old was too young. Five is how old his son Skip was when Jack told him The Story and it hadn't stuck, didn't seem to make any impression whatsoever. Which got Jack wondering: How old do you have to be to retain an event for the rest of your life?

That was the thing about memory: After a

1

certain point, you just knew something. How you came to know it didn't matter.

"Okay, here we go," Jack says. "But promise me you won't let it scare you."

Hazel sits up on an elbow. "I won't be scared," she says solemnly. Jack knows it's true: Nothing scares Hazel. Not when she can learn something. She's the kind of child who would burn her right thumb on a hot stove, then come back the next day and burn her left in order to compare.

In an odd way, it made Jack proud. Hazel's brother Skip wouldn't touch the stove in the first place, always so cautious of everything. But Hazel was willing to give up a little skin for adventure.

"It begins with a mystery, a riddle," Jack says, and he can hear his father's voice, his father's words, so clearly. Dad's been gone five years now, but the memory of his last days is so vivid, it could have been thirty minutes ago. "If you figure the riddle out, you can stay up all night. If you can't, you need to go to sleep. Deal?"

"Deal," Hazel says.

"Close your eyes while I tell it to you," Jack says, slipping into The Voice, the same one his own dad used to use, the one Jack now uses on his TV show, where every week he explores the world's most famous conspiracies: Who killed JFK? Why did FDR have a secret fraternity known as The

Room? Or his favorite during sweeps: Outside of every Freemason meeting, there's a chair known as the Tyler's Chair; what are its true origins and secrets?

It's a show Hazel isn't allowed to watch. Jack's wife Claire worries the show will give Hazel bad dreams. But Jack knows that Hazel revels in nightmares, just like Jack used to: Something chasing you in your sleep was always far more interesting than fields of cotton candy.

"This story begins a hundred and fifty years ago, with a farmer," Jack says as Hazel leans farther forward on her elbow. "The farmer woke up early one morning to tend his fields, and a few yards from his house, he found a young man on the ground, frozen to death."

Hazel was fascinated by freezing—Jack and Claire constantly found random objects in the freezer, everything from dolls to plants to dead spiders.

"The farmer takes the body inside his farmhouse, puts a blanket on him to thaw him out, then goes and rouses the town doctor, bringing him back to look at the poor chap.

"When the doctor gets the dead man back to his office, he begins a basic autopsy. He's trying to find some identifying details to report to the mayor's office. But as he cuts open the man's chest, he

3

makes a surprising discovery..." And here, Jack does the same thing his own father did, and gives Hazel two brisk taps on the center of her breastbone, gives her a real sense of the space involved. "Right there, on the sternum and on the outside of his rib cage, he finds a small object the size of a deck of cards. It's encased in sealing wax. And as he cracks the wax open, he finds a miniature book."

"Would it even fit there?"

"Remember Grandpa's pacemaker? It'd fit. It's pocket-sized."

"What kind of book?" Hazel asks, eyes still closed.

"A bible. A small bible, perfectly preserved by the wax. And then, the man...opens...the... bible...up," Jack says, laying it on thick now, "and sees four handwritten words inside: *Property of Benedict Arnold.*"

Jack stops and watches Hazel. Her eyes have remained closed the entire time, but she keeps furrowing her brow, thinking hard. "So?" he says. "How did it get there?"

"Wait," Hazel says. "Who's Benedict Arnold?"

Don't they teach anything in school anymore?

"He was a soldier," Jack says. "During the Revolutionary War."

"A good guy or a bad guy?"

"A complicated guy," Jack says.

"Was the bible put in the man's body after he died?"

"No."

"How do you know?"

"There would have already been a wound on his chest."

"Was it his bible? Like, did he own it?"

"I don't know," Jack says, thinking, *Well, that's not a question I'd ever pondered.* Hazel's eyes flutter open, then close again tightly. She's checking to see if he's lying.

Hazel stays quiet for thirty seconds, forty-five, a minute. Then, "Why does it matter how it got there?"

"Because it's a mystery," Jack says. "And mysteries need to be solved."

Hazel considers this. "Do you know the answer?"

"I do."

"How many guesses do I get?"

"Three per night," Jack says.

She nods once, an agreement sealed. "Okay," she says, "lemme think."

Jack stays with her another ten minutes, then heads to his own bedroom, where Claire is up, reading. "Did you get her to sleep?" Claire asks.

"No," Jack says. "I gave her a riddle."

"Oh, Jack," Claire says, "you *didn't.*"

*　　　*　　　*

Hazel waits until she can hear her father and mother talking down the hall before she opens her eyes.

She gets up, walks across her room, opens the closet where she keeps her stuffed animals. The fact is, she doesn't really care for stuffed animals, thinks they're kind of creepy when you examine them closely: animals with smiles and fake shines in their eyes, no teeth, no real claws either. She quickly finds Paddington Bear, undresses him from his odd blue rain slicker, fishes out a pair of scissors from her desk, and then, very calmly, cuts open Paddington's chest.

Inside is nothing but fuzz, white and clumpy. It's nothing like how she imagines a body will be, but that doesn't matter. She pulls out all of the stuffing, leaves it in an orderly bunch on her bedroom floor, and then fills Paddington's empty cavity with a Choose Your Own Adventure paperback, the one where you pretended to be a spy, but where you mostly ended up getting run over by trucks. She then packs the bear back up with stuffing, staples his fur back together, makes Paddington look smooth and new and lovable, then puts his jacket back on. Adjusts his red cap.

Hazel then tiptoes out to the kitchen, finds the

stepladder, and slides it in front of the freezer. As she climbs up and examines the few packages of frozen food, she decides Paddington would be best served back behind the old flank steak that's been in the icebox for nine months now.

When her father asks her how the hell Paddington Bear ended up in the freezer, disemboweled and filled with a book, she'll give him her answer. *It's impossible*, she'll say.

Nothing is impossible, her father will say, because he is a man of belief.

Then it must have been magic, she'll say.

There's no magic, he'll say.

Then it must have been a person, trying to fool you, she'll say.

And she will be right.

1

Summer, Utah
Now

"Let's see what this old bruiser can do," Jack Nash says. He's behind the wheel of his '77 sky blue Cadillac Eldorado with a trunk big enough to lie down in, and he's hurtling down Highway 163 through the Utah desert. It's not even 10 a.m. and Hazel's sitting next to him, Skip's in the backseat. There's a lifetime of polish and pain between them all. But isn't that how it always is? He presses the gas and the Caddy thunders forward.

"Maybe take it down a notch, Dad?" Skip says. Jack catches a glimpse of his son in the rearview mirror. He's looking a little peaked. Thirty-nine years old and he still gets carsick. "You get a ticket at your age," Skip adds, "you're liable to lose your license."

Your age. How old does Jack feel? In his mind, he's still in his thirties—sometimes he feels like

9

he's a teenager even—but Jack knows his brain is a liar. His body has been telling him the truth for some time now. No one ever says seventy is the new forty. Seventy...that's the line where if you die, people don't get to say it was a tragedy.

"Just keep an eye out for cops," Jack says.

Hazel rolls her eyes, rubbing absently at a small knot on her forehead, a bruise just below her hairline. A wound from a fight she'll never talk about.

"The speedometer only goes to eighty-five?" Hazel asks.

Jack rolls his eyes, knowing all too well how easily his daughter finds trouble. But that was the nice thing about these old cars built to go fifty-five. Eighty-five seemed extravagant. Cars these days went to 140, 160, sometimes 170. Or their speedometers did, anyway. A false sense of a new horizon, that's what that was.

This stretch of the 163 is one of Jack's favorite swaths of land. It's all red today, from red sand to red glare, everything the color of dried blood. It's the beauty and grace of the natural world: The massive sandstone spires are the result of millions of years of erosion and pressure, alongside the forbidding truth of the desert, which is that you're always one wrong move from something that could kill you.

A rattlesnake.

A scorpion.

Even the very air itself, which could end you with heat or cold, it didn't discriminate. Out here, dying from exposure was just dying.

Beautiful. Made you feel alive.

The first time Jack and his kids were here was decades ago. Same car. Back then, Claire was up front next to him, both of the kids in the back, the tape player screaming out the Rolling Stones, Jack's favorite band. "Jumpin' Jack Flash" was his song, of course.

Skip was a teenager and in the midst of another season of *The House of Secrets* alongside his famous father. From the start, everyone knew it was a ratings ploy, like introducing a new baby on a sitcom, and like the worst of those, they started calling Skip "Scrappy" from *Scooby-Doo*. Still, it put his face on posters in *Tiger Beat*. A mistake? Probably. No, surely. But Skip loved it. Hazel was just a kid, but ready for the world...just a world different from the one Skip was living in.

They'd driven from Los Angeles to Zion to Bryce to Moab, Claire's hand on Jack's thigh, tapping out the beat. If he concentrates, he can still feel it there, *bump-bump-uh-dun-uh-duh-dun-uh-duh, But it's allll right now*...

Jack eases off the accelerator. "We need to talk," he says, "about the future."

*　　　*　　　*

Jack Nash has three rules. He came up with them when he started in TV news, before he got into the mystery business. He'd read a bunch of autobiographies and found that every successful person had some sort of code.

The first was that there was a rub in every deal—a snag or a drawback; there was always a catch. Once you understood that, there were no bad deals.

The second was that nothing goes missing. Everything is *somewhere*.

This was actually a rule of Claire's, from when the kids were still young. Whenever they said they'd lost something—a toy, the dog, their favorite shirt—she very calmly explained to them that just because something was gone didn't mean it'd ceased to exist. But then Claire got sick, and he couldn't help but wonder if that rule needed some amending, because while she was still there, she began to disappear a bit every day. First it was her hair. Then her teeth. And then one morning, he woke up and she was gone entirely.

For a while he still felt her presence in the house, like she was just in the other room, or out in the yard, and he'd absently call out to her, habit somehow getting in the way of grief. Eventually, that feeling went away and now Jack only feels her in the place between sleep and waking, can almost feel her sitting on the edge of the bed, watching him.

Claire's been gone ten years now. How Jack wishes she were here. She's *somewhere*. Jack knows this. He found her in the first place, he'll find her again. He thinks maybe he's closer to her now than ever, particularly with how every day he feels a little shorter of breath, how there are days when he can't feel his fingertips. His doctor told him it was a blood flow problem.

He needed to take his meds.

Eat right.

Get exercise.

Slow down. He got a second opinion, a third; they all told him the same thing. Can't feel your fingertips? Take a nitro. The nitro doesn't work, call 911. Can't get to a phone? Get right with your soul.

He was trying by practicing his third rule: Honor the people who love you.

Jack realized early on that rules one and three didn't quite work together. Sometimes the rub is that the people who love you wouldn't recognize your logic, not when it comes to matters of business. So maybe they aren't *rules*, Jack considers today, all these years later. Maybe they are *truths*.

And the thing about truth, well, it doesn't always need to be fact based.

Indeed, when Jack picked his son up in Las Vegas, where Skip had been signing autographs at a convention, and where he'd been living—"for tax purposes," Skip told him—and when Hazel flew in from some anthropology conference, Jack wasn't even sure if he could go through with his plan to lay it all out. *It was an anniversary trip*, he'd told them, *for Claire*, which got both of the kids to grudgingly agree to check out of their own lives for a week. But the fact was, he wanted to put a bow on another part of their lives too.

"I'm done," Jack says. "I'm ending the TV show."

"What? *Why?*" Skip asks.

"Time to live like a normal person."

"Isn't it a little late for that?" Hazel says.

Probably, Jack thinks. "Maybe I have fifteen years left," he says. "I'd like to enjoy them."

"Don't say that," Skip says. "Soon as you put a number on things, you start counting toward it. That's bad juju."

Now Jack was the one rolling his eyes. *Skip.* A childhood nickname that stuck. No man should enter his fifth decade still saddled with a nickname, Jack thinks, unless it's something like Alexander the Great, except even Alexander the Great was dead at thirty-two. Skip's real name was Nicholas, but it was Jack's own father who'd crowned him years before. As in, *Maybe it will skip a generation.*

"You're finally being smart. You should've done it years ago," Hazel says. "You outlasted Jacques Cousteau. Go ahead—pull the plug and enjoy."

Hazel. She'd taken after her mother in so many ways that it was often hard for Jack to be around her anymore. Her face, her voice, even her hand gestures, reminded him of Claire so much that it hurt to be near her. They also had the same temper—and the same reckless attraction to destruction.

How many times had Jack been woken by the police, Hazel in the back of a squad car? How many phone calls had he made, even in the last year, to keep charges from being filed against her for assault...or mayhem...or whatever charge the police wanted to hang on her? Jack tried to harness it—in his line of work, especially the parts of his life he hid from everyone else, fearlessness was what kept him alive. But then Claire saw what he was doing, and that was the end. *I will not let you put her in that business.* Over the years, Hazel had found her own business. She was a pilgrim, a professor, and never exactly risk-averse.

"But the fans..." Skip said.

"*Don't,*" Hazel warned, her temper already

showing. "When was the last time the fans were ever happy?"

She was right about that too.

For the first few seasons, it was enough to find some old NASA employees who swore the moon landing was fake...or the woman who woke up one day and suddenly could speak Latin. All Jack had to do was nod and show that perfect amount of empathy. Just because something seemed implausible didn't mean it wasn't true.

But then people started to need more, something a bit less static. And that meant Jack had to go into the field, begin actually *investigating* the mysteries of the world, even solving them when he could. That was the thing about the mystery business: Every now and then, you had to unravel one, or else the viewers would begin to think everything was fake, or, alternatively, that the world really was a series of vast, unending conspiracies meant to keep them from knowing the truth.

That's what it always boiled down to. People weren't happy unless they believed at least part of the world was some grand hoax. It's what had made Watergate so compelling. Everything everyone suspected *was* true: Government was corrupt, the world was being manipulated, nothing was on the level...and it took a couple of guys named Bob and Carl to figure it all out. But as Jack knew, most times, mysteries didn't have satisfying endings. Like the death of JFK. No one wanted to believe Oswald acted alone, because then that story was done.

The world was so different now. Anyone could see anything. And the government? Between the robots, drones, and Navy SEALS, they had more people working for them than against them. Whatever Jack Nash could find hardly mattered. He was a cog. The machine was so big now, it could withstand a few loose screws.

"Can you even be happy?" Skip asks. "Away from it?"

As soon as he found the book. No, not just a book. A bible. *The* bible. It was so close to him now. If he closed his eyes, he could see it, right in front of him, there in the desert, swirling in the wind.

"That's the last mystery," Jack says, his words slurring.

"Dad, you all right?" Hazel asks quietly. She's looking at him strangely, he thinks. Like she's studying him, cataloguing him, breaking him into parts, like she does. She puts her hand on his elbow. "You look flushed."

"Never better," Jack says. Outside, the desert suddenly blooms white, the sand so luminous that it reminds Jack of the Sahara. "There's something else I want to tell you."

"We know, Dad," Skip says. "Honor the people who love you. You've told us a million times."

"Your color isn't good," Hazel says. "Your face is red. Why don't you pull over? Let me drive."

"Everything is red here," Jack says, but no, no, it's white now. Everything awash in light. Is he on a beach? He thinks he might be. The salt on his lips. The waves in his ears. Yes. He's not driving a car. He's asleep on some further shore. Wasn't he about to say something?

"Dad!" Hazel shouts, grabbing the wheel. "Dad, can you hear me!?"

He feels the waves settling in his chest, not a bad feeling, no. The light has turned from red to white to a brilliant yellow, the desert transforming right before his eyes. Do the kids see it? They must. They must see it.

He hopes they finally do.

2

Los Angeles
Eight days later

"—azel-Ann? Hazel-Ann, can you hear me?"

Hazel-Ann Nash blinked through the darkness, squinting at the blinding light.

"*She's alert!*" a man called out. White coat. Doctor. Hospital.

The doctor was shouting questions in her face, but as she anxiously glanced around, her eyes...*Why weren't her eyes working?* It was like they focused only for a second, pinging from the bed she was in, to the dead TV, to the hand sanitizer on the wall, to the whiteboard with the handwritten words:

I am Hazel-Ann Nash and I am feeling

_____.

Was that really her name? *Hazel-Ann?* Something was wrong. How could she not know her name?

BRAD MELTZER AND TOD GOLDBERG

Her heartbeat pulsed in her tongue, her gums, her ears. Her instinct was to run, though that didn't make sense. Why would you run from a hospital?

"Can you feel this, Hazel-Ann?" the doctor asked, stabbing parts of her body.

The problem was she could feel *everything*. She wasn't entirely sure why she was in a hospital, though judging from the way every part of her felt as if it had been set on fire and then extinguished using a brick, she guessed she'd been in some kind of accident.

"Can you feel *this*, Hazel-Ann?" the doctor asked. He poked the bottom of her foot.

"Hazel," she blurted, suddenly sure of only one thing. She didn't like being called Hazel-Ann. She ran her tongue over her top teeth. They were all there. A couple of jagged edges. That wasn't good.

The doctor was about her age, thirty-five, maybe a few years older. As he leaned over her bed, Hazel could see that he'd missed a spot while shaving that morning. Right above his Adam's apple was a clump of long hairs. She wanted to reach up and yank them out, show him how it felt to be yelled at and stabbed, but her arms were immobilized, hooked to a latticework of IVs. And besides, the doctor had kind eyes, deep blue.

"Hazel," he said, "do you know where you are?"

Did she? Where had she been that day? Utah. Yes. Monument Valley. With her brother...Skip, his name was Skip—and her father, Jack.

She could remember eating fry bread at a highway stop. A Navajo man dusted it with cinnamon and slipped them a few extra pieces when he recognized her father—the famous Jack Nash—from his forever-running TV show, *The House of Secrets*. As they ate, her mother was in the dirt parking lot, banging the horn from the passenger seat—

No.

Wait.

Her mother was dead. Ten years now. Brain cancer. She could remember her mom in the casket, could remember the sun so hot that day that everyone at the graveside was sipping ice water from red Solo cups.

But that wasn't today, couldn't have been today. It was as if there were two memories occupying the same space.

"Moab?" Hazel said.

The doctor turned toward a nurse Hazel hadn't noticed before, or maybe the nurse had just walked in. Nothing was firing right. The nurse wore a blue V-neck smock and had a clipboard in her hands, but she was just staring at Hazel with honest concern. Hazel's father once told her that if she was ever scared on a plane, all she had to do was look to see if the flight attendants seemed worried. If they did, buckle up.

"I need a seat belt," Hazel blurted, though she hadn't meant to speak. Her voice sounded all wrong.

"Hazel, you've been in a car accident," the doctor said as Hazel noticed he had a bit of pepper stuck above one of his incisors. It was all she could focus on, that lack of attention to detail, the failure to realize that he'd left a mess in his own mouth. "Do you remember anything about an accident?"

She could see her father's hands on the steering wheel of his Cadillac, Skip reaching for her from the backseat, the smell of her father's ever-present mint gum.

"What hospital is this?" she asked, hearing her voice shake.

"UCLA Medical Center. In Los Angeles. I'm Dr. Morrison. I'm taking care of you. Everything is going to be just fine."

Los Angeles was where she'd grown up. She knew that.

"What else do you remember?" Dr. Morrison asked. His tone made Hazel feel there was something bad in the answer.

"I need to see Skip," she said.

"We'll let him know you're awake again."

Again.

"How long have I been out?"

"Intermittently," he said, "for eight days."

Her heartbeat pulsed faster than ever. Nothing made sense. Maybe she *should* run. But she could hear her dad's voice. *Nothing good comes from panic.* Old instincts kicked in. Look around. Examine. Assess. She turned to the nurse, trying to gauge her reaction.

"I need to see my father," Hazel demanded.

"Everything is going to be fine," Dr. Morrison said for the second time. "Can you tell me what you do for a living, Hazel?"

"Anthropology professor. At San Francisco State," she said. Yes. That's right. That's where she honed her skills. Examine. Assess. "I study death. All its rituals."

"That's good," Dr. Morrison said. "Can you tell me your parents' names?"

"Jack and Claire."

"What about your grandparents?"

"Cyrus and . . . and Patricia," Hazel said, naming her dad's parents. As for her mother's parents, their names were lost in her brain. "I can't remember my mother's parents."

"That's okay," Dr. Morrison said, shining a light in her eye. "I should tell you," he added, an odd tic

Hazel noticed, that he seemed to be forewarning, subtly preparing her for whatever he was going to say next, "these next few days will be hard."

"I need to see my father," Hazel said, gripping the sheets because she had to grip something. Find calm. Observe. Assess. *I am Hazel-Ann Nash and I am feeling* _____.

"Janice is going to take care of you," he explained, motioning to the nurse.

As the doctor stepped out into the hallway, he was approached quickly by another man, this one in a black suit, white shirt, maroon tie, who stepped beside the doctor and examined the chart too. They both had their backs to her, but she saw the way the doctor shook his head. His hand went absently to his throat, his fingers lingering on those missed whiskers.

The man in the suit put his hands on his hips and pushed his jacket away from his body, which is when Hazel saw his holster. And gun.

A SIG Sauer, Hazel thought, though she had no idea where the hell that thought came from.

"Where's my dad?" Hazel repeated.

The nurse bit down on her lip and Hazel saw tears well up in her eyes. "People..." Janice said. "People loved your father."

3

Shanghai, China

The Bear gets the call. He's at a French café on Yongkang Road, eating his *pain au chocolat*. He lets himself have one a week, after he does his roadwork. No sense running ten miles without a tangible reward at the end.

"She'll live," he's told through his cell phone.

The Bear considers this, trying to figure out if it's his problem yet. "She's in the hospital?" he asks.

"Yes. Los Angeles."

"What's her present condition?" He never says the name Hazel. Or Skip. That way, if some idiot happens to be eavesdropping, they won't hear anything remotely compelling, or, better, they'll think he's a doctor.

Today, the only other person in the café is a young woman hunched over a laptop. She has giant headphones over her ears, and The Bear thinks how funny it is that for a while everyone wanted headphones to be small and inconspicuous and then, suddenly, they wanted them to be huge, so that everyone could tell you wanted your privacy.

"Stabilized."

The Bear isn't surprised. Brawlers like Hazel don't go down easy.

He gets the full list: broken rib, a bruised sternum, deep lacerations to her face and hands—all standard, the sort of injuries caused by seat belts as much as by the accident itself—and then the one that's had her out for so long: her brain's been scrambled, something with her amygdala. Her wiring crossed. Not amnesia, of course, because no one actually gets amnesia, The Bear knows. It's like all of the myths of childhood that have turned out to be complete bunk. It's too bad. If he could give himself a tap on the forehead to selectively erase a few things, well, he'd pick up the nicest hammer on the market.

"When will she be released?"

"Unclear. We're trying to figure out what she remembers." A pause. "There are additional problems."

The Bear listens intently for another few minutes. "I will take care of these issues," he says, "and then our association is complete, correct?"

"Correct."

The Bear swipes his phone off, which is always so unsatisfying. In the old days, he'd have yanked a cord from the wall, wrapped it around his fist, and watched his hand turn purple, a good way to harness and control anger. But now he was just staring at a bucolic photo of a pink rose in bloom. He needed to figure out how to change that. The photo and his anger management.

He pulls up his email, reading the newest file. It's a scan of a typed letter on government stationery, filled with terrible misspellings, a total disregard for the difference between *your* and *you're*. It's also filled with classified information. From the FBI.

The Bear wolfs down the rest of his *pain au chocolat*, savors the buttery aftertaste on his tongue. The Bear thinks he will run an additional mile or two. Thinks it would be good to get his endurance up. He can't be groggy; his body isn't so finely tuned anymore. Age. A real sonofabitch, indiscriminate in its application.

His phone buzzes. More emails. A plane ticket. Directions. Orders.

There's also a photo. From New Brunswick, Canada. Of course. The onetime home of Benedict Arnold.

The Bear steps outside, finds the sun.

He loves Canada in the early summer. But not as much as Los Angeles.

Lovely. Perfect.

He's been in hibernation for too long. Time to sharpen the claws.

4

UCLA *Medical Center*
Two days later

W hat's your favorite color?"
"Red?" Hazel said from her hospital bed. That's the color she saw when she closed her eyes. She could imagine a little red dress, her shoulders bare. She was walking into a room as people turned to look at her. A dance? No. A cocktail party. Italy? Yes. Italy. That's what it was.

"You hate red," Skip said, blowing steam off his coffee.

"How can I hate a color?" Hazel asked.

"You can learn to hate anything," Skip said. "Believe me." His face was still a bit black and blue from the accident—he'd broken his nose and had an orbital fracture, minor injuries compared to Hazel's—and it looked like maybe he was wearing concealer under his eyes. He'd been on TV since he was seven years old. Hazel guessed that made him an expert on more things than she could imagine.

"How come I can't remember you, though?"

"You know I'm your brother."

"I know, but the *details* of our lives together…the last time I saw you…where you live…any meals we might've eaten…Those memories are gone. I don't even know my favorite restaurant, or favorite crappy movie, or even if I like you or not."

"With looks like this, what's not to love?"

"I'm serious, Skip." On the whiteboard, it now read: *I am Hazel and I am feeling frustrated*. It was a generous word. *Disbelief* was more like it. Or *pure shock*. The doctors told her to give it time, that maybe her memories would come back. Or not. It'd already been two days. Two days with barely any sleep. Two days where she couldn't taste anything (though they said that may not be permanent), but still, two days of her not knowing what to say when the nurses asked which Cheerios she liked better, plain or Honey Nut? *How the hell could I not know that!?* she wanted to scream. But something told her to keep her calm in front of the doctors, the nurses, and even Skip.

Was that her relationship with her brother? According to the nurses, for over a week now, even when Hazel was unconscious, Skip was here every day, bringing old photos and sitting by her side, rubbing her arm the way she likes it. If that wasn't love, what was it? Skip was being the perfect brother. So why was she so guarded around him? Is that how she dealt with everyone? The scariest part was, she didn't know that either.

"It's the same with Dad," she explained. "Online, I found an article from a year ago. It said Dad passed out in a grocery store in Encino. Full tachycardia followed by a stent in his heart. Where was I for all that?"

Skip took a sip from his coffee. "Wherever it is you go," he said. "Beirut, I think. Maybe Iran. Digging in the sand. Mom used to call it your *continental drift*."

For some reason, that sounded like her mom. *Continental drift.* "What about what they're saying online? About Dad getting too close to the truth?"

"So now the *government* killed him? Or maybe the Illuminati, the Masons, the Bilderbergs, or those damn poorly dressed pilgrims from the lost colony at Roanoke. Some even say," Skip began, and suddenly he was their father, his voice a perfect imitation, "it could've been...*dark magic!*"

Hazel burst out laughing. "He did love invoking a good Nazi curse." She'd caught the tail end of a *Secrets* marathon the night before on the TV in her room. If there was one thing she'd learned, it was that if a mystery's solution was a little shallow, muddy the waters with lore.

"The coroner said it was a heart attack. But even if you disagree, do you know how many people it takes to run a worldwide conspiracy?" Skip asked. "How many man-hours? People get bored, take other jobs, focus on their families, get old, get colon cancer, whatever, and then you gotta get new people and pay for their training. So get these giant organizations out of your head. No one wants to rule the world anymore. That's a horrible job."

"So you don't think it's someone you and Dad met... *in the House of Secrets*?" Hazel said, using her father's voice now too, not even on purpose. Right there, she realized *this* was the lexicon of her relationship with Skip: the mocking, the teasing, thirtysomething brother and sister still peppering their conversations with the tiny triggers of their childhood. It made her happy. A piece of her showing up when she least expected it.

"One last question," Hazel said. "Do I have any friends? Why hasn't anyone come to visit me? Am I not a nice person?"

"That's three questions," Skip said. "It's like you have a brain injury."

It was a joke, but Hazel felt Skip evading her, as if he were pretending he hadn't heard her.

"Skip," she said, "I need to know."

Skip looked at her. "Do you remember Darren Nixon?"

Hazel thought for a moment. "I don't know who that is."

"I figured."

"So who is he?"

"No one. Friend from childhood," Skip said, grabbing the remote and putting on the TV.

Hazel didn't know much about her brother. But she knew a lie when she heard one.

"You brought him up for a reason, Skip. Tell me who Darren Nixon is."

"Will you stop? Since when are you so paranoid?"

For Skip, it was yet another joke, but all it did was remind her how much her brain was misfiring. Facts were easy for her, especially her research. If she closed her eyes, she could practically recite the Edwin Smith Papyrus, an ancient Egyptian medical manual. But when it came to *people*—to memories, especially about herself— there was so little she could recall. It was like looking through gauze. So yes, maybe Hazel wasn't paranoid in her old life. But she certainly didn't feel like someone who apologized for being who she was, whoever that was.

"Skip, there's a computer in the waiting room.

Plus every nurse on the floor has a phone with a Web browser on it. You can tell me now or I can go out there and look him up myself. Now who's Darren Nixon?"

"I'm telling you, it's nothing. He's someone who knew Dad."

"Knew him how?" Hazel was about to ask. Instead, she glanced out into the hallway. There he was again, the man in the dark suit. The one with the gun. The SIG Sauer.

Skip looked out into the hallway too, then back at the remote.

But as Hazel saw the man lock eyes with Skip...as her brother shot this stranger a quick look right back, one thing was clear: These two men knew each other. And they were keeping that information from Hazel.

"Hey! You! Guy in suit!" Hazel shouted.

The man kept walking, like he didn't have a care in the world. This was a hospital. If you're here, you have a care.

"I'm talking to you! *Who's Darren Nixon!?"* Hazel called out.

"What're you doing?" Skip hissed.

The man turned the corner by the nurses' station, nearly out of sight.

"I know you heard me!" she added, louder than ever. "I'll keep yelling until someone puts it

into Google! Darren Nixon! *Darren Nixon!* Spelled *D-A-R-R-E-N—!*"

The man with the gun stopped. Without a word, he turned, heading straight for Hazel's room. Skip twisted in his seat, refusing to look at him.

"Ms. Nash, I think you made your point," the man said.

"Don't tell me you're Darren Nixon," Hazel said.

"No." He shut the door, then reached into his jacket for— Not his gun. His ID. He flashed a shiny gold badge. From the FBI. "I used to work with your father."

5

"Skip, call security," Hazel said.

Skip stared at her.

"Skip, you hear what I—?" Skip was still silent. "Wait," she said to her brother. "You know this guy, *don't you?*"

"I didn't say that."

"You don't have to! I see it on your face!"

"Haze, before you go explosive—"

"Don't. I was trying to like you, and now you're *lying* to me?"

"I'm not lying! I met him last week. I swear on my eyes. He came up to me in the hospital cafeteria, flashed his shiny badge, and asked me about Dad. Wanted to know if I knew this guy Darren Nixon."

"And you didn't tell me this?"

"You're kidding, right? You can't come up with your favorite color and I'm supposed to tell you that the FBI wants to chat?"

"Ms. Nash, I can explain," the man in the suit said. According to his ID, his name was Trevor Rabkin. He was over six feet tall, wide across the shoulders, and handsome in a bland way. His black hair was short, his blue suit nice, though not expensive. More Jos. A. Bank than Brooks Brothers. And it was wool—too hot for the summer—which meant it was probably what he had, not what he wanted to wear.

"I used to work with your father," Rabkin said.

"You said that already. What kind of work?" Hazel asked.

Agent Rabkin didn't answer, which made Hazel think he wasn't just a guest on her father's show.

"Haze, he just wants to ask you a few questions," Skip said.

"And I just want to know what kind of work you did with our dad, because even with my brain not working, I feel like I'd remember if he was doing favors for the government."

Rabkin was still silent.

"Oh, c'mon, can you please spare us the tough-silent-guy thing?" Hazel said, fighting her urge to kick him out on his ass. Just by being here, the FBI was interfering with her recovery. But if Hazel wanted answers—if she wanted to know why the FBI was suddenly sniffing around—there was only one way to find out. "You obviously were doing something with our father, you couldn't get what-ever info you wanted from Skip, and you wouldn't be here if you didn't have something you were hoping to get from me. Now who's Darren Nixon?"

Rabkin stepped deeper into the room, scan-ning each corner. At the foot of her bed, he picked up her chart and paged through it, the way people who don't read do, as if by fanning the pages some fascinating aspect of the story would be revealed to them.

Hazel wondered why he was alone. Didn't the FBI always travel in pairs? And why did she know that?

"Do you know where your father was the week before he died?" Agent Rabkin asked.

Hazel shook her head. That memory, like so many others, was gone.

"Filming," Skip said.

"Exactly," Rabkin said. "Filming yet another sea-son of *The House of Secrets*, this one a special episode about some new scientific breakthrough that they hope can help them authenticate the Shroud of Turin."

"What's this have to do with Darren Nixon?"

"The show was filming in Tucson, Arizona, where the science lab is. But for one of the days, your dad took a day-trip to Spokane, Washington..."

"Can you please stop doing that thing with your voice?" Hazel said. "You sound like my father doing a tease before a commercial break. We get it. My dad went to Spokane."

"And while in Spokane, he went to visit a man named..."

"Darren Nixon," Skip said.

Hazel shot an annoyed look at Skip.

"Two days after that, Darren Nixon was found dead in New Brunswick, Canada, facedown in a mini-golf amusement park, of all places. Your father was Nixon's last known visitor."

Skip took half a step back. This was news to him too.

Hazel felt herself indexing the evidence Agent Rabkin was presenting about himself. His white button-down shirt had metal collar stays, held down by magnets. A nice touch, offset by the fact that his red tie looked like it hadn't been untied in ten years. He had a day's worth of beard and a little cut on his neck, like his razor was dull. No cologne. A tan line where his ring should be. Like he'd just taken the ring off for the occasion.

"Does your wife know what kind of cases you work on?" she asked.

Agent Rabkin stared at Hazel for a few seconds, not speaking. "Not anymore."

"So now you come in here and want us to

believe that my father might've killed this man Nixon?" Hazel asked.

"I didn't say that; you did. What caught our attention was the cause of death. According to the coroner, Nixon's body was cold to the touch and thawing out. Like he'd been frozen. And then, when they cut Nixon open . . . well, just under the skin of his chest they found a—"

"Book," Hazel said.

Rabkin looked at her. "Not just a book—"

"A bible," Hazel blurted. "A bible that belonged to Benedict Arnold."

Skip turned her way. Rabkin took half a step to the side, like he was ducking a punch.

"Hazel, how the hell'd you know that?" Skip asked.

6

"ho told you about the bible?" Rabkin asked.

"I don't know," Hazel said, still in the hospital bed. She closed her eyes. Tried to focus.

She'd heard this story before.

Mysteries need to be solved.

A dead body.

Something hidden inside it.

Some of the details were so clear; others were lost.

She opened her eyes. Agent Rabkin and Skip were still staring at her.

"I think my dad told it to me," Hazel said.

"He didn't tell it to *me*, that's for sure," Skip said, standing from his seat and walking over to the window, but never taking his eyes off Hazel. His voice was shaking. "I'd remember something gory like that."

"So you think this bible, you think it was something your dad was *searching* for?" Rabkin asked, glancing back down at Hazel's chart. "Or was it something he already *had*?"

Hazel looked away, toward her reflection in the TV above her bed. Rabkin wouldn't be here if he didn't think Hazel knew something. "I'm not sure," she said, meaning it completely. "But New Brunswick, Canada—where you found the body: Wasn't that where Benedict Arnold lived right before he died?"

"He died in London," Rabkin said. He had an unblinking intensity that Hazel found familiar, as if everything he said he'd read somewhere else. Which was probably true. "After the Canadians got tired of him."

"Time-out," Skip said. "Why would you think my dad had this bible?"

"That's classified," Rabkin said, Hazel watching him work through those words for a second before he uttered them. *Classified.* Like he liked saying it. He was still new at this. "What I can tell you is: Two weeks ago, on June 19, your father had a private meeting in Spokane, Washington, with a young man named Darren Nixon. Two days later, Nixon was found dead in one of the last places Benedict Arnold lived. And three days after that, your father was dead too. So either we've got a hell of a coincidence, or..."

"You think someone murdered my dad," Hazel said.

Rabkin didn't say a word.

"I thought they said it was a heart attack," Skip said. "We saw it happen. I saw it with my own eyes." Skip paced the room. "You telling me the coroner lied to me? Is that what it's come to now?"

"Sit down, Skip," Hazel said, but he didn't. To her left, on the side table, was a framed photo Skip had brought to the room. The doctors said old photos might jar some memories. This one was of her and her father at a Dodgers game. She must have loved LA as a kid. That's what the pictures seemed to show, anyway. If she'd loved it here, though, wouldn't she have stayed? Why would she spend most of her adult life studying other cultures, digging into unchangeable history? What had she been looking for all this time?

It didn't matter, Hazel realized, because the government didn't send FBI agents to Los Angeles hospitals to say hi to anthropology professors. This was about her father. About what he knew. About what he'd left behind. About the last mystery. And then she heard those words too: *That's the last mystery.* And then. As the car swerved...the red.

"Can I just say," Skip began, "I don't get who

Darren Nixon is, but if my dad really was going all holy grail on Benedict Arnold's bible, I'd know. I talked to him every day. I knew what made his nose twitch. Anything JFK-related? Sure. Thomas Jefferson–related? Check. He also had a true soft spot for Jack the Ripper and, for some reason, life-after-death experiences—we did over two dozen shows on that. But never—not *once*—did he mention Benedict Arnold or his bible."

"Maybe this was the secret he kept from everyone," Rabkin said.

"Then you don't know my father. He was on TV for four decades. He outlasted Jacques Cousteau, Crocodile Hunter Steve Irwin, even that guy from *America's Most Wanted*, and he did it for one reason: He didn't chase anything unless he could put it on television. So again: What's so special about Benedict Arnold's prayer book? Who gave it to Arnold? Where'd it come from?"

"Now you're asking the right question," Agent Rabkin said. "The bible was a gift to Arnold. From a man named George Washington."

7

T hat's the absolute stupidest thing I've ever heard," Skip said. "And I've spent half my life in meetings with Hollywood executives."

"Skip, be quiet," Hazel said, swinging her legs out of bed and standing up, despite the pain. To Rabkin, she added, "Tell me the story about Benedict Arnold."

"You should look it up. The last moments between Benedict Arnold and George Washington are among the most heartbreaking in U.S. history," Rabkin said. "It starts when Benedict Arnold is revealed as a traitor. Right there, Benedict realizes the gig is up—he's been found out, and it's all happening right as George Washington himself is about to arrive at Arnold's home for a visit. Good china is on the table. Linens are washed. The best wine is ready. Two old friends, you understand, that's what they were." He paused. "Of course,

Washington hasn't heard the news yet. He has no idea his dear friend is a turncoat. But in a panic, Benedict Arnold races out of the house. He leaves his wife and kid behind, jumps on his horse, and rides away, toward the British."

Hazel knew the details were right, but what gnawed at her was that it sounded like Rabkin had just looked the story up himself. He had the facts, but he didn't have the emotions. For two days now, that exact feeling pained Hazel more than anything. She saw a commercial for Corona beer, but couldn't remember the last time she had one; she found a scar on her shoulder, but didn't know how it got there. Without the emotional context, it was like she wasn't living in her own head; she was occupying someone else's. Indeed, as Rabkin was proving, emotions were the key to understanding the historical relevance of something. People did horrible things to each other, the same kinds of things over and over again. It was the *why* that mattered. Rabkin only had the *what*.

"I'm confused," Skip said. "Why didn't Arnold take his family with him?"

"It was war," Rabkin said. "You don't bring your wife and kid to war."

"So where's the bible come in?" Skip asked.

"When Washington learns what's happened, he's devastated," Rabkin said. "He trusted Arnold.

They'd fought together, lost the same friends, even loved the same people. And on top of that, Arnold wasn't just trying to hand over the country. He was handing over Washington himself. If the plan had worked, the British would've hung George Washington in public. When Washington hears the news, they say it's the only time the father of our country is ever seen crying."

"Who's *they*?" Skip asked. "Who's the mysterious *they* that always knows everything?"

"Historians," Hazel said. "Go on."

"Then Alexander Hamilton shows up," Rabkin said, "and delivers a handwritten letter from Benedict Arnold to George Washington. In it, Benedict asks his old friend for three things: 1) He wants Washington to protect Arnold's wife Peggy Shippen, who everyone in the country wants to see with a noose around her neck. 2) He said that all of Washington's aides are innocent and had nothing to do with Arnold's treason, so please let them live. And 3) In one of the oddest requests a person could make in such a moment, Benedict Arnold asks that his *clothes and baggage* be sent to him."

"What's so important about his baggage?" Skip asked.

"That's the question, isn't it?" Rabkin said. "Benedict Arnold has just put a knife in the back of his best friend, become one of the most hated men since Judas, has basically abandoned his life, and his wife is in danger of being murdered—and what does he ask for? He wants his *luggage*. He says he'll even pay for the freight, if need be."

"If I were George Washington," Skip said, "I would've lit it all on fire. Burned it like it was Atlanta."

"Wrong war," Hazel said. Not that it mattered. If there was one constant in history, it was that the victors torched property, salted the earth, destroyed all the old idols. No sense warehousing the past when you could obliterate it entirely. Which made this all the more curious.

"Most people would've taken revenge," Rabkin agreed. "But for some reason, Washington obliges. It's a moment no one can explain. Washington hates this man. He spends the rest of the war hunting him and calling for his death. So why in God's name does he send Benedict Arnold a final care package?" He looked at Hazel.

"You want my opinion?" Hazel asked.

"I want your theory."

"People in traumatic situations," she said, well aware of the irony, "are unreliable. Washington acted one way when he was feeling emotional, another way when he was feeling pragmatic. It's called being human."

"That's a theory."

THE HOUSE OF SECRETS

"It's more like my life right now."

"Or maybe George Washington was a class act," Skip said, "and all that was in the luggage were clothes and belt-buckled shoes."

"That's another theory. And some say that's *exactly* what was in there. A bunch of clothes, undergarments, and a few tins of wig powder. Others say it was a stack of old letters and books, since Benedict got his start as a bookseller. But another theory that's persisted for years is that among those books was a very special volume. Benedict Arnold's personal—"

"Bible," Skip said, glancing over at Hazel, who was trying her best to be unreadable. Because she couldn't believe anything she was hearing. Couldn't fathom how she'd woken up from a coma to find herself in this life. She tried to imagine her father spending time at this job. Tried to imagine the choices he'd made, him searching for this bible. Tried to remember any hint of this secret life, or her new fear. Her real fear. That she was a part of this life too.

"There's also this," Rabkin added. "During the Revolutionary War, George Washington used to use old books to send coded messages. Paper was hard to get and very expensive back then, so they'd write on the interior pages of any book they could get ahold of, including bibles."

"And that's true?" Skip asked.

"They'd take them off the dead redcoats if they had to," Rabkin said. "It was war."

"So now we're supposed to believe that when Washington handed over Benedict's belongings, he was actually sending a hidden message?" Skip asked. "You're starting to sound like an old *House of Secrets* episode, and not one of our good ones."

"That's not the only thing bibles were used for," Hazel said, feeling something click into place, like she was in the classroom, piecing together some bit of history. It was a brand-new sensation, but also one that felt...comfortable. Felt right, which was a sensation she'd been missing for two days. She walked over to the rolling side table next to her bed, opened the top drawer, pulled out a faux-leather bible with the name of the hospital—UCLA Medical Center—embossed on the cover.

She flipped it open to the back pages, which were lined for notes but were empty. "Back in the 1700s, if you're living out in the country, there was no local library. So the Bible might be the only book you had, right? Instead of just using it for its intended purpose, people also used them as both diary and ledger. They'd keep birth dates, marriage dates, business deals, whatever." *All the blessed events*, she thought. "If you go back through history, that's where people recorded everything they

wanted to record, because it was the one possession they'd always take with them. People kept
their histories in their bibles." She closed the hospital bible, put it back in the drawer. "For better or
worse."

"Do you believe that, Hazel?" Skip said.

"It's not about believing," she said. "It's what
people did. It's what people *do*."

"Listen to your sister," Rabkin said. "According
to a number of historians, the secret in Benedict
Arnold's bible was that he had an illegitimate son
he was trying to protect. An even crazier theory
says it wasn't Benedict's illegitimate kid—in fact,
what they were really hiding was an illegitimate
child sired by George Washington himself."

"What historians?" Hazel asked.

"Government historians," Rabkin said carefully.
Patently *not* ignoring her, Hazel noticed.

"We did two *House of Secrets* episodes on Washington's secret-kid thing. I didn't believe it then,"
Skip said, "and I'm having a hard time believing it
now."

"Do you believe this, which came from a team
of professors who studied Benedict's later life:
What if Benedict Arnold's greatest secret was
that he *never* switched sides? What if his so-
called 'traitorous acts' were actually planned by
Washington, making Benedict the ultimate triple

agent, infiltrating the British and always reporting back to us? Imagine that," Rabkin said.

He stared at Hazel for a few seconds, not speaking. She wondered what had prepared Rabkin for this job, what had made him memorize these facts. She'd spent her own life inside ancient texts. Agent Rabkin looked like he'd spent his life contemplating how to shoot people. Except...his hands. He had the smoothest hands. And then there was that tan line where his ring should be. Someone had loved this man. He'd picked out vows to say. He'd gone on a honeymoon. Maybe he was divorced, maybe his wife was dead, but at some point, someone was worried about this man.

"Everyone thinks Benedict Arnold is the bad guy," Rabkin said, "but maybe he's the hero of the story."

Hazel sat with that. On her left, she noticed the photo of her and her dad at the Dodgers game.

"I still don't understand what this has to do with my father," Hazel said.

"That's because you haven't seen the body," Agent Rabkin said. From his suit pocket, he pulled out an envelope with a photo and slid it onto the table.

8

The Bear lands in Dubai, that shithole, then sits on the tarmac for two hours.

The pilot says something about a backup at the gate, and it will be just a few more minutes, then the flight attendants start coming down the aisle with the drink cart. It's the United Arab Emirates, so The Bear figures the airport is like a police state anyway.

The Bear gets it.

No problem.

Security first. Besides, he emailed in a tip hours earlier, on the layover in Frankfurt, saying that a flight coming in forty minutes before them had a passenger presenting with some Ebola-like symptoms, which would take the attention of the Americans who were here too.

"You'd think they'd know that we all have somewhere to be," the man sitting next to The Bear says. His name is Arthur Kennedy. He has about five hours to live, by The Bear's estimation. He's wearing a Hawaiian shirt, tan shorts, and sandals with socks, which The Bear thinks is a good look on precisely nobody, but particularly not on this fellow, with his strangely hairless legs. It's a plane filled with tourists from all over the world. The closer they got to Dubai, the drunker the passengers got. Back in economy, it's like a dance floor in Ibiza.

"Where do you need to be?" The Bear asks, though he knows the answer.

"Boulos Al Qasr," Kennedy says, referring to a posh hotel that actually translates as *The Palace*.

How original, The Bear thinks. *As original as the name Arthur Kennedy. Or Darren Nixon. Was that really the best they could do? Dead Presidents?*

The Bear is not the sort who speaks to people on planes. He used to buy out the entire row when he flew. But all of the new regulations have made things more difficult, so The Bear has practiced restraint recently. But this is work, so he's been talking to Arthur Kennedy, with his rum-and-Coke breath, off and on for hours now, letting Kennedy nap, which gave The Bear time to spike his cocktail with a dash of Lotrum, a drug you can only get in Russia these days, primarily for use in controlling behavior in animals.

In humans, as Kennedy will soon learn when he gets off the plane and tries to walk for more than a few meters, it causes profound muscle weakness. He'll look drunk. In fact, his respiratory system will be failing. And then, two hours from now, The Bear will dispose of this man.

"That's where I'm staying," The Bear says.

"You ever been?"

"First time," The Bear says.

"It's supposed to really be something," Kennedy says. "It's not like one of those new glossy places on the Palm, where you could be anywhere, right?" He shakes his head. "No, it's the full Arabian experience. They tried to make it an honest re-creation of what it would have looked like a hundred and fifty years ago to be in a castle, but with a spa and steak house and golf course." He shakes his head again. "Not a lot of respect for history anymore."

"Then why are you staying there?"

"Irony," Kennedy says, laughing at his own joke.

Arthur Kennedy is a loose end. A mistake from another decade. The Bear shouldn't have to take care of this problem, but Jack Nash's death—and what happened to Darren Nixon—has turned on a few too many lights, shaken cages, aroused the sleeping animals. The Bear will feed them, get them to go back to sleep. Then he can deal with Hazel.

Arthur Kennedy hasn't lived a life deserving of his fate. But few do. He looks out the window. "So typical. The FAA. The TSA." Kennedy shakes his head again, slower this time, a string of saliva slipping from his mouth. "It's like they forget the T stands for *transportation*, right?"

The Bear opts not to tell Arthur he's not in America anymore. Instead, he says, "If you had taken this trip a hundred and fifty years ago, the authentic experience would be that you arrived nearly dead from scurvy. If you arrived at all."

The Bear checks his phone. It's two in the afternoon. As planned. He scrolls through social media, looking for mention of the Ebola flight. It's nowhere.

Disappointing but predictable.

Real problems—even when they weren't real—tended to take more time to really gain traction. Unlike Hazel and Skip Nash, for instance. A picture of Hazel walking the hallway with her brother, dressed in her hospital gown and shorts, had gone from an Instagram account belonging to @cotslipping to the front of Reddit in just over twenty-four hours. Now, her hospital gown had its own Twitter account with four thousand followers.

It takes so little these days, The Bear thinks, to divert attention.

"I have a car coming," The Bear adds, "if you need a ride to the hotel."

"Yeah? You wouldn't mind?" Kennedy asks.

"It would be my pleasure," The Bear says, meaning every word.

"Tell you the truth?" Kennedy leans toward The Bear, as if he has any choice: The Lotrum soon will render him functionally unable to lie. "I've actually got a date. Sounds crazy, right? Guy like me? I mean, take a look at me. Pushing fifty, could probably lose fifteen pounds, and here I am, flying to another country to meet a girl. I know I'm not some supermodel. The Internet is the great equalizer, right? Met her a week ago, and now here I am. Just a real estate guy from Connecticut chasing love in the United Arab Emirates. Isn't that a thing? Crazy."

The Bear feels the slightest pang of guilt. There was no girl. There was just The Bear at a keyboard, writing to Arthur Kennedy for the past week. Through their emails back and forth, Kennedy revealed himself to be a rather romantic man. But he was also a loose talker on all topics, and that simply would not do. The climate had changed.

BRAD MELTZER AND TOD GOLDBERG

If it had been solely up to The Bear, he would have handled this quietly, in Kennedy's home in New Haven. But decisions were being made outside of his realm. And that was too bad.

An example needed to be made.

9

Hazel had seen plenty of dead bodies before. The first was in college—a girl who lived down the hall from her in the dorms hung herself. Jumped out of her dorm room window with a rope tied around her neck on one end, her bunk bed on the other. She hung there for an hour while firefighters were called to cut down her door. Hazel didn't know the girl at all. Is that why she remembered her now?

Then a body in a river in Egypt. Another stranger.

And then all the pictures of bodies she'd studied while trying to figure out the balance of cultures, why people killed each other, as important to her studies as why people loved, a fact that she imagines now must have been disillusioning. But there they were in her mind, a bibliography of bodies, civilization's worst.

She knew there were other dead bodies. Her

mother for one, but Hazel had no mental picture. There had to be others. The dead who Hazel cared about, all of them now lost.

This had to be the first dead body she'd ever seen in a mini-golf playground, however. It lay facedown between a six-foot-tall water geyser shaped like a star and another, inexplicably shaped like a smiling purple and gold pig. It was a particularly unsettling sight. Which was probably the point. Suffocation turns a body ugly.

Except Hazel, to her own surprise, wasn't unsettled. Skip, on the other hand, jumped back from the table like he'd been shocked. "Jesus," he said. "A spoiler alert would've been nice."

"That's Darren Nixon," Agent Rabkin said. "Thirty-six years old. Quiet life. No wife. No kids. Worked in Spokane at a chemical plant as a maintenance engineer for a time. Bounced at a pub on the weekends. According to his Netflix queue, he loved your dad's show. Then, for some reason, your father made a personal visit to him the week before your accident. Either of you know anything about that?"

"I never even heard of Darren Nixon until you asked me last week," Skip said.

Rabkin looked at Hazel, who closed her eyes, trying to think. Nothing. Always nothing. "When do they think he was killed?" she asked.

"Hard to pinpoint because of the freezing," Agent Rabkin said. "Best guess is about two weeks ago. Around the time your father went on that trip."

"That doesn't mean my dad did anything. I could've killed him too," Hazel said, trying to take pressure off her father, but quickly realizing she was moving in the wrong direction.

"Hazel, don't say that," Skip snapped.

Hazel was staring at the photo, trying to make sense of it. The man was facedown in maybe two inches of water. He had on a scarlet military jacket with four brass buttons and gold cuffs. Like something from the 1700s.

"The jacket looks familiar," Skip said.

"It should," Rabkin said, pumping his bushy eyebrows, which could use a little manscaping. That's what happened when your wife was gone. "I just found out this morning, that jacket belonged to your father. It's supposedly Benedict Arnold's coat from Fort Ticonderoga. I assume you knew he had something like that."

There it was, Hazel thought. The real reason Rabkin suddenly showed up. *That* was the trap he'd been setting, and Skip walked right into it, an occurrence, she imagined, that wasn't a rarity.

Skip took the photo from Hazel. He looked at it for a few seconds, set it down, then shook his head, like he was trying to clear the image. "If you say so," he said.

"Take another look. It's important. You're not in trouble if you recognize your dad's jacket. But if it's *not* his, we need to know."

Hazel put her hand over Nixon's head, so Skip wouldn't have to see Nixon's tongue lolling out of the side of his mouth. "I guess it looks like his," Skip said. "Someone gave it to Dad. It was probably a fake, like that huge statue of Anubis—the Egyptian god who guides souls to the afterlife—that he has in his living room." People gave Skip and his father all kinds of crazy things over the years. The nail that held Christ to the cross. The Sword of Damocles. Amelia Earhart's flying gloves. *Impossibilities*, Jack called them. "There's a thousand of those jackets out there, and all of them belonged to Benedict Arnold, you know? Dad got it years ago. Just one of those things."

"You know what it reminded *me* of, Skip?" Rabkin asked. "When you got caught selling one of your dad's old Civil War swords. You remember that?"

"That was a misunderstanding," Skip said, more to Hazel than to Rabkin. Like maybe she didn't know the truth. And she didn't.

"You told the buyer it was from Gettysburg," Rabkin said, "that it belonged to General Lewis

Armistead. That's in the court records, Skip. Are you saying the court records have been falsified?"

"I'm saying," Skip said, "that I was in a bad place."

"Did the rehab help?"

"I haven't gone back, have I?"

Hazel was wrong. *This* was the actual trap. And for the second time, Skip had his leg in it. The FBI wasn't just here for information; this was an interrogation.

"You accusing me of selling my dad's coat to this dead man?" Skip asked.

"Not just a dead man. A dead ex-con. Two years ago, Nixon spent time in prison."

"For moving stolen merchandise?" Hazel asked.

"Nope. For forging his boss's signature on company checks, then trying to burn the place down to cover it up. That's fraud and arson," Rabkin said, watching both their reactions. "Darren Nixon wasn't the nicest of guys," he added, his thumb tapping where his wedding ring used to be. *Agent Rabkin's wife hasn't been gone long*, Hazel thought. That explained the overgrown eyebrows too. Probably divorce. If Rabkin were a widower, maybe he'd have a softer edge. As it was, he seemed jagged to a fault, as if he was ready at any moment to put his fist through a wall. Or into a person's mouth.

"You don't think it's odd, that when it comes to Darren Nixon, your father's jacket was found on someone he certainly wouldn't associate with?" Rabkin asked.

"It wasn't my father's jacket!" Skip practically shouted. "It was Benedict Arnold's!" He breathed hard. "My father came into possession of a jacket like this. Maybe it was even this one! Maybe it wasn't!" He stared down at the grisly picture. "I swear to you, I've never seen this guy. I don't know him. And if it helps, my dad knew that that coat, I mean the one he owned at least, was a fake."

"You seem more confident now."

"You asked me the story of the jacket, that's what I know about the jacket. It was fake," Skip said.

"Then do you have any idea why your father would go pay Nixon a personal visit? Or did he regularly go visit ex-cons who binge-watched his show and wore his old clothing?"

"Watch your tone," Hazel warned. Was this new, her protective feelings about Skip? Or did this come from some proven trust she couldn't quite remember? "He's telling the truth: That jacket is worthless. It's a fake."

"I thought you said you didn't recognize the jacket," Rabkin said.

"I lied," Hazel said.

"No surprise there."

"What's that supposed to mean?"

"Have you even heard the doctor's latest theory about your injury, Ms. Nash?" Agent Rabkin asked.

"Dr. Morrison said I have a traumatic brain injury. They're still doing tests to see the extent."

"That doesn't mean they don't have a theory. Apparently, the problem's in your left amygdala. Way I understand it, our brains are like power grids. Blow out one transformer and you can black out an entire city—or part of it, which is what happened in your case. They said it produced a condition that's like the opposite of PTSD."

"They don't know what they're talking about," Skip said. "She remembers her studies...her anthropology research."

"I'm sure she does. But tell me about your brother, Ms. Nash. Do you admire him? Are you jealous of him? Or better yet, what about your dad? He died almost two weeks ago. But have you cried about it yet?"

Hazel didn't say anything. She looked out the window. Tried to imagine how the people out there in the real world would respond to this line of questioning. The kids walking on the campus at UCLA. The tourists shopping in Westwood. Hell, even the doctors and nurses downstairs in the cafeteria, whiling away their breaks over a slice of

German chocolate cake and Instagram. A chill ran through Hazel. The room was suddenly cold. "I loved my dad," she said. She meant those words. Even if she couldn't remember all the contours of their relationship, some things could be felt. "I did love him."

"I'm sure you did. But according to Dr. Morrison, there's the issue," Rabkin said. "In post-traumatic stress disorder, your emotional memories get heightened, which is why soldiers duck for cover when they hear a loud noise. For you, it's the opposite—your emotional memories got scrambled. So you can recall cold data like your address or license plate number, or even the Wikipedia facts of an ancient papyrus—but anything you have an emotional connection to, whatever info was in the emotional part of your brain, well . . . that's why you can't remember your best friend. Or your first kiss. Or what made you happy."

"So she has no emotions?" Skip asked.

"No, of course she has emotions. She can love, hate, feel, or experience the quiet terror that she's probably feeling right now. What she lost is her *attachment*—to people, to objects. So what she really lost, when it comes to the people she cared about, is her memory of their relationship. Isn't that right, Ms. Nash?"

Hazel stayed silent, the room now freezing.

"So she knows I'm her brother, but she doesn't know how she used to feel about me?"

"They said it's amazing she even recognized you. From here on in, she can walk into a bar, meet someone new, even be attracted to them, but have no idea they once broke her heart. It's the same with her memories about herself. With the gaps she has—the files now gone from her mental hard drive—she's still not sure what kind of person she is, much less who she was."

Hazel sat with that. Like any truth, she knew it as he was saying it.

"Want to hear the most interesting part about the amygdala?" Rabkin asked. "It's the size of an almond, only a few centimeters in size. Plus or minus. Tends to be a little larger for folks with anxiety disorders or who have undergone extreme stress. A little smaller for others."

"Like who?" Hazel asked.

"Sociopaths," Rabkin said. "Serial killers. A millimeter in either direction can signal problems."

Hazel wanted to sit back down on the bed. But she didn't move. "Where do I fall?"

"Dr. Morrison said your structure hasn't changed," Rabkin said carefully. "According to your last MRI, you were normal."

Were.

"When was that?" Hazel said.

"That's the *exact* same question I asked," Rabkin said. "It was six months ago. Checked yourself into the ER in Santa Cruz with someone's teeth stuck in your forehead from a headbutt. That ring any bells?"

"No."

"You told the doctors it was a skydiving accident. It was a fairly serious concussion."

Hazel wanted to argue, wanted to scream again, wanted to say it wasn't her. But for two days now, this was her life. Simple facts? Those were easy. Emotional memories? File not found.

In this case, she knew she skydived. She remembered that. But jumping out of a plane and ending up with someone's teeth stuck in her head? It seemed the sort of thing that would get hardwired, but again, file not found. It was the same last night, when they gave her an hour to go online and she found a mention of an old drunken brawl (that she had started) in a bowling alley in Oakland. What the hell kind of person did she used to be?

"Want to hear Dr. Morrison's final piece of advice?" Rabkin asked. "He said that depending how you look at it, maybe this is a gift. You get to be anyone you want now. *Anyone.* This is your new life, Ms. Nash. Maybe it's time to associate with better people. And make safer choices."

"What if I want my old life back?"

"He said that once your brain starts to make associations—when you smell something, when you see something—you'll find your way. But you have to proceed under the assumption that what's gone is gone."

"Nothing is ever gone," Hazel said. "Everything is somewhere."

Rabkin actually smiled then.

"Listen," Skip said, turning the photo over, so he wouldn't need to see it again. "If you worked with my father, wouldn't you know what he was up to?"

"Your father was a cautious man," Agent Rabkin said.

"Did you even know him?" Hazel challenged.

"No," Rabkin said.

"Who did?" Skip said.

"Clearly not you," Rabkin said.

"It was a rhetorical question," Skip said. He finished his cup of coffee, then looked at the bottom of the cup like it contained some magic. "This is crazy."

Hazel agreed, still replaying Rabkin's words about her amygdala and the PTSD. At least now she had a theory—an explanation—for where so much of her life went. More important, according to the doctor, as her brain makes associations, some of it could come back. For that alone, the room wasn't as cold anymore. Still, there was that word Rabkin used: *Sociopath.*

Hazel glanced back at her hospital bed. On each of the side railings was a reinforced metal loop, welded into place. She hadn't noticed the loops before, but she knew what they were there for. Handcuffs. This was the kind of bed they use in prison. The kind of bed that Darren Nixon probably slept in at some point.

I am Hazel-Ann Nash and I am feeling like I need to know what the hell is really going on.

"So you have no idea *why* or even *if* your father was searching for Benedict Arnold's bible?" Rabkin asked.

"Let me tell you a secret about my dad," Skip said. "Stories like this Benedict Arnold one, they're *everything* and absolutely *nothing*. Most people are content to just go live their lives. Some people need to *need* something else, something that isn't right in front of them. Maybe that's God. Maybe that's quantum physics. Maybe it's atheism. That's the mystery. If Dad wanted Benedict Arnold's bible, or his jacket, or his jockstrap, that's the reason he chased it."

"That explains a chase. It doesn't explain what could be a secret obsession he hid from his own family."

"All obsessions are inexplicable," Skip said,

"until you go out into the world and find out there's ten million people shouting from their basements about the same thing. Then it's just culture."

"That's the problem," Rabkin said. "Your father shared his obsession with one guy—a guy he shouldn't've been around—and that guy is now dead. Then your dad died three days later."

Hazel flipped the photo faceup again. "Why didn't he turn over?"

"What?" Agent Rabkin said.

"Unless you're at sea, or you don't know how to swim," Hazel said, "it's actually pretty hard to drown. That whole drowning-in-a-teaspoon-of-water thing is pretty much a myth. I don't see why this guy Nixon didn't just turn over."

"He'd been poisoned," Rabkin said with a new tone in his voice. That was another test. One that Hazel passed. "We found a paralyzing agent in his blood. A pretty significant dose."

"That's even harder," Hazel said, "historically speaking." Hazel thought about how the tribes of the Amazon were frustrated when they tried to use poisonous leaves and bark to kill people. The formula was hard to get right, people's body chemistry imprecise. "To just kill a person you're confronting," she continued, "one-on-one, in an open space? It's easier to just shoot them, or, if

71

you're worried about the noise, stab them in the chest. Poisoning someone and then hoping they drown? That takes work. And the outcome is a gamble."

The words tumbled out of Hazel's mouth before she even understood what she was saying, like she was an actress standing in front of a class, playing a teacher. Again, it felt right. And then she realized why Agent Rabkin had at first seemed familiar. He reminded her of herself. Or some version of herself.

"Why the hell do you know that?" Skip said.

"While you were on TV," she said, "I was in school." She slid the photo back to Agent Rabkin. "Tell me more about the poison in Nixon's body."

"It wasn't something we normally run across. A drug called Polosis 5," he said. "The only other place it's shown up—in a smaller quantity, but it was definitely there—was in your father's body."

"So someone *poisoned* our father?" Hazel said. Skip couldn't even speak.

"I didn't say that," Rabkin said. "What I'm telling you is your dad was at Nixon's house. Then, a few days later, he died out in his car while he was with you."

"Then why'd they tell us it was a heart attack?" Skip said.

"Skip, stop talking," Hazel said. There was

something starting to work in her mind, some wire twisting loose.

"You look like you have a theory, Ms. Nash."

"Hnh," Hazel said. "I'm just thinking, maybe this isn't about Darren Nixon being a bad guy. Maybe he's just a collector, but for this purchase, maybe he bought more than a coat. Whatever he found, maybe someone came looking for that, then came after Dad. Or maybe while Nixon was up in Canada, Dad arrived at Nixon's place, accidentally ingested some remnant poison, and it took a few days to kick in," she said. "Where'd you say Nixon lived again? Spokane?"

"That's classified."

"Except you already told us," Hazel said, thinking Agent Rabkin wasn't real solid on what was and wasn't secret.

"I see what you're doing, Ms. Nash. And I appreciate it. But let me remind you: You can study death all day long; it doesn't make you a federal agent."

"That's not—"

"I'm sorry your father's dead. I truly am. But if you and your brother want to help us, the best way to do that is by telling us all you know, then let *us* do our job, while *you* recover from your accident."

Hazel nodded, still wondering how a bible could even fit in someone's chest. Plus, why was her father spending time with someone as sketchy as Nixon? And more important, why would someone even want a bible that belonged to Benedict Arnold? That seemed to be about more than just money. Was there really something hidden inside? Some old secret? Whoever had it, they had it for a reason, right? It couldn't be a good one. Who does anything for peace anymore?

"Can I ask you one last question, Ms. Nash?" Rabkin said. "Did you kill your father?"

"Hey!" Skip shouted.

"You have a feeling, Ms. Nash. So what's your gut tell you?"

Hazel thought for a moment. Weighed the evidence. Considered her knowledge of obscure poisons, like the one that apparently killed Darren Nixon. "No," she said, thinking, *I don't* think *I did*.

"That's good to hear. Then you have nothing to worry about," Rabkin said. He opened the door, then walked out without looking back. "I'm glad you're feeling better, Ms. Nash."

10

Johannesburg, South Africa
2011

SEASON 23, EPISODE 12 (2011): "THE CON-
SPIRATOR OF JOHANNESBURG"

Jack Nash is sixty-five years old, sitting at one of
five stools in a 150-year-old pub in Johannesburg
named The Gun Hall. He's waiting for the end of
the world...and a woman calling herself Emily to
come out of the bathroom.

No.

The toilet. That's what they call it here, not even
the *loo*. He wonders what the etymology of that
word is, what the rub on that deal is, and remembers that he has all of the world's knowledge in his
pocket and he could probably just ask Google for
an answer. It used to be that he needed to employ
a staff of researchers to figure out the most mun-
dane questions, kept university librarians around

the country on speed dial, met his assistant Ingrid that way—or thought he had, anyway. But now he never needed to speak to anyone if he didn't want to, which meant that days like today were getting more and more rare: a face-to-face meeting with an actual human source.

Emily walks through the pub, and Jack sees that she's nervous. She kneads her hands together. Touches her nose. A series of common human tics that convey anxiety. "I'm sorry," she says, and sits down beside him. "Dr. Horton doesn't feel comfortable meeting you here."

Jack glances around. No one's noticed him yet. He has on his best disguise: a baseball cap, a bit of beard, and his back to the room.

"You're safe here. This place has been a sanctuary since the nineteenth century," Jack tells her, though back in the nineteenth century, The Gun Hall used to be…rough. Even during apartheid, it was rough. Today, it's all cleaned up, filled with tourists snapping photos of their food, the sort of place you held a wedding.

"He's been burned by the press," Emily says.

"I'm not the press. I'll let him tell his story the way he wants." That was true. Jack wasn't a reporter; he didn't chase truth; he chased ratings. And right now, Emily's boss, Dr. Stephen Horton, was predicting that asteroid HM13 was going to slam into us, bringing about the end of the world. Most years, it'd be a *good enough* story. Today, as we approached 2012 and the Mayan doomsday, this is a two-hour special. Shark Week for the paranoid.

"I'm sure you're aware," Emily says, "that forces are at play who would like to keep Dr. Horton quiet."

Jack sips his beer. He's known Emily for twenty minutes and already knows that she's a liar. It's not a problem, on its face. Liars are dependable. You always know what their rub is, which makes it easier to figure out their next steps. Which is what Jack likes. Unweaving the fiction. Is the world going to end next year? Probably not. But raging asteroids weren't the only thing Jack was here for.

"I'm staying at the Saxon," Jack says. He drops some cash on the bar. "Dr. Horton wants to talk, he can find me there."

Jack steps out into the street, but he doesn't hail a cab. It's beautiful in Johannesburg today, and if Jack's going to die, his last moments shouldn't be in a car.

He's thinking of his daughter—of Hazel—home sick from work with a sore throat. Jack called her three times, checking to make sure Hazel got a doctor's appointment. Everything should get looked at. Everything, he always tells her. Indeed, he's about to go for call number four when some-one recognizes him.

"Excuse me, Mr. Nash?" Jack turns around. There's a man in a button-down shirt, black pants, sunglasses. "You are Jack Nash?"

"I am," Jack says.

"Could I get your autograph?" The man has a piece of paper and a pen in his hand. Jack won-ders how long this man has been following him.

"For my son," the man adds.

"Of course," Jack says, that old paranoia falling away. He takes the paper and pen from the man, smiles big. "What's his name?"

"Bethel," the man says.

Jack looks up, hearing the word. The magic word. *Bethel*. The great old city where the first great spy story happened, back when it was still called Luz. "I know a man from Bethel," Jack replies, using the recognition phrase his supervi-sors had him memorize.

"He is a great man indeed," the man with sun-glasses says.

Identity confirmed, though Jack smiles to him-self at the melodrama. The Bible passage—from the Book of Judges—is about a man who lets killers into the city of Bethel, betraying everyone he loves. They used to call that passage *The Trai-tor's Creed*.

Jack looks around to see if anyone else is watching.

By the time Jack turns back, the man with the sunglasses is gone, the crosswalks on both sides of him filled with hundreds of people. For a brief moment, Jack is standing on the corner alone...and then the crush is on him, behind him, to his sides.

Jack is impressed. The autograph was a nice touch.

Bethel. Home to a great traitor. Though not nearly as great as the man who betrayed George Washington.

Jack looks down at the paper. He flips it over. There's something written on the other side. It's an address, a few miles away. Not a great area. Naturally. They'll never bring the prize where everyone can see it. Still, isn't this why he came all the way to Johannesburg? It was never about a meteor, or even a TV show. For Jack Nash, it was about locating another page of Benedict Arnold's bible.

11

UCLA Medical Center
Today

H ow's your pain? One to ten, where are you?" the night nurse, Dexter, asked.

Hazel's entire body throbbed. Sitting up in bed, she was at about seven, with an eight rising in her neck. "Two."

"You're only hurting yourself, you know," Dexter said.

"I don't want anything else in me. I just want to feel...authentic."

"You're a good sister, a good daughter. Nothing's more authentic than that."

Hazel smiled a thank-you and flipped open Skip's laptop, which she'd asked him to leave behind.

Ten minutes ago, she sent Skip after Agent Rabkin, telling her brother to follow the FBI agent out of the hospital—and most important, see who else he stopped to chat with. She knew Rabkin wasn't a novice, but with Skip gone, it'd at least give her time for this.

She closed her eyes. Like an echo, she heard Agent Rabkin's news that her dad was poisoned. Heard his warning to stay away.

Mysteries need to be solved.

Three guesses per night.

In her mind, she was in bed, her old bed, in the dark, with her father sitting beside her. What was he saying?

She opened her eyes. It was right there, so close. Still, one detail, one feeling, stood out more than anything else. The love her father had for her. Whatever it took, whether Hazel's brain was working right or not, nothing would stop her from finding out if someone killed him. She needed to pay that love back.

Adjusting the laptop, she was all set to run searches on her father, on Agent Rabkin, and of course on ex-con Darren Nixon. But as she launched Skip's homepage...

Browser history.

She couldn't help herself.

With a click, there it was, her brother's digital footprint, most of it centered around Facebook, Twitter, Instagram, BuzzFeed stories like *Who has the hottest NHL wife?*, the ESPN hockey pages (Did her brother even like hockey? There was so much she couldn't remember), and based on the list under *Recently Visited*, far too much time on HOS-MB: *The House of Secrets Message Boards*, where fans were leaving tributes to their dad. Every few entries, Skip would reply with a quick *Thanks for looking out for us!!*

She clicked further back and found Skip's own Google searches for *Trevor Rabkin, Darren Nixon,* and even *Jack Nash death conspiracy*, which took him to the corners of the Internet reserved for what looked like their dad's most dedicated fans.

The only thing that really caught her eye was under the *Recently Closed* tab, where Skip had landed on the Contact page for Longwood Funeral Home. A dull pain that had been squatting in the back of Hazel's neck exploded in a burning fire. She'd been unconscious for eight days. Had she really missed her dad's funeral?

Hazel glanced at the clock on the laptop. Skip would be back soon. This was her chance to dig into her dad's poison, Benedict Arnold's bible, and all the craziness the FBI just dumped in her lap, but try as she might, she still couldn't get that word out of her head...

"*Sociopath*," Hazel whispered to herself, logging in to her own email account.

Mysteries need to be solved. Time to see the life she'd left behind.

Onscreen, she had fifty new emails. One from the chair of her department at San Francisco State—*I'm happy to hear you're doing better. Some of us were very worried about you*—one from a reporter at the *Los Angeles Times* asking for an interview, and dozens from people she'd never heard of, each with a variation of the subject line "SORRY ABOUT YOUR FATHER."

She deleted them all.

She had a little over three years of mail stored up: Hundreds of messages back and forth with students. (Student: *Prof. Nash, I'm going to be about four days late with my paper. Is that cool?* Hazel: *No.* Student: *Three days? Is that cool?*) An inordinate number of emails flagged as important that she sent to herself, usually reminding her of dental appointments or kickboxing class. There would be some weeks when she and Skip seemed to be in constant contact—photos, jokes, weird sightings of their father (*Check out this old clip of Dad on That's Incredible!*)—and then months where there was nothing.

She couldn't find a single email from anyone who looked like a friend.

And then there were the messages from her dad. Dozens. So many unanswered:

Haven't heard from you in weeks, Hazel-Ann. I left a message on your home phone and at school.

Was she avoiding him?

Was thinking of your mom today and wanted to see your face. Can we Skype later? Love you.

"Love you too," she whispered. But had she Skyped him? File not found.

Thought of Tim Knollberg today. Have you heard from him?

Tim Knollberg. At the sight of the name, she was moving backward, and a memory was rolling over her.

Every year when classes started, Hazel fought to keep a low profile. She could remember that. Let Skip be famous. Hazel preferred the quiet. She never advertised who her father was, but somehow the college kids always knew.

So when nineteen-year-old Tim Knollberg came to office hours and said, "Can I ask you something about your dad?" Hazel assumed he was another superfan. Until he handed her a flyer and added, "That's my sister Rachel. She disappeared when she was nine. I took your class on the off chance that maybe your dad could help us find her."

Her father had helped. Of course he had. They

did a whole episode on the modeling technology that existed to accurately age missing children, set up hotlines around the country, even helped identify three long-lost children who'd been abducted and murdered. But they never did find Tim Knollberg's sister.

Where in the world are you, Hazel-Ann? Are you there? Is it a full moon? Are you out there howling, my werewolf? Call me.

My werewolf. She knew that name too—it's what her dad would call her when she didn't understand why he had to constantly leave and chase UFO leads, or meet with witnesses at Loch Ness. Why, she used to wonder, were fake things more important than real things?

"Big things are coming for you," he used to promise her. "Because one day? You'll be the werewolf." It was a term of endearment, his way of telling her that she mattered, that one day she'd be some unknowable thing people wanted to figure out. It was a funny thing between the two of them, except it had grown to mean something entirely different to Hazel.

She replayed Rabkin's words: An amygdala of a certain size indicated killers and other types of werewolves.

"Sorry to interrupt..." a man's voice said, calling out from the hospital hallway.

Hazel looked up, saw a suit, thought it was Agent Rabkin himself. But it wasn't. Just a lanky Asian man, his face masked with worry, like he was lost.

"Sorry," the man said, already backtracking. "Wrong room."

"No worries," Hazel replied, thinking, *Not a big deal. Nothing to worry about.* But then another thought came to her: What if that man was someone who was actually threatening her? What if someone who was truly dangerous had raced into her room? What would she do? What would happen to him?

And then another thought—a dark, brutal thought: *He would have met the werewolf.*

12

It was nearly 10 p.m. when Dr. Morrison walked to his reserved space on the first floor of one of the hospital's nearby parking structures. The day he got it, he was excited, until his ex-wife asked, "How come people don't feel good until they get their name on something?"

That's why she was his ex. She could ruin even the easy days.

Just like someone else.

"You don't answer your phone anymore?" a man called out.

Dr. Lyle Morrison lived alone in a leaky Spanish revival in Santa Monica Canyon. He had a golden retriever named Rolex who pissed all over his floors. And he still owed $127,000 on his student loans from Yale. But of all the headaches in his life—including alimony—none was as bad as the man in the dark suit currently leaning against Morrison's silver Lexus. Agent Trevor Rabkin.

"Sorry to be late," Rabkin said. "Skip was trailing me. Took an elevator ride to lose him."

"I know you spoke to her. You think I'm stupid?" the doctor hissed.

"She's in better shape than you said. Nearly at full speed."

"If you interfere with her recovery—"

"I just want to know how she's doing."

"You don't care how she's doing. You want to see what she knows, what she remembers."

"And that's a crime? You know how long her father worked for us? Even longer than you."

Dr. Morrison went silent.

"You think I didn't look you up, doc? We all have a moment we'd regret. You got caught and made a deal to get out of yours. Jack Nash was no better—and if I had to bet, based on Hazel's file, neither is she. So you can act as high and mighty as you want, but there's a reason you're standing here in the dark, passing me confidential information. Just like there's a reason you never told Hazel how well you know her family."

Morrison clenched his jaw and shook his head. "This is the last time I'm doing this."

"Your help is always appreciated. Now. Hazel.

What're the chances of her memories coming back?"

"That's the issue. You saw. She doesn't even know what she knows."

"What about her therapy?"

"The grief counseling was a waste. Without memories, she doesn't have any grief. So of course she hasn't even begun to mourn her father. I don't know if she knows how."

Rabkin considered that. "Maybe that's better."

"It's not."

"You worked with her father too. How's she compare?"

"That was years ago," Dr. Morrison said. "Jack Nash was a reckless man, but also a kind one."

"And she's not?"

A security guard in a golf cart rolled by and tipped his cap at Rabkin and Dr. Morrison, just three guys in a parking lot, doing their jobs.

"You realize I could lose my practice for having this conversation?" Dr. Morrison growled.

"Then keep your voice down."

The doctor looked around the parking lot, sighing to himself, as if he couldn't quite make sense of the experience he was having. "I feel like I'm supposed to tell you to follow the money now."

"Don't worry. We're the good guys," Rabkin said.

"We just—" Rabkin's phone vibrated. So did Dr. Morrison's. A new text for both of them.

Dr. Morrison pulled out his phone first. Read it.

"What's wrong?" Rabkin asked.

The doctor held up his phone. On it was a message that Hazel's hospital bed was empty.

"No one knows where she is."

13

You okay? You in pain?" Skip called out as he pulled up to the bus bench in one of their dad's old cars, a 1966 Chevy Impala Super Sport.

Hazel was always in pain.

"I lost Agent Rabkin," Skip added.

"It's okay. Just get us out of here," she insisted, sliding into the passenger seat and ducking down. They were four blocks from the hospital. Skip took off. *Was this their relationship?* Hazel wondered. Is this what he regularly did? She'd get in trouble and he'd bail her out?

Hazel stayed silent until they got home. Or at least to this home: the 1926 Spanish-Moorish revival house in Studio City that sat protected behind closed iron gates.

This was the house she grew up in. Her father's house.

"Ready to see your old life?" Skip asked.

She nodded, slowly opening the car door and staring up at the front walk. There was so much she wanted to ask him, about Rabkin, about their father, about the poison. Instead, she went with "Skip, was there a funeral? Did I miss Dad's funeral?"

"It wasn't a big deal."

"What does that mean? How could it not be a big deal?"

"It was a memorial. Just friends and family," Skip said, and then stopped. Hazel could imagine him playing those words back in his mind, hearing how they sounded. "It was small. Private. Just..." He paused again. "I didn't know if you were ever coming back out, Hazel. I was operating under the assumption that I'd be having a memorial for you next."

She nodded, still sitting in the passenger seat, mentally picturing her dad's funeral, a packed cemetery with tons of mourners, all of them crying. Then she pictured her own funeral, with just Skip—and whoever was paid to do the service. She couldn't help but wonder if being dead would bring less pain than what was burrowing through her belly right now.

"You're not okay, are you?" Skip said, like it was a question he'd never asked before, like he'd become accustomed to her being bulletproof.

"I'm fine," Hazel said, still picturing Skip alone standing over her grave. Empty funerals didn't come from bad luck. They were earned. "I need you to tell me..." she added. "You heard what Rabkin said. If Dad was poisoned—"

"Stop. Just stop, okay? You didn't kill our father."

"Skip, was I a good person?"

"Why don't you come inside?"

"No one has come to visit me," Hazel said. "You didn't answer me the last time I asked. I need to know. Now."

"That's what made you leave the hospital?"

"I've been going through my email—"

"Don't do this. You've been on the news for two weeks. Your life isn't what it was before."

"You think I don't know that?" Hazel asked. "A half hour ago, I read an old online interview I'd given to the alumni magazine of my college. You know what I said?"

"Hazel-Ann," Skip said, "we really don't need to do this."

Hazel-Ann. It didn't sound like he called her that. Ever.

"I told them I studied death and dying because it was the one thing about humans I actually liked. That they died. I said that. Out loud. You Google my name? It's right there. Who talks like that? What *kind of person* talks like that? If I had friends, wouldn't someone have called, at least? Sent flowers? I mean, who would have come to my funeral?"

He was silent for a moment, then said, "Butchie."

"Butchie? I can't remember someone named Butchie? I'm doing worse than I thought."

"You need to get some sleep," Skip said, climbing out of the car.

In no time, they were both at the front door, a heavy one made from a thick slab of mahogany with an antique brass doorknocker shaped like a dragon. Skip stood there a moment, his hand on the doorknob. "You sure you're ready for this?"

Hazel nodded, but as Skip opened the door, his sister just stood there.

"How about I go inside and give you a few moments?" Skip added. "Come in when you're ready."

Hazel nodded again, not really listening, not hearing anything.

She was there for five minutes, ten minutes... Then finally, she stepped inside.

Her father's house was filled with the dead.

The walls were covered in framed photos of their mom. Claire at twenty-five. At thirty. At forty. Frozen in time, before she got sick.

In the living room, like a sentry next to the butter yellow sofa Hazel could remember from her

THE HOUSE OF SECRETS

childhood, stood a six-foot-tall marble statue of Anubis.

Dad's library was filled with books. Autobiographies. History. Folklore. Shelves devoted entirely to UFOs, Bigfoot, the sinking of the *Titanic*, 9/11. There was a desk in the center of the room, with a Tiffany lamp shoved to one side and the rest of the space covered in books. Every book was lived in. They had pages bent down, passages highlighted in black, blue, red, and green. Notes were scribbled in the margins, and some paragraphs were marked with sloppy asterisks beside them. God knows what his system was. A volume of Thomas Jefferson's letters was marked in three places with ticket stubs from a recent movie.

But it was his shoes that got to Hazel.

They were scattered throughout the house: loafers in the kitchen, sandals under his desk in the library, tennis shoes in the hallway, shiny black tuxedo shoes by the sliding glass door to the backyard. Hazel hadn't noticed them when she first arrived. Now, they were all she saw. Even when she stared out at the dark yard, she could make out a pair of battered old hiking boots in the rose bed beside a trowel still poking into the dirt. *He was coming back*, Hazel thought. He had always come back.

95

"Here we go," Skip said. A flash of light lit the kitchen; he handed her a lit sparkler.

"I like sparklers?" she asked.

"It's July Fourth."

Hazel had no idea. In her mind, it was still June. It might always be June.

"Dad's favorite holiday," Skip added. "I thought we'd celebrate in his honor. Honor the people who love you."

Hazel recognized that—*Honor the people who love you*, that was her father, wasn't it?—as Skip waved his sparkler like a conductor, making an infinity symbol in the air.

The sparklers were technically illegal in Studio City, Hazel thought, suddenly remembering that from nowhere too.

"Make 'em last," Skip said, still conducting.

Hazel let the sparkler burn down, down, down, until the last lick of flame smoldered between her thumb and index finger, until Skip leaned over and blew it out.

"Try not to kill yourself," Skip said. "You're all I have left."

She watched the ember. "Can I ask you something and you won't be offended?"

"Sure," Skip said.

"Do I like you?"

Skip laughed. "You revere me."

"Even when you were on the show with Dad?"

"Especially then," Skip said. "It was actually kind of awkward. I'm not a hero."

He kept his face straight for almost a full twenty seconds. He was a better actor than she thought. He yanked open a cabinet, pulled out two coffee mugs, and set them on the marble island between them.

"You didn't hate me," Skip said. "We had a few odd years there. Plus, you weren't into the show, that's for sure."

"What about recently?"

"Does it matter?"

Just as Hazel started to answer, someone banged loudly on the front door.

Hazel looked at Skip, close enough that she could really see his face. He was a boyish thirty-nine, but time wasn't always going to be his friend. There were deep lines around his eyes. Worry lines. It was almost midnight. "You expecting someone?" she asked, quickly thinking they had that front gate for a reason.

Skip shook his head. She was starting to see his pattern. Skip had nothing; he always had nothing.

Bam-bam-bam!

"Open the door! FBI!"

Hazel lunged forward, looking through the peephole. At the sight of him, Hazel's first inclination

BRAD MELTZER AND TOD GOLDBERG

was to back up quietly and pretend no one was home, get to a phone, call 911, run out the back as fast as she possibly could.

"Ms. Nash," Agent Rabkin said from the other side of the door, "if that's you standing there, you need to open this door before I kick it in."

14

W hat do you want?" Hazel challenged.

"No one knew you were checking out of the hospital," Agent Rabkin said, stepping through the living room, then the dining room, as he scanned the house. Hazel saw what he was really doing, picking apart what had been turned into a time capsule of her dad's life: a photo of him shaking hands with President Reagan, a still from the time Skip was on *The Love Boat* (he couldn't have been more than ten), and Hazel playing field hockey, blood on her right knee, a stick in her hands, and a look like murder in her eyes.

"I didn't know I had to tell you," Hazel said, "especially since I don't know you."

"I'm not your enemy, Ms. Nash."

"Then why're you here?"

"To make sure you and your brother are safe."

"And that's it?"

"That's it."

"Then I suppose you'll be on your way," Hazel said, motioning to the door as Skip handed her a fresh cup of coffee. She took a sip. It tasted like warm dirt, but brought a memory of standing under a spindly tree in the sub-Saharan savanna, sharing a cup with her guide. Hazel had been there to study a group of Bushmen who had death rituals that were unique even among the tribes of the region: When someone in the clan died, they would pick up camp and move, never to live in the spot of death again. Still, something more was starting to work at her now.

"You have a good night, Ms. Nash. You too, Skip," Rabkin said. "And don't forget: If you interfere in this investigation, I will arrest you."

Hazel watched Agent Rabkin leave, followed him out the front door past five pairs of shoes, and didn't say a word as his black Suburban rolled backward out of the driveway.

She'd grown up on this tree-lined street. Movie studios used to set up on the end of the block to shoot establishing shots. Dozens of horror movies started in her safe, sun-dappled neighborhood, and only cut away when the monsters showed up, or someone with an ax came out of the bushes. Except Hazel knew there was a secret in every house on the block, a creature under every bed.

The sky blue Cape Cod across the street. Who lived there way-back-when? They weren't close, so the memory was clear. The Caswells. Their father walked out on them. The yellow California ranch house next door? The Laramors. Oldest son died in a car accident, hit by a drunk driver. Down at the end of the block? The two-story Brady Bunch house that had been remodeled, with a wrought iron fence now wrapped around the whole place, including a call box. Who lived there? The Sorensens. The mother used to walk down the middle of the street in her robe and nothing else, cops would get called, and then they wouldn't see Mrs. Sorensen for a few weeks, maybe a month.

It was summer in Los Angeles, the time for serial killers and wildfires, but being outside was suddenly the only place Hazel could stand to be. The inside of her father's house was closing around her like the walls of the hospital, like the walls of her mind.

Mysteries need to be solved.

Three guesses per night.

"Hazel? You okay?"

She turned around. Skip was standing behind her.

"There's a rub in every deal," Hazel said. There was a memory she couldn't grasp, some lost piece of time, a thread that, pulled tight, would end up in her hand. "In the hospital, Rabkin never answered our question about what work Dad did with the government."

Across the street, the garage door of the Cape Cod opened and two teenage boys came rolling out on skateboards. Under the driveway spotlight, they were shirtless, tan, and in mid-sentence. Hazel caught something about a party in the canyon. It was the middle of the night and no one was stopping these kids from doing anything.

"This isn't a conversation for the front lawn," Skip said.

"Dad lived here for our entire lives. Whatever secrets he had, they managed to stay on this block."

"Maybe I should go on TV and tell everyone that Dad was a spy," Skip said. "I bet we'll get some answers then."

"That doesn't mean they'll be the right answers."

Skip started to reply, then stopped as Hazel's words sank in. "Dad was decapitated in the car accident," he said. "Last week, when I first met Rabkin, he told me that. I wasn't sure if you heard. I thought you should know."

"Hnh," Hazel said. "Was Dad already dead?"

"If he was alive, it wasn't in a significant way," Skip said.

Hazel nodded, thinking she knew a bit about what it might be like to be alive insignificantly.

Over the past week, what had she seen when she was in that coma? Blackness. If she wanted light, if she wanted answers about her dad and Benedict Arnold's bible, there was only one place she'd get them.

15

The Bear stokes the fire. The problem when you burn clothing is the unpredictability of fabrics, which is why The Bear prefers to wear silk. It's hard to ignite, burns slowly and erratically, if at all—and in the situation where someone might try to set you on fire, a significant amount of accelerant would be needed. *Make them work to kill you*, The Bear thinks. *Make them leave evidence.*

It seems to The Bear that he's dealing with an acetate today, what with the acrid smell and the molten black sludge that's filling the bottom of the firebox. He'll have to chip that off when it cools, flush it down the toilet, then have housekeeping come in early, before he checks out, make sure they give the toilet a good scrubbing.

The housekeeping staff at the Al Qasr hotel has been very attentive thus far. He'll leave them a nice tip when he checks out in a few hours. Will fill out a comment card.

He tosses a pair of socks in the fire. They sizzle and melt. Nylon. Arthur Kennedy had enough money to sit in first class, and still, *nylon*?

It's five o'clock in the Eastern Time Zone, so The Bear gets online and watches the feed of the local New Haven, Connecticut, news. A reality TV star has been arrested for tax evasion. The Friends of the New Haven Animal Shelter will host a pet adoption in the parking lot of the IKEA tomorrow at 11 a.m. There was an earthquake in Plainfield, of all places.

No mention of local man Arthur Kennedy's body being found in Dubai. In truth, The Bear is surprised. He'd left Kennedy outside the mosque in Sonapur, the old burial ground that the Emirates had turned into a camp for the workers of the high-end resorts. Just a few miles from the most expensive and lavish destinations on the planet and yet it was a squalor of tenements and shanties. *A bad place to die, a worse place to live*, The Bear thought, knowing a little light wouldn't be such a bad thing to shine on that shadowland.

But he's spent more than a day waiting for someone to find the body and put the word out.

He checks the *New Haven Register*. Nothing. Checks the *Hartford Courant*. Nothing. Widens

it out to the papers in Boston, New York, even
Philadelphia. Nothing. He checks crime blotters.
Checks Twitter. Checks Facebook. Checks Insta-
gram. He checks the social networks in the UAE,
Russia, China, everywhere. Spiders through the
credit reporting services, the banks, everything.

Quiet.

He reads the obituary for Jack Nash, celebrated
TV host of *The House of Secrets*. There's plenty of
noise there. Whole websites are claiming it was
murder, assassination, cover-up.

He looks for the man known as Darren Nixon,
who was found with a bible in his chest.

Quiet there too. That much he expected. People
were still good at their jobs occasionally.

Then he looks for Hazel. And Skip.

Skip is easy to track. On Twitter, someone
named Tommy2unes posted: "Just saw Skip Nash
at Starbucks. Gave condolences. Super nice.
#HouseOfSecrets." For twenty years, Skip had
been on TV. Wherever he went, someone saw
him. He was a living alibi. This made The Bear's
work easy. The bait was set. When word got out,
Skip and Hazel would come running.

The Bear does 100 sit-ups, 150 push-ups, another 100 sit-ups, another 150 push-ups. Then
he orders crème brûlée from the room service
menu.

The Bear eats his crème brûlée. Looks for Arthur Kennedy again.

Refreshes.

A hundred crunches.

Refreshes.

The Bear calls the New Haven police from one of his three cell phones, not that they'd be able to trace him all the way to Dubai. Not the locals, anyway. It was up the chain that was the issue. "Would it be possible to check on my cousin? He hasn't answered his phone in days and I'm starting to worry. His name? Yes. Arthur Kennedy. Yes, I'll hold."

He hangs up, tosses his phone into the fire, watches it melt.

That should do it. Maybe Skip wouldn't come running.

But Hazel would.

16

I don't think you're ready for this," Skip told her the following morning. They were getting off the highway now, on the turnoff for the airport and its giant *LAX* sign. "For all you know, this is exactly what Rabkin wants you to do: to go searching like Dad did. Maybe he's using you."

"No one's using me," Hazel said. Part of her thought that was true. Another part of her thought about Darren Nixon, about Benedict Arnold's bible, about her father. Mostly about her father. Whatever was really going on, she had to know who her dad was, even if she didn't quite know who *she* was yet.

"You should throw away your cell phone," Hazel told Skip. "Burn your computer too. Whatever's going on, I'd rather do it without the FBI."

"I don't know, Haze," Skip said. "All those years I was on the show, Dad never said a word to me about searching for anything that belonged to Benedict Arnold. Don't you think one night, when we were in a hut in Asia, or out in Africa, doing that show on Bushmen and their precognitive dreams, he would have said something?"

"You were a kid."

"I'm not a kid anymore." He looked in the rearview mirror, then pointed over his shoulder. "You think Dad wanted us to be followed?"

Hazel turned around. There was a black Suburban behind them.

"That's an airport shuttle," Hazel said.

"How do you know?"

"Because it's obvious," Hazel said. "Skip, I meant what I said about your phone."

Skip pulled up to the curb at LAX. The black Suburban passed them. It had a giant sticker in the back window advertising Luxury Limousine Transport.

"*See?*" Hazel said.

"You think it would say *surveillance?*"

The Suburban was far away now, fading from view.

"I can come with you if you want," Skip said.

She didn't answer. She didn't have to.

Skip didn't say a word for almost a full minute. Finally, "Why aren't you scared?"

"I don't know," Hazel said.

"It doesn't mean you shouldn't be."

"What's the worst that could happen?"

"You could die," Skip said.

"I've already been dead," Hazel said, thinking, *I'm already dead.* "How long were we out there in the desert before help came?"

"An hour," Skip said. "I don't know. Maybe more."

"If someone wanted us gone, we'd be gone."

Skip got out of his car, popped the trunk, and pulled out Hazel's bag. It was a bowling ball bag with a Skippy peanut butter logo on it, the kind of gross, hip thing you buy in LA and never use again. Hazel knew it wasn't hers, and knew there were barely any clothes in it. Two shirts, two pairs of pants, no shoes. Those had been cut off her when she was brought into the hospital; she bought flip-flops in the gift shop. She wanted to go home to San Francisco, get some clothes of her own. And get some other things too.

"Are we people who hug?" Hazel asked.

"We aren't," Skip said. Hazel made a face, then reached out and wrapped her arms around him. "Don't do anything stupid, okay?" he said.

"That's the plan," she said.

17

I recognize you," the man sitting next to Hazel on the flight to San Francisco said. They'd been in the air for thirty minutes. Hazel's head was down, her earphones in, as she watched her father on the iPad she had grabbed from his house. This was precisely how she'd spent nearly every free moment since she left the hospital: trying to learn everything her dad knew.

Onscreen, there he was, in the Everglades, 1981, searching for a hundred-foot python that locals said had eaten a missing girl. He never found a giant python. Nor any bones of a young girl.

Hazel took one earphone out. "I'm sorry?" she said.

The man was staring at her like he knew her, his face too close to hers. He was in his forties, dressed in a suit, but not like the kind Agent Rabkin wore; this one was tailored, and it didn't look like he had a gun. He wore a dress shirt, one with a white collar and blue stripes, which made him look like a network anchorman. Or an asshole. He had a watch that would let him know the hour in two other time zones she was pretty sure he couldn't identify.

"I said I recognized you," he said. "You're a woman who doesn't want to be bothered."

"Perceptive," Hazel said, and started to put her earphone back in. The man tugged the cord out of her iPad.

"I'm Tony Champion," he said and extended his hand. Hazel didn't take it, because she thought she might break his wrist. "Name isn't familiar to you?"

"No," Hazel said, feeling her anger rising, but unsure how to stop it.

"Tony Champion's Tri-City Ford? No? Nothing?"

"I'm not from the area," Hazel said. Whatever area he was from.

"Ah," Tony said. "I recognized you in the airport, actually." He winked at her. Actually winked. "No worries. I'm not one of those people, right? That annoying guy who talks to you on a plane and then you're worried he'll follow you out to your car or something? I'm not that guy. I'm more like the guy who sits down next to you and talks nervously because he's afraid to fly." He paused. "That came out wrong. I mean. Let's start over. Can I start over?"

"You can try," Hazel said.

"I look over and I see you, and I'm like, okay, I know that girl, she's the one from that car crash in the desert, I mean, I know you're more than that, but I eyeballed you at the airport—Jack Nash's daughter—and then I look down and see your father there on your screen and I know for sure. And I think, *What are the odds?* We should have a drink. Do you want a drink? You have a drink with me, I'll give you back your earphones. How's that for a deal?"

"I don't want to be bothered," Hazel said.

"I get it," he said. He rolled her earphone cable around between his thumb and forefinger. Then tugged it again—hard—so it ripped from her ear. "But what choice do you have now, right?"

Hazel turned her whole body toward Tony, leaned into him, past the armrest. They locked eyes, and Hazel gave Tony a good deep drink of her black glare. Let him see the fire he'd started.

Hazel saw his pulse beating in his throat. If she wanted to, she could go for blood right where he sat. He'd be unconscious before he could even ring for the flight attendant. How many ways could she do it? She could snap her headphones apart into sharp points. She could use her seat belt buckle to clip his throat. She could use her bare hands…and wouldn't that be satisfying about now?

Slowly, Tony Champion's smile faded. Hazel could see his face turning pale, could smell the fear coming off him, hear his breath quickening. Her earphone cable slipped from his fingers.

He wasn't half as terrified as Hazel now was. It was one thing to protect herself, but her thoughts, the violence, had come so fast, so intensely, so…naturally. Who the hell was she in her old life?

Her hands now shaking from the adrenaline rush, Hazel took her earphones back and plugged them in.

She wondered, though, did she usually act this way? Maybe Skip had been right that morning, when they were together in the house, watching old episodes of *The House of Secrets*, seeing their dad aging in hour increments on the screen of the iPad. For years, Dad had Skip right by his side: a sandy-haired boy in Libya searching for remnants of the dragon slain by St. George; at thirteen and awkward, talking about the power of crystals in Santa Fe; at seventeen in Philadelphia, all sinew and nonchalance, walking the underground tunnels of the city, looking for ghosts.

And then Skip was gone, on teen-idol cruises to Mexico, reality shows in Japan, conventions anywhere, sharing stories about what NASA told him about aliens, where he thought Jimmy Hoffa was buried, overseeing dives for sunken Revolutionary War treasures, coming up with an odd gold coin. He was, Hazel realized, only a couple of generations removed from selling miracle elixirs at a sideshow.

Hazel tried to focus on the TV show, tried to keep her concentration.

Onscreen, Jack was sitting on the porch of a falling-down river house, talking about the python with a Haitian woman who was no more than twenty-five. The missing girl's mother. Her eyes were so wide with fear, it was a wonder she managed to put one word after the last. In her studies, Hazel had seen it a thousand times, when she was interviewing survivors of a thousand different horrors. Fear brought out precision in language. You didn't have the benefit of metaphor or equivocation when you were in the middle of an unending trauma. She wondered what that did to the amygdala.

"I have a daughter," her father says to the young mother, then reaches out, touches her on the wrist. *"Hazel-Ann."*

"Pretty name," the mother says.

"If she were missing, I'd never stop looking for her," Jack tells her. *"Ever."*

Hazel hit Stop. Scrolled back. Listened to her father's words again.

Again.

Again.

"I'll find your daughter. She is somewhere," Jack says.

Again.

Again.

In fifteen minutes, the plane would swing toward San Francisco, where a woman named Hazel-Ann Nash lived. She'd gone missing in a car accident. That didn't mean she wasn't somewhere.

18

FBI Building
Los Angeles

Trevor Rabkin was taping up his old life when his phone buzzed. A few months back, he'd given away the last of his ex-wife's clothes, what she'd left behind in the dryer when she walked out. A couple of shirts. Jeans. A scarf he'd purchased for her at a market in Kabul. Now, at his desk at FBI Headquarters, he was sealing a box filled with toys for his daughter. Get it into the mail. Be ready for the next part of his life. It was almost noon. Hazel would be arriving in San Francisco any minute.

"Your girl is in the wind," his new boss, Special Agent Louis Moten, said.

"Sir?"

"Hazel. Did you know she's in San Francisco?"

"I'm aware."

Moten made a noise, like a grunt. A

surprised but content grunt. "You knew she'd go," Moten said. It wasn't a question. "Good job, Agent."

"You asked me to handle this. I'll handle it," Rabkin said.

Last month, Trevor Rabkin accidentally blew the cover of an FBI agent involved in a bank robbery syndicate by shooting him. The FBI was in the process of kicking Rabkin to the curb. So what was next? Law school? No. Too many people. He wasn't great with people. Maybe he'd look into veterinary medicine. Specialize in farm animals. Horses and cows. Not as much emotion wrapped up in those.

Except he'd already thrown away so much. He could say *lost*. But that wasn't true. He'd thrown it away.

That's when a man he'd never seen before entered his office. Older, late sixties at least, a gut, white linen suit, like he was just in from a courtroom in Mississippi in 1967. The man's nose looked like it'd been hit a few times. No obvious guns on his body. Not even a bulge on his ankle. *Paper pusher*, Trevor had thought, though the guy carried himself like a cowboy, all his weight back on his heels. He had a file in his hand.

"You Agent Rabbit?" Louis Moten had said.

During his military training, they didn't call him

Rabbit just as an easy nickname. It was also because he was fast, though these days he wore the name because he kept jumping around—this would be his third transfer within the FBI in as many years. And most likely his last.

"You still interested in being an actual agent?" Moten had asked. "Maybe use what you learned in Afghanistan."

Trevor tightened his gaze. He hadn't told Moten that he'd served, much less where he'd been stationed. No, Moten wasn't a paper pusher. He was the kind of guy who burned papers.

"I'm in from Bethesda," Moten had said. "You ever been out to Bethesda, Agent?"

"No, sir." Bethesda was the command center for half a dozen different operations. The kind that didn't exist. Line items for million-dollar staplers? Those were in Bethesda.

"It's a swamp," Moten had said, a thin smile spreading across his face. "You got a wife? Kids?" he'd asked.

"No," Trevor had said. "Not anymore. My wife took my daughter with her."

"That doesn't mean you don't have a kid."

"I was just—"

Moten cut him off with a wave. "You got anyone you tell your secrets to? Therapist? Dog?"

"No."

"Then we share a very good belief system," Moten had said, pressing his palms together so his rings clinked: a gold wedding ring on his left hand...and on his right, a class ring from somewhere, one of those gaudy numbers that made it look like you won the Super Bowl for graduating college.

"Everyone deserves a chance at redemption, don't you think?" Moten added. "How'd you like a job?"

"Depends what kind."

"How about one that doesn't treat you like a moron?"

Trevor nodded. He liked this man and his ugly suit. But what he liked even more was the chance to once again be the rabbit who was fast.

From there, Rabbit got files on Jack Nash, the poison in his body, and all Jack's work with the FBI. He also got files on Jack's kids. The dumb one named Skip. And the one they didn't trust. The wild one. Hazel. Dad traveled a lot. Hazel did too.

"There's something else," Moten said today through the phone. "I'm sending it to you now. Could be nothing. Probably nothing. But I need you to look if it becomes an issue."

There was a ping on Rabbit's computer. He opened the file.

An American man named Arthur Kennedy was found outside a mosque in Sonapur, dead from what the UAE authorities were calling natural causes: respiratory failure, likely from a stroke.

Which meant he dropped dead. Happened to people every day.

The problem was, there was no one to claim his body, which meant by UAE law he'd be buried in an unmarked grave at the paupers' cemetery, since no one was paying to ship his remains around the world.

Case closed.

Until New Haven cops got a call from someone purporting to be a cousin of Kennedy's. When they couldn't get a return on the phone number, they kicked it to the New Haven FBI field office for some help, and then it pinged and pinged and pinged, until it was in Rabbit's email.

Rabbit looked closer at the details in Kennedy's file:

Connecticut driver's license. Forty-six years old. Height: 5'8". Weight: 211 lbs. Brown hair. Brown eyes. Organ donor.

From the photo on his license, he was mostly bald, not bothering to comb anything over, just an island above his forehead, sidewalls. He's smiling, his teeth terrible, crooked, jagged, like his entire mouth is a crumbling Greek city.

He had a real estate license since 1996. Owned three properties in New Haven, including a warehouse and the adjacent parking lot. If you want to make money, build a parking lot, even if it just means paving dirt and painting lines, and then you can charge people to leave their cars on it, money out of nothing, every day.

What caught Rabbit's eye was that there was no next of kin, no will on file.

Not with an attorney. Not with a lawyer or a bank trust.

There was an OkCupid profile with a hundred personal answers, none of which looked terribly personal. Didn't smoke, didn't drink, but didn't mind if you smoked or drank. Enjoyed American history, considered himself middle-of-the-road politically, but "didn't believe the liberal media." His typical Friday night included "wine, good friends, and some spirited debate."

Rabbit had set up his own profile a few weeks after his wife Mallory left. It was the middle of the night and he was sitting in Powell Library at UCLA, surrounded by students cramming for a future they thought was assured. He'd gotten through fifteen questions, then decided he'd be better off trying to find another agent to date. That hadn't worked either.

Onscreen, Rabbit clicked open the medical

examiner's photos and tried to make sense of what he was seeing.

Arthur Kennedy may have died of natural causes, but he'd been left outside for a while, long enough for the sun to get to work on him before anyone found him. There were no obvious signs of trauma. Kennedy was sitting up, head bent back, mouth open wide, gravity working on his face, making it look like he was mid-scream. The flies didn't help matters.

It was gruesome—but it was how people looked when they died. It was the one thing he'd never really gotten used to in this job. All the bodies he'd seen, he always ended up mentally cutting and pasting loved ones' faces onto them, imagining what they'd look like after their final moment.

There were, however, two things that seemed unusual about Arthur Kennedy. The first was his clothes.

He wore a military uniform—blue wool jacket with gold piping on the lapels, gold buttons down the front, long white socks, black shoes—like something you'd see in a Civil War reenactment. No, not Civil War. Revolutionary War. A tricorn hat was knocked off his head. All he was missing was a musket.

How the hell did the UAE cops not flag something like this? Unless they were told not to flag it.

The second thing was that, underneath Kennedy's jacket, his chest was bare—except for a dark red line at the center of his breastbone. A jagged new scar with an oblong lump. Like there was something hiding underneath.

19

San Francisco

I thought you weren't coming back," the manager of Hazel's apartment building said. They were walking down a long hardwood hallway in her building off 16th Street in the Mission District, one of those refurbished San Francisco tenements. That meant it had all the brick and wood of the past, all the shiny metal of the present, the whole world now a Pottery Barn.

Hazel couldn't remember the building manager's name, wasn't sure if she'd ever known it. She had to buzz him to get in, since she also had no idea where her house keys were.

Probably on the floor of the Utah desert along with the rest of her.

"Then with all that publicity and such," the manager was saying, "I thought, well, better change the locks out front, in case someone comes snooping around, pretending to be a relative. Didn't know there'd been a celebrity living in my building all these years."

"Did anyone come?" Hazel asked.

"Couple reporters. But I didn't let them talk to anyone." Hazel thought his name was Hal. Maybe Charlie. One of those. "Your friend came too."

She cocked an eyebrow.

"The one with the pit bull. Butchie," the manager said. "Couple looky-loos too. People left some candles out front for your dad, some flowers, stuffed animals. For a bit I was worried it was going to be a Princess Di thing, and I'd have to figure out what to do with ten thousand teddy bears. That didn't come to pass, thankfully."

"I hate teddy bears," Hazel said.

"Never trust anything with buttons for eyes." They came to unit 106 and he handed her the key. "Here you go. Good to have you back."

"Can I ask you a question?" She felt like Dr. Morrison, offering forewarnings during simple human conversation. Something she understood better now.

"Sure," Hal-or-Charlie said.

"Were we friends?"

Hal-or-Charlie didn't think for even half a second. "I wouldn't say that, no."

"Have we ever even spoken before?"

"You had a problem with your shower that one

time. Then those times when you thought someone was stealing your mail. Other than that, I
guess not really."

"When was that, with my mail?"

"Last time? I don't know. Two months ago?"

Last time.

"So only when I had a problem?"

Hal-or-Charlie shrugged. "That's how it is sometimes."

"Why did you look out for me then?"

"Isn't that what people do?"

"Do they?"

"I guess I just think most people are good," he
said, watching Hazel open the door to her home.
"Pay that back and maybe when the wolves are
gathering, someone will shoo them away from my
door too."

20

Hazel's apartment was small. Seven hundred square feet. Galley kitchen. Two plates still in the sink. A glass. A coffee cup. The refrigerator was filled with things she couldn't imagine she enjoyed: condiments, half a dozen plastic bottles of blue Gatorade, and unopened packages of pre-sliced, pre-packaged lunch meat—salami and roast beef—not even any bread to put the meat on.

Hazel cracked open a Gatorade, drank it down. Unwrapped a package of salami, shoved four pieces into her mouth. *Guh.* Couldn't taste anything. She needed something spicy, something to taste, something to remind her she was human.

She stepped into her living room. There was a single couch that looked like it had belonged to someone else first, Hazel was pretty sure it was a remnant of that phase when everything was shabby chic. There was also a glass coffee table covered with textbooks—*Understanding Cultural Rituals of Death*; *Introduction to Anthropology, 25th edition*—magazines, and a stack of ungraded student papers.

She picked one up and read the student's name. Dakota Shepherd.

Hazel could picture her exactly, which was a relief. She sat in the front row and asked on the first day that she be called "Cody," which was probably one of the only reasons Hazel remembered her, with or without a brain injury, because three days a week, whenever she saw her, Hazel repeated *"Call her Cody"* in her mind, sensitive to people being called what they wanted.

As Hazel skimmed the paper, she saw that Cody had written about the Buddhist tradition of spending forty-nine days after the death of a loved one working through the stages of *bardo*, chanting sutras to help ease the dead toward happiness in their next state. To Hazel, that was a good idea. Maybe she'd do that next, instead of working through the facts of her present existence.

Her walls were covered in framed photos...of herself.

There she was skydiving, it looked like over Santa Cruz if her topography facts were still right. As always, facts were easy. But people...emotions...

experiences? Next to her in a circle of jumpers was a man with a tattoo on his throat. It was of a pit bull, the name *Butchie* scrawled across it in Old English. The man's helmet, and Hazel's, read *Butchie'z Airborn Adventurez!* The photo looked recent. Still, file not found.

There she was in Egypt, head wrapped in a yellow scarf, actually atop a camel. There's a cut over her left eye, nothing serious but a wound nonetheless. She reached up, felt the skin above her eyebrow, felt the slight raised edge of a scar. File not found.

And then in Africa, a man she couldn't remember standing next to her. His right arm was wrapped around her waist, his thumb and middle finger squeezing her hip, his shirt unbuttoned one too many spots, revealing his red burned skin. A name appeared in her head. Karl. Karl with a K. And then, out of nowhere, she could feel his breath on her neck, could remember a scene in a tent village on the savanna, the two of them screaming at each other deep into a desert night, and then him saying, "It's called an affair for a reason."

That's all she had. Hazel pulled the photo off the wall, tossed it into the garbage, and went into her bedroom.

Her bed was unmade, the outline of her body

right where she left it weeks ago, a tangled depression in the sky blue sheets. The walls of her bedroom were filled with even more photos of herself. Hazel tried to remember some concrete detail about each trip. Beirut: *Interviewing the living survivors of the Lebanon bombings.* Paris: *Complex mourning rituals of runaways.* New York: *Lunch with her father at Tavern on the Green.* Who was on the other side of the camera? Strangers. Now and then.

The best thing, she realized, was that she didn't care.

No. That wasn't true.

She knew she *did*. But the benefit of her injury was that she didn't *have to* anymore. She could throw away every old photo. She could keep feeling nothing about the past, could only accumulate *new* feelings. That's what Dr. Morrison's advice was. According to Agent Rabkin, that's what Morrison wanted her to know. That when she walked out of the hospital, she wasn't bound by the person she'd been, by the people she'd grown up with. She could walk away.

She could forget about all of this.

She could get back into the classroom.

She could teach the realities of the world.

The things we all have in common, and the things none of us do.

The unchangeable history.

Except, she now was beginning to understand, history wasn't fixed. Only its reporting was.

There was a single book on her nightstand. *Ancient Poisons*. She picked it up. There were dozens of dog-eared pages, highlights in yellow and orange, arrows, underlines, questions: *At what quantity is tissue poisoned? Check re: temperature at which full dissipation occurs.* Was this who she was? Was this her specialty? Being a recluse sociopath?

Flipping to the index, she searched for Polosis 5, the drug they found in Nixon's body, in her father's body. She didn't know what surprised her more: that it wasn't in the book, or that she was thankful it wasn't there.

Her cell phone began to ring. She looked at the number. Agent Rabkin. She should answer the call, find out if he had anything new...except all she heard in her mind was: *Run. Don't look back.*

She turned off her phone. There was a reason she came home. The memory she didn't share with Skip. The memory of what she'd hidden here.

Hazel opened her closet door. Hanging shirts, T-shirts, long-sleeve T-shirts, all arranged precisely by color, starting with white, ending with black. The labels indicated she'd spent a lot of her free time inside J.Crew. On the bottom, she had her pants and shorts, ordered by season, also by color. There was a chest of drawers in the closet too, an antique highboy, the kind you lug to every place you ever live. It was a classic. Indestructible.

She pulled open the drawers.

Socks.

Underwear.

Pajamas.

Sweatpants.

And then, in the bottom drawer, arranged neatly, just like everything else, were her guns.

21

Hazel tore up her apartment looking for a concealed-carry permit. She didn't remember one, which worried her even more. Cold facts—like the facts from her anthropology research—wasn't that something she should recall? But, as she was learning, when it came to the "facts" of her personal life, from the pictures on her wall to the clothes in her closet, once something entered the so-called "emotional" part of her brain and became part of the intimacies of her life, all the details became jumbled.

Pulling open drawers, she found loads of other stuff—an old PalmPilot, birth control pills, a vibrator, even her passport—but she still couldn't find the permit.

Wouldn't she at least remember the bureaucratic parts of the process? Getting background checked? Learning if the state thought she had high enough moral character?

Maybe she didn't have any moral character.

Maybe that's why there was no permit.

Maybe that's why, with each episode of *The House of Secrets* that she watched over the past few days, she found herself rooting for the myth *not* to be figured out conclusively.

Rooting for the bad guy.

Rooting for whatever was hidden to stay that way.

It made her think of Johannesburg.

It was a doomsday episode, where Dad came back, as he always did, and where the world didn't end, because it never did. She'd watched it last night with Skip, who told her that when Dad finished filming there, his heart stopped working for the first time, but not the last time. Now, something told her to put it on again.

Hazel opened her computer, found the episode on YouTube. Like last night, her dad looked sick. Worn down. Dilapidated.

She stared at her father's face, his skin. Pale, even with makeup on. The whites of his eyes, the sclera, almost cream in color. Infection. Maybe jaundice. Hard to tell. Hands, trembling.

Where had she been when he'd fallen ill?

Drifting.

Her passport said Lebanon. Then Ireland. Then Iran. All in a month's time.

As she studied the screen, Hazel's eyes slid toward the right-hand column. The videos "Up next."

The House of Secrets—Moscow (1985). Two million views.
The House of Secrets—Kabul (2002). Four and a half million views.
The House of Secrets—Iran (1980). Seven million views.

Hnh.

She remembered that episode. She'd watched the Iran one a few days ago, where he talked about a Bakhtak, a creature in Persian legend that sat on your chest while you slept, turning dreams into nightmares. But now . . .

She reached for her passport. There was a stamp for Kabul in there too.

And Moscow. All in the same month.

What had she been doing there? Lebanon, she remembered, interviewing bombing survivors. Kabul was to study war and its survivors. But Iran? She stared at her passport, details coming back. The secret dance clubs of Tehran, DJs spinning into the morning, the taste of her own sweat, the burn in her eyes, the sense of doing the wrong thing, in the wrong place, with the wrong people.

Her dad had been to all of those places too, over the years. On YouTube, she looked at the date of the Iran episode. 1980. Americans still being held hostage, Carter still in office, Hazel only a year old, and he'd gone to Iran?

She clicked on the episode. There was her dad, younger than Hazel now, meeting with people cloaked in shadows, telling Bakhtak stories. Then these men—they were always men—walked with him through shaded courtyards, Jack absently pulling dates off trees, shining them on his shirt, small children running at his feet, kicking a soccer ball.

That image repeated.

Every episode, at some point, small children encircled Jack, playing, laughing, shouting, acting like kids.

Walking through the streets of Belfast in 1984.

Moscow in 1985.

Beirut in 1999.

Kabul in 2002. Didn't matter. Jack would get on one knee, whisper something in a child's ear, muss up their hair, and then they'd run off squealing in delight.

At the height of the show, he was so famous, adults and small children in countries that vilified the United States, like Russia and China, still loved him—because he was the guy who could say uncomfortable things about America. How many times had he done an episode about corrupt Presidents? Or given credence to things like secret wars, or the CIA using acid trips for mind control? Jack Nash was the guy who pulled the veil back. It didn't matter where you lived, there was always a veil. So he could travel the world with impunity.

And wasn't that ironic.

What had Hazel been doing all these years? Traveling the world with impunity too, going to those same places. Places normal people didn't visit. And for some reason, she knew those visits weren't with her dad.

Hazel felt a pressure on her chest, like a Bakhtak, she imagined. For the past two days, she'd been focused on Agent Rabkin's revelations, that her father had been working for the government. Like he was some sort of spy. But now, eyeing her passport and feeling her stomach twist, Hazel had to wonder: the guns, the poisons, even her continental drift... Was her dad the only one working for the government, or was *she* working for them too? Even worse: If this had something to do with Darren Nixon's criminal past, if Nixon was threatening her father or even Skip, would Hazel hold back? Would anyone hold back to protect their family? Or to put it another way, when some-one forced Darren Nixon's face into the water, drowning him, was *she* the one watching his body twist in his fake Revolutionary War jacket?

She shook her head. She was a professor and re-searcher, but she wasn't a murderer. She was just a woman who'd made some bad choices. Wasn't she?

Her passport was open, shaking in her hands. All those places—Iran, Moscow, Kabul. And again that thought: *Places normal people didn't visit.*

She had no memory of being afraid there, won-dered if werewolves ever feared anything. Silver bullets were pretty rare these days.

And then there it was.

Some clarity.

Where had she gone? Eventually, everywhere Jack had been.

What had she been doing? Researching the cul-tures of death? Reasoning with the end? No. Something worse.

A cold sweat gripped her ribs, working up to-ward her neck. Hazel headed into her bedroom, stripped out of her clothes, crawled into bed nude. Her body slid into a perfect notch in her mattress, the sheets felt just right pulled up under her chin, her pillow cradling her head exactly.

She closed her eyes, hearing her dad's voice still talking onscreen in the next room.

Could she see herself interviewing people in a thatched hut or a war zone somewhere?

Could she see herself sitting up late, drinking coffee, typing, reporting her findings?

Could she see herself in this apartment?

She couldn't.

She knew those things were true, but they were gone.

Could she imagine herself holding a gun, maybe that sleek silver SIG Sauer, the one with the grip so smooth that when she hefted it up an hour ago, it felt like her own skin?

Could she imagine herself sliding the clip in, hearing the satisfying click, lowering it down by her leg, moving around a corner?

Could she imagine herself firing it to protect her father?

She could.

22

FBI Building
Los Angeles

There's not enough here, Rabbit thought. He was staring at his computer, clicking through the tabs of various government databases. This is what *investigation* amounted to these days. Clicking. He wondered if more of his colleagues were sidelined by being shot at or by carpal tunnel.

In the bottom left of the screen, he'd minimized the gruesome photo of this newest victim, also inexplicably dressed in another Revolutionary War coat: Arthur Kennedy, found dead in Dubai with a bright scar on his chest. The Dubai medical examiner hadn't yet opened his chest, was waiting for someone to claim the body. If there was no next of kin, then who cared? Put it in a potter's field, save everyone a night's work.

Did that make sense to Rabbit? Of course not. People dressed like that don't just drop dead with no one noticing. If no one noticed, it's because at the time of death, no one was supposed to notice.

And c'mon. The name. *Kennedy*. First Nixon, now Kennedy? That defied all logic and had Rabbit thinking that one, if not both, of those names might be fake.

But the thing that kept coming back to Rabbit was that at forty-six, Kennedy wasn't just an orphan—that was normal, parents die—but he had *nobody*. Not a cousin. Not a second cousin. Not someone who'd married into some corner of the family. No one. Didn't even have a will on file, which, okay, that happens. Still, Kennedy should have friends. At least on the Internet.

Rabbit again started clicking, started looking.

No Facebook.

No Twitter.

Rabbit again thinking, *There's not enough here. Something's missing.*

Parents. That's what was missing. Rabbit clicked back to the case file, looking for Arthur Kennedy's birth certificate. It wasn't there. He had a Social Security number, so at some point, he had a birth certificate. Unless *Arthur Kennedy* was a fake name. Still, there'd be a record someplace, some piece of paper that helped him get through school and live on a day-to-day basis.

Agents in New Haven should have pulled his

passport application. No doubt, it was a low rung being assigned to the New Haven office. Probably the only thing of note they did was spy on students at Yale, try to infiltrate Skull and Bones, realize they didn't want to piss off someone who might be President one day.

Back to Kennedy.

No arrests.

Not on any obvious government watch lists.

No taxes due.

First-class airfare purchased using a credit card, not trying to hide. Reserved a room at the Al Qasr, paid up front, never checked in to his hotel. But his body wasn't found for two days. That didn't make sense.

Where had he been?

What had he been doing?

There were many ways to find an answer. But as was his preference, Rabbit chose the most direct route. He picked up his phone, dialing a now-familiar number.

No one picked up until the third ring.

"What?" Skip asked. "What'd I do now?"

23

San Francisco

Hazel woke up the next morning, showered, put on fresh clothes, swallowed a handful of medications, then walked six blocks to a convenience store, bought a disposable cell phone, and called Skip.

Tried to, anyway.

He didn't pick up. Which wasn't a problem, since all she had to do to find him was look online. Not even 10 a.m. and already, according to Twitter, Skip was at a Jamba Juice in the Valley. He even retweeted a photo from there, drink in hand, a girl on one side of him making that stupid duck face. Things were beginning to clarify for Hazel. One thing she was certain of: Skip needed to keep photos of himself off the Internet.

From there, Hazel walked down 20th, found a bench inside Dolores Park. It was a sunny day, kids were playing on the slope of grass, rolling,

rolling, getting up, running up the hill, rolling again. There was a playground at the bottom of the hill with a little putting green. Hazel thought about what it must have been like to be Darren Nixon, drowning in the middle of a park three thousand miles from home. What was the last thing he saw? His killer walking away? A blade of grass in the distance? From her vantage point, Hazel could see downtown San Francisco, the fog burned off, nothing but glittering metal and stone in the distance, but Hazel focused on what she could really see. What was true. What was no longer conjecture in her mind.

She closed her eyes, tried to feel the place, tried to imagine herself here before, and there she is. Could see herself sitting on a bench, could see herself at sunset, with a man and his dog.

Butchie.

Could remember telling him a fact she'd learned. A small bit of anthropological significance in the space where kids jumped in a rented bounce house that night, had a picnic, a birthday party.

"This place," she's saying to Butchie—and there's his dog, off the leash, running, Butchie clapping, the dog running back, standing right by his side—"used to be a cemetery."

"What?" Butchie says back. "You gotta be shitting me. Like *Poltergeist*?"

"No," Hazel says, "they moved the bodies. It was a Jewish cemetery. This land became too valuable, so they just dug them all up and moved them to Colma."

"I don't even know where that is."

"Across the bay," Hazel says. "It's where they moved all the dead when they eventually decided there shouldn't be any cemeteries in the city."

"That's some dark shit," Butchie was telling her, and yeah, she thought now, it's what happened. Sometimes, the dead got moved, paved over, and forgotten.

24

Where are you?" Skip asked through Hazel's new phone. He sounded frazzled, the opposite of the photo she'd seen of him minutes earlier, when it looked like he was having the time of his life at Jamba Juice. "I've been trying you all night!"

"I pulled the cord from the wall. So I could sleep," Hazel explained.

"So you're in San Francisco? You arrived okay?"

Hazel didn't say anything.

"Hazel, are you being held at gunpoint?"

"No," she said. "I just…I don't feel safe saying where I am."

"You need to contact Agent Rabkin."

"I don't feel safe doing that either," Hazel said. Two kids came running past, a boy and a girl, six, maybe seven years old, their candy bars melting in their hands. There was grass in their hair, and

Hazel thought, *They look like summer*. "I found guns in my apartment, Skip. A lot of them."

"That's not something I need to know about, Haze."

"What if I'm the one who killed him?" Hazel asked.

"Who? Dad? I don't care what they say, Dad had a heart attack."

"I'm talking about the man wearing Dad's red-coat jacket. Darren Nixon. Do you think I might have killed him?"

"They checked your records. You haven't been in Canada," Skip said.

"Maybe I helped plan it then." She told him about the book of poisons, about her passport, about her memories. "It's like I major in death, Skip. There's something not lining up."

"You had nothing to do with it," Skip said. "Remember what Dr. Morrison said? These days will be hard. Not everything is going to make sense."

"That's not helpful. How do *you* know what *I* don't know?"

"Because I knew him, okay?"

"Knew who?"

"Darren Nixon. The man they found dead. I met him."

"What're you talking about?" Hazel asked.

"I spoke to him once or twice. He was a crank.

So if Nixon had contacted you at some point, believe me, I'd know. He would have sent me a hundred emails about it."

"Why didn't you tell Agent Rabkin this?"

"Are you planning on telling Agent Rabkin about your specialty in poisons?"

Hazel was silent.

"Exactly," Skip said.

"So now you spend time with criminals? Tell me how you knew him," Hazel demanded.

"I met him at a convention. In Long Beach, I think. It was around a year ago. He was a huge fan of Dad's. I got to know him a little bit. Few drinks. I didn't know he was a convict. I thought he was a normal person."

"I thought you said you talked to him once or twice."

"It wasn't a big deal. He wanted to buy some mementos from the show. Then he asked me about Benedict Arnold's bible."

"What?"

"I didn't even know what it was. It gave me something to talk to Dad about. Then it got weird, and I cut it off. End of story, until the FBI entered our lives."

"Back up. Weird *how*?"

"Nixon started sending me letters," Skip explained. "The usual kooky conspiracy crap.

Multinational governments chasing Benedict Arnold's bible, using it as some talisman. He had charts and graphs going back to the 1800s, crazy stories about the KGB and the Cubans in the eighties, then Al-Qaeda and 9/11 in the 2000s. You know, whatever people were scared of, that's what he got obsessed with. Dad had that Revolutionary jacket he wanted to get rid of, maybe I told him about it. It was dumb—you know, don't poke a bear—but I just thought, maybe that'll get rid of him."

"Were you ever going to tell Agent Rabkin this?"

"You really think he doesn't know? He's like Dad on the show. The only questions he asked were the ones where he knew the answers."

Hazel tried to arrange it all in her mind. "If everything you say about Darren Nixon is true, that he was a crackpot and everything he believed in was bullshit, why did someone kill him and stick a bible in his chest?"

"I don't know, Hazel. Why do you have guns in your house?"

"To protect myself," Hazel said. "Or at least to protect my family."

"You really think I knew he was a criminal? You think I'd knowingly let someone dangerous near Dad?"

Hazel didn't answer. She looked over at the

young boy and the young girl, who were halfway across the park now. "Skip, I need a few hours. Can you give me that? Can you stall Agent Rabkin if he contacts you?"

"That's what I've been trying to tell you. I talked to Rabkin. He's called me five times in the last twenty-four hours."

Hazel didn't know her brother, but she knew that tone. "About what?"

"They found another body. This one in Dubai. The victim was wearing another Revolutionary War jacket..."

"...and had some sort of miniature bible hidden in his chest," Hazel said.

"How'd you know that?"

"I was just—" She stopped herself. "It wasn't a hard guess."

Skip went quiet.

"So what do we do now?" he finally asked.

"I have something to do here first, but then I'm thinking of going to Spokane, where this guy Nixon lived. I'd like to see what he knew, talk to some neighbors," Hazel explained, still hearing Rabkin's warning to stay out of the way.

"You shouldn't go to Spokane."

"I'll be fine."

"Want me to come with you?"

"I'll be fine."

"That wasn't the question," Skip said.

"Maybe you should talk to Rabkin. See what else you can find out about the new body. The one in Dubai."

"Or maybe while you're in Spokane, I can *go* to Dubai," Skip said. "Maybe bring some cameras with me."

"And that helps us *how*?"

"You really never went with Dad when he was filming, did you? Whenever he showed up with those cameras, people would come running, especially to me. Lovable Scrappy-Doo, remember? When I arrive, people take pictures, it gets folks talking. If someone saw something, or knows something, they'll tell me. Isn't that what we want?"

Hazel shifted her weight on the bench, noticed a few more kids running by. Of all the questions Skip asked, this was the hardest. When it came to her brother, she didn't know what she wanted. Keeping Skip close meant he'd be underfoot. Plus, considering how often he got recognized, they'd lose all element of surprise. At least in Dubai, especially with cameras, they might get some answers. And even if they didn't, he'd be far *and* safe. Probably.

"You really think going to Dubai is a good idea?" Hazel asked.

"You think it's any worse than going to Spokane?"

"I don't know. I'm upside down, Skip. What if I get up to Spokane and find evidence of myself—that *I* was there—what happens then?"

"You won't."

Hazel wasn't so sure. She needed to talk to someone who might be.

"You realize," Skip said, and Hazel thought she heard something in his voice that was actually close to glee, even in this situation, "that you believe we're part of a giant, multilevel conspiracy, right?"

"It occurred to me, yes," Hazel said.

"Welcome to the family business, Haze."

25

Hazel found an open booth in the back of Jim's Restaurant, a diner that had been in the Mission forever and looked like it, its wood-paneled walls covered with old black-and-white photos of the city, along with strange inspirational art. Hazel thought the one that read *Life Is A Mystery To Be Lived, Not A Problem To Be Solved* was an outright lie.

"I'll have the chicken-fried steak and eggs," Hazel said. She then tacked on the biscuits and gravy for another five bucks, figured what the hell.

Her waitress, a woman in her forties wearing jeans and a green apron smeared with splotches of what looked like Thousand Island dressing looked at her quizzically. "You don't want your usual?"

"What's that?"

"The Hangtown Fry."

Hazel looked at the menu. The Hangtown Fry

was an oyster, bacon, and mushroom omelet. The idea of oysters, bacon, and eggs together roiled her stomach, even if she still couldn't taste much of anything. "No."

"We're real busy is the thing," the waitress said. "So if you don't like it, it's a pain in the ass to make you something new. Manager doesn't want a problem again."

Again.

"I'm good," Hazel said, but then she had a thought. "Maybe a plate of peppers. Jalapeños? You have those?"

"Seriously?"

"Yeah," Hazel said. "And some Sriracha. Just bring the bottle, and I'll be great."

Her server shrugged and muttered, "You say that now," then walked away.

Hazel took out her new phone and made the one other call she was waiting to make. UCLA Medical Center. "I'm looking for Dr. Morrison, please."

"I'm sorry, he's unavailable right now."

"It's Hazel Nash."

There was a pause. "Hold one moment for me."

Hazel was transferred five times, each time thinking she was picking up another bug along the way, figuring she'd have Agent Rabkin, half of Quantico, and probably the Super Friends listening in too. Superman, Wonder Woman, and the

Wonder Twins would all be getting ready to mobilize by the time she was finally patched through to the doctor's cell phone.

"Hazel," Dr. Morrison said, "I've been worried about you."

"Everyone keeps saying that. I'm trying to figure out if that's true."

Silence. Hazel could imagine him, always in a blue shirt, staring down at his feet.

"I'm not exactly sure what you're getting at," he finally said.

"Dr. Morrison, can we talk about my father?"

26

D id you know my dad?" Hazel asked.
"I did," Dr. Morrison replied through the phone.
"How well?"
"Not very."
Dr. Morrison cleared his throat. It was something humans did. You couldn't stop your throat closing when you felt tension, couldn't train yourself out of it, Hazel knew. You could only recognize the sensation and then not do anything about it. "I worked with him on an episode called 'The Murderer's Hand,'" he explained. "It was a brain injury where a woman's hand...Well, it doesn't matter." He paused again. "He called me sometimes, used me for research. I'd talk him through things. Purely professional."

"So if I had research questions," Hazel said, "you'd answer them for me? That would be a service you could supply? Or was it limited to my father? And maybe Agent Rabkin, I'm guessing."

Again, silence. Hazel's father wasn't the only one doing private favors for the government.

"Hazel," he said, "you need to come back. You need more treatment. More counseling."

"I will," she said. "But can you answer another question first?"

"You shouldn't call here," he said, but didn't hang up. "Go ahead."

"I was reading online and found that there was some kind of syndrome where people came out of traumatic brain injuries thinking they were aliens," Hazel said.

"Well, no," Dr. Morrison said. "They actually think everyone *else* is an alien. Aliens, replicants, impostors. It's changed over the years, depending upon what's been ingrained into the culture of the time. But yes. Capgras syndrome. And then there's Cotard's syndrome, where patients believe they've actually died and are now ghosts or, lately, zombies. Same thing. Whatever is culturally relevant, that's what they believe." He paused. "You don't believe either of those things, do you, Hazel?"

She didn't *believe* people were impostors. That had proven to be true. She didn't *believe* she was dead. It had been proven that a part of her was, absolutely, dead. She lowered her voice, though the diner was so loud with people now, she could have been speaking into a bullhorn and no one would have cared.

"Is there a syndrome," Hazel said, thinking of the guns in her apartment, of all the books of obscure poisons, thinking of everything she knew about death, "where a person thinks they're a hired killer?"

Dr. Morrison didn't answer for a long time. Maybe thirty seconds. "Paranoid schizophrenia," he finally said.

"If I'm lucid enough to ask the question, though, that would mean I'm not a paranoid schizophrenic, right?"

"You've been through a traumatic experience."

"Have I? I know I was in an accident. I know my father is dead. I know my brother is alive. But what about my mother, Dr. Morrison?"

"Pardon?"

"You heard me. My mother."

"She died years ago."

"I know," Hazel said. "In your hospital."

"It's a hospital, Hazel. People die here. She had cancer."

"The first day," Hazel said, "you asked me to name my grandparents. Why did you do that?"

"It's a standard question to check cognitive function."

"No. It's not," Hazel said. "Show me a picture of an animal, ask me to name it, that's a cognitive check. Asking for the names of grandparents, that's not on any scale. I know that. Unemotionally. You know why? Because they usually have nicknames. Nana, Pop, whatever. Nicknames. And you'd never know the right answer, anyway. I could have said anything. Unless you already knew them."

"Hazel," Dr. Morrison said, "you're not sounding rational."

"Did you treat my mother?"

Dr. Morrison took a breath.

"Did you treat my mother?" she repeated.

"I consulted," Dr. Morrison finally said.

Hazel stopped. "Did *I* know you?"

"We met. Yes. We met."

"How many years would you say you've been 'consulting' with my family?"

"Ten," he said. "Maybe more."

"Have you ever heard of Benedict Arnold's bible? You were working for the government too, weren't you, when they needed help?"

"Hazel, I'm going to recommend that you call 911," he said, though Hazel could hear a catch in his voice. A new speed. *Panic.* "You're having an episode. It's to be expected. Are you somewhere safe? Why don't you give me an address, and I'll have an ambulance sent to you."

"I haven't felt this clear since you shined the light in my eyes," she said. "You kept me for two days, not telling me what was wrong. But you were talking to Rabkin that whole time, weren't you, updating him on my condition?"

Silence.

"You knew who I used to be, what kind of person I was, but you acted like I was just another innocent stranger in a car wreck. Was that Rabkin's idea—to take advantage of my memory loss, to smooth out my bumps and reformat my hard drive—or was that yours?"

Silence.

"And it wasn't just you, was it? The grief counseling you made me do...they told me I was a good daughter. And what about the extra-friendly Nurse Dexter who did the same? Does he still even work there? Did you sign off on him too? Someone must have. Because he wasn't caring for a single patient other than me, was he?"

Silence.

"Didn't you take some oath? Not to do any harm?" Hazel asked.

The waitress came and dropped off Hazel's chicken-fried steak and eggs, came back a second later with the biscuits and gravy and a plate of dark green peppers. Dr. Morrison was still not speaking, but Hazel could hear him breathing, could hear the slap of his shoes on tile. The doctor must be moving rapidly through the hospital, chasing the reflection of the halogens on the floor. She could imagine him thinking, asking himself the questions he probably didn't care to spend much time dwelling on.

Who was Dr. Lyle Morrison? She'd researched him briefly when she was in the hospital, just so she'd know who was inside of her head, so she'd be sure she could trust the person working on her hard drive, or at least giving it a decent system restore. Then she'd spent a bit of the last night reading about him too, when it became clear to Hazel that everything she thought she knew was up for interpretation.

She saw he'd graduated from Yale. She found his political donations, examined photos of him from social events—he looked good in a tuxedo, usually with what appeared to be his mother on his arm—found his Facebook page, private, except for the photos other people had tagged him in: surfing; once at a Jimmy Buffett concert at the Hollywood Bowl, a fin on his head; eating dinner with a big group of people, his arm around a woman in a black dress. Then there were all the listings of the finest neurologists in the country.

She found his age: forty-seven. Older than she thought by almost a decade.

Time wasn't something she had a handle on these days.

She even found his house in Santa Monica Canyon, examined the satellite photos of it, imagined him walking through the hallways, standing in the yard, doing things like watering his lawn, all the normal human things people do to make up a life.

The things that mean nothing and everything.

She cut into the steak and it bled out into her eggs, turning the entire plate an off-shade of pink. She stuffed the bite into her mouth, prepared to taste nothing, but instead got a hit of copper in the back of her throat. She took a bite of biscuit, hoped she'd get another rush, but it was just like most things: moist sand. So she ate a pepper, felt a rush of sensation, no taste, just pain. She ate another.

"What was your price, Dr. Morrison? Or did they have something on you?"

"I need you to hang up. Do you hear me? Hang up."

"Tell me I'm not crazy," Hazel said. "Tell me you know I'm not crazy."

"I will lose everything," Dr. Morrison said. "Do you understand, Hazel? I will lose my entire life."

She heard the whistle of a wind gust, the roar of traffic, the doctor outside now, probably, Hazel thought, on Westwood Boulevard, the busy artery that ran directly in front of the medical center.

"I am not who I think I am. Am I?" Hazel asked.

"You're not," Dr. Morrison said.

"Thank you," Hazel said, but the connection was lost. Hazel called him back, once, twice, three times, each call going straight to voicemail. A woman's voice: *You've reached Dr. Lyle Morrison. If this is an emergency, hang up and dial 911.*

Hazel looked down at the table and ate another fiery pepper, then another. More and more pain, but at least she was feeling something. Finally, Hazel decided, it was time to dial a brand-new number.

27

T his the place?" the cab driver asked.

Hazel looked for herself, up at the sign at the end of the strip mall.

BUTCHIE'Z AIRBORN ADVENTUREZ!

One of those inflatable air dancers was out front, in full skydiving gear, goggles, everything.

"I think so," Hazel said, picturing the photo on her wall. She'd seen herself falling from the sky holding on to Butchie. She was low on people she trusted. He seemed like the only person who might reasonably be one of them.

Hazel got out of the cab, approached the front door of the shop, and peered through the glass. Lights on. But no one was there.

"Anybody home?" she called out, pulling open the door. A wall of helmets of all colors, including the Raiders and 49ers, was on her left. Harnesses on her right. Straight ahead, past the glass counter, was the menu: $230 for *Xtreme Weekend Divez Over The Pacific!* and $109 for *XtremeUltra GoPro Videoz of Your Jump!*

Could she really be friends with someone this attached to Zs and exclamation points? Another sign read, *We'll Beat Anyone'z Price$!* Hazel wondered how the hell a skydiving store even stayed in business. It seemed like piano and waterbed shops, the kind of places you only went to once.

"Butchie, you here?" she called, noticing the security camera above the cash register. Hazel looked directly at it, smiled thinly, waved two fingers.

A door in the corner, marked *Employeez Only*, burst open, and out came a thirty-year-old Hispanic man, beefy and aware of it, in a tight black tank top that showed a lattice of tribal tattoos twisting up his shoulders, across his neck. The straps from his tan cargo shorts hung down toward his flip-flops. He stood there, unspeaking, like he was unsure of what he was seeing.

"Hey," Hazel said.

Butchie rushed forward, grabbed Hazel, pressed her against his body, pulled her away, held her face in his hands, stared into her eyes, and then kissed her forehead, her eyes, her chin, her whole face...other than her lips...then did it again.

"Girl," he said, "I thought you were dead."

"I did too," Hazel said.

He looked over her shoulder. "You by yourself?"

"Yeah."

He was still holding on to her, but he'd tensed up, again glancing outside. "You sure?"

"Can I just ask: You a drug dealer or something—?"

Butchie put his hand over Hazel's mouth, not hard, not threatening, just to stop her from speaking.

"You carrying?" he whispered.

"I'm supposed to answer that?"

"You don't got your knife?"

Hazel heard the word *knife*, and her first thought was this: *There was no sense stabbing someone if you didn't intend to kill them.* If you cut open someone's liver and they live? Same amount of prison time in California as making them dead, as long as it was in a fight and not some premeditated hit.

Hazel almost made this statement out loud, managed to stop herself, because she didn't know why she knew this information. Didn't even know if it was true. Was too scared to ask.

"No knife," she said.

He reached under the counter, came out with a nine-inch blade, serrated, the kind of knife you might use to gut a deer. Or a man.

"Go out the back door," Butchie said, slapping the knife into her hand. "Meet me at our spot in an hour. We'll figure this out."

"Our spot?"

"The range," he said.

Nothing.

"What happened to you?" Butchie said.

"Something's wrong in my head."

Butchie hit a button on the cash register. It spit out a paper receipt, which he tore off, wrote four words on it, held it up. DRIVING RANGE. HARDING PARK. "You know that place?"

Hazel nodded.

He crumpled up the paper, threw it away. "See you there."

28

The driving range at Harding Park was just on the other side of San Francisco State, which, Hazel knew, is where she taught. Maybe she should've gone there first.

"Sit," Butchie called out, pointing at a little stool next to him. There were dozens of golfers lined up, every ten yards or so. Butchie was in the last spot, next to the net fence, the only one not dressed in pastel colors.

"We should be good here," he said. He had a bucket of balls next to him. "But keep an eye out."

"For what?"

He didn't answer. Hazel tried to remember.

She'd jumped out of planes with him. She knew that.

Which meant there was trust between them. And the way he'd kissed her, the way he'd grabbed her? They were close. She understood this. She wasn't sure how close.

He lined up and swung—*thwack!* The ball slanted to the right after about fifty yards in the air. "The hell happened?" Butchie asked.

"I was in the hospital."

"I know that." *Thwack!* "I get the news too, you know." He pointed his club at her head. "What's the story in there?"

"I've got this thing in my brain," Hazel said, and then explained the injury to her amygdala as best as she could. Butchie listened intently, still hitting balls.

"You get any superpowers with it? You psychic now or able to move shit with your mind? Open a garage door or something?"

"I know we know each other," Hazel said. "I know we're friends. But I've got no idea what that means. Were you my boyfriend?"

"You ever had a sex change?"

"I don't think so."

"Then I was never your boyfriend." *Thwack!*

Gay. Got it.

"So, you got amnesia or some shit?" he added.

"No, I can remember things. Facts especially. But personal experiences...people...those're harder. I just can't quite order them up right. I get little snatches. Bits of memories. I need to stitch them back."

Thwack! "You know I came to visit you?"

"Where?"

"UCLA. They wouldn't even let me near your hospital room. Some big burly fuck put his hand on my chest and told me I didn't have clearance to see you and I almost came back with a Molotov cocktail of clearances, you know? Burn the whole place down just so I can make fun of your paper gown."

"That wasn't my doing," Hazel said, happy to hear there was at least one person who tried to come visit her. Maybe there were others—though she somehow knew there weren't. "I was in a coma."

Butchie pulled out a nine iron, stepped to one side, and took a few practice swings. "I came to get your mail, water your plants. Then your building manager called 5-0. You believe that? Can't people do nice things for people anymore? Shit. Cops ran my license, put me in the back of their car, made sure I wasn't robbing you. Lucky for us, they didn't get to your drawers, or we'd be seeing each other at our arraignments. So I just waited, right? Saw you on TV. Then people started looking for you."

"Who?"

"If they left a name"—*thwack!*—"I would have handled it already. Wasn't students with late papers, I'll tell you that." Butchie stopped midswing, looked over his shoulder at her. "Your hair is too short. You look better with it long."

"It was burned. They cut it in the hospital."

"That's a bitch," he said. *Thwack!* "Dammit. I've been slicing like crazy lately. You remember how to fix that?"

"Make sure your palms are parallel," Hazel said. "Maybe invest in a pair of golf shoes."

Butchie gripped his club, adjusted his hands, and let it fly. "Better," he said. "So you still know that."

"You and me," Hazel said. "Are we in some kind of business together?"

"Not together. It's my business, with the planes," Butchie said. "A little import." *Thwack!* "Oh, that was clean. A little export."

Hazel thought for a moment. "So you *do* sell drugs?"

Thwack!

"Guns?"

"I don't sell. I ship"—*thwack!*—"whatever people don't want to use FedEx for. Sometimes it's chemo meds that someone's niece can't get in Mexico. Other times, well, I don't open the packages."

"Do *I*?"

"You've been known to be curious on occasion, yeah."

"What kinds of occasions?"

"There was a chiropractor in Long Beach. You had a bad feeling. Sure enough, he was sending photos—the worst kinds of photos, of little kids with...Anyway, you know what kinda photos. He was sending them to fellow monsters across the country. When you opened the package, you sent half the pics to the chiropractor's wife, the other half to the police. Then you did the same to the recipients." *Thwack!*

"Sounds like a good way to make enemies."

"That's your specialty," Butchie said. "Manuel Leyva got thirty years in Montana, no parole, for what you sent about him. He knows it was you."

She was tempted to ask, but there were only so many problems to deal with. "So you don't know who was looking for me at your store?"

"Whoever it was, they were polished. Maybe Feds, maybe someone private. Definitely a pro," Butchie said. "I told them I didn't know where you were. Now I can't tell them that."

"I'm out of here later today."

"To where?"

"Spokane," she said, knowing she shouldn't tell anyone that, but also knowing this was the first person she'd met who felt...right.

Hazel thought about her medical records, about the teeth that were yanked from her head, about her various injuries, about all her trips, about what the hell all this drifting meant. Wondered how she could speed up her learning curve. Dr. Morrison was right—she still needed therapy, but that wasn't going to solve the problems she had now.

"This is going to sound crazy," Hazel said, "but did I ever mention Benedict Arnold to you?"

"You really asking me this?"

"Butchie," she said, "I've had a confusing week."

"Get up," he said. She did. "Turn around." She did. "Pull up your hair." She did. Butchie put his hand on the back of her neck.

Her arm twitched, getting ready to go for that knife.

"Easy," Butchie said. "If I was going to hurt you, I wouldn't have given you a weapon first." He pulled his phone from his pocket, aimed it at her neck, and clicked a photo. "You've been walking around with that for as long as I've known you."

Hazel looked for herself. It was a tattoo, along the nape of her neck, under her hair. Simple script, all lowercase, no punctuation:

a wretched motley crew

A quote. From Benedict Arnold.

29

Trevor Rabkin got on a plane in the morning, made it to Hazel's San Francisco apartment in no time. Tried her phone again. No answer. Not that he expected one. According to her credit card, she bought a new prepaid cell phone this morning, got some breakfast, then took a cab ride to a strip mall near her office.

Human things.

Nothing to worry about. Except this was Hazel.

Naturally, Skip was no help. He swore he hadn't heard from his sister. Said he was just as worried as Rabbit. That this behavior was not the person he knew.

No one knew her, that was the problem. Apparently, not eve Hazel knew Hazel.

"You must b Mr. Charles," Rabbit said, flashing his FBI ID.

"Can I help you?" the manager of Hazel's

building asked, though Rabbit knew what the answer would be. Nineteen years ago, the manager did two years for stealing a car when he was seventeen. He'd been clean since, which made him the kind of guy you wanted managing your apartment complex, because he wanted trouble like he wanted smallpox.

"Are you familiar with Hazel Nash?" Rabbit asked.

"I know she came back yesterday. She in trouble?"

"Did she tell you she walked out of the hospital, even though she was receiving mental health treatment?"

"Mental health?"

"Mental health," Rabbit said. "As in, real problems."

The manager scratched at something on his right earlobe. "You know, as long as she lived here, I thought something was off. But I keep to my own, let other people keep to theirs."

"I'm the same way," Rabbit said. "Everything she's been through, last thing you want is a person becoming a danger to themselves and others. But that's what she is right now."

The manager tugged at his earlobe some more. Trevor saw that he had a crease in it, and that he was working over a patch of dry skin. "You ever hear that old wives' tale about earlobe creases?" Rabbit asked.

"I don't know many old wives. Know a lot of single mothers and deadbeat dads, though."

"They said it was a sign of having a big heart," Rabbit said, leaving out the part where your heart gets so big, it explodes in your chest and kills you.

"Truth," the manager said. "Poor girl doesn't know what's coming next for her. I've been there. Let me get you the keys."

30

UCLA Medical Center
Los Angeles

D r. Lyle Morrison had spent most of his life trying to save people. He'd devoted nearly twenty-six years on this planet to the practice of medicine.

But now, standing on the roof of the UCLA Medical Center, the wind whipping his lab coat behind him like a cape, he couldn't figure out how he'd never managed to save himself.

Oh, he'd tried.

Over a decade ago, he wrote himself a quick prescription. Just one time, he'd promised. A little Adderall to keep things moving. Over the next few years, he'd blown through even more prescription pads, trying to find some happy middle ground. But every day was a tug-of-war, and he was the rope.

In his coat pocket, his phone buzzed.

Decline.

He looked over the edge. An ambulance

screamed up the street. Students walked through Westwood, eyes down on their phones. Cars raced through intersections.

So many accidents about to happen, then narrowly avoided.

Dr. Morrison wondered whether his life would be different if he'd been a worse doctor. If he hadn't gone to Yale, hadn't been spotted early on as an expert on the human brain, would life be better? Is there a richer reward for doing worse? What about if he'd never gone to the NA meetings—Narcotics Anonymous—if he'd never told that group in the church basement about his problems? That's how the government found him. So if he hadn't sought help, would he still be this man he'd become?

Buzz.

Decline.

What did he know right now? He knew that Hazel Nash would be the end of him.

He knew that she wouldn't stop until she found the truth—about her dad and what Dr. Morrison did for the government. How many times did Jack Nash come back from his bible searches needing medical attention that should've been reported to the CDC? How many times had Dr. Morrison taken bullets out of men while they were chained to toilets? They'd used blackmail to get Morrison to do those jobs. Would anyone believe that? Maybe. But then when his drug issues got out? Morrison's current life would collapse.

He knew that in a few days, once Hazel started pushing open the doors to the past, the hospital he was standing on top of would disown him, that it wouldn't matter how much he'd helped the government, or how many favors he'd done.

Most of all, he knew that he couldn't undo the truth: He'd done harm. Forget the drug issues. He'd lied to Hazel, worked to keep her in the dark. He'd harmed her. And as long as the government knew about his addiction, he'd continue to do harm. The one thing he swore he'd never do.

There was no pain worse than realizing you're a lesser man than you think you are. Except for the pain that you can't change it.

Buzz. Buzz. Buzz.

Dr. Morrison dropped his phone off the side of the building. He watched it sail through the air, so light, pinwheeling past all the floors he'd walked on, past all the emergencies he'd tended to, past all the patients he'd treated as their brains turned against them.

The phone crashed to the pavement, disintegrating on impact. A few people looked up, but then kept moving on, the world still spinning, nothing permanent except energy.

And what was the brain but energy? Maybe he didn't need this body anymore. Maybe it was time to test his beliefs, test thermodynamics, see if the cure to this pain was as simple as losing the vessel. Maybe he could escape this prison he'd built around himself.

The wind gusted again, and Dr. Lyle Morrison let his arms go slack behind him, felt his lab coat pull from his body in the wind, felt it peel off and away. It was that simple: Who he was was torn off his back. How free he felt, finally.

And then he took a step forward.

31

A wretched motley crew.

"You recognize the quote?" Butchie asked.

Hazel nodded. "It's what Benedict Arnold called his men, the ones who helped him fight against the British," she said.

"Not just *fight*. Win."

She nodded at that too, an old lesson flashing back. Who taught her this? Her dad, or did she read it? "The British navy had them pinned down in Valcour Bay," she said, hearing her words like they were coming from someone else. "It was a tremendous assault, but Arnold trained his men so well, they lived through it, sneaking away in the middle of the night, and living to fight another day," she explained. "The so-called 'wretched motley crew' took on the superior force, outwitted them, and eventually won the war, all under the hand of their inscrutable leader, Benedict Arnold."

It was the kind of story they make movies about. Except for the problem of that inscrutable leader. The liar and cheat no one trusted.

"Butchie, have I ever killed someone?"

Butchie turned and looked at Hazel. He didn't answer.

"I need to know," she said.

"Girl," he replied, putting his nine iron back in the bag, then coming out with a new club, "first thing, you need to keep your voice down. Second, I need you to do a pirouette for me, real slow, so I can see if you're wired up."

"People don't get wired up anymore. They just leave the voice recorders on their phones on."

"Still," Butchie said. He faced her then, golf club in his hand. It was a Big Bertha Driver, which she knew could collapse her head in a few strikes, not that she needed any more blows to the brain. "Take a couple swings," he said. "Let me hold your phone."

Hazel handed Butchie her phone, then stood in front of him, let him pat her down.

"Satisfied?"

"I had to ask," he said. He eyed the other golfers. "Take a swing. Make this look normal."

"I messed myself up pretty bad. I don't know if I can."

"It's all muscle memory," he said.

Hazel recognized that Butchie hadn't answered her question. Maybe he never would. What she also recognized was that she felt comfortable for the first time since she'd woken up, that she felt authentic, that whatever was happening with Butchie, it was something she *did*. Something she *enjoyed*.

Hazel lined herself up over the ball, felt her back angle down to about forty-five degrees, shifted her weight, her pelvis screaming, her ribs and shoulders screaming, her neck screaming, then swung back and powered through the ball, sending it high up in an arc, 150 yards away.

"See?" Butchie said. "Your body took over." Hazel took another swing. This time, the ball shot out sideways. "See, you thought on that one. Gotta detach."

"You don't need to answer my question," Hazel said as she sat back down.

"You shouldn't have asked it," he replied, lining up.

A thought occurred to her: "Where's your dog?" she asked, referring to his pit bull.

"Butchie? Had to put him down," Butchie said.

"What? When?" Hazel said.

"A couple weeks back," he said. *Thwack!* "He had cancer everywhere. I've been pissed off about turtles and parrots and shit living eighty years. I'm like Mr. Bojangles over here now."

"Jesus, I'm sorry," Hazel said. Then: "You and your dog had the same name?"

"It's a cool name," Butchie said. "Love yourself first, right?"

"I'm trying that out."

Butchie gave her a frown. "Well, at least I got you back."

"Part of me, anyway."

Butchie thwacked a few more balls into the distance. Up in the sky was the *whoop-whoop-whoop* of helicopters. Two Apaches flying low, out over Lake Merced, heading toward the Pacific.

"Butchie, how'd we meet?"

"A mutual friend told me you wanted to learn to skydive. Four, five years ago."

"I think I already knew how to skydive," Hazel said.

"You knew how to jump out of planes strapped to somebody's chest."

"Who was the friend?"

"Your pal from Africa."

Hazel remembered the photo from her apartment. The man breathing in her ear, his hand squeezing her hip. "Karl with a K."

"You remember him?" Butchie asked.

"Not until I saw his picture in my house. Even then, he's a blur. Where's he now?"

"Wherever you left his ass," Butchie said. "You

really don't remember this shit? I met him while I was doing ecotours in Costa Rica. Couple years later, he brings you into my shop, says you're good people, but even then I was like, that girl's got bad taste."

"Thanks."

"At least *he* had good taste," Butchie said. "Smart dude. Just not real great on the human-to-human level."

"How long did it take you to trust me?"

"About fifteen minutes."

"Then trust me now," Hazel said.

Butchie stared at Hazel for a moment, like he was seeing her for the first time. Above them, the helicopters came swinging back toward the course. They'd been crisscrossing the sky for a while now, training for the eventual moment when they had to go attack a city again.

"Tell me what you need," Butchie said.

"I need to find out if someone hurt my father. Whoever my dad worked for, whatever's going on, this thing on my neck? That's not random."

"Can't disagree. You got a plan?"

Hazel went silent for a minute, rethinking it yet again. For days now, she'd been searching for alternatives, searching for *anything* that would help her better understand herself. All that was left was a desperate choice. A true Hail Mary. But that's who throws Hail Marys. Desperate people. "Tell me something," she said. "How difficult would it be to get your hands on some sodium pentothal?"

"Sodium *what*?"

"Truth serum. To use on me."

32

The first thing Rabbit did once he entered Hazel's apartment was find her guns and empty the clips. There were more bullets somewhere in this place, he was sure of that, but even so, he didn't think Hazel was the kind of person who went on shooting rampages, certainly not in her own apartment. Rabbit figured she was angry, confused, unsure. It was time to figure out what else she was feeling.

Rabbit checked Hazel's computer, saw YouTube, clicked the Back button, then Back again and again, to see what she'd been watching.

Johannesburg...Iran...Libya...Philadelphia. All of her dad's greatest hits. She was searching.

Rabbit was still thinking of Hazel's reaction when he told her about the first body—Darren Nixon—dressed in Revolutionary War gear. No shock, no sadness, and full of uncanny information. Then that second body shows up, in Dubai.

Late last night, Rabbit had done a search through every police and Bureau database, looking for any other victims who'd been dressed for a Revolutionary War battle. Almost all of them were attacked outside Colonial Williamsburg. Ten years ago, there was a reenactor who came home from work, walked in on a robbery, and ended up with a bullet in his head. Six years ago, another killed herself by hanging. Her parents found her swinging on the tree in front of their house. Five years ago, there was also a domestic violence case, a husband shot his wife, he in full colonial uniform, sitting in the front seat of their Subaru wagon.

None of them had bibles buried in their chests, like Darren Nixon and Arthur Kennedy. And none of them had ties to Jack Nash and his family.

Sure, Hazel and Skip's dad was beloved by millions, but underneath the fan love, Jack Nash was an actor. More important, according to Rabbit's new boss, Moten, Jack had made a few enemies himself. And so, apparently, had Hazel. Professors have good veneers, but scratch a little deeper and you'll find obsessions.

So how'd this all tie back to Benedict Arnold? Did Rabbit even believe *The House of Secrets* stories, of hidden truths about our first President, or covert messages tucked into centuries-old books? Did he even believe that a bible could *fit* in someone's chest?

When did people get so damn gullible? Life wasn't a popcorn movie. It didn't have a neat and tidy ending. Every country in the world was soaked in blood, democracies and dictatorships alike. Yet, as Rabbit knew, most people only cared about what they could see on the surface. It didn't matter if *The House of Secrets* stories were *factual*, it only mattered if people believed them to be true.

Sliding a thumb drive into Hazel's Mac and copying her files, Rabbit again mentally took the pieces apart, then put them back together: Forget the fact Darren Nixon was a criminal. Nixon was found facedown, in a Revolutionary War coat that once belonged to Hazel's father. There was a lie being told there, he knew that much. Then the second body showed up, poor Arthur Kennedy in Dubai. Another lie, right there on its face.

To report the body, someone had to call the New Haven cops all the way from Dubai. Someone who must have known the cops would kick it to the Feds, and that the Feds would see what Rabbit had learned in the last twenty-four hours, which is that Arthur Kennedy didn't actually exist until the 1990s.

No immunization records.

No high school records.

No selective service form.

Then all of a sudden, he gets his real estate license, starts living in New Haven, same house now for two decades.

In Rabbit's mind, whoever Arthur Kennedy really was, there's no way he was always named Arthur Kennedy. Same with Nixon. But to have those names—two Presidents—they either named themselves together or, more likely, were named by the same people. People who thought their connection would never be noticed. That was the key, Rabbit realized, and now he was again thinking of his boss Moten and the great Jack Nash.

For years, Moten supervised Jack's work with the government. That was a fact. When Jack was in a foreign country, the TV star was proud to use his celebrity to help Uncle Sam. That's a fact too. And yes, during those times, Jack's missions included a search for the missing pages of Benedict Arnold's bible. The only question was: What did Jack find—and how did it relate to these two bodies now?

All this time, Rabbit had assumed Jack was looking for the treasure. But certainly Jack couldn't be the only one. Nixon was a criminal.

Was Kennedy too? What if they're the ones who found the bible—or treasure, or whatever it was—first, or maybe even went and stole it? Is that why they died—is that why Jack died too?—at the hands of someone who wanted his property back? Or maybe someone taking personal revenge? There was a reason Nixon's and Kennedy's chests were cut open. That was most definitely a message. But to whom? Nixon and Kennedy didn't just appear from nowhere. They lived real lives. Maybe hurt real people.

According to the files, though, Kennedy didn't have a past. So who was he? An informant? Someone in witness protection? Moten would tell him if that was the case. Kennedy's most profound online interaction was his fantasy baseball team, the WarEagles, who were still in first place despite the fact that he'd been dead for days, a detail the rest of the league was oblivious to.

Rabbit got into Kennedy's OkCupid account, found that he'd made a connection with a woman named Alexis. Her profile said she was a travel agent—a convenient job that Rabbit thought didn't really exist anymore—and they'd made a plan to go visit Dubai together after a week of messages that made Rabbit miss those drunken nights with his ex-wife. The website domain name for Alexis's travel agency was purchased a few weeks before she started talking to Kennedy. Now the site was empty, and Alexis's profile was stripped clean, no photos, nothing.

It smelled like a scam even before Kennedy ended up dead, but for what? People got scammed every day. People like Arthur Kennedy, who seemed utterly, absolutely alone in the world? They got scammed every minute. The thing was, best as Rabbit could tell, the only thing they took from Arthur Kennedy was his life.

Rabbit ran the airline passenger list to Dubai, looking for any known bad actors. Nothing. Then there was the time of death. If Arthur Kennedy really was killed in Dubai in the past few days, Hazel and Skip were innocent. They had both been here. Rabbit saw them himself each day at the hospital.

A new player then. A big player had entered the game. Or was he here the whole time, waiting for his next orders?

Rabbit went into Hazel's living room. He saw the empty Gatorade bottles, the meat wrappers, the outline of Hazel's body still on her couch. He smelled people's food cooking, could hear music lilting out through open windows, barking dogs, a crying baby. Real life was happening in Hazel's apartment building.

On Hazel's wall, there was something missing,

a perfect discolored square that caught his eye. He opened her trash, found a photo of Hazel and some man in a desert, noticed the way the man's hand rested low on her hip, wondered who he was, why he'd been the one thing from her past Hazel decided had to go.

The intercom next to Hazel's front door began to buzz.

"Hello?" Rabbit said.

"That you, Butchie?" a voice replied. It was a woman. One who didn't sound surprised.

"Yup," Rabbit said. He looked over at the wall of photos and saw the one of Hazel in midflight. *Butchie*. He tried to imagine what a guy named Butchie sounded like. Realized it didn't matter. If the woman on the intercom already thought he was Butchie, he was Butchie. With a grunt, he added, "Who's this?"

"I-It's Mel," she stuttered. Rabbit tried to place her accent, thinking maybe she was Hawaiian. "There's a— I got a delivery for her."

"Great. C'mon up," Rabbit grunted. With the push of a button, he buzzed her in.

Sometimes real life was a carnival game. Hit the buzzer at the right time, and you get a prize.

33

Butchie drove Hazel across the bridge into Berkeley, out toward the racetrack known as Golden Gate Fields. He knew a vet out there who'd be happy to get Hazel what she needed, the so-called "real-life" version of truth serum. "They use that shit to calm the horses down if they break their legs," Butchie told her, "before they shoot them between the eyes."

They were in his thousand-year-old Range Rover, the color impossible to tell, maybe it didn't have any paint on it anymore. The back of it was filled with everything from camping gear to parachutes, GoPro rigs, an inordinate number of Frisbees, boxes of Clif bars, and plastic jars filled with jerky. "Do you live in here?" Hazel asked.

"Never know when I might have to."

As they arrived at the track, Butchie pulled into

a full parking lot—it was a race day, plus that night there was a dollar concert, a Bon Jovi cover band named Bon Jersey, according to all the flyers littered on the ground—and two minutes later, a woman in red scrubs was knocking on Butchie's window.

Her nametag read *Drea*. Hazel wondered when she'd lost the first two letters of her name, how she decided she couldn't live with them anymore, how Hazel's own parents never called her Hazel-Ann, how she'd been Hazel forever, her mother telling her they thought one day she'd be Hazy, if she was lucky.

Drea had blond hair pulled tight from her face and back into a ponytail, hoop earrings that were too big, a brown bag in her hands.

"If someone ends up dead," Drea said, "that's going to be a real problem. Is one of you planning to kill yourself?"

"Nah," Butchie said. "Recreational use only."

"Some party." She waited a few seconds, sighed, then handed Butchie the bag. "That's pentobarbital. That dose is going to put you out in about three minutes. You're not going to want to be alone afterward. In case your heart stops."

"That happens?" Butchie said.

"That happens," Drea said. Then, to Hazel, "Do I know you?"

"No," Hazel said, just hoping Drea would go away.

"Don't bullshit me," Drea warned. She was pissed now. "You a cop? If you're a cop, I'll—"

"I'm not a cop," Hazel said, thinking that if Drea threatened to snitch on them, she could reach across Butchie, grab Drea's ponytail, and pull her into the front seat, smother her with a parachute, have Butchie drive up to the Delta, dump her there, where someone would find her, but not for a while.

"You still look familiar to me," Drea said.

"She's got one of those faces," Butchie said.

"You were on the news," she said. "Your dad was famous. Mr. Spock or something?"

"Something," Hazel said. If need be, she could rip those hoops from her ears, shove them down her throat.

"Small world," Drea said.

"It'd be cool if you didn't talk about this," Butchie said.

"Yeah, like I'm going to tell people I sold drugs to Mr. Spock's kid?" Drea said, and then headed back the way she came.

As they drove off, Hazel shot a look to Butchie, apologizing for thoughts he'd never see. In truth, Drea got lucky. But like before, Hazel sat there in silence, in disbelief about how fast, how over-whelmingly, her bloodlust hit—and how intoxicat-ing it felt. Biting her lip until it hurt, she thought, *Drea, I'm sorry.* Then: *Maybe this isn't so bad.* And: *This is trouble.*

34

Rabbit stepped out into the hallway of Hazel's building and headed toward the elevator. Whoever was visiting Hazel—whoever this friend Mel was—Rabbit wanted a good look first. If Mel had flowers, chocolates, and a card signed by everyone in the Anthropology department, he'd let her go. If she was carrying something else, he wanted to be ready.

Two minutes later, the elevator doors opened. A thin sixtysomething Hawaiian woman stepped out, hair thin and scraggly, looking more like a cleaning lady than a friend. She had some dry cleaning draped over her arm. Harmless enough, but that cleaning bag was a good way to hide something underneath.

"How you doing?" Rabbit asked her when he walked by.

"Fine," she said, not the least bit suspicious.

Why should she be? Rabbit was a guy in a suit. Looked like a broker coming home for lunch. "Have a nice day."

"You too," Rabbit said, then stepped into the waiting elevator, let the door close, but didn't hit any buttons. He counted to ten, punched the Door Open button, stepped back out. Sure enough, Mel the Hawaiian woman was at Hazel's door.

"If you're looking for Hazel, she's not home," Rabbit called to her.

The woman turned, confused. "How do you—?"

"Maybe I can help you instead," Rabbit added, watching her right arm, still hidden by the dry cleaning.

The woman backed up just slightly, her build slight, like you could sneeze her over. "How do you know Hazel?" she asked, her voice breaking.

"We're dating."

"You don't look like one of her dates."

Rabbit pulled his badge, held it out.

"I knew you didn't look like someone she'd date," Mel whispered, her voice going softer, like you could tear it. "What'd she do now?"

"What's in the bag?" Rabbit asked, pointing with his chin toward the dry cleaning.

"Clothes."

"I can see that. Why's Hazel need your clothes?"

"Not mine. They're—" Mel stopped, her voice lower than ever. "I had a job interview. Billing coordinator for a company that translates Web pages. That's a job apparently. Anyway, Hazel let me borrow..." She held up the dry cleaning, too embarrassed to make eye contact. "She said I needed something good to wear. That these might fit."

Rabbit studied the clothes. They weren't just nice. Based on the tags, they were brand-new. "She bought these for you?"

"I heard she got out of the hospital. I wanted to say thanks." Mel turned to walk away, then stopped. She still didn't make eye contact. "Whatever you think she did, Hazel Nash isn't a bad person," she added. "In my book, that bitch is downright glorious."

35

United Arab Emirates
Today

Four a.m. in Dubai and The Bear is wide awake, tracking Skip Nash online through the hotspots of LA. Skip's grabbing sandwiches at Nate 'n Al's deli. Then he's shopping, high-end retail, overpaying for V-neck T-shirts on Rodeo Drive. Then he's at the valet stand at the Grove, waiting for his car, taking a photo with Clara and Mickey, who are visiting the city from Louisville, and who the day before were "wowwwwed" by the Hollywood sign.

Skip should be on a plane. Skip shouldn't be in public. And he should be with his sister, wherever she's hiding. Maybe the broken Hazel is smarter than she seems. Certainly smarter than Skip, which isn't saying much.

Still, things are not working out as The Bear would prefer. If there's not the movement he desires soon—if Skip and Hazel don't head his way soon—he'll post photos of Arthur Kennedy on Twitter, then he'll get on a plane back to the States, finish this.

And then, 4:21 a.m., just as he's dressing for his run, he gets a ping. Cops called to an apartment building in San Francisco. Sixteenth Street. The Mission. A 911 call that someone might've been using a fake FBI badge to get inside. Hazel won't go home to that. And this should get Skip running too. They have the best and worst of their dad in them; they'll want to investigate. Things are starting to happen. At last.

The Bear checks the flights leaving Los Angeles for Dubai. There's a 9 p.m. British Airways flight. Eighteen hours of flight time, a layover in London. If The Bear understands the world, he'll have Skip Nash here soon enough. Hopefully Hazel too. Then the real fun would begin.

The Bear got ready for his run. *Ten miles today,* he thinks. *Make sure I'm ready for all the blood.*

36

This gonna work?" Butchie asked. He'd strapped Hazel into a papasan chair, one of those big rattan numbers with a flat circular pillow in a satellite-dish-shaped seat. They were in a storage unit in Oakland, down on MacArthur, where no one could hear.

Hazel tried to move. Pushed forward, then side to side. She thought it was the first time in history someone had found a good use for a papasan chair. Bungee cords secured her in place, arms crossed, so she could plunge the drugs into the basilic vein at the notch of her left forearm. "I'm good."

Butchie flipped on the GoPro helmet that was strapped to Hazel's head. She was facing a mirror, so she could film her own reaction. She needed to see herself, see what her body was doing when she answered.

"This is some real evil-scientist madness," Hazel said. "My dad would be proud."

"You really think this was his life? That he was out there working for the government, doing James Bond shit?" Butchie said. "Skiing in the Alps and then shooting someone? Sleeping with women covered in gold?"

"He was married to my mother," Hazel said, but that got her thinking: Did she know how her parents had met? Had she even seen photos from their wedding?

Dr. Morrison hadn't shown her any. Nor had any of the therapists. Neither had Skip. There weren't even any photos in Jack's house.

Maybe it didn't matter.

Of course it did.

"My dad was a showman, not a fighter. And he certainly wasn't James Bond."

"Whatever he was doing, he wasn't alone," Butchie said, opening the brown bag and pulling out a single syringe.

"What do you mean?"

"You said you watched those episodes in Iran, Moscow, all those places? Especially then, he needed help getting there. You know anyone who worked with him back then?"

The only person Hazel remembered was just a name that was in the TV show credits: Ingrid

Ludlow, an assistant. When was the last time she'd seen her? It'd been years. Hazel sorta remembered Ingrid being a part of their lives as children, always around, and then...gone. She'd ask Skip about her, see if she came to Dad's funeral.

"Did I ever talk to you about my dad?"

"Sometimes," Butchie said, ripping open the plastic packaging, freeing the syringe. "It seemed to annoy you, so I didn't make a habit of being like, 'Oh, remember that time your dad did that alien autopsy?' That one pissed you off. You said it was a personal affront. Got all Professor Nash on me."

She'd watched that episode and had a flash of memory. Her father had actually called her, asking for some of her expertise. And even then, the episode?

It was...an embarrassment.

Her entire life was devoted to the real stuff, and here was her father, cutting open a doll and doing The Voice: "If aliens really did come to our planet, this is what we think their organs would actually look like." *I should've told him it would all be white fuzz*, Hazel thought.

Wait.

White fuzz.

What was that?

And then she was in her bedroom, holding the

scissors, cutting open the bear, shoving the book in. The book. No. Wait.

There was a story.

A man.

Frozen.

An autopsy. Something shoved in his chest.

Benedict Arnold's bible.

She remembered something else. Benedict Arnold's full name was actually Benedict Arnold V—the fifth one born—though in truth, he was really Benedict Arnold VI. They named him the fifth when his baby brother died. A historical glitch. A trick.

Agent Rabkin said it earlier—maybe Benedict Arnold wasn't the bad guy in the story. But now Hazel wondered this: In all *these* stories, was her father the *good* guy? All those trips he made abroad...always with children. Everyone saw Jack Nash as the hero. But what if his trips had a darker purpose?

"What I'm saying," Butchie said, "is that maybe they made up that stuff about your dad doing work with the government...maybe that was just to get you riled, to see what you'd do."

"I almost pulled Drea through your window and smothered her," Hazel said, now wondering just how much darkness runs in a family.

Butchie raised his eyebrows, but he didn't say

anything for a minute. "Drea's a good kid. She helped me put down Butchie."

"You put your own dog down?"

"People you love, you don't want them going out seeing some stranger. It's a blessing to be there when someone passes." Butchie held up the syringe. "You ready?"

"Not really," Hazel said, her body tensing against the ropes. She clenched her teeth. A Hail Mary. "Do it," she said. Butchie pulled a small vial from the brown bag.

"You're gonna incriminate yourself, on film," Butchie said. "You realize that?"

"I need to know what's real. Especially about myself."

"You're the worst criminal ever," Butchie said, as he stabbed the syringe into the vial, pulled back the plunger. "How do you even know this truth serum shit works?"

"I saw an episode of *House of Secrets* once," she said, "where my dad debunked it."

37

Druzhba, Russia
1985

SEASON 9, EPISODE 3 (1985): "THE MOSCOW DIAMONDS"

Jack Nash can't believe his luck. He's traveled six thousand miles, across two continents and one ocean, over the rutted back roads outside Moscow, paying off locals, drinking vodka, eating solyanka, and still he hasn't been killed.

He has thirteen people, a full production team, in a tiny hotel a few miles away, waiting for his phone call. This episode of *The House of Secrets* is about a cache of jewels, found sewn into a dress, that just might be the famous Romanov diamonds, missing for nearly a century. But that's not the reason Jack's here.

He's outside a farmhouse, chain-smoking Belomorkanals with a man named Dmitry Volkov, a professor from the university in Moscow. Jack's waiting for his researcher Ingrid to come back outside to let him know what she thought of their offer.

Dmitry is probably KGB.

Well, no.

There's no probably.

He is KGB. But he's also a professor of history, a celebrated voice in the Soviet world. The Kremlin rolled him out whenever they needed a friendly academic face for the West. And judging by the pristine black car—a Volga—he rolled up in, a well-compensated face too. On TV, he seems more refined, but up close Jack sees that his teeth are a little crooked, the bottom row obviously capped, the top row slightly angled to the right, like italics. The bags under his eyes are thick and black.

Dmitry is the cover story for why this American TV show is let into town, the bit player who will show the world how refined and cooperative the Soviets are. For the next two days, for the benefit of the cameras, Dmitry and the famous Jack Nash will put on a relentless search for the Romanov diamonds. But behind the scenes, for the benefit of their governments, these two men will be trading something far more valuable.

"Don't worry," Dmitry says, "no one can hear us out here."

"You can hear us."

"I'm an academic, not a general. Not like your Benedict Arnold."

Jack rolls his eyes. Was there a single Russian who understood the meaning of subtlety? Yes, Jack was doing a favor for Uncle Sam—"just a lil' errand," the man with the government badge and Texas accent had said. Jack had done a few of these errands before, including during a trip to East Germany for a show about what was stolen from Hitler's bunker. The errand then? Jack was to leave a manila envelope under his hotel mattress. Two days later, a Generalleutnant in the East German army would be staying in the same room and would retrieve it. Today's errand? Jack wasn't just a delivery boy anymore. He was authenticating and picking up a potential new page from Benedict Arnold's bible. But that didn't mean Dmitry had to blurt it all out loud.

"Why such fascination still with the man?" Dmitry asked.

"People like a bad guy," Jack says.

"Not so bad," Dmitry says. "One of your finest warriors. In Russia, he would be a hero. We'd just leave out his last actions. Rewrite the books, make it look like he'd been framed, blame it all on someone else. Assign blame and you create a martyr. Keep reminding people of how he didn't believe in your cause, you only remind the world why your cause shouldn't be believed in."

"I think we've done all right."

"History," Dmitry says, "it is not constant. Maybe a rewrite is due?"

"Well, when you guys take over, I'll put that in your hands."

Dmitry chuckles, then breaks into a series of phlegmy hacks. He pulls a handkerchief from his pocket, wipes his mouth, then examines what he's left on the cloth, turning it this way, that way. "I had a part of my lung taken out a few years ago," he says after a while. "A tumor the size of my thumb."

"Cancer?"

"No, no," he says. "They said it was benign. But I always wonder: Was it the entire thumb? Just the tip of the thumb? The bones that connect down to the wrist? They were never clear."

"I'm sure it was just the tip," Jack says.

"What is the difference between being sure and believing?"

"I'd need evidence before I believed—and before I make any deal," Jack says.

Now Dmitry is the one rolling his eyes. He understands what Jack is saying. When it comes to this page of the bible, there's no deal until they can authenticate it.

"This is why I think, yes, you will win this Cold War. Because Americans, you will wait out anything, even those things that seem impossible." Dmitry coughs some more. "The woman inside, what is her name?"

"Ingrid," Jack says.

Dmitry pulls out his pack of Belomorkanals, offers another one to Jack. They're like smoking industrial waste.

"I don't actually smoke," Jack says.

"I don't either," Dmitry says.

Ingrid steps out of the farmhouse and waves to Jack that all is okay. There's nothing urgent about her movements. She adds a thumbs-up. Everything checks out. This page of Benedict Arnold's bible is real.

"Looks like we have a deal," Jack says.

"Your friend Ingrid?" Dmitry says. "We keep her here for a few days, just in case."

"That wasn't part of the agreement," Jack says.

"Consider it an addendum. Until we both get what we want."

A teenage boy steps out of the farmhouse then and stands beside Ingrid. Jack hadn't seen the boy before, and doesn't know where he showed up from.

Even from a hundred yards away, Jack can tell the kid is sick. It's the way he's standing, like he's missing something from the middle of his body. Jack has seen that before, when he's been in hospitals visiting kids with bone cancers, kids who have a couple of days to live, who want to spend some of those days talking to him about whether or not ghosts are real, just like Hazel always wanted to know. *This kid*, Jack thinks, *will know before I will*.

"I need something from you," Jack says.

"You are getting it. Your bible, yes?"

"No, something different. Something that gives us another reason to talk. For one of our episodes. Truth serums and lie detectors. We'll meet somewhere tropical, the Dominican Republic maybe, sit down, have a drink, pretend we're interrogating each other. Show that it's crap, you and me, tougher than the spies."

"I like it," Dmitry says. "Let me talk to the university."

"Let me talk to the CIA," Jack says.

Dmitry is silent for a moment, then starts laughing hard, which turns into hacking again, now he's bending over at his waist, a shudder working up out of him.

"You should get that checked out," Jack says.

Ingrid is still standing in the doorway. She won't

be happy about needing to stay behind, but when it comes to the crew, she's the only one who knows the true secret of the bible.

"I hope you can sleep tonight," Dmitry says, walking slowly back to his car, leaving a dwindling trail of smoke behind him.

38

Oakland, California
Today

Butchie flicked a switch on the GoPro camera strapped to Hazel's head. "Okay. You're running hot now." He put his iPhone in her left hand, already open to the video with her questions. She'd recorded ten of them, spaced out at ten-second intervals; that way, if she started to babble, she'd interrupt herself. That was the hope, anyway. "How long you want me gone?" he asked.

"A mile away," Hazel said, "then turn around and come back."

It made no sense to Butchie, Hazel arguing that if he stayed and could hear her answers, maybe she'd lie. No sense at all! If this so-called "truth" serum worked, she'd have no choice but to tell the truth as she knew it. But Butchie knew some things deserved privacy.

"When you get back, if I'm dead or in a coma or

something, call Skip. Tell him who you are; he'll take care of it. Then..." Hazel tried to figure out the best thing to tell Butchie. She decided on the truth. "Get out of town."

"Girl," Butchie said, "I already thought you were dead once, and I stayed right here. If someone wants me, they can come get me."

"Also, if I'm knocked out when you're back, don't watch the video. You have to promise me."

"I promise you."

"One mile," Hazel said.

"One mile," Butchie said, and backed out of the storage unit, pulled the rolling door down after him, and hit the padlock.

Hazel sat and stared at the phone screen, waiting to hit the Play button on her video. The storage unit was 10×20 and packed meticulously with Butchie's belongings. Furniture, boxes of books, racks of clothes, bikes, skydiving paraphernalia, but also pictures in frames everywhere, stacked up, leaning on the wall. In each one, Butchie was with people, always with people, smiling, a drink in his hand, his dog by his side. Hazel wondered if he had a boyfriend, if whatever his secret life was had room for love, since it didn't seem hers did. She wondered how it was that she'd ended up alone, bungeed to a papasan chair in a storage unit, getting ready to shoot herself up.

Hazel waited two minutes, then looked down at the needle and shoved it into her arm.

39

This time, there was a soft yellow glow and then it was gold and warm and like summer vacation, like flying, like being back in the air, like jumping from the top of El Capitan in Yosemite and floating, never coming down, never landing, just keep moving, keep on moving, never wake up, everything gold.

40

You got spotted," Moten said.

"I didn't," Rabbit told his boss. He was inside Hazel's apartment. The local cops were leaving, a few neighbors were gawking, and Hal, the building manager, was smoking outside. "*I'm* the one who called 911."

"*What?* Why would you do that?"

"You think Hazel isn't keeping an eye on this place? I want her to know we're here. Once she hears that, she's not coming back. Now we've got her running. Off balance. The perfect time for her to make a mistake."

"So we're putting our hopes on what the cleaning lady tells her?"

"First, she's not just the cleaning lady. If I'm right—and I'm telling you, I'm right—she's a friend. Second, Hazel's not stupid. You want to see what she's up to, we need to be smart. Smarter than just skulking around in the shadows and hoping for the best."

Moten didn't say anything for a moment, but Rabbit could hear him *tap-tap-tapping* with something. It was late on the East Coast. This time of night in Bethesda, Rabbit imagined Moten was at home with his wife, catching a ball game, eating some dinner, maybe wearing a robe. "Skip's about to go on a plane," Moten said. "According to his phone, he's headed to LAX."

"I saw. The moron is flying under his own name, on a flight to Dubai that leaves at nine," Rabbit said. "He'll be in Dubai tomorrow night. I checked the manifest. There's a cameraman scheduled to join him on a later flight. They think pulling out TV cameras will get folks talking. Not a bad plan—though I wouldn't trust Skip with anything."

Tap-tap-tap. "I didn't know about the cameraman. Good work on that, Rabbit."

"You hired me for a reason, sir. Whoever killed Jack Nash, we'll find them."

"Just tell me where Hazel is."

"I'm betting with someone named Butch Vasquez," Rabbit said. "His name wasn't in her file, but I make him as a friend, maybe sometime coworker." The fact was, the only name in Hazel's file was her own. Everything else was redacted. "A local cab driver said he dropped Hazel at Butch's shop this morning. I'm on his place next." Rabbit was staring at a photo of Butchie now, of Butchie and Hazel breaking gravity. Butchie had a plane. Keep an eye on that.

Tap-tap-tap-tap. "Now do you want to hear what went wrong here today?" Moten asked.

Rabbit didn't answer.

Tap-tap-tap-tap. "Did you talk to our friend Dr. Morrison recently?"

"No," Rabbit said.

"Hazel did. When you get to her, find out the tenor of her conversation, okay?"

"Why's that?"

"I'd like to know why he had a sudden change of heart."

"Pardon me, sir?"

"I just got a call from UCLA Medical Center. Seems Dr. Morrison is no longer in our corner."

"What makes you say that?"

"He jumped from the hospital roof. They're now scraping what's left of him off the sidewalk."

41

As Hazel came to, all she saw was stars. Except they weren't actually stars. They were glow-in-the-dark stickers on the ceiling, all the major constellations, and for a second she thought she was ten and at a sleepover somewhere. She half expected to look over and see a bunch of stuffed animals, but instead she found Butchie.

"There you are," Butchie said. His hands were clasped in front of him.

"Were you praying?"

"Something like it."

"Where am I?"

"A place I keep," he said. Hazel let her eyes adjust. They were in an old warehouse space, broken up by three-paneled shoji dividers and a wall of windows, half of them open, a light breeze billowing in through white blinds. It was like waking up in a dream. "You remember me coming to get you?"

"No. Did I say anything?"

"You asked for a cheeseburger and a glass of water," Butchie said. "Then you started talking gibberish about a stuffed bear. That's when I knew you'd be okay."

"How long have I been out?"

"Couple hours. It's late. Figured better not to have the entire world see me carrying a body in here."

Hazel propped herself up on her elbows, her entire body pulsing now. She needed her medication. She was overdue, even with the horse tranquilizers in her body. "This is where you live?"

"This is where I hide."

She was woozy, maybe still asleep, now that she considered it. The ceiling glowed down on her, covered with stars.

Butchie pulled Hazel's phone from his pocket and set it on the nightstand. "Your phone's been going crazy. Anyone got this number?"

"Skip," she said. Hazel thought about that, how easy Skip was to follow. "Maybe also divisions of the federal government."

"I disabled the GPS," he said, "and all the other tracking shit. Maybe you should call your brother back, let him know you're alive."

"I need to see the video first."

"It's here," he said. "Go back to sleep. You don't look so good."

She didn't feel good. Everything was beginning to swim before her eyes. She tilted her head back again and spotted the only constellation she remembered. Ursa Major. Based on the Greek myth of Callisto, who was attacked by Zeus. The woman never got to fight back.

"Did you watch it, Butchie?"

"Nah," he said.

"Are you lying?"

"I know what I'm guilty of," he said. "I don't lie to you. Not ever."

42

Hazel dreamed of her mother.
No, she was awake.
No, the twilight in between.
She'd open her eyes and see Butchie, still in the chair beside her, hands still clasped together. She'd close her eyes and see her mother in the car in Utah. See her in her open casket. Cutting the crust off a peanut butter and banana sandwich, the two of them eating and laughing, the taste so clear in Hazel's mouth, tangy and rich at the same time. Reading *Where the Sidewalk Ends*, holding her hand in a crowd, always holding her hand, there in the classroom, in the back row as Hazel gave her first lecture.

Though that's not true, Hazel realized, this was a lucid dream. A lie. Her mother was dead by then. She'd imprinted that impression, overlaid something she hadn't seen with something she wished she'd seen. Perspective was a thing you never really had until you lost it and tried to figure out where it went.

"This continental drift of yours," Claire is saying to her, and Hazel recognizes she's remembering something, that there's some connection her brain is making again, wonders if it will be gone when she's awake. Her mom is sitting outside on a chaise longue, so skinny Hazel can see the acromioclavicular joint at the top of her shoulder. Hazel's standing behind her, clippers in hand, shaving her mother's head, just finishing chemo's job. "This drift is going to get you killed if you're not careful."

"So if I'm careful," Hazel says, "I'll be fine?"

"Make no mistakes, and you won't have much of a life." The breeze picks up and as soon as Hazel shaves a strand of hair, it blows away, Claire follows its path with her eyes, and again Hazel thinks, *No, the perspective is wrong, you're making this up.*

Then Claire says, "I'd like to be buried in my hometown."

"I know. In Mission Valley," Hazel says, referring to the small town outside of San Diego.

Claire smiles weakly. "Ask your father when I'm gone. Have him tell you the truth. My real hometown. In Berlin."

43

Three hours later, Hazel woke up. Something was poking at her throat. It was the corner of a piece of paper, safety-pinned to her shirt, a note from Butchie:

Downstairz having coffee. Look out the window. Then cloze it.

She got up. Her legs felt pretty good, but her head felt like it had been scooped out using a backhoe. She walked to the bank of windows, looked down.

Butchie sat at a table across the street outside a coffeehouse. It was seven thirty in the morning. A line of people already spilled out into the street around him. Butchie had sunglasses on and was reading the newspaper, but as soon as Hazel appeared at the window alone, he lifted a single finger, then put it back down.

Message received.

She closed the window and drew the blinds. Walking into the kitchen, she found a banana. The first bite was like eating mud. *–ffgh!* She opened the fridge, found some Tabasco, and doused the banana. As she took another bite, she felt the pain, felt the rush.

The GoPro was hooked to a laptop on the counter, and there was a note next to it. *Just hit enter. It'z queued.*

So she did.

The video rolled. There she was, tied to the chair, helmet on her head, ready for battle. "Yes or No," her own voice asked onscreen. "Did you kill your father?"

44

Q: Did you kill your father?

A: I didn't.

Q: Have you ever killed anyone?

A: I tried to. Yes.

Q: Did you kill Darren Nixon?

A: We all did. We're all to blame.

Q: Did you know Dad was working for the government?

A: No.

Q: Have you been working for the government?

A: No.

Q: Have you seen Benedict Arnold's bible?

A:

Q: Did you love your family?

A:

Q: Are you lying to yourself?

A:

Q: Hazel, stay awake! Don't let the drugs knock you out! Do you trust your brother?

A:

Q: Do you trust Butchie?

A:

45

What Hazel saw?
Someone she didn't recognize.
Someone who looked at peace.
Someone telling the truth.

The video was twelve minutes long. During the first three, she was waiting for Butchie to get far enough away. In the next three, the drug hit and she was answering her own questions. But the weird thing was that she didn't look angry.

Didn't look sad.

Didn't look worried.

She answered the questions with a smile on her face, a giggle working out of her throat, and then she was asleep, out cold in four minutes. Then Butchie, bless him, his face filling up the frame as he ripped the camera from her head, stopped the recording. She doubted he'd gone more than a block away. Maybe he hadn't left at all.

Did she kill Darren Nixon? *"We all did."* What did that mean? Who else was she referring to?

She wondered who she'd killed. Or did she just try? Was that Nixon or someone else?

Realized it could've been accidental. But no, it wasn't accidental, was it?

Realized that Dr. Morrison was right about her. She was not who she thought she was. Not at all.

Realized if she killed anyone, they probably deserved it. Hopefully deserved it.

Realized she was fine with it.

Realized that everyone has a job.

Realized that there definitely used to be something wrong with her, that she didn't need to be that person anymore, right? She could start over, be who she wanted to be. Maybe she'd start over and end up in the same place.

Fair enough.

But there was Skip to consider.

She found her phone. There were a dozen missed calls, but no messages. She figured that once she called her brother, with or without any GPS, whoever was looking for her—the government or anyone else—they'd be able to find her somehow. That's how it had to be. Everyone serves someone.

Except, Hazel knew right then, she served her family first. *Honor the people who love you.* That was one of her father's rules. It was a good one. She hadn't answered the question about whether or not she loved her family. At that point in the video, she was already gone, and maybe now it didn't matter.

Why? Because as far as she could tell, she'd spent the past few years retracing her dad's steps, wearing Benedict Arnold's words on her body, but did it on her own. She wasn't working for the government on whatever they had her dad doing. No, whatever Hazel's life consisted of, it was hers.

But...

That didn't mean she wasn't interested. She'd been with Jack and Skip in that car in the Utah desert, she'd been with her father when he died, and maybe one day she'd remember those last moments as her own, not as the broken movie reel in her mind. But she'd been there with her brother, they'd survived, and Skip hadn't left her side since. She had walked away, pushed him away, and still he waited for her. If that wasn't the definition of someone loving you, she didn't know what was.

Honor the people who love you.

Yes. She'd do that. No matter what it took.

46

Skip answered on the first ring. "You all right?"

"Never been better," Hazel said. "What about you? You somewhere safe?"

"I'm in London, waiting for my connecting flight. I spoke to the network. They're thinking of sending a full film crew with the cameraman," Skip said. "To get it started again."

It. "That's what they told you?"

"You were right, Haze. Whatever happened out in Dubai, this is our chance to find out."

"Unless we're doing exactly what whoever did this wants us to: Split us up, so they can pick us off." She paused. "Maybe you should come back."

"I'm not coming back."

"Skip—"

"Listen, I've been thinking. This thing? Maybe it's also an opportunity for me. On TV."

"Skip, that was Dad's life. It doesn't need to be yours."

"Then what do I do with the rest of *my* life?"

"Get a job."

"I have a job," Skip said. "I'm not like you. I don't know how to do anything other than be Skip Nash." He stopped. "Crap. I just spoke of myself in third person. That's a bad sign, isn't it?"

"It's not a good one," Hazel said. "Skip, did you know about my tattoo?"

"You have a tattoo?"

"On the back of my neck, under my hair."

"No," Skip said. "What is it? Some death rune? An Iron Maiden logo?"

"Something Benedict Arnold said. *A wretched motley crew.*"

Skip was silent for a moment. Hazel heard an announcement being made over the PA in the airport: Boarding for Dubai would start momentarily out of Gate 62B. "The last couple weeks," Skip said, "is the most time I've spent with you since we were kids. You could be covered in tattoos, Haze, and I frankly wouldn't know any different. You're a stranger to me, and not because I wanted it that way."

"Did Dad know me?"

"Whatever you two had was between you two. It was like you spoke the same language, one different from the rest of us."

She knew Skip was right. "I don't think Agent Rabkin has been entirely truthful with us," she added.

"About what?"

"He told us Dad did work for the government, as if that were Dad's choice. But what if it wasn't? What if the only reason Dad was with them was because they found something bad about Dad, something they could use against him?"

"Like what?"

"I don't know. I'm not there yet. But maybe Dad did all this because he *had* to. Do you think he wanted to put his life at risk going to those crazy places? He had kids. A wife. Who would do this willingly when they had so much to lose?"

"I would do it. I want to do it."

"You have nothing to lose," Hazel said. And there it was. Another announcement rang out.

"I need to get on a plane, Haze. You go to Spokane, find what you find, then come out here too. We'll do it together."

"I will. I promise," Hazel said, worrying deep down that those were the last words she'd ever say to her brother.

47

Butchie drove down the main drag. The Mission was as busy at 10 a.m. as it was at 10 p.m. People were already standing outside, smoking, texting, looking at their feet. Everything the same as it ever was, except legendarily rough bars like the Elbo Room were now filled with people who lived in modernist condos and preferred chardonnay to a beer and a shot.

"Stop here. In front of the noodle place," Hazel said. They were still a few blocks from her apartment building, but she didn't want to get closer until she knew what they were walking into.

"You really think someone's watching?" Butchie asked.

"Only one way to find out." She pulled out her phone, a new one that Butchie had at his place, and dialed a number.

Butchie looked out his window. Across the

street, an old Asian woman was walking a poodle. "How soon you think until I can get another dog?"

"A year."

Butchie considered this. "When does reincarnation kick in?"

"When the soul is ready," Hazel said. "That's what the Hindus say, anyway."

"Any of these religions got a damn clock?"

The woman with the poodle crossed the street, and the poodle started going crazy, barking and snarling at a passing old man.

"*No, Astro! No, Astro!*" the woman shouted.

"No kind of name for a dog," Butchie said.

Hazel focused on her phone, which was ringing until—

"Hello?" a man's voice said. The manager of Hazel's apartment building.

Hal, Hazel decided. *Definitely Hal.* "Hey, Hal, it's Hazel Nash. Sorry to bother you, but I've got a leak in one of the toilets. Can you come up and take a look?"

Hal coughed out a half syllable, then stopped himself. "S-Sure. No problem. I'm just glad you're okay. We were worried about you."

"*We?*"

"M-Me. And your cleaning lady. Mel, right?" he stuttered, an evolutionary tell. When something scares you, a few million years of practice tells you to run. Another couple of million years and it gets wired to your emotions, even your speech, which is what Hal had going on. A polysensory experience. Proof that your premotor cortex was alive and well.

Hazel hung up the phone. "Something's wrong. Get us out of here," she told Butchie.

"If you want, I could just keep driving. My plane is out in Concord. I could have you over the Channel Islands in a couple hours. Get you to San Nicolas and you could be like that native girl in the 1800s. Live off the land and shit, except I'd come and visit."

Juana Maria, the last of the Nicoleño tribe. Eighteen years she'd lived alone on the island after the rest of her tribe died off. Finally, in her fifties, she was found and brought to the mainland, where she lived at the Santa Barbara Mission. Became a children's book and everything.

A good story.

But the truth was also that she got off the island and no one understood her language. No one could figure out what the hell she was talking about. So they fed her, baptized her, and in under two months she was in the grave, dead from dysentery.

A bad ending. It didn't sound all that different

from the situation Hazel currently found herself in.

"You got enough gas in your plane to get me to Spokane?"

"You might need to jump out," Butchie said, "but I'll get you close."

48

It was a forty-minute trip across the bridge into the East Bay, Butchie driving nice and slow as Hazel eyed any car that followed them for more than a few minutes.

By the time they turned off for Buchanan airfield in Concord, they were alone. No one behind them.

But that didn't mean someone wasn't already waiting there.

"Yeah, I see them," Rabbit said into his phone as he watched them scurry from Butchie's car, still searching every direction of the airport. They didn't spot Rabbit across the way, tucked into a maintenance hangar that smelled of gasoline and Fritos.

Sure, Rabbit could shut down the airport, put Butchie in cuffs, arrest Hazel just for the guns he found in her apartment. But as Moten himself had said, there were better ways to find the truth.

Within a half hour, out on the runway, Butchie's black and yellow Beechcraft—the Bumblebeez—took off, heading north.

"Absolutely. I promise you, sir," Rabbit said into his phone. "I'll be there before they land."

49

Hazel didn't like this place. She knew it the moment she realized that Darren Nixon—the man found dead wearing her father's colonial coat—hadn't actually lived in Spokane. He lived twenty miles north, in a town called Deer Park, population 3,500.

When Hazel pulled up to Nixon's white one-story house, she didn't see a soul in the neighborhood. It was late afternoon and everyone was still working. She probably had a few hours until any of the neighbors came home. *Good.* Hazel took one last look over her shoulder. At least this was going right.

Nixon's Arts and Crafts house was right off Main Street, walking distance to a Christian bookstore and a used car lot that had three cars and a tractor for sale.

According to Agent Rabkin, Hazel's father had

been here in June, before the family trip to Utah.
When Hazel thought it was Spokane, she imagined her dad in a city, a cab dropping him off, but
Deer Park was rural and small, and if Jack Nash
had showed up in town, much less visiting an ex-
con, people would have known about it. Someone
at the gas station would have had him sign a dollar
bill. Hell, he might have stopped into the Christian bookstore just to see if they had his book. But
Hazel had looked online: There was no mention
anywhere of anyone seeing Jack up this way.

Hazel knocked hard on the door. It was wood,
just like the rest of the house, making Hazel think
about Nixon's crimes. His arson charge. Was the
place he lit on fire made of wood too?

No one answered. No surprise. From her
pocket, Hazel pulled out the lock pick and tension
wrench that Butchie had given her back on the
plane. At first, she didn't know what to do with
it, but as she inserted it, muscle memory kicked
in, leaving her wondering what other locks she'd
picked.

Had she been here before? Could she be the
one who followed Nixon up to Benedict Arnold's
old home in Canada, then slipped him poison
and stood on his neck to make it look like he'd
drowned? *We're all to blame*, she heard herself saying. But what did that mean? Would she do that

to protect her father? To protect Skip? Was that something she was capable of?

Of course she was.

But was it something she'd done? She turned the tension wrench. There was a muted click, and the door slid open. If she was right, she'd know soon enough.

The first thing Hazel noticed were three tall bottles of olive oil on the kitchen counter, a taste she wondered if she'd ever have again. In the living room, there was a bulky old color TV with a screen so covered in dust, Hazel could have etched her initials in it, a sofa that sagged in the middle, and a coffee table covered with books, reams of paper, and three cups with withered tea bags stuck inside them, all surrounding an IBM Selectric typewriter.

Hazel went straight for the books: a Stephen King about JFK's death, a biography of John Adams, a volume about the exodus in Syria, and there, at the bottom of the stack, *Secrets of the House* by Jack Nash. Her father's autobiography, which had come out a few years ago. She couldn't recall him writing it. He probably hadn't.

Hazel flipped to the title page with a feeling of dread. She didn't actually remember her father's handwriting, but she knew it the moment she saw it, clean block letters that read: FOR DARREN, SO NICE MEETING YOU! —JACK NASH.

Had her dad signed it when he was here? For some reason, she didn't think so, despite the fact that the ink looked fresh, like it was done recently. Hazel flipped through the book, but didn't see any bookmarks or folded-down pages. Yet somehow, from the way the spine was cracked, the book looked like it'd been read. Completed.

Hazel carried the book with her, heading for the bedroom. Nixon's queen bed was pressed against the wall in a corner, so that only the left side was accessible, the way little children slept, or people who'd spent time in captivity, like prison, not wanting their back exposed, not even when they were asleep in their own home. There were stacks of books in here too—biographies on Bill Gates, Steve Jobs, and Cornelius Vanderbilt; Nixon clearly liked his businessmen—and another IBM Selectric, identical to the one in the living room.

There was only one apparently personal item in the room, on a shelf. It was a faded color photo that looked like it had been cut from a magazine. There was a beautiful woman, sitting, holding a baby in her arms, looking down upon it with nothing short of reverence. Behind them was a splash of red, from what looked like a flag, though most of it was blocked by the edges of the frame.

Hazel unscrewed the back of the frame and slid the photo out. It was definitely sliced from a magazine. The paper was thick and glossy, but nothing like a real photograph. There was no writing on the page, but now she could see the full flag revealed, draped lifelessly on a stand in someone's library or office. Red, black, and green. The national flag of Libya.

Libya.

Hazel had seen that episode just the other day. Her father was tracing the history of a dragon slain by St. George.

It was, as all of these things were to Hazel, absurd. After looking at paintings in Libya and replica bronzes in Croatia, Dad finally determined that the dragon was likely a metaphor...*or was it?*

Hazel rubbed the back of her neck and looked back down at the photo. A small child. There was always a child. Was that young Nixon in the photo? Maybe? Probably? All she knew for sure was that her father had been in this house. Soon after, Nixon was found dead in Dad's Revolutionary coat. And in between? There was still so much missing.

In the dragon episode, there wasn't any mention of Benedict Arnold. And wasn't that what this was all about? That's what Agent Rabkin had said. Naturally, Hazel refused to take his word for it. She'd looked it up herself. George Washington *did* send Benedict Arnold his belongings, including what many agree were books and most likely a bible. But even then, what made Arnold's bible so important?

According to Rabkin, there was something inside, something in its pages, some kind of message. Or. Maybe the bible *itself* was the message. Maybe it contained a code, or itself was a code. Or a message. Was that why her dad was in all those countries? Was he sending a message? Or maybe receiving one? Whatever the bible really contained, it was important enough to take someone's life. Someone who had committed his own crimes—and had just been visited by her father. Is that what Darren Nixon figured out? What Jack Nash was really up to?

For the next two hours, Hazel pulled open drawers, looked through closets, and peered under beds and couches, sifting through Darren Nixon's life, unearthing him like she was digging out a body, sweeping away the dirt and sand one grain at a time.

She expected to find guns. She expected to find poisons. She expected to find detailed blueprints for her father's house. However, the most dangerous thing she found was a new set of knives in the kitchen. They were all there, none of them missing.

In a second bedroom, which had been turned into an office, there were reams of white paper, boxes of ribbons for Nixon's typewriters, manila envelopes by the dozen, sheets of stamps, and, in the only evidence of twenty-first-century technology, a desktop photocopier and scanner.

And yet Darren Nixon didn't have a landline, didn't have a computer.

Throughout the plane ride here, Hazel had imagined herself walking into Nixon's house and the walls would be covered, serial-killer style, in crazed drawings of Benedict Arnold, Jesus, and maybe maniacal clowns, just for the fear factor. There would be an arsenal of weapons. There might even be a secret message from her father scratched into a mirror, or a pool of dried blood seeping out from under a false wall that led to a stone chamber filled with hundreds of copies of Benedict Arnold's bible.

That would have made things easier.

Now, standing in Nixon's makeshift office, all she knew about the man was that he had a healthy aversion to modern technology. The fact that his TV wasn't even plugged in confounded her more. If he'd been a fan of her dad's TV show, if he'd stolen or even purchased Benedict Arnold's jacket from her father, or had contact with him, wouldn't Nixon have some better connection to the world? Rabkin had mentioned a Netflix account, but there was no place to watch it. She supposed he had a computer at work, and a phone—maybe he even had a friend or two who might eventually come looking for him, but here he was, living in a tiny town, with just books and two typewriters?

No. Pieces were still missing. But. Everything is somewhere.

Hazel sat down in Nixon's desk chair. It was high-backed, with faux leather upholstery, the armrests pulling apart at the seams. Nixon had covered a few spots with black electrical tape, but on the end of the left arm, it felt like he'd picked at the tape until it pulled away, and now there was a bald spot surrounded by a fluff of white fuzz and sticky fabric. Hazel could feel indentations where he'd dug in his fingernails.

Hazel spun slowly around in the chair, trying to take in the room as Nixon saw it every day, see what his eyes fell on, what talismans Darren Nixon kept.

A silver metal garbage can in the corner. An empty carton of Marlboro Reds lay in the bottom of it, though the house didn't smell like smoke. There were a few balled-up Kleenex and last month's bills in there too.

There was also a corkboard on the wall.

In the middle of it, held in place with two thumbtacks, was his inmate release form from the Washington State Department of Corrections. A simple one-page document stating that he'd been released from prison two years ago on July 18, satisfying the terms of his conviction. The signature of the Governor. The seal of the State of Washington, with George Washington's thin, unsmiling lips, his hooded eyes, his white hair. The only other item on the board was a yellow Post-it that said, *Buy chains*, a reminder for the winter that he'd never see.

Next to the corkboard was a window, sunlight glowing through the cheap white shades. But what caught Hazel's eye was a hole that was drilled below the bottom right corner of the window. Through the hole, a bright yellow extension cord was stapled to the window frame and ran down to the ground, eventually plugging into a surge protector.

Surge protector. In a house that barely used electricity.

Hazel followed the cord, pulled the shade up, opened the window, and looked out into the backyard. Running down the outside of the house, the yellow extension cord was stapled to the wall, then disappeared, buried in the dirt. The yard had a fire pit, a single folding chair, and an old wooden side table. Beyond that was a quarter acre of dirt and wild grass. Nothing that required electricity.

So where'd that cord run?

Hazel went outside. Everything is somewhere.

50

It was warm outside, maybe eighty-five degrees, and the metal folding chair felt hot to the touch when Hazel reached it. That chair had been green once, but most of the paint was chipped away, revealing the rusted metal beneath. This was where Darren Nixon spent his free time, judging from the corona of cigarette butts on the ground, the mountain of ashes in the fire pit, and the dented Pepsi cans along the ground. Hazel could see why: It was peaceful—silent, save for a wind chime somewhere in the distance and the chirping of birds.

The fire pit was about four feet wide and ringed with river stones, not a professional job, but it looked like it'd been built with some care. Nixon liked fire. He used it as a weapon. And when it came to the fire pit, he clearly put time into it, building it nice, so that he could sit outside under the stars, smoke a cigarette, drink a Pepsi, and, judging from the circle of footprints in the dirt, pace around the flames.

It was natural, Hazel knew. Humans were wired to walk in circles, unless they had a firm and distinct point of reference in front of them. It was how people got lost and died in the desert and the forest alike, even when civilization was only a few miles away. True north to the human body was an ever-tightening circle.

For Nixon, this was a good place to sit, walk, and make plans.

Or type. The wooden table had a few dozen sheets of paper on it, now damp and ruined, held down by two rocks, and beneath it, no electrical port anywhere.

So where did the yellow cord go?

Hazel walked back toward the outside of the house, gripped a section of the yellow cord in her hand, and tugged. The staples popped from the wall. When she got some length of the cord in hand, she pulled harder, yanking it from the ground. Bits of dirt and stones burst upward, like a burrow when Bugs Bunny would travel underground.

She walked slowly across the yard, pulling the yellow cord from the ground, unspooling it like a thread in an old sweater, letting it lead her.

Eventually, it stopped, dead-ending at a wooden fence on the far right side of the property. No. Not dead-ending. She tugged the yellow cord. It kept on going underneath the fence.

To the house next door.

Hazel looked through the fence. Even from here, she could see it. Across the yard, behind an old house with peeling gray paint, the yellow cord poked out from the dirt and snaked into a small hole that was cut into the side of a prefabricated shed.

A most perfect hiding place.

51

Hazel darted to the house next door, leaping up onto the front porch. There was a business card and a magnetic refrigerator calendar from a real estate agent shoved into the crack of the door.

Hazel knocked, waited. Tried the doorbell. Nothing. She peered into the front window, but couldn't see anything through the thick brown curtains. She pulled the card and calendar from the door. The paper was stiff and the agent's face—a woman named Lori Lord who promised to provide "110% Customer Satisfaction!"—was washed out from the sun. No one had been through this door in weeks, at least. Maybe months.

Hazel heard a door slam across the street, turned around, and saw a teenage girl walking outside. She picked up a ten-speed bike from the pockmarked front lawn, hopped on, then seemed to notice Hazel for the first time.

"You the calendar lady?" the girl called out.

"No," Hazel said.

"Too bad. Ours slid under the refrigerator and now I never know what day it is."

Hazel walked down the front steps and into the street, holding up the magnet. "You can have this one." The girl pedaled over and took the calendar from Hazel's hand. She was maybe fifteen, with hair down the length of her back, fake diamond studs in her ears, and a black Ramones T-shirt. "Nice shirt," Hazel said.

The girl gathered up the hem of her shirt, pulled it away from her body. "Someone left it in the house on July Fourth." She shrugged. "I thought it was cool." She let go of the shirt, let it fall back onto her body. "Probably some friend of my pop's. How does that happen? You go somewhere and forget your shirt when you go home?"

"Beer," Hazel said.

The girl laughed. "There was plenty of that."

Hazel thought she was wrong. The girl was maybe eighteen or nineteen. Hazel imagined her sitting in the back row of one of Hazel's classes, raising her hand, asking if whatever Hazel was talking about would be on the test, Hazel thinking, *Sweetheart, it's all on the test*.

"Do you know who lives here?" Hazel asked.

"Nobody," the girl said.

"For how long?"

"A year? Maybe two, now that I think about it. Since before Ms. Nixon died, anyway. She moved out when she started to go cuckoo."

"Right," Hazel said.

Ms. Nixon. Darren lived next door to his mother. Now Mom's house was vacant, save for that shed out back. A good hiding spot for sure, Hazel thought. Especially for someone who'd already been busted by the cops, who probably hated them. If someone kicked down Darren's door, they wouldn't find the shed, at least not right away.

"Do you know Darren?" Hazel asked.

"You from the IRS or something?" Definitely not fifteen. Maybe she was twenty.

"No, no," Hazel started. "Darren's my cousin."

"Oh. Cool. I've been knowing him since I was ten. He used to let me and my brother play hide-n-go-seek in his backyard. He was a paranoid guy. I'd see him watching us."

"I haven't been out here in forever," Hazel said, careful to slip into a bit of dialect to let the girl know Hazel was just like her, whatever that meant. "I knew his mom lived in one of these houses, I just couldn't remember which one." She pointed at her rental car down the street. "I came by to get some stuff for Darren. He's sort of in a bad spot. Got in a car accident in Canada. Messed up his head."

The girl brushed her hair from her eyes. "Shit," she said. "Wow. Crazy."

"Yeah," Hazel said. "Does he use this house too? I want to make sure I get anything he might want."

"Not since his mom died, I don't think. My dad helped him move all the furniture out and he gave us some silverware and a bunch of dishes. Bone china. Said that wasn't him. My dad said he's lazy. We sold it on eBay." She picked up her bike, got on it. "He might have some stuff in the shed out back, I think. I hear him out there a lot. I'm warning you, though. He's a bit of a weirdo."

"Aren't we all?" Hazel said, heading for the backyard. "I'll check it out. Glad to see you. I don't want anyone thinking I'm robbing the place."

52

The prefabricated shed was 10 × 12, the top of its door spotted with a freshly spun spiderweb. No one had been here in a bit. The shed looked like wood but was made from vinyl. *Harder to burn*, Hazel thought, now wondering if this was where Nixon plotted his crimes, or if this was what he built after.

As Hazel pulled on the door, she expected more typewriters, more paper, more books. Instead, it reminded her of one of the medical labs from the hospital: The three walls were covered in white dry-erase boards; there was a desk with a laptop computer, a printer, and two lamps. A portable fan stood in one corner, and all the electric devices were plugged into a surge protector that was connected to the yellow cord. There wasn't a single piece of paper in the room.

On the dry-erase boards, Nixon had listed every

episode of Jack's show, nearly three hundred in total, including the various specials and miniseries that they did when the ratings sagged. There were columns for the original airdate, the approximate date the episode was filmed, the location, the mystery, all of it in tiny handwriting, a scrimshaw-like precision that Hazel immediately and somehow found familiar: It was how captives wrote, how the imprisoned passed notes, scribbling onto tiny pieces of paper, compounding as much information as possible into the smallest space, in case they needed to transport the information in unconventional ways.

You'd already been to prison, Darren Nixon. So what was left to be afraid of? What scared you when you slept?

He'd crossed out certain episodes: the one with the alien autopsy, the five separate episodes that concerned Billy the Kid, any about the possibility of ESP or computers becoming sentient. He'd circled more than a dozen episodes that took place in different countries. Iran in 1980. Libya in 1983. Northern Ireland in 1984. Russia in 1985.

According to Hazel's passport, all the places she'd recently visited.

Beside those episodes, in his tiny writing, were two letters with a question mark: B.A.?

Benedict Arnold.

He'd also put stars next to a few episodes: an episode in Florida about the Bermuda Triangle, one in Boston about Bobby Kennedy and the Mafia, the one in Philadelphia in the underground tunnels. But there were no B.A. marks next to any episodes in America, and there were a good three dozen over the years that had some concern with George Washington and the Revolutionary War.

Finally, on the far left of the boards were a few drawn lines connecting various episodes, with questions running along the top:

International burials?

Cross check with census/naturalization

Military action?

Hazel didn't know what any of it meant. She took out her phone and snapped two dozen photos, getting the boards from every angle.

She turned on Nixon's laptop, was surprised to see it had Internet, then saw that it was connected to a secure network called PrettyFlyForAWifi. The signal wasn't strong, just three bars. Hazel looked around the shed but didn't see a router or modem. Nixon was stealing his Internet from his neighbors. It made sense. If someone tracked him online and cops pulled up to his neighbors' house, Nixon would still have time to run out the back door, pulling the electricity with him.

But why would they be coming for him now? What was he paranoid about?

Hazel clicked through his computer, looking for documents that might be of interest, but everything she came up with initially looked like homework assignments. Darren apparently was enrolled in a night class at Spokane Community College, a course in genealogy.

Complex guy, Hazel thought.

He had a family tree assignment for Stephen Colbert, with effusive notes in the margin from the instructor: GOOD JOB! GO TO THE THIRD COUSIN—COULD GET JUICY!

He had other family trees for Barbara Bush, Henry Winkler, even Jesse James.

And then, he had three more.

One for himself:

Darren Nixon.
   Born 1979 in Sirte, Libya.
   Mother: Mona Haql, changed her name to Nixon upon immigration to the U.S. in 1983 (Deceased).
   Father: Unknown.

There was a tree for Hazel's father:

Jack Nash.

Born 1946 in Rochester, New York.
Mother: Patricia Nashier (Deceased).
Father: Cyrus Nashier (Deceased).

And one final tree:

Hazel Nash.

53

Dubai, United Arab Emirates

The Bear watches Skip Nash eat lunch.

Skip is sitting under a cabana, poolside at the Al Qasr. The resort sits directly on the beach, overlooking the Persian Gulf, nothing to disturb the discerning traveler but blue sky, the sound of lapping waves, and the smell of coconut oil, yet there's an infinity pool, just in case that's not enough.

A lithe young man and a lithe young woman, both in white polo shirts, each with impossibly long legs stretching out of tan shorts, appear as if by magic every few minutes, drop off food and drinks, pour glasses of water, then disappear again, until you think of them and they magically reappear.

It makes The Bear think one could almost forget about the ongoing wars stirring across the region, the beheadings, the crucifixions, the drone strikes, the journalists being flayed alive, the tourists happy to come visit the resorts of the United Arab Emirates and forget it all. So perhaps it is no surprise that even a dead American named Arthur Kennedy, dressed like a Revolutionary War soldier, could be kept out of the local press. Better to keep that quiet—send it directly to the Americans—than to risk the money of tourists from the West staying away.

Still, Arthur Kennedy is now a problem, a bother for someone else, as it was designed.

Not that Skip Nash seems bothered.

The Bear found him online. There were three photos of Skip at the airport in Los Angeles, on his way to London, two in Heathrow Airport, then one as he got into a private car in Dubai and headed to the resort.

He shouldn't be surprised Skip came here. He's tracking the death of Arthur Kennedy. But for Skip to come so quickly means someone told him where Kennedy was scheduled to stay.

The Bear looks down at his phone, swipes back to the photo of Skip getting into the car at the airport. It was curious that he was traveling without his sister. He tried to imagine a situation by which they would be separated, what the FBI agents who had controlled Jack Nash were thinking.

Perhaps The Bear didn't understand their motives as well as he thought.

Perhaps he didn't understand Hazel. That seemed impossible. She'd been injured, sure, but that wouldn't change her fundamental nature.

Perhaps it didn't matter. Skip was here. It changed The Bear's focus, altered what he thought was true, but not the imperative.

The only question is, who else knows that Skip is here? Then, on Twitter, a post from @MarcoPolo69: a photo of Skip sitting in his cabana, drink in one hand, phone in the other, a chewed straw jutting from his mouth. A nasty, disgusting habit.

"Is there anything you'd like, sir?"

The Bear looks up from his phone. The young man in the polo shirt is before him. His gold nametag says he is called Marco. He has a tray in his hand, a leather order book open and ready.

He has a bright, white smile. Good dental care. No pimples on his skin.

A man who has made some money for himself. Surely not just from dropping off drinks to tourists.

"Do you recognize that man?" The Bear asks, nodding toward Skip.

Marco looks over his shoulder, then back at The Bear. "I don't recognize anyone," he says, in a way that makes The Bear understand that Marco recognizes everyone. His English is perfect. Barely any accent.

"Tell me your age, Marco," The Bear says.

"Sir?"

"You asked what I'd like. I would like your age."

"Twenty-two," he says.

"What is your real age?"

Marco shifts his weight. "Sir?"

"You're lying. I'd like you to not lie. That is the second thing I'd like. What is your real age?"

"Twenty-seven," he says.

"Do you have a family of some kind?" The Bear asks. Marco looks like the sort of man who is untethered by such things as wives and children, the sort of man who seems parentless, as if he sprang from the dirt one day fully formed.

"Doesn't everybody?" Marco says.

"I'd like you to treat my friend over there like your family. That means his privacy shouldn't be violated."

Marco looks over his shoulder at Skip, who is taking a photo of himself, then back at The Bear. "He doesn't seem to care much about privacy."

"I care." The Bear reaches into his pool bag, comes out with five one hundred dollar bills. "I'd like you to not recognize me," The Bear says and hands Marco the cash.

"No problem," Marco says, fully engaged now. Not betraying the slightest bit of skepticism, anger, or fear. What kind of people must come to a resort like this, The Bear wonders, that this is a normal day for this man? "Anything else you'd like?"

Skip has gotten up from his cabana and walks to the edge of the pool, looks around, like he's waiting for someone to join him.

"Yes," The Bear says, and then hands him another five hundred dollars. "I need a small favor. I'd like the straw that gentleman was chewing on. And a few other items." He takes Marco's pen from his tray, writes down a brief list, hands it to him. "Those possible?"

"Possible, yes," Marco says.

The Bear writes down the address of the house he's staying in, a few miles away. "Delivered here. Do you know this place?"

"I don't think so," Marco says. "Maybe you can help me find it?"

He hands Marco a few more bills.

"Oh, yes," Marco says, "I know this place."

The Bear didn't like to get his hands dirty. It was much easier to have others do these small jobs. But greed? He did not appreciate greed. Marco would learn that in time.

54

Hazel's birthday was written there: *December 18th. Born in Los Angeles, California.* Her brother's name was there: *Nicholas "Skip" Nash.*

Her father's name was there: *Jack Nash.*

And of course, her mother's name was there: *Claire Nash.*

Yet as Hazel read and reread her family tree, as laid out by Darren Nixon, she couldn't take her eyes off that final line:

Mother: Claire Nash.

Why didn't it say *Deceased?*

She flipped back to her father's family tree, to her grandparents:

Patricia Nashier (Deceased).

Cyrus Nashier (Deceased).

But under her own family tree, there it was:

Mother: Claire Nash.

Her mother was dead. *Wasn't she?*
Hazel clicked through the other family trees, searching for one for Skip. Shouldn't there be one for Skip? She wanted to see if Skip's tree said the same. Maybe it was just something Nixon accidentally left out. But as far as she could tell, the only Nash family trees Nixon had made were for herself and her father. Nothing for—
Click.
"Hazel, I was really hoping it wouldn't come to this," a male voice said.
When Hazel turned, there was a gun in her face, just as she had known there eventually would be.

55

Y ou're not listening," Agent Rabkin said, his gun trained on Hazel. "If you move, I *will* shoot you."

"Nice to see you too," Hazel said. She put her hands in the air.

Rabbit had a duffle bag at his feet. He unzipped it, came out with a pair of zip ties, tossed them at Hazel. "Put these on."

"How?"

"It'll come back to you, I'm sure."

Hazel wrapped the ties around her wrists, then yanked them tight with her teeth. "Satisfied?" she asked. "Or do you want me to do my ankles too?"

"We're not adversaries, Ms. Nash. I'm trying to be your friend."

"I don't have a lot of friends who make me zip-tie myself," Hazel said. "Or threaten to shoot me."

"I've looked up some of your friends. Where's your pal the pilot?"

"I sent him home."

"If he comes waltzing in here," Rabbit said, glancing around, studying the whiteboards, "he's going to get shot. He's not my problem."

"I told him everything I know. So if something happens to me, he truly is your problem, the way I see it."

It's how Rabbit saw it too. But the fact was, if Hazel really was as dangerous as Moten and Dr. Morrison said, she would've left a trail of damage behind her these past few days. So maybe she'd changed, or maybe she hadn't. That wasn't Rabbit's job. His job was to close this loop and figure out who killed Jack Nash and Darren Nixon.

Rabbit scanned the room. Hazel had been here for at least an hour. She could've poured bleach on the computer, wiped all the whiteboards clean. Instead, she was sifting, still probing.

Rabbit holstered his gun. On the computer screen was a family tree with only a few staircases of names. Rabbit's ex-wife had been the archivist for their own family's history, a hobby Rabbit didn't understand, constantly digging into the past, trying to figure out who begat whom, as if it had any real relevance to life today.

"Hazel, back at the hospital, you said people

used to write their histories in bibles. I don't suppose any of the histories in these family trees have the contents from Benedict Arnold's bible?"

"I think they all do, in a way," Hazel said. "All part of the same obsession."

"Which is what?"

"Figuring out the past. Our dead man, Nixon...he's a pretty good genealogist."

Rabbit leaned toward the laptop screen. Though Hazel's wrists were tied, she moved her hands up and clicked on another file: the family tree for Darren Nixon. Rabbit read it once, twice, three times. It didn't make sense. "*Libya?*"

"I thought the same," Hazel said.

"And Nixon did this?"

"Far as I can tell."

Rabbit reread it again. "It's wrong. Darren Nixon was born in Spokane."

"How do you know?"

"I've read his file," Rabbit said.

"Files can be faked."

"Kennedy's too?"

"*Kennedy?*" Hazel asked.

"The other victim. Arthur Kennedy."

"You're joking, right? Those're their names, *Nixon* and *Kennedy?* You think that's just coincidence?"

Rabbit knew she was right. Nixon and Kennedy

were tied together, then tied again with Jack Nash.

"Maybe they had their own mission with the government. Or maybe another government."

"You're watching too many of your dad's shows. If Nixon was some foreign sleeper agent and was killed, he wouldn't have been left in some park in Canada. One day, he would have just been gone. He was raised right here. His records go back to childhood. Immunization forms, grades in the local public school. He *lived* here."

"Maybe he did," Hazel said. "But have you seen his birth certificate?"

"I would've known if he was a Libyan national. That would've been flagged."

"What about his mother?" Hazel asked.

Rabbit started to say something, then stopped. He didn't have anything on Darren's mother. Only that she was dead. He'd need to get access to the government databases to cross-check Mona Haql with Mona Nixon. Figure out where the hell she came from, who she was married to, who Nixon's father might be.

At least he had one parent on record, unlike Arthur Kennedy, whose parents didn't seem to exist.

"You found this all here?" Rabbit asked.

Hazel pointed to the whiteboards. "Darren

Nixon was a smart man. Not so bright, maybe, if he's setting buildings on fire and living in this town for this long. But he's a fine researcher. He makes good logical leaps."

"To what?"

"I think," Hazel said, "he figured out that my dad was doing work for the government. Maybe even something in his homeland of Libya."

Rabbit turned and looked at one of the whiteboards, then turned to the one that was behind them. Moten had told him that Jack Nash had done some favors for their office, even done some shows on topics that made Uncle Sam look good. But to see these countries: Lebanon, Iran, the USSR, Afghanistan, Iran, and yes, Libya. So many enemies. Why spend so much time in places we were so hated?

Something started to wiggle free in Rabbit's mind.

He reached down to his ankle, came up with a tactical knife.

"Show me your hands," Rabbit said.

"Now you believe me?"

Rabbit stayed silent.

"Agent, when we were back in my dad's house, and you told me not to interfere in the investigation"—she extended her hands, cuffs at Rabbit's chest—"you knew I'd come to Spokane, didn't you? Was that your test? To throw out some clues and see what I'd do?"

"Ms. Nash, I don't think for one second that *you* knew what you were going to do, so far be it from me to make my own guesses about your life."

With a single *zzt* of his knife, Rabbit slit through the left cuff, freeing Hazel's hands.

"Do you trust me?" he asked.

"No. Not at all," she said without hesitating.

"Then maybe you won't believe this," Rabbit said. He slit the other cuff. "I think it's time to figure out who killed your father."

56

Hazel watched as Agent Rabkin stood there for a long time, studying the whiteboards, his jaw working, grinding his back molars.

They called it *bruxism*.

Habitual grinding was found in people worldwide, across cultures and throughout time. In mummies pulled out of graves in Egypt and frozen bodies dug up in the Aleutians, you could see the same wear pattern in their jaws as in the mouths of finance guys in Manhattan who were put into the ground yesterday.

Hazel was tempted to tell Rabbit to relax, it wasn't worth the stress on his body. We're all going to end up in the same place eventually; better not to wear his teeth into pegs first. But right now, she didn't think he deserved any favors.

"So these episodes...?" Rabbit finally said,

pointing to the ones Nixon had circled on the whiteboards.

"They've got nothing in common—not ghosts, or aliens, or even Benedict Arnold, since my father didn't do a single episode on him."

"Then what are all of these B.A. notes?"

Hazel didn't answer.

"You don't know, do you?" Rabbit asked.

"And you do?" she said.

From the look on Rabbit's face, he was just as lost.

If she wanted, they could keep playing this game, sparring to see who knew what. But Hazel knew that if Rabkin really was the enemy—if he had anything to do with Darren Nixon's death—she wouldn't have been in those plastic cuffs. She'd have a bullet in her head. Butchie too. And they would've never been allowed in the air. You couldn't board a commercial flight with a bottle of water. The FBI wasn't going to let suspected murderers into the skies above.

"Tell me why you let me come here," Hazel finally said.

"It was my boss's idea. He said you'd either burn the place down or we'd at least be able to cross you off the suspect list. Personally, I think he was interested in what you said about the photos of Nixon's body."

"Your boss sounds like a manipulative prick."

"Isn't that the job of being boss?"

Rabbit waited for Hazel to laugh. It never came.

She didn't trust Agent Rabkin. Not yet. But he seemed different now. Like he was off script. He'd put a gun on her a few minutes ago, but hadn't patted her down. Which meant he wasn't scared of her, wasn't worried she was going to do something to him or try to run.

It meant, she realized, that he trusted her. He was lost because she was lost.

"So these B.A. notes don't mean anything to you?" Hazel asked.

"Maybe Nixon thought that's where your dad was looking for the bible. In fact," Rabbit said, looking down at Nixon's family tree, then up at the whiteboards, "based on when the name change happened, it looks like Nixon's mother was in Libya when your dad and Skip did their episode there. Nixon would've been there too."

"He would have been a toddler," Hazel said. "He wouldn't have any memory of the place."

"Maybe not. But his mother surely would."

There it was. That's what Hazel was looking for. "Tell me, Agent Rabkin, what was my dad really doing in Libya?"

"That's classified," Rabbit said absently, still studying the boards.

"I thought you wanted to solve this thing."

"No, I mean, it's truly classified. I don't know either. The information I gave you, that's exactly what they gave me."

"Who does know?"

"Above my pay grade. All they told me was that your dad did us a few favors: When he was filming a show in Yugoslavia once, they invited him to stay in some government palace. We apparently had him bug his own room. Then, a month later, the Secret Service launched a money laundering sting in that same room, were able to listen in, and voilà, they had all the proof to show some dirty player in the Yugoslavian government. Once, in Mexico, he did the same thing with the DEA for an ambassador who was helping run drugs between Phoenix and the border. But Iran? And Libya? Like I said, above my pay grade."

"What does someone like you get paid?"

"You looking to change jobs?"

"No," Hazel said, "I'm trying to figure out why all this is worth it to you."

"It's not about money," he said.

"Then what?"

"Doing right," he said. He bent his left ring finger down into his palm, rubbed his thumb over that tan line. A habit, Hazel thought. Or maybe a tell. Doing right for the people he loved.

"Ever hear about my dad doing anything with kids?" Hazel asked. "In all his shows, there's always...I don't know...there're lots of kids around."

"What're you saying? You think your Dad—?"

"I'm not thinking anything," Hazel shot back.

Onscreen, Rabbit again eyed Nixon's family tree. *Father: Unknown.* "You think your dad could be Nixon's father?"

Hazel didn't answer, though something in her gut didn't think so.

"What about your brother? You said he was in Libya for that episode. Think he'd remember anything?"

"I can ask, but I doubt it." Skip would've been only seven back then. Old enough to have a memory. Probably not old enough to make sense of it. "Maybe my dad's assistant Ingrid would, if she's still alive."

"She's alive," Rabbit said.

"You've checked recently?"

"Not in the last hour, no," he said. "But unless she's taken a fall, she lives—"

"In Hartford, Connecticut. I know. I looked her up," Hazel said. "Maybe send someone to her house."

Rabbit glanced at her. Then something seemed to dawn on him, something that worried him. "Anyone seen you since you were here?"

"I talked to a kid across the street. Maybe not a kid. A young woman."

"She saw your face?"

"I wasn't wearing a mask."

Rabbit started moving, walking slowly around the room. "What have you touched in the house and shed?" he asked.

"Everything."

"You talk to anyone else?"

"No."

"You didn't stop for gas? Didn't get a sandwich? Nothing?"

"No, nothing."

"Where were you planning on going next?"

"Depended upon what I found," Hazel said.

Rabbit pulled at the skin under his chin, the sympathetic nervous system kicking in. Hazel knew he either thought she was lying or was feeling profound uncertainty.

"If you had anything to do with Darren Nixon's death," he finally said, "you need to tell me."

He wasn't just asking about her memory anymore. He was asking what she knew, what she'd found out.

"I think we were all to blame," Hazel said.

"And that means *what*?"

"I gave myself truth serum—that was my answer. I think it has to do with my dad and whatever was in this bible, but...I don't think I killed Nixon."

"What about your father? You kill him?"

"No," Hazel said, but the fact was, she had no idea. "I don't know. I don't think so. I wasn't ready to die, I know that much, so if I'd done something to him, I wouldn't have done it in a car I was in too."

Another pull at the skin. Then a release.

"You and I," he said, "we're off the record now."

"What's that mean?"

"It means something isn't right. And now you've left your DNA all over this house and this neighbor can ID you."

"Everyone can ID me. After that video of our car crash, one of the rolling hubcaps has its own Facebook page," Hazel said. "And let's not forget, it was your big mouth that brought me here. I wouldn't even know to sniff around if you and your boss didn't think it was such a good idea."

Rabbit went silent. "I've been wondering about that too," he finally said. "For me not to know Nixon had Libyan parents, it's because someone didn't tell me. Or because someone wanted you to find it."

"Above your pay grade, huh?"

"That's what we need to find out."

We. He was using "we" now, Hazel noticed.

That'd be useful. "Can we talk to your friend Dr. Morrison?" Hazel asked.

Rabbit shook his head. "Morrison is dead."

"No, he's not. I just spoke to him."

"I'm sure you did. And then he jumped off the roof of the hospital."

57

Hazel closed her eyes, picturing Dr. Morrison's blue shirt. The stray hairs on his neck. The pepper in his teeth. She focused. She could hear a dog barking. She could also smell Agent Rabkin's cologne. All this going on in the world, and he still managed to put a dash of something on his neck.

All this cloak-and-dagger crap with her dad?

All of his old secret government trips?

All of this death so close to her?

She was still sitting inside a stranger's shed. Someone with a history. With a life.

"What do you go by," Hazel said, "when you're not at work?"

"Trevor. Though . . . Rabbit."

"Rabbit?"

"It's short for—"

"I got it," she said. "Why was Dr. Morrison giving you all the details about my treatment?"

"He didn't have a choice." Rabbit took a breath. "He was a drug addict. Started with an addiction to Adderall, then began writing his own prescriptions."

"How long?"

"Fifteen years. Maybe more. Longer than I've been employed, though apparently he'd been going to NA meetings—Narcotics Anonymous—for the past few years."

"But you knew who he was. You knew he worked on my mother. And consulted with my father. He probably knew more about me than I do."

"What else did he tell you?"

"I'm not a good person."

"No," Rabbit said. "You weren't."

"I've killed people."

"Your file is unclear on that."

"It wasn't a question," she said. "That's something I've figured out. At the very least, I tried to kill someone."

"Were you successful? Do you know who?"

"I was hoping you could tell me—I mean, besides Dr. Morrison."

"You didn't kill him," Rabbit said.

"Really? Because I'm not feeling that."

"You feel something?"

"I'm not a robot," Hazel said. "Why didn't Morrison just quit? When you came to him and told him you needed him to hide my old life from me, why didn't he just quit his job, get in his car, and keep driving?"

"I thought the same thing when I first approached him. I hated using his addiction against him, just as much as he hated seeing me. But there's no quitting. For either of us," Rabbit said. "Just choices of how you want to live."

"You have a shitty job," Hazel said.

"Yeah. I'm starting to see that." For a moment, Rabbit just stood there, looking at nothing, thinking about his new boss, Agent Moten. Then he reached into the duffle, came out with an iPad and a bag filled with Hazel's medication. "I got these from your apartment. I don't know what helps anymore, but even for the pain meds, you've missed almost an entire day."

Hazel watched his thumb go to that missing ring again. He had no idea he was doing it. He was just doing right.

She took a handful of pills and swallowed them with no water. "I have a tattoo on my neck," Hazel said. "That in your secret files on me?"

"No," Rabbit said. "But if we're telling secrets, I have one on my shoulder."

"Is yours a quote from Benedict Arnold?"

"No. It's a birch tree with a hawk in it."

Hazel turned away from Rabbit, pulled up her hair, and let him read it.

"What's it from?" Rabbit asked.

"It's what Benedict Arnold called his men."

"I didn't like American history. Would've failed it in high school if I wasn't so determined to get away from my parents. True story."

"I was just as determined. But I never got anything less than A," Hazel said, "in anything."

"What do you think it means?"

"Probably," she said, "that I'm not someone you want to creep up on from behind." She let her hair fall back down, turned and faced Rabbit again. "What does yours mean?"

"That I'm not someone you want to creep up on from any angle," he said. He handed her his iPad, facedown. "One last question: We found a new body. I'd like to know what you see."

"And then what?"

Thumb. Missing ring. A pause. "And then you stay or go."

Her father was dead. Her mother was a mystery. Her doctor was dead. Darren Nixon was dead. Her own memory was a vacuum. *I should run*, Hazel thought.

But she didn't.

58

A dead man, mouth agape.
Lit upon by flies.
Outside, a hard sun.

Not a pretty sight. But this was her sweet spot. Hazel knew this business of death. Muscle memory, the muscle being her brain.

"I don't know him," Hazel said. "Is that what you need to know?"

"Never heard the name Arthur Kennedy?"

"Not until you told it to me ten minutes ago," Hazel said. "What's his story?"

"Businessman from New Haven."

"That's not far from where Ingrid lives."

"Could be a coincidence."

Hazel didn't think so. Maybe she would have yesterday, but not today. "Where did you find Kennedy's body?"

"*We* didn't," Rabbit said. "He was found outside

a mosque in Sonapur." When Hazel cocked an eyebrow, he added, "Slums of Dubai."

"Where Skip is. So this is the body he went to check out. You think he's safe?"

"As safe as you are here."

It was a fair point. Skip said he was also bringing a cameraman, someone who'd have an eye on him. Still, the best way to keep her brother safe was to figure out who had done this in the first place.

"Tell me what you see," Rabbit said, pointing back to the photo.

"Was he murdered?"

"Tell me what you see."

Long way from home, was Hazel's first thought. A modern experience. A Western one, specifically. Most people died within shouting distance of where they'd been born.

Most murder victims weren't left in places where people easily found them. That was against the whole point of killing someone. Even in cultures without strict law enforcement, murderers still didn't go around leaving bodies stacked up in obvious places. You only left a body in a public place if you wanted to get caught or you wanted to scare the population. From the earliest tribes of the Amazon to the terrorist sects working today, if there was one constant ritual for the dead, Hazel knew, it was to use their brutalized bodies as a warning.

THE HOUSE OF SECRETS

Except this man didn't appear brutalized.

Hazel expanded the photo. He was older than Darren Nixon, pushing fifty by the looks of the folds around his mouth, evident in death, even with the flies. Pattern baldness, but kept trim, sideburns squared.

Terrible teeth, but not yellowed, which meant he had dental care regularly. Had a watch on his left wrist, a nice one, not too expensive, an Invicta, white gold band, blue face, a diver, though he didn't look like the kind of guy who went diving.

No blood anywhere.

"Well, he's not homeless," Hazel said. "Teeth are too clean and his watch is too new."

His eyes were closed, but that didn't mean anything. Most people died with their eyes closed. It didn't matter if you fell out of a tree or died of cancer, or where in the world you were, Hazel had found. The body was good about closing out stimulus right before the end.

"Another Revolutionary coat? A copycat?" Hazel said, pointing to the man's jacket. It looked a bit like the one on Darren Nixon—her father's coat—though she could tell just from looking at the photo that this one wasn't old. The buttons were too shiny, which meant they likely weren't lead or pewter.

"Definitely a costume. The fabric looks acrylic or polyester. Probably something you can get on-line, or in a good Halloween shop."

Hazel flipped back through the photos. There were only three, all of them clothed. She'd need a shot of the body nude on a table to get a really good look.

"He was dressed after death," she said.

"Based on what?"

"The body was found outside?"

"Yes, just as you see it."

"Full sun?"

"For a few hours, maybe," Rabbit said. "But it was hot. Almost a hundred degrees, even at night."

"You sit outside dead, you're going to leave fluids everywhere. See how clean his clothes are? This man was dressed maybe twelve hours after death, that would be my guess."

The flies and rigor mortis made it look horrible, but as Hazel looked at Rabbit, she knew—he'd seen worse.

"He wasn't strangled," she added, pointing to his neck. "And I don't see any wounds. Those would be leaking too."

"The report says respiratory failure. Stroke, maybe. Heart attack."

"They find a rental car?"

"Nope. Nothing. Never checked in to his hotel either."

"The hotel where my brother currently is—thanks to the fact that your office told him where this dead guy was planning to stay."

"Trust me, I don't like it either."

"So Arthur Kennedy's body was dumped in a public place, dressed in a crappy Revolutionary costume, and no one noticed?"

"That's the problem I'm having," Rabbit said.

"And somehow these pictures just show up in the FBI's inbox by chance?"

"Right. It's impossible," Rabbit said.

"No. Someone's baiting you. Or trying to fool you."

"There's something else," he began, but Hazel wouldn't let him finish, because when she heard those words—of someone *trying to fool you*—she already knew, could feel it coming up from behind her, like she'd already been told the story.

Because she had. She remembered the details. Just like Dr. Morrison had said, with the right association, certain details would come back. She remembered it all now. Including the answer.

"I know," she said. "They found another bible in his chest."

59

Trevor Rabkin was thirty years old when he first heard The Story. He was in a dead criminal's shed. Hazel had just remembered it, remembered all of The Story, so she repeated it, twice, to make sure she got all the details.

A farmer. A frozen body. An autopsy. Benedict Arnold's bible concealed in the body's chest. It wasn't the sort of thing you told a six-year-old, that much he figured out right away.

"When did your dad say this happened?"

"A hundred and fifty years ago. It was a bedtime story. I thought it was, anyway. He could have said three hundred years ago, it wouldn't have mattered to me. The point was, it's all a trick. In the story, after the autopsy, they say that the bible was put inside the chest before the person died. But that's the point. It can't be. It's impossible. And once you accept it's impossible, then you can solve it: Whoever did the autopsy is lying, or the narrator of the story is lying, but someone's lying. The only way a bible gets into someone's body is because someone puts it there. It's a message, a symbol, a whatever the excuse is. But at base, it's a trick."

"Who else knows that story?"

"It was just something my dad made up one night," Hazel said. "Ever heard anything like it?"

"No," Rabbit said. And neither had Moten, unless he chose not to tell Rabbit. A continuing presumption that was now begging to be tested. "Does Skip know the story?"

"You heard what he said. If Dad told it, it wasn't to him. He just— Growing up, I think it was something my dad made up to get me to stop asking him questions."

Or to start, Hazel thought. It was an idea she wasn't sharing with Rabbit, but it was one she could no longer ignore. All these history details in her head, from Benedict Arnold living in Canada, to bibles being used to hold family trees, to all the nonsense with a book inside someone's chest...All these years, she assumed her father was *entertaining* her. But what if it was more than entertainment? What if, over time, he was *testing* her? Or better yet, *training* her?

Hazel considered this, rolled it through her brain. It was, of course, ridiculous. Why would a father train his six-year-old daughter?

"You're thinking something, aren't you?" Rabbit asked.

"No," she told him, now remembering a new detail—that her father had been through almost the same thing. Her grandfather was in this business too, used to work in radio and for the Army Signal Corps, telling Loch Ness and Sasquatch stories in a weekly radio show to entertain the troops. Then her dad came along and put those stories on TV.

From there, Hazel had a new theory. A better theory. *Why would a father train his six-year-old daughter?* Because he wanted to make sure she didn't make the same mistakes he did. Because he wanted her to stay away from these silly tricks, wanted her to leave the family business behind. Because he wanted to give her a chance at freedom—to be different from her brother—so she wouldn't get trapped like he was in this life.

Why would a father train his six-year-old daughter? Because he loved her.

"Y'know your dad taught you that story for a reason."

"I'm starting to realize that."

"Whoever killed Arthur Kennedy—and Darren

Nixon—they wanted you to know. Not me. Not the police. *You.*"

"That part, I believe," Hazel said. "But why do it in Dubai...or even Canada? Why not make it easy and kill him here?"

Rabbit thought for a moment. "Let's assume Canada was for its tie to Benedict Arnold. That at least makes sense as a way to lure Nixon there. I mean, look around here. He was clearly on the paranoid side," he said, motioning around the shed. "But for Dubai, maybe they knew we were watching you. Maybe it was to lure you out of the country."

"And instead, now Skip's the one out of the country." She went silent for a minute. "Or for all we know, Skip's the real target."

"What're you talking about?"

"We still off the record?"

"Hazel, if you know something—"

"The first victim: Darren Nixon. Skip knew him."

"How well?"

"Not too well," Hazel said. "He figured you and your bosses knew it."

"I didn't," Rabbit said. *Add it to the list*, he thought.

"Skip had heard about Nixon's charts and graphs, said he would write these crazy letters, always rambling about my dad and his old shows.

But Skip didn't sell him Dad's jacket. I'm telling you, I believe that."

"So you think your dad was the one who brought the jacket here? I saw the flight records myself. He was definitely here."

It was the one detail that still didn't fit anywhere. Last month, her dad was in this house—maybe even this shed—dealing with a known criminal. Why would her dad make that trip? Did he come here on his own? Did Nixon figure something out? Or did someone else send Jack Nash here?

"Rabbit, who do you work for?"

"The taxpayers," he said. "And an office in Bethesda."

"You have an actual boss? Someone you answer to?"

Rabbit hesitated, but not for long. "His name is Louis Moten. That mean anything to you?"

"No."

"From what I can tell, he was your father's handler."

"Do you think he'd ever do anything to purposely hurt my father?"

"What makes you say that?"

"Look at the whiteboards. Even just the Libya one. I watched that episode. Skip was on that trip—*at just seven years old*. Does that make any logical sense? When the TV show went to danger-ous places like Libya, that's when we think Moten and my dad were doing their magic and searching for the bible. So if that's the case, if Moten really cared about my father, considering how dangerous Libya was back then, why would he ever let my dad take Skip on that trip? Moten was in charge, right? Then why would he let a young kid like Skip walk into jeopardy like that?" She paused, and Rabbit could tell she was working up to some-thing larger, something Rabbit had avoided.

"That doesn't mean Moten is now putting bibles in people's chests."

"I didn't say that. But whoever it is, it's someone who knew what was happening during those covert Benedict Arnold trips my dad was taking. That narrows it to Moten, to Skip, who was seven years old, and to my dad's assistant Ingrid Ludlow."

"Unless there's another player we don't know about."

Hazel looked at each of the whiteboards, at the shows with B.A.s next to them. Lebanon. Johan-nesburg. Iran. Moscow. "In those countries, my dad must've made enemies."

"Of course he made enemies. But as for bringing Skip into war zones, for all you know, that was your dad's idea."

Hazel sat with that, though not for long. "Rabbit, is your father still alive?"

"Last I heard. Why?"

"What's his job?"

"Retired now. Used to fix cars," Rabbit said. "Spent a lot of time screaming at people on the TV to either buy a vowel or solve the puzzle."

"What about your mother?"

"Lives in Flagstaff, has a nice little place behind a gate that keeps my father out."

"Would they have let someone else put you in jeopardy? Would they have trained you for a job that might get you killed?"

"No," Rabbit said. "I did that all on my own."

"And my father would?"

"Maybe he thought you'd be good at it."

"Or maybe he wanted me out of it," Hazel said.

Rabbit got up, pushed the door of the shed open. It was almost dinnertime. The neighbors would be coming home soon. Kids would be out. Two strange cars in the neighborhood would be noticed. If Darren Nixon was actually from Libya, if his mother was from Libya, if somehow he'd intersected with Jack Nash there, in the 1980s...then where the hell was new victim Arthur Kennedy from? And how did the three of them fold into each other?

And why hadn't Moten told him anything?

It was, Rabbit considered, a full-blown international conspiracy...or, as Hazel said, a simple trick. From the very start, if the authorities needed a suspect, they had easy ones in Hazel and Skip Nash.

Or, he realized, now that his fingerprints were all over this place, maybe even himself. The new guy in the office, brought in for reasons never explained.

"We should get you out of here," Rabbit said, letting the door close.

"No," Hazel said, "what we should do is get you in a sit-down with your boss Moten."

"That's exactly where I'm headed. And no offense, you're not invited."

"I didn't plan on joining. I'm calling my brother, then going to Connecticut."

"To find Ingrid?"

Hazel nodded once. As Dad's assistant, Ingrid Ludlow was on the payroll back then. She should know things no one else did. But this wasn't just about Ingrid. "Someone wanted me to find Arthur Kennedy. I'm going to do that too. And you should know, if I find something important, Butchie will know. He needs to be protected, and the only way that's going to happen is if he has something to bargain with too."

Rabbit pulled out his phone, took his own

pictures of the whiteboards, then promised Hazel, "I can get a security detail put on your brother. He won't be hard to find in Dubai."

"I appreciate that." She shoved open the door, light again flooding the room. "One last question," she said. "If Ingrid really does know something from back then, why isn't she dead?"

"Maybe no one cares what she knows anymore," Rabbit said. "You said you looked where she lived, right? No kids. Never married. No siblings. You kill someone that no one cares about, what's the use?" It was, Rabbit realized, a sad, honest truth. He needed to make some changes in his life, fast.

60

Dubai, United Arab Emirates

Marco shows up to The Bear's rental house right on time. He's got four ziplock bags, just as The Bear requested, stuffed inside a sack from the Al Qasr spa.

"Any issues?" The Bear asks.

"No problems," Marco says, because Marco, The Bear has learned, is a man who can make things happen. He is also a man with friends in the housekeeping department, the only ones in every hotel who have access to even the most secure corners, people always happy to let someone clean up their refuse.

The Bear examines the contents of the bags.

There are two straws, well chewed, probably all the genetic material The Bear needs.

Clumps of hair, matted together. "From the shower and his hairbrush," Marco says, "just like you asked." Another bag, with another two dozen or so hairs, roots and all. "His pillow."

Fingernails. Or maybe they're toenails. Nails, regardless. "Side of the bed," Marco says.

The Bear wasn't expecting such an excellent DNA haul. He figured he'd be lucky to get a few strands of hair, which wasn't optimal. He wanted nuclear DNA, which meant he'd need to get complete follicles. Just the hair itself, he'd only have mitochondrial DNA, which was less useful. To make a full profile, he'd need everything. Now he had saliva, a bit of skin from the nails, the nails themselves, and hair. Scientists were cloning humans with less.

The Bear slipped the bags into his suitcase. He'd be on a flight in two hours. Right after he took care of this.

"Do you smell that?" Marco asks. He starts sniffing, going to every corner of The Bear's living room. "Ammonia? Do you smell that?"

The Bear doesn't like to cut people's throats, thinks it's an uncivilized way to kill a person. There's the issue of the mess, and then there's the issue of knowledge, the person aware—at least for a moment—that they are about to expire. Barbaric. Only actual psychopaths took any joy in that. It's why he much preferred poison.

But alas, sometimes there's no time for that. So

he steps behind Marco, who has his head thrown back, nose to the air like a dog, and slices his carotid and internal jugular. The blood supply to the brain is cut immediately, making it much less painful, much more clean, theoretically.

The Bear goes through Marco's pockets after making certain he's dead, finds that Marco has spent only a few hundred dollars of The Bear's money, probably given to his friends in house-keeping. He takes the cash out of Marco's wallet, plus a voter ID card. His name is not Marco, The Bear sees.

His name is Mahfuz Radawi.

He is twenty-three.

A good liar, The Bear thinks. Admirable.

He stuffs the cash—plus another five hundred—and Mahfuz's ID into an envelope. He'll drop them into the mail on his way out of town, in case Mahfuz has a wife or children at home. Or a mother and father.

They won't need to worry about burial costs. The tub full of lye he dumps Mahfuz's body in should take care of that issue.

Now, thanks to the phone call he just received, The Bear is off to the airport. To Connecticut. Lovely this time of year.

61

Hazel spent the entire red-eye from Spokane to Philadelphia reading the Arthur Kennedy file that Rabbit had copied for her. Tomorrow, she'd get a connecting flight to New Haven, but for now, in the back of this plane, as she was trying to draw an anthropological portrait of the man, all she saw was a picture of absence.

How was it possible that a man of forty-six, with a bank account of substance, of seeming normal desires and abilities, was also the sort that not a single soul missed once he'd died? No wife, no husband. No girlfriend, no boyfriend. No lover, no friends. No social media. Just his dating profile, which was full of lies, and his fantasy baseball league, which he was still winning. Nothing that distinguished an entire life...and yet, he was on a plane to Dubai to meet a woman he'd met online?

Over Omaha, with a grid of lights beneath her and then nothing but darkness to the edge of the world, she thought about it. It was, she realized, a choice.

A choice made by a person with nothing to fear. Which meant he was comfortable in who he was—he could fly to another country without setting off any alarms.

A choice made by a person with nothing to lose. Which meant he'd experienced enough in this life to leave a little skin behind. Maybe it was a lark, just for the sex. So what?

A choice made by a person who could afford not to come back. Which meant the life he had was one that didn't find its value in a place.

A person like the first victim, Darren Nixon.

A person a lot like herself.

Or the herself she used to be.

Things seemed more permanent now. Dr. Morrison had killed himself to protect his own secrets, but maybe to help keep hers too. Had tried to steer her mind toward a better version of herself.

Butchie had put himself out for her, had proven to need little more than her word to believe the most preposterous series of events.

Skip loved her, needed her, wanted her beside him at the moment when life might turn upside down for them both.

Even Agent Rabkin—Rabbit—had trusted her enough to put his career, maybe his life, in her hands too.

And here was Arthur Kennedy, another life devoted to hers, if after the fact. A person who lived—and was killed—in a way that maybe only Hazel was supposed to recognize.

If that was true, if he was a message to Hazel, what was she meant to see?

His dead body? An obvious warning: This is what can happen to you.

The Revolutionary outfit? An exclamation point. What were Benedict Arnold's purported final words? She'd looked them up. "Let me die in this old uniform in which I fought my battles. May God forgive me for ever putting on another," though here was Kennedy, dressed in a cheap imitation.

An impossibility.

A person trying to fool you. To get you to make a dumb mistake, to go somewhere you shouldn't.

Hazel shook out a handful of pills. Examined each of them, imagining what they were doing in her body: the Morovin righting her balance, half of a Norco, smoothing out the sharp edges of her pain, Xanax for lowering her anxiety—a complex cocktail of avoidance. Was she in pain? Yes. Had her balance ever been off? At first. But now, no. She didn't think so. She'd never felt like the world was actually tipping over, just metaphorically.

Had she felt anxious? She had, but recognized that she used to be the kind of person for whom anxiety was just a mouse in the corner of the room, not the elephant in the middle. Which was healthy. It was the people who lived absurdly happy lives, the eternal optimists, who never saw the monster waiting for them under the bed, whereas those with at least a tad of healthy fear admitted the possibility existed.

Which meant, as the monster came closer, they could prepare to fight.

Hazel wanted to be prepared to fight. She tossed the pills on the floor, crushed them under her shoe.

Hazel looked out the oval window of the plane, found the moon in the darkened sky. It wasn't full, wouldn't be for another few days, she thought, but she felt the claws lengthening in her fingers, pressing through her skin, could feel the sharp tips of her incisors against her tongue, the muscles across her shoulders relaxing, stretching, coiling, the world around her turning slow while she sped up, her vision so sharp now, it was as if she could see through the roof of the plane, could see ancient stars collapsing, could see the folds of time and space.

The werewolf was coming.

62

Louis Moten lived in a large whitewashed brick Colonial just off East-West Highway in upscale Chevy Chase, Maryland. Like two other houses on the block, his home had black shutters and a red door. Classic.

What's a house like this cost? Rabbit wondered, parked in the long driveway, which wrapped around the front of the house in a half circle like a moat. *Two million? Three million?*

Not a bad life for Louis Moten, Rabbit thought. Yet when Moten came walking out at 8 a.m. to pick up the morning's *Washington Post*, a cup of coffee in his hand, a brown terrycloth robe from the previous century hanging off him, he didn't look happy. He spotted Rabbit's car and headed straight for it.

"What are you doing here?" Moten hissed.

"I was looking up some files," Rabbit said. "But

so many of them were classified. Especially the ones on Darren Nixon and Arthur Kennedy."

"Son, I'm warning you. This is where I live."

"I called you last night," Rabbit said. "You didn't answer."

In fact, Rabbit had called him a dozen times at work. The phone rang and rang and rang; Moten wasn't the kind of guy who used voicemail. Rabbit imagined the janitor who cleaned the office in Bethesda—there's always a janitor, someone getting paid fifteen bucks an hour to clean up the top-secret world—walking through, a phone ringing in an empty office, middle of the night, just thinking, *Man, you're never going to get anybody at this hour.*

"My wife was sick," Moten said. "I took the night off."

"I didn't know there were time-outs."

"Family first," Moten said. He looked up and down his street. "You need to get out of here, Agent. Everyone on this street can see you."

"Am I in hiding?"

"You're not. No. Not yet."

"I need to talk to you," Rabbit said.

"I don't pick up the phone, you fly across the country?"

"I need to know what Jack Nash was doing in these places." He handed Moten a list of all the

314

B.A. episodes from Darren Nixon's wipe-off boards: Lebanon, Iran, Moscow, Libya...

Moten's front door opened and a bald woman walked out. "Everything okay?" she called.

"Fine, fine, honey," Moten said. "This gentleman is lost. Just giving him some directions. I'll be right back in."

Moten's wife smiled wanly, then went back inside.

"I'm sorry," Rabbit said. "I didn't know."

"She's got a couple months," Moten said. "Maybe longer, but I'm not banking on it. It's in her pancreas."

"Is she in pain?"

"What do you think?" Moten shook his head, as if he couldn't believe Rabbit had even asked the question. "You start to die, in my experience? It hurts." He looked at the list of episodes, then crumpled it up, tossed it back into Rabbit's car. "You'll need to be elected President for answers to those."

"I know about Benedict Arnold's bible."

"Do you?"

Rabbit thought about that. "Why am I on this job?" he finally asked.

"Do you think Skip or Hazel killed their father?"

"I don't know if anyone did," Rabbit said.

"You think that poison just ended up in his system by magic?"

"No," Rabbit said. "I think it might have been planted."

"By who?"

"I don't know," Rabbit said. "Maybe Skip. Maybe Hazel. Maybe you. Maybe the President. Maybe it was me. I was there too, when they brought back the body."

Moten nodded. "Do you know who killed Darren Nixon?"

"No," Rabbit said.

"You think it was twenty different people from those twenty different countries, all holding a grudge against Jack Nash, each injecting Nixon with a little bit of poison to keep him quiet about something?"

"No," Rabbit said.

"Then what makes you think this is about something from decades ago? Sure, Jack used to help us on missions—I told you that from the start. But whoever killed Jack was searching for that bible in the present, not thirty years ago."

"Darren Nixon was Libyan," Rabbit said, then explained to Moten what Hazel had found, the family tree, about what it appeared Nixon had figured out, that Jack was doing things with the government in dangerous places. "His mother was Libyan, sir. Mona Haql. Her family line runs back two hundred and fifty years in Sirte. There's something with that."

"Where's the proof?" Moten said.

"There's nothing," Rabbit said.

"Nothing isn't proof."

"*Nothing*," Rabbit said, and he could hear Hazel in his head, "is impossible." Rabbit uncrumpled the paper. Held it up. "This paper? It's possible. Darren Nixon didn't come from Libya for no reason. Which is why I need to know what Jack was doing on these jobs. Nixon seemed to think they were searching for pages of Benedict Arnold's bible in every place on this list. If he'd figured out that Jack was working for the government— or that something went wrong on one of these missions—maybe Nixon was blackmailing him. He was a criminal, right? Nixon could've heard about something Jack did in the field. Mistakes happen; people screw up. Maybe that's why Jack killed him. Maybe that's what this all is. Covering up Jack's past messes."

Moten took the paper from Rabbit's hand. "Was Nixon also blackmailing Castro? The Ayatollah? Gorbachev? You find a time machine among his belongings, Agent?" The front door opened again, Moten's wife poked her head out, Moten waved. "Just one sec, honey," he said, shook the paper. "Can't make heads or tails of this address." She closed the door, no smile. "What do you want, Agent?"

"I want the missions," Rabbit said.

"You won't get them."

"Do you know what he was doing?"

"No," Moten said. "I just sent him where they told me to send him."

"Who were *they*?"

"CIA," he said. "NSA. Anything with an A. You need to understand, Agent, it wasn't like things are today. When they told us to do something, we did it. Today, being a terrorist is easier; being an actual nation is harder."

Rabbit thought for a moment. "Skip Nash is in Dubai," he said carefully. "Hazel says he's bringing a TV crew, for a new show. He's about to announce it, tell the world he's out there looking for Benedict Arnold's bible. He wants to see what happens, see who comes out of the woodwork."

Moten stared at Rabbit for five, ten, fifteen seconds without blinking. "He'll just become bait."

"Or you'll save him and catch whoever comes," Rabbit said, "and we'll get this circle closed. That's what you want, right?"

Silence again for fifteen seconds. Thirty. "Where's Hazel Nash now?"

"Still in Spokane," Rabbit said. It was a lie. But a lie he felt he needed to tell.

"Get her on a plane to Dubai."

"Is that the safest place for her?"

"I don't care what's safest. It's smartest. Skip will listen to her. And to you," he said.

"Anything else?"

"You like my house, Agent Rabkin?"

"It's very nice, yes, sir."

"You know how I got it?"

"I don't."

"By following orders," he said. "Don't come here again. And don't fucking call me until you're in Dubai."

63

The Drawing Room, Hazel's hotel in New Haven, Connecticut, had been upcycled from an old Radisson, the inside redesigned to look like it was still the 1700s. Dawn in America every day...except with twenty-four-hour room service and specialty cocktails in The Franklin, the faux dive bar that hosted karaoke night every Wednesday.

Today, The Franklin was filled with the attendees of a tech conference, everyone in matching lanyards, polo shirts, and tan pants, their conversations bleeding out into the lobby over the thump of classic rock, Journey telling everyone to keep believing.

Hazel sped past a couple asking the concierge for dinner reservations somewhere "casual but with fancy food," wishing it was all so easy.

Arthur Kennedy had lived in this city.

That wasn't a mistake.

Just like it wasn't a mistake that Darren Nixon had been lured to Canada to be killed.

Messages were being sent.

"C'mon, where are you?" Hazel whispered into her newest burner cell as the line rang for the third time.

"You're alive?" Butchie finally answered.

"Still," she said, now outside, with the afternoon sun on her face.

"Where's the 203 area code? Area 51?"

"Connecticut," Hazel said.

"Same difference."

"You have no idea. You somewhere better?"

"Camping out in Humboldt," Butchie said, referring to the Redwoods park four hours north of San Francisco. "You ready to come home?"

"Not yet," she said, heading for the parking lot a few blocks down. No way was she parking near the hotel. "I need another favor."

"Good. This nature shit is boring me to death. What's it this time?"

She told him what she knew about Arthur Kennedy, this man with no past. Told him about Nixon, about Agent Rabkin, about the family trees, and her suspicions.

Butchie listened intently, then said, "You want me to come get you?"

"No," Hazel said. Since the moment she landed, she'd been reading and rereading the files Rabbit gave her. "I have bits of Kennedy's life; what I want is his full history."

"Define *history*."

"Airline records. I need you to get me proof of any flight Arthur Kennedy ever took." She thought for a moment. "Run train records too, just in case. I want to know where he's been going, who he's been seeing."

"You said there were no records of Kennedy's childhood?"

"Nothing," Hazel said. "Not even his parents' names. So if he just sprouted from the ground fully formed in 1996, in time to get his real estate license, that means Arthur Kennedy's name..."

"...had been changed," Butchie said.

"Just like Darren Nixon. Which would leave a paper trail. Somewhere. But just like Nixon—and his mother Mona—there's nothing."

Sure, Hazel wanted to know *who* Kennedy had been, that was important, but she also needed to find out *what* he'd been, why he'd died. And with those names—Nixon and Kennedy—who named them so uncreatively? Right now, that was the only way to find out what Kennedy's connection to Benedict Arnold's bible might be. "I want to know foreign countries, I want to know if Kennedy took a cruise on the Mississippi, I want to know if he flew to New Orleans for spring break to flash his tits in college. He was here in New Haven for a reason. If he's been somewhere else, there's a reason for that too."

"Girl," Butchie told her, "this will cost you. You want someone to break into the airlines? That's high-level hacker shit."

"How much?"

"Enough for a lawyer down the line," Butchie said.

"How *much*?"

"Someone legit? Keep their mouth closed? Twenty. At least."

Hazel had money in her bank accounts—she found those in her apartment: about ten thousand dollars in savings, another five in her checking account. But if she was who everyone said she was..."Do I keep money somewhere else?"

Butchie made a *tsk*ing sound. "You're lucky I'm an honest person," he said. "You got a spot hollowed out in your closet, behind that big-ass chest of drawers. You keep a stash."

"Can you get to it?"

"You really want me going in your place while someone might be watching?"

"You must have loose change somewhere."

"Now you want my retirement fund?"

"Butchie, when I get home, whatever I have is yours. And if I don't ever make it back for some reason, it's still yours."

"You don't make it back," Butchie said, "we all got problems." Hazel heard a car alarm going off in the background.

"You're not in Humboldt, are you?"

Butchie sighed. "No one likes the outdoors."

Hazel cut through the parking lot, found the gray rental car she'd rented, using the fake ID she'd found in her purse. "Please tell me you're not in the city," she said.

"Just tell me when you need this information by."

"Two hours?" Hazel said.

"You know even hackers got lives. It's not like they're just sitting at home waiting for illegal business opportunities."

"One last thing," Hazel said. "I need better contact info for Ingrid Ludlow. My dad's old assistant. In Hartford."

"You don't have Google?"

"I tried. She's not picking up."

"Give me ten," Butchie said. He called her back in five. "This woman's gonna be hard to reach. For the last two weeks, she's been at some place called the Institute of Living."

"That a co-op or something?"

"That's what I'm trying to tell you," Butchie said. "Lovely old Ingrid—she's in a psychiatric facility. That's where her mail's being forwarded to, anyway."

"Hnh," Hazel said, wondering if she should even be surprised. "I'm headed there now. And Butchie? After you send me Kennedy's airline records, I want you to send them to Agent Rabkin. But wait for a bit. Give me a head start on it."

"You want me to email a fed? Girl, I'm not comfortable with that."

"Things go wrong," Hazel said, "he won't be a fed by the time he gets the message."

"I don't like it."

"I don't either," Hazel said. "But that's where we are."

"Haze, before you go…" Butchie paused. "Why're you really going to see this woman Ingrid?"

"I think something bad happened on one of their old missions, something when my dad was searching for Benedict Arnold's bible. And I think someone found out about it. Maybe Ingrid will remember some detail I can use."

"Again, why're you really going to see this woman Ingrid?"

Hazel paused. "To ask her about my father. And my mother."

"You prepared for the answer?"

"She's in a mental home. At this point, I'm prepared for anything."

64

Belfast, Northern Ireland
1984

SEASON 8, EPISODE 9 (1984): "THE GHOSTS OF BELFAST"

Jack Nash doesn't have much of a stomach for blood.

Ingrid Ludlow? No problem at all.

Usually.

But the wounds they're seeing today—missing limbs, burns, bullet and shrapnel holes—have her rattled.

"What happened to these people?" she asks.

Jack, Ingrid, and the rest of the crew have been in the city for twenty-four hours, finishing an episode on the haunted history of Ireland, from the ghosts seen walking the halls of ancient castles, to the sounds of shrieking children outside the old match factory, to the whimsical story of a dog who followed its master, even after death. But that's not the real reason for this trip.

Jack knew he'd be getting an invitation to visit the hospital from the mayor of Belfast. It'd look like a small goodwill mission, the sort of thing he was always happy to do, sharing a joke with the children in pediatrics, the newspaper photographing him with a bald child. The sort of thing that helped balance the scales in his mind.

"The IRA exploded a car bomb outside a market," the mayor says. He's a tall, angular man in a black suit, an impressively knotted tie. Jack thinks he probably hasn't slept in a week, maybe two. The bags under his eyes sag nearly beyond his cheekbones. "Twenty people died. An absolute tragedy."

The dead are the lucky ones, Jack thinks. No one in the ICU has even lifted his eyes, and Jack suddenly feels like he's in the wrong place, like coming here was a mistake. Talking to the kids, the choreographed photo ops, that was fine. People seemed happy to see him, and maybe someone sick got a shot of adrenaline from the experience. But here, where life and death were separated by threads, he felt like an impostor.

Once again, the search for Benedict Arnold's bible had brought them to hell.

"Did they catch the bomber?" Ingrid asks, knowing the answer.

The mayor stays silent, knowing it as well.

They're led out of the ICU and down a long hallway, through a set of double doors, then downstairs and through a labyrinth of hallways, until they're in a waiting room with leather couches and filled with the smell of brewing coffee. Two men with machine guns slung over their arms are guarding a door.

Jack didn't know he'd be in Ireland until two days ago, which is when they heard someone was offering a brand-new page of the bible. Within forty-eight hours, Moten's unit scrambled, throwing the trip together and coming up with a good enough TV topic so it looked completely logical for the great Jack Nash to be filming in Ireland. Now all they needed was to close the deal.

"Mr. Nash," the mayor says, "we have a patient who would very much like to see you. But only you. Is that all right?"

Ingrid gives Jack the look. The same one she gave him in Libya. The one she's been giving him for almost ten years now. The look that says no.

"I would prefer to have my assistant nearby," Jack says. "Maybe out in the hall?"

The mayor looks to the armed men. One of them, the shorter of the two, nods almost imperceptibly. "I guess that would be fine," the mayor says. This "patient" isn't going anywhere.

Jack and Ingrid are led into a room that looks into another room, where there's a man hooked up to a hanging matrix of IV lines and monitors. He's missing one arm up to his elbow, and Jack can only make out a single eye.

"You have fifteen minutes. Doors will be locked, so if there's a problem, best to make noise," the guard says.

"What's his name?" Jack asks.

"Shitbag," the guard replies. "But his given name is Dermot. He answers to both."

"Do you want me to talk to him first?" Ingrid asks Jack once the guard has left and locked the door behind him.

"No," Jack says, "it's fine."

Jack walks into the room, sits down in the chair next to the bed.

"You know me?" Jack asks.

"I know you," Dermot says, but it's as if he can't believe what he's seeing. He tries to turn his head, as if he's forgotten he only has one eye, but that's not happening. "You're the ghost-and-goblin man."

"That's right," Jack says. At first Dermot looked bald, but in fact his hair has been burned off.

"Seen you on my TV. You and your boy."

"That's right," Jack says again. Where would Skip be now? Asleep in his bed at home. Where he belonged.

"I'm a family man too," Dermot says. "I have a daughter. Five years old."

"A good age," Jack says. There's a chain running down from the bed to the floor, padlocked to the ground. Dermot is shackled.

"I'll probably never see her again." He runs his tongue over his lips. They're dry and cracked.

"You probably should have thought of that before you detonated that bomb," Jack says.

"Two hundred years ago," Dermot says, "I would have been a hero to you." He closes his one eye for several seconds. Jack watches him, thinking he might be fading out from the drugs running through him, but then Jack sees that his lips are moving silently. Dermot reaches up with his good arm and feels for something at his neck, pulls out a cross, brings it to his lips, and kisses it. "I have a page from your bible," he tells Jack.

"I know," Jack says. "Where?"

"In my home," Dermot says. "My wife will give you what you need. She has my demands as well. You know how valuable it is."

"Our deal has already been made."

"No," the man says. "Not yet."

Jack stands up.

"Where are you going?" the man asks.

Jack doesn't answer. He leaves the room. Ingrid is waiting for him outside.

"We set?" Ingrid asks.

"He wants to renegotiate," Jack says. He checks his watch. He was in the room for three minutes. "You have twelve minutes. Will you need more than that?"

"Not if he's cooperative," Ingrid says.

65

Rabbit didn't sleep anymore. He was beginning to think no one did.

Used to be, back before his wife left, he had a schedule. Once he walked out of his office, he was done working for the day, unless it was a matter of national security. He'd turn off his work cell phone, go to the gym for an hour, reacclimate to being around people not involved in either perpetrating or solving crime. Then he'd head home to his house off Coldwater Canyon, less than a mile from Jack Nash's, maybe five minutes away. That was the thing about the real world. You never knew who your neighbors were.

He'd kiss his wife, play with his daughter Candace for a bit, maybe read her a book or watch a cartoon for twenty minutes. After they put Candace to bed, he'd tell his wife about the office politics, because that's all he could tell her about.

Maybe he'd do a crossword or watch a ball game to settle his mind, then he'd close his eyes and, presto, eight hours later, he'd wake up just before the alarm.

It was a skill he'd learned from his time in the military, where you slept anywhere, anytime. It didn't even need to be particularly safe. He'd catch thirty minutes propped up against a Humvee, an hour in an Apache hustling between air bases. Once he even took a ninety-minute nap strapped into the cargo hold of an AWAC.

For a while, after his wife packed up and walked out, he tried to keep that same schedule, but it was pointless. He'd end up sitting in the dark watching TV, replaying old fights in his mind.

The thing was, it wasn't like she'd been wrong about anything. Her demands had been simple. Be present and be loving. He'd been bad at both. And then one day two years ago, she told him, "Today's your daughter's birthday." The next night, he came back from work, and she and Candace were gone.

Even now, sitting at a red light on 10th Street in Washington, DC, Rabbit was still picturing the note—his wife's block handwriting laced with hidden rage.

Rabbit was headed downtown, to an address Moten had given him, though Rabbit knew it by heart: 935 Pennsylvania Avenue. Headquarters of the FBI. They'd give Rabbit a new ID and a plane ticket on United Airlines, leaving for Dubai in just a few hours.

Three weeks ago, when Moten came to him after Jack's accident, Rabbit saw it for exactly what it was. An opportunity. A chance to actually fight the bad guys, to put some good in the world. He'd lost so much—his job, his wife, his daughter—this was his chance to write a good chapter for once, to rebalance the scales and prove he could be that person, that amazing person he used to be but somehow lost sight of.

A person of potential.

Like the great Jack Nash.

Of course, as Rabbit scratched at the shiny veneer, he quickly found out, yet again, that something he loved—Jack and his *House of Secrets*—was just another lie.

But the more Rabbit scratched, the more he realized that it wasn't just Jack Nash who was a mess. Rabbit was thirty years old, and the majority of his days were spent attempting to stop nightmares from happening, and where had it gotten him? Alone in the world, not a single damn friend, a wife who still wouldn't speak to him, a daughter who still didn't know him, and the one person he'd had a decent conversation with in the last six months was Hazel Nash.

Slowly, a few of Hazel's memories had come back. If she eventually found out what else was in her head—tomorrow, next month, fifteen years from now—maybe he'd end up needing to stop her from making some nightmares too. If what Rabbit had seen in her file was just a quarter of her real life, what would happen when the other 75 percent came back to her?

Or came looking for her?

From here on out, it wasn't Rabbit's problem. Now his job was to follow orders. Get on the plane. Find Skip. Close the loop and keep things quiet.

But as Rabbit made a left onto Pennsylvania Avenue, circling past the concrete, bureaucratic hulk of a building that was home to the FBI, he couldn't help but notice another building, diagonally across the street, where massive Corinthian columns were draped with gold and blue banners.

Rabbit should've headed for the parking spot that was waiting for him at the FBI. Instead, he drew up to the curb and lingered on Pennsylvania, squinting at the banners.

MAKING THEIR MARK: STORIES THROUGH FAMOUS SIGNATURES

Underneath was the massive signature of John Hancock, as well the building's ID.

THE NATIONAL ARCHIVES

Rabbit stared at the building and took a deep breath through his nose.

Then this thought. *Go to the airport; get on the plane.*

Then: It's not that he didn't trust Moten...he just didn't know if he trusted whoever worked above him.

Yet for a man who'd spent his entire adult life in intelligence, Rabbit couldn't shake the feeling that he'd never known what it felt like to truly be fooled.

Ten minutes later, he was in the lobby of the National Archives, approaching the sign-in desk.

"I'm sorry, sir," a female guard said. "We're not open to the public until ten a.m."

"I have an appointment," Rabbit said, flashing his badge. "Now who do I talk to about Benedict Arnold books in your collection?"

66

Hartford, Connecticut

T he Bear parks his rental car—a Buick LaCrosse, because no one notices someone who drives a Buick LaCrosse—next to Ingrid Ludlow's driveway, and waits to see if a light goes on, if a shutter opens, if a dog barks.

Nothing.

He calls Ingrid's telephone. It rings and rings. No voicemail. No answering machine.

She lives in an old neighborhood in Hartford, one of those filled with cottages built in the 1800s that sit right next to teardowns with elderly owners waiting to die. The area might be called charming, but The Bear thinks it's probably infested with rats.

He walks up to the front door, rings the doorbell, waits. He presses his palm against the center of the door, feels it give. He thinks: *Termites.*

A threat to structural stability, surely, but it was

not as bad as once having an order for your head from the KGB, or a death warrant issued against you by the IRA, or the half-dozen fatwas that chased her across the Middle East and North Africa. There was a time when Ingrid Ludlow would be worth a mint dead. Now? Old wounds tended to heal when you stopped picking at them. Not even the termites seemed to be in a rush.

The Bear steps back around the side of the house, takes a photo over her fence with his phone, sees if there's an attack dog, finds instead that Ingrid is growing tobacco and marijuana, just a few stocks of each, right there in view.

Pushing seventy years old. Doing what she wanted. Wasn't that nice.

She's earned it, The Bear supposes. All those years devoted to Jack Nash. She was a researcher and historian. Compulsive. A fine team put together by the government. Practical and accurate. The Bear doesn't think there are many other academics running around the world with as much blood on their hands as Ingrid Ludlow.

Well, maybe one.

The problem with Ingrid, The Bear thinks now, is that technology erased the need for her skill sets, or at least made them both functionally less important. A Google search eliminated hours in a library. And a drone strike from thousands of miles away was much more effective these days than an American with a knife.

So here was Ingrid today.

"Can I help you?" a man calls out, getting out of a Subaru wagon across the street. He's in his thirties, with messy hair in the style of scientists and people in bands. The Bear sees that he has a tattoo on his calf. It looks to be the Chinese symbol for patience. The Bear wonders: *Why doesn't he simply have the English word* patience *tattooed there instead?*

"Just doing a welfare check," The Bear says. "Have you seen Ms. Ludlow lately?"

"I think she's away," a woman says, getting out of the car, popping the trunk, unloading bags from Whole Foods. She shares a look with the man. "For a bit."

"Do you know where?" The Bear asks. He takes an awkward step into the middle of the street, hunches his shoulders, tries to look smaller, less threatening, opens his hands, palms out. Tries to become the kind of man who does welfare checks.

The couple share another look. "She's in the hospital," the man says.

"Oh, no," The Bear says. "Did she fall?"

Another look. "Just a checkup, I think," the woman says. "Are you from the city?"

"Yes. I'm her physical therapist. From when she took that fall last year," The Bear says, using a key piece of information from Ingrid's insurance file. Both strangers now smile, everyone at ease. The woman is also in her thirties. She's wearing a tank top and yoga pants. She has the same tattoo as the man, though hers is on her bicep. The Bear wonders if the tattoos are messages to each other or to the rest of the world. Patience. A noble pursuit. Though if you needed to remind yourself of it so often that you ended up putting it on your flesh, it was likely a failed pursuit.

"She's up at the Institute of Living. On Barry Square?"

"Oh," The Bear says. A psychiatric hospital. "Permanently?"

"No," the woman says, "she said it was just for an oil change."

"Tell him what she really said," the man says. "It's hilarious."

"She says she likes the food." The woman laughs, so does the man, so does The Bear, or at least pretends to.

As the two of them go into their own house, The Bear goes back to Ingrid's front porch, puts on a glove, pulls out one of the straws Skip chewed on—then drops it through the mail slot.

"The Institute of Living," The Bear repeats, looking it up on his phone. It couldn't be that far from here.

67

National Archives
Washington, DC

Y ou must be the Benedict Arnold fan," the
archivist whispered.

"I'm not sure *fan* is the right word," Rabbit said, standing from his seat at a long wooden
table and offering a handshake. They were in the
second-floor reading room, which felt like the
1750s, what with the banker's desk lamps, ornate
chandeliers, and the eerie quiet. Libraries were
the one place people still kept alive the monastic
virtue of silence.

"Don't be ashamed," the archivist whispered,
laughing a quiet laugh. His name was Beecher
White, an archivist who specialized in "Old Military." He had short cropped hair and looked like
he had a black eye, though Rabbit imagined
archivists didn't get into too many fistfights.
"When it comes right down to it, we're all fans,
aren't we?" Beecher asked.

Rabbit nodded, noticing the archival box he was holding. It was the size of a ream of paper, but he carried it like he was carrying the crown jewels.

"I just told them I was looking for something interesting," Rabbit said.

Beecher leaned in closer. "Everyone here, they want the dark, mysterious Benedict Arnold. Me? Personally? I like looking at people's stuff."

"I do too," Rabbit said.

"Beautiful. Wonderful." Beecher opened the box. "Then I think you'll like this one."

68

Hartford, Connecticut

H ome. That's what Hazel was thinking about now, watching all of these people mill around the back lawn of this place where none of them wanted to live. They looked tranquil, even happy, some of them enjoying the sun, a few playing bocce, all of them surrounded by nurses and orderlies who would tackle them to the ground if they made a run for it.

"They're bringing her down now," an orderly with a rash of freckles across his nose told her.

Hazel nodded thanks, strolling around the circular fountain that was the centerpiece of the Institute of Living's golf course–sized back lawn. The fountain was broken and its marble base was drained of water, but Hazel still circled it, over and over.

Ingrid Ludlow didn't live far from Arthur Kennedy. Barely an hour away. Both of their homes were close to the Connecticut birthplace of Benedict Arnold himself.

From her pocket, Hazel pulled out the tourist brochure from the hotel, listing nearby historical sites.

Benedict Arnold's bookstore was labeled with a bright yellow star. That star was now a strip mall, meaning the most notorious traitor in American history was now haunting something called Pizza Bomb, a Super Speedy Printing shop, a UPS store, and a nail salon. And wasn't that the way? The horror of history was not that it was repeated or forgotten, it was usually that it was ignored in favor of pizza by the slice and next-day shipping.

On her phone, Hazel pulled up Skip's Twitter page. He'd posted a photo of himself three hours ago from the balcony of his Dubai hotel room, along with an update: *Good things happening! Stay tuned! House of Secrets coming back! #LostAnd-Found.* It had been retweeted 603 times.

She clicked through his updates, his photos from LAX, from London, from the Al Qasr beach, in each one his smile wide across the screen, life treating Skip Nash right, no matter where he was at any given time. It was, she knew, a lie.

She clicked through the photos other people had posted with Skip, so many taken without him knowing: Skip at an airport coffee shop with a donut shoved in his mouth. Skip asleep aboard a plane. Skip standing in the shallow end of a pool surrounded by cabanas, with the Persian Gulf in the background, paradise manufactured out of the desert.

She lingered on that last photo for a moment, staring at her brother. He was shirtless, wearing sunglasses. Both of his hands were flat on the surface of the water. He wasn't smiling, wasn't frowning, wasn't outwardly doing anything but being still.

It was probably just a trick of the photo, a single frozen moment in Skip Nash's life when no one thought to bother him. He looked...at peace. It seemed all at once familiar and completely alien. Hazel tried to remember the last time she'd seen him being totally serene. Certainly not since she'd woken up after the crash.

Hazel studied his face, trying to find a match in her brain, and there he was, standing in the shadow of the Three Gossips, a 350-foot sandstone tower in the middle of Arches National Park, outside of Moab. Time and the elements had cut the stone into the rough shape of three people, deep in the middle of a secret, their heads tilted toward one another, listening, for the last million years or so.

When was this?

A few weeks ago. The day before the crash.

An entire lifetime ago.

Now she remembered. She and Skip had gone hiking, each in a different direction. Hazel spotted Skip when she came up out of a wash to the west of the towers. Skip was standing alone, his head tipped back to the sky, sunglasses on, his palms down. He stood so still that for a moment she wondered if in fact it really was Skip she was seeing, or if it was a scarecrow, placed out in the middle of the desert as some kind of joke.

She watched him like that for a minute, maybe two, thinking she should turn around, walk away, let him have his silence, and right when she made that decision, Skip dipped his head and saw her.

"How long you been standing there?"

"I just walked up," she lied, and she knew, from the slightly embarrassed look on Skip's face, that he knew too.

He pointed at the Three Gossips. "Pretty incredible, isn't it?"

"Please don't tell me that aliens carved it with their lasers, as a warning."

"Naw, Haze," he said. "That's just erosion." He took a swig of water, then gave her a smile that didn't seem all that joyful. "You remember the trip we took out here when we were kids?"

"Barely," Hazel said.

"Same here." He looked back up at the massive sandstone towers. "I remember those, though."

"It kills three," Hazel said. Skip cocked his head, like he wasn't sure what Hazel meant. "Gossip. It kills the speaker, the listener, and the one who's being talked about. Everyone loses."

"You come up with that?"

"No," Hazel said. "It's in an old book."

"I should probably read more old books." He gave her that smile, the one that was in *Teen Beat*, the one that he'd worn on TV everywhere. Hazel realized now, frozen on a lawn in an insane asylum, that in every memory of her brother, he was wearing the same mask.

She tried to rewind her life back to the crash, but all she saw in her mind was the color red. Twenty-four hours after their conversation, Jack would be dead, Hazel's memory would be scattered, and Skip would be the only one left standing. And then? Three more dead people. First Darren Nixon, then Dr. Morrison, and now Arthur Kennedy. Everything starting the moment that poison stopped Jack's heart.

But . . . no.

That wasn't true. It began when Jack started working for the government. That was the thing to remember. It was a series of dominos, tipping over across time. Benedict Arnold's bible may have been one of Jack's obsessions, but in the scope of his entire life, what did it really matter? It didn't define him. It wasn't larger than his children. His family.

But maybe she was looking at things wrong. Dr. Morrison didn't kill himself because of Benedict Arnold's bible, he killed himself because he was a man with secrets, a drug addict, a person whose life would crumble if the truth about him were known. He would be stripped of his license. He would be sued. He would live in infamy, which didn't have much appeal these days for those who didn't want to get their own reality TV show. His life wasn't altered by something as ephemeral as a secret plot. It came from something concrete and tangible. Something bad—a regrettable human error that would take away everything if people found out.

Was it the same with her father? Did something happen on one of his bible-finding missions? Something where he made a mistake? Something where he hurt someone he loved?

"Son of two bitches. Look at you," a female voice called out.

Hazel turned just as the institute's back door swung open.

"Hazel, Hazel, c'mon inside," her dad's former assistant Ingrid called out. "You know I hate the sun."

Hazel put on a smile, wondering what could possibly make this old woman insane.

69

Sirte, Libya
1983

Season 7, Episode 12 (1983): "The Dragon of Libya"

How did Jack get here?

It's because his ratings were in the toilet. That's what the network guys had told him. He'd seen the numbers. How was he going to compete against *Joanie Loves Chachi* and *The Dukes of Hazzard*? Never mind *Monday Night Football*, which Jack would prefer to watch too.

"Maybe it's time to pull the plug," Jack had said, because the truth was, walking away would be better for his health, better for his life. Maybe get a job doing the weather in LA, where he'd just look into the camera and say it was going to be about seventy degrees.

"Why not bring your kid on a few episodes," someone had suggested.

Maybe it'd get kids watching. Then maybe they'd try a Saturday morning cartoon with Skip. In a year or two, they'd get him into *Tiger Beat* and *Teen Beat*, anything with a beat. Could he sing? They'd make him bigger than Shaun Cassidy if he could carry a tune.

A silly idea. Dumb.

But it worked.

They'd done an episode on Alcatraz—that went fine, Skip a bit tentative at first, but he warmed up as the shoot went on. By the third day he was hamming it up, and Jack had to rein him in.

Then they did a show on the old Winchester Mystery House in San Jose, and Skip lit up. Even Claire could see it.

"He's a natural," she whispered to Jack as the two of them watched Skip run up a stairwell that dead-ended into a brick wall, chasing a phantom's footsteps. Claire never came to the shoots, hadn't in years, but she wanted to make sure Skip was okay. "He doesn't even see the camera."

"It's because," Jack told her, "he actually believes."

But how'd Jack get *here*—today—with his son, in the palace of a dictator in Libya?

Jack blamed Egypt, which is where he and Skip were filming an episode, a real episode, about the riddle of the Sphinx, or the labyrinths of the pyramids, or whatever else they could get B-roll for. They'd use it in half a dozen episodes over the next year. He took Skip as a treat—his first trip abroad—a reward for his recent hard work.

But then Jack got the call from Moten last night in Cairo saying they needed to make a stop in a city called Sirte, on the coast of Libya. *Libya, of all places!* Of course, Jack said no. Not with Skip there. No way.

Moten wouldn't hear it. This was bigger than Skip, bigger than Jack, bigger than anything they'd tried before. They'd been contacted by the brother-in-law of Muammar al-Gaddafi, who had something to offer, something that would keep millions of people safe.

"Another page of Benedict Arnold's bible?" Jack had asked.

"Not just any page. *The* page. The big one— the one we've been searching for, Jack. This could help us win a war," Moten had said, which was exactly what the officers had said two centuries ago, when George Washington made his trade and sent back the so-called "belongings" of Benedict Arnold.

"I won't do anything that puts Skip in jeopardy," Jack told Moten.

"You think anyone wants Skip getting hurt?" Moten said. "I wouldn't ask if lives didn't depend on it. This is how you'll change the world, Jack."

So here they were, in Libya, pretending to film a show about dragons and preparing to trade for the most valuable page of the bible. It was the opportunity of a lifetime.

"I'm bored," Skip says.

"Settle down," Jack tells him. His son is fidgeting between Jack and Ingrid at an absurdly long black table inside an ornate dining hall. Ingrid had told Jack to leave Skip at the hotel. Jack trusted the hotel even less. At least here he could keep an eye on Skip himself.

"How much longer? I'm bored," Skip said.

He was only seven years old. He should be starting second grade this week. Instead, he was waiting on a meet and greet with the brother-in-law of a known killer.

"Maybe we can get some juice for the boy," Ingrid says, pleasantly, to their hosts, though Jack thinks the sum total of her patience is nearing zero.

"See this table?" the Libyan official asks. Except she's not Libyan. She's a six-foot Ukrainian woman named Yusra. Jack had thought it was just some insane rumor that the dictator of Libya surrounded himself with lethal Eastern European women, like some bad Bond villain, but no, in fact, it was true. "You might be interested to know it is the largest table in all of Africa. It was handcrafted using Brazilian rosewood, which is exceptionally rare. It has been stained by using actual ox blood."

"In real life?" Skip says.

"Yes, absolutely," Yusra tells him.

"Do you know how much longer?" Jack asks.

"Ten minutes," Yusra says, which is what she's been saying for an hour and a half.

"Then you should bring him some juice," Ingrid says.

"In ten minutes, if His Eminence is not yet arrived, we will certainly have some juice, yes."

"Let's do three minutes," Ingrid says.

"It is not a negotiation, Ms. Ludlow," Yusra says.

But Jack knows: Everything is a negotiation, everything has a rub, especially here.

Last night, Jack reassured his wife, "Claire, he'll be fine." Jack's hoping he's right.

Even now, Jack thinks, Skip seems happier out here in the wilds than he ever does at home. Calmer. Centered. More like a normal kid. His fidgeting now feels like a welcome change from his worry and anxiety about the world. Boredom, Jack can handle. Existential pain? He's not so great with that.

Besides, Skip is about to have a story he'll be able to tell for the rest of his life.

70

National Archives
Washington, DC
Today

I don't understand what this is," Rabbit said.

"You see the signature, yes?" Beecher the archivist asked.

Of course. Right at the top, handwritten. *I Benedict Arnold Major General do acknowledge...*

"It's not his will, is it?"

"It's called an Oath of Allegiance," the archivist explained, his white-gloved hand touching the corner of the mottled parchment, which was the size of an envelope. "When the war began, George Washington had all the officers of his army swear that they'd be loyal to the cause. He needed their promise. In fact, we still use these oaths in our modern army, when our officers have to swear they'll defend the Constitution. But back then, at Valley Forge, all the officers lined up and signed on the dotted line.

"See this number here," he added, pointing to

the handwritten "5" in the top right-hand corner. "That was the order they signed the oaths. The first person to sign was..."

"George Washington," Rabbit said.

"Exactly. We have his here too. It's labeled with a number 1 in the corner. But think of that moment. These men lined up, all of them ready to swear their allegiance to our new country. Washington is first. Then comes two, three, and four. And then fifth in line is this man, who takes his pen and writes his name—*Benedict Arnold*—on this very sheet of parchment."

Rabbit leaned toward the document, which indeed said that Benedict Arnold would defend the United States against King George, the British, and all their heirs.

"We usually only take this out when a bigwig comes. Y'know, like the President... or my college roommate's kids."

"It's definitely interesting," Rabbit said. "But I'm also wondering, your catalogue downstairs said you have some of the letters that Benedict Arnold wrote directly to George Washington."

"We have over sixty of them, some digitized, some originals."

"Do you have the one where he asks George Washington to return his belongings to him?"

"Excuse me?"

If Rabbit wanted to know what Jack Nash was chasing, he needed to know more about this bible and what was really sent. "After Arnold went on the run, he wrote a letter to George Washington asking for his books and supplies. Do you have that letter?"

"I know that particular letter, but it's at the Library of Congress. Here at the Archives we have a digitized copy." Beecher was annoyed now—he'd gone out of his way to pull this document. He looked at his watch. It was an old Hamilton watch with a JFK half-dollar as the face of it. "All of the Founders' letters are accessible online," Beecher said, pointing to a nearby computer terminal.

"Listen, I'm not trying to waste your time. I'm just wondering…It's for a case we're working on…Is there any sort of document that might show *exactly* what Washington sent to him?"

"I know Arnold was hiding on a ship called the *Vulture*. There should have been a shipping manifest at the time."

"Yes, yes. Something like that."

"If it even exists, I bet it's more likely in England. I could see about getting a scan, though. Is there something specific you're wondering about?"

"To be honest," Rabbit said, "I'm most interested in Benedict Arnold's bible. Do you know anything about that?"

"No. I've never even contemplated it. Is that an actual thing?"

"It is. To some people."

It was the simple question that kept circling around Rabbit's mind. If Hazel's father had spent his life looking for Benedict Arnold's bible, if Darren Nixon was poisoned because he had some theory about it, if Arthur Kennedy had died for it too…why did no one else seem to care about it?

In Dubai, Skip was about to announce to the world that he was going to go in search of the bible, and Rabbit imagined that the news would be met with…silence. Who cared enough to look for the book if it didn't even make it into one of Jack Nash's *House of Secrets* episodes? He knew the legend Moten had told him, if a footnote in history could be called a legend at all, that when Benedict Arnold asked for his belongings, what he was really after was his bible—and what was written in it. But what Rabbit didn't know was how Washington responded to Arnold's request. What *had* Washington sent back?

"Hmm," Beecher said, standing there for a moment. Then he looked up, twinkle in his eye. "Be right back. I've got an idea."

71

Twenty minutes later, Rabbit was still waiting, eyeing the double doors at the far end of the reading room that were marked *Staff Only*, thinking how odd it was that words on a door stopped people from so much.

"Sorry it took me so long," Beecher the archivist announced, coming out through the doors. "Good news is, I think I found something."

Rabbit expected another archival box, but the only thing in Beecher's hand was a yellow Post-it.

"What's this?" he asked.

"A phone number. For the head of special collections for Sterling Library at Yale."

"Yale?"

"So odd, right? One of the most revered colleges in America, and it's an architectural ode to a country—England—that used to be our mortal enemy. In two hundred years, will there be new

American universities built to resemble the crumbling streets of Kabul?"

Rabbit was lost. "I'm not sure I—?"

"Benedict Arnold was *from* Connecticut. They've got one of the best Arnold collections in the world. If you hurry, you can catch her. She'll be happy to talk. They don't get many calls up there."

*   *   *

"I appreciate your patience," the librarian known as Carrie said through videoconference.

Rabbit watched her onscreen as she set a file down on the table. Carrie was in her mid-fifties and looked like she'd robbed a Casual Corner in 1979.

Rabbit didn't like teleconferences, but as Beecher explained when he brought Rabbit into this conference room on the fourth floor of the Archives, this was the best—and fastest—way to see the Yale collection up close.

"So this is what we have regarding his belongings." Carrie pointed at one of three stacks of paper. "You have the contents of the home he shared with his wife Peggy Shippen and their son Edward near West Point. Most of which was eventually burned, as you might imagine."

Carrie pointed at the second stack, another cat-alogued list of items, like a giant ancient grocery list. "Then you have the contents of his office at West Point, all of which were retained and pored over, looking for evidence. But as you'll see, what they found there was primarily books, documents, and, funny enough, a pair of slippers."

And then the third stack. "Those were the items his wife and son took with them when they were banished from the Colonies, which is mostly the clothes on their back."

Rabbit sat there, reading through the document list that she'd emailed.

"Where did you find this information?"

"I believe these items are actually there at the Archives, though they just have so much stuff there, it's easy to get drowned," Carrie said, flash-ing a small smile and a bit of librarian pride. "They're part of his trial documents. We have a copy here as well."

"Is there a list of what Washington sent to Arnold?"

"No," Carrie said, "but from the remaining household items, it doesn't seem to be a signifi-cant number of things. President Washington was a gentleman, though. Can you imagine? Sending your greatest enemy his belongings?"

"A different time," Rabbit said, still reading the

list. Here were the minutiae of an eighteenth-century life, Benedict Arnold's as boring as anyone's: Clothes. Pots. Pans. Furniture. Rugs. Two hundred and thirteen books, though none listed by title. Candles. Salted meat. Pounds of sugar. Bottles of Madeira.

"Any mention of a bible?"

"A few," Carrie said. "He had four bibles in his office at West Point, which is not unusual for the time. His wife and son had a bible with them when they departed for the *Vulture*." She pulled out an old newspaper clipping from a clear protective sleeve. "I found this in a search, a witness narrative that appeared in a paper in New York, saying that Peggy clutched a bible to her chest as she got on the boat to depart. Of course, we can't verify the authenticity, but what a vision. I suspect he would have had several more bibles in his home. The ones that weren't burned were probably stored somewhere or given away. So he might have had, gosh, ten bibles. That wouldn't be odd."

"Ten?"

"Maybe more," Carrie said. "Don't forget, he got his start as a bookseller and even owned a bookshop at one point. He could very well have had twenty, for all we know."

"So, there's no record of a bible with Arnold's

handwriting, or a family tree in it? Nothing like that?"

"Oh, there're probably several," she said. "What we have access to here, it's just a small percentage. The Arnold family tree is a long one, so many of his personal items have been kept and passed down over the years."

"You have that collection there?"

"Yes, both his family and strangers have donated things over decades. Clothing, personal papers, even a plate or two. People are always interested in touching something real, so we've been actively acquiring. Indeed, that's the benefit of being in New Haven. People turn things up in the walls or attics of their house all the time. You'd be surprised. We have many local benefactors."

A thought occurred to Rabbit. "Do you happen to know my friend Arthur Kennedy?"

Onscreen, Carrie brightened. "We love Arthur! How do you know him?"

"He's a dear old friend," Rabbit said.

"Oh, then you'll love this . . ."

72

Hartford, Connecticut

The last time Hazel Nash saw Ingrid Ludlow was last night, in a YouTube clip. Ingrid chain-smoking in a darkened library while Jack examined documents using a magnifying glass, like he was Sherlock Holmes. The two of them were in a castle in Transylvania, searching for actual vampires.

The clip was from 1986, Ingrid looking like she'd escaped an episode of *Dynasty*, her hair an ode to Linda Evans or to cubist art. She was wearing a silver overcoat; Jack was in a sweater with too many colors, a black trench coat with the collar up, as if maybe that would stop any bloodsucking fiend from getting to him.

Now standing in the lobby of a psychiatric hospital, watching Ingrid being led down the hall by an orderly, his tattooed arm looped through hers, Hazel wished for a moment that vampires were real and could maybe give Ingrid back her youth and beauty.

Ingrid limped on her right leg, and her left leg dragged half an inch behind, like maybe she'd had a hip replacement that didn't quite take, and though Ingrid had glasses on, Hazel could see her eyes darting about.

"You're coming back?" the orderly asked Ingrid.

"A few days," Ingrid said.

"I look forward to it." He handed Hazel a set of car keys. "She still has her license, but me personally? I wouldn't let her drive."

When the orderly was gone, Hazel said, "Wait. They let you just walk out of here?"

"Sweetheart," Ingrid said, and she straightened herself up a bit, eyeing the keys in Hazel's hand, "this was a tune-up—from when I heard your dad died. I checked myself in, I can check myself out. Now, you comin' or not?"

73

The Bear is three cars ahead of Hazel as she pulls onto the interstate, headed toward New Haven.

Now The Bear knows for sure.

He knew Hazel would come here.

Now he knows where she and Ingrid are going.

He's close to them now. Closer than he's been in some time.

The Bear doesn't like surprises, then thinks, *Does anyone?*

Certainly not a surprise like the brutal one that's coming.

74

Y ou know how Arthur is," Carrie the librarian said about Kennedy. "He never wants credit for anything." She looked around the room, pointed to the wall. "He donated *that*." She turned the teleconference camera, aimed it at a framed document. "It's a bill of sale, signed by Benedict Arnold, for a brigantine."

Rabbit leaned in, squinting at the screen. It was almost impossible to read the document until Carrie readjusted the camera and pulled in. There at the bottom was Arnold's distinctive signature: a wide loop through the arm of the B, a period, and then his last name in precise script, every letter perfectly readable. "When is this from?" Rabbit asked.

"Before the war. Which makes it less interesting to some."

"He was just a man then," Rabbit said.

"That's precisely what Mr. Kennedy said. Though that reminds me, I haven't seen him for a bit. He usually comes in once or twice a month."

"He's traveling," Rabbit said.

"Oh?"

"Last I heard, he was abroad," Rabbit said. "Shopping for antiques. Dubai." Where Rabbit should be headed right now. A 6 p.m. flight.

Another thought came to Rabbit then. "Has anyone else ever come to look for this information? Anyone who might also be interested in your collection?"

"Truth is, aside from local students during term paper time, we don't have many—" She cut herself off, flipping to the archival box that held the old newspaper clipping they'd been looking at. "Here, we can check right here." Attached to the outside of the box was a sleeve with a computer printout tucked into it. "According to this list, in the last six months, beside Mr. Kennedy, only one other person has requested this document."

Carrie held the printout up to the screen. Rabbit read it, then read it again, the same name listed three days in a row.

Darren Nixon.

Rabbit felt the tip of his tongue go numb, realized he'd been pinching it between his teeth for the last minute, that if he wanted to, he could bite

THE HOUSE OF SECRETS

right through it now, his body prepared for trauma, a bit of fight and flight at the same time.

"Agent Rabkin, you okay?" Carrie asked onscreen.

He barely heard the question. He pulled out his phone, started dialing. How had he not seen it?

Both victims: Nixon and Kennedy. All this time, they weren't looking for Benedict Arnold's bible. They were looking for something far more precious.

75

Sirte, Libya
1983

T he door at the end of the dining room opens, flooding the room with bright sunlight, followed by a sudden bustle of people. Three more very tall Ukrainian women walk in holding cameras, like newspaper photographers from the fifties, and then a phalanx of security personnel walking in a reverse triangle pattern, all of them with Kalashnikov rifles.

In the middle of them all is the brother-in-law of the dictator—Tariq—head of Libya's state security.

Jack, Skip, and Ingrid rise.

You got lucky, Ingrid says with just a look to Yusra.

Tariq is in his forties, slim, and is dressed in full military regalia, white pants and a white jacket, covered in medals and ribbons, a green sash across his chest, also covered in medals. He steps through his guards and walks straight for Jack, hand extended.

"Jack Nash," Tariq says, "such an honor."

"Thank you, sir," Jack says, knowing Tariq expects pleasantries before he'll name his price and trade for the bible.

Tariq's handshake is light, almost imperceptible. Flashbulbs go off.

"Have you enjoyed your time in my country?"

Flash.

"Yes, sir, yes," Jack says.

Flash.

"Have you found the dragon? For your show?"

Flash.

"Not yet," Jack says.

Flash.

"There is tomorrow."

Flash.

Tariq takes a knee, so that he's at eye level with Skip, Jack thinking it was an odd thing for a man like this to do. "And this must be your son."

76

W hat sort of help do you need?" Ingrid asked from the passenger seat. They were on I-91, heading toward New Haven in Ingrid's ancient Ford Taurus, the interior a ruin of old newspapers and the smell of cigarettes. "Research? I was always good with research."

Hazel watched the other cars on the interstate. Kids in backseats, parents on their cell phones. A whole other world, right there beside her. Hazel wondered what this parallel life was like, if anyone cared about anything other than getting to and from work. Maybe that's all she was doing too.

But Hazel couldn't shake the feeling. Like someone was behind them, watching.

"I need to know what you and Dad were up to," Hazel said, "back in the day."

"Making TV."

"Beyond that. I need to know about Benedict Arnold's bible. About the trips you took looking for it."

"No, you don't," Ingrid said. "No one does."

Hazel checked the rearview mirror, still not getting much of a read from this old woman. "Ingrid, did anyone tell you how my father died?"

"Heart attack, wasn't it? That's what I read in the papers." She turned and looked at Hazel. "I wanted to come to the funeral."

"The government said my dad was poisoned. That's why I'm here. They think it's related to the bible."

Ingrid was silent for a long time. "The drug they think he was poisoned with, what was it?"

"I know this sounds crazy."

"It's okay, sweetheart. I've already been committed."

Hazel told her about her dad's body, and about Darren Nixon and Arthur Kennedy, whose warehouse they were now going to in New Haven. According to Kennedy's tax records, he'd rented in a few places, always moving around the city. But this warehouse was his one constant. To Hazel, that made it the first thing worth checking out.

Ingrid listened intently, her eyes shifting back and forth from the road to her side-view mirror. Like she felt someone watching too. Hazel studied

Ingrid's expression to see if she showed any surprise or recognition, but Ingrid betrayed nothing, not even a hint of skepticism.

"How old are you?" Ingrid asked when Hazel finished.

"Thirty-six."

"Have you had a happy life?"

"I don't really know," Hazel said.

"Do you want one?"

"I suppose I do."

"Then go back to your hotel. And then don't ever come back here."

"Sweetheart," Hazel said in her best Ingrid impersonation, "it's too late for that."

Ingrid laughed. A real laugh. "You're different from how I remember you. Nicer."

"I'm just trying to figure out the world these days."

"Your father," Ingrid says, "he thought you were pretty special."

"Like a werewolf?"

"No. They're only special once a month." Ingrid inhaled, and Hazel saw that her whole body shuddered. Parkinson's, maybe.

"Can you tell me something, Hazel?" Ingrid asked. She popped open the glove box. Inside was a tin of tobacco along with some rolling papers. She pulled them out, started hand-rolling a jagged cigarette. "Why does everyone think Benedict Arnold is the only person who ever turned on this country? He just has the benefit of scale and a name that's easy to remember. Does anyone remember the name of that boy who went and fought with the Taliban? Or all of the Americans who've been caught spying for the Russians? Or all the technological fraud that happens now, when our secrets are broken down into tiny numbers, data flying all around us, everything always being stolen and used against us. Everything!

"Every email you send, it's being stolen and routed elsewhere. Or all the cameras that are watching you every day? All of it is treason. But that will never end up in the history books. That makes it easier to just assume the one bad person, the one traitor of merit, happened in the 1700s and after that, well, it was just Candyland and cupcakes. It's not true. History is being written right now, but no one is updating the old books. So why is Benedict Arnold so important?"

"He's not," Hazel said. "In the scope of the history of the world, he's a particle of dust."

"No," Ingrid said, her voice slowing down, "he is the *shorthand* for a particle of dust. A signifier. That's his role. As a code. That's the final trick." Ingrid looked in her side-view mirror again.

"You think someone's following us too?" Hazel asked.

"I'm not going to lie to you." Ingrid tapped her own forehead. "I've been having problems these last few years unseeing things. You know what that's like?"

"I have the opposite problem."

"What do you remember about me? You can be honest."

"Most of it's gone. But I saw a picture at my dad's house. Of all of us," Hazel said. "I don't think my mother liked you."

"She didn't."

"Why's that?"

"She thought your father and I were too close."

"Were you?"

"Intellectually," Ingrid said. "Which was probably worse in your mother's view." She lit her cigarette, took a long drag from it. "I still want to know what you remember about me."

"All I have is what I feel now. I think I'm scared of you," Hazel said.

"You were always the smart one," Ingrid said.

"Something bad happened on one of your missions, didn't it? The one in Libya."

"If I tell you about Benedict Arnold's bible, you're going to be like me. Wanting to forget. Is that what you want?"

"I want what's true," Hazel said, "and then I'll choose who I want to be."

Ingrid craned up and checked the side mirror, saw a car that most definitely might be following them. "Benedict Arnold's bible isn't a book. It's a person."

77

Sirte, Libya
1983

N icholas," Jack says, using Skip's given
name to be more formal. "Shake his
hand, Nicholas."

There's another flash from a camera.

Skip does as he's told, but Jack can tell his son
is nervous.

"Very firm grip," Tariq says, placing both of his
hands on Skip's shoulders. "And this is your wife?"
he says of Ingrid.

Flash.

"No," Ingrid says. "Colleague."

Tariq nods, a little too appreciatively, though
Jack's larger concern is the way he's touching Skip.
Jack doesn't like to see this man's filthy hands anywhere near Skip. When Claire sees the photos,
she'll lose her mind.

"Your wife must be beautiful," Tariq says, "if
this is merely your colleague." He gives Skip's

shoulders a squeeze. "Is your mother beautiful, Nicholas?"

"Yes, sir," Skip says.

"Beautiful women," the dictator's brother-in-law says, "are a blessing and a curse, yes, Mr. Nash?"

Flash.

Moten had told Jack how important it was to make this deal, to get this "bible," this person, and bring him back to the United States. They'd moved so many people like this over the years, shuttling them out of so many hot spots around the world, hiding them among Jack's film crew. Moten told Jack to agree to everything today. To show the utmost respect. To let this preening man...preen.

The problem is, it's not quite Jack's nature.

"Personally," Jack says, "I think beauty is a disguise. Intellect is what matters."

Tariq raises his eyebrows in surprise.

Jack thinks most people don't have personal opinions around this man, unless they don't mind their personal opinions being the blunt instruments of their own demise.

"Come with me, Mr. Nash." He raises his chin toward Ingrid, and like that, three of his men slowly surround her. Nothing overtly threatening, which in itself is reason for Jack to worry. "Your colleague can stay here. Don't you want to see who you're trading for?"

78

G o back. You said the bible was a person. So who was the person? This Libyan Tariq? Or was it someone else?"

"Do you remember the episode?" Ingrid asked, still watching the car's side mirror. "'The Dragon of Libya.'"

"I saw it," Hazel said, tugging the steering wheel toward the highway exit. According to the GPS, Kennedy's property was just ahead. "I watched it a few days ago. Skip and my dad—they weren't in a palace. They were running around museums, looking at statues."

"Then you understand the lies."

"The lies about what? The location? The people? You said he brought a kid into a war zone. My father would never do that."

"Sweetheart, I promise you one thing. You have no idea what your father was capable of."

79

Washington, DC

B utchie, where is she?" Rabbit demanded, holding his phone with one hand, starting his car with the other. "Where's Hazel?"

The other end of the line was silent.

"Butchie, I know you're there. This is Agent Trevor Rabkin. I need to reach Hazel. It's an emergency. Full 911."

Butchie still didn't say anything.

"I know she's in Connecticut. I know she checked Ingrid out of the hospital," Rabbit said. Outside, a police cruiser rolled down the block that Rabbit was parked on and crept slowly past, the officer staring directly at Rabbit. Then it sped up, turned right, and disappeared. "I've been calling her and she's not picking up. I know she's contacted you."

"How?"

"How what?"

"How you know she contacted me? You on my phone?"

"I am," Rabbit said. He wasn't.

"Just so I'm clear on this," Butchie said, "Eliot Ness needs my help with something? Is that where we are with this? Because I want to make sure I got the details right for when I'm sitting in my prison cell at Pelican Bay."

"Butchie," Rabkin started, but he didn't get the rest out.

"Friends call me Butchie. How about you call me Mr. Vasquez," Butchie said. "I'd like to hear that."

"Mr. Vasquez," Rabbit said, "just give her a message for me. Tell her they knew each other."

"Who?" Butchie asked.

"Darren Nixon and Arthur Kennedy. They spent time together in Connecticut."

"Probably Kennebunkport too," Butchie said. "Maybe Camp David."

"What're you talking about?"

"Check your email," Butchie said. "She told me to send it to you too."

Rabbit clicked open his email. Butchie had sent him two documents. "Before I open these," Rabbit said, "I need to know if I'm breaking the law."

"You could probably plead down on it."

Rabbit clicked open the file. The first page was

Nixon's behavior record from the Washington State Department of Corrections, which read like a list of ways to never get out of prison: fighting, hoarding materials for weapons, refusal of commands. Darren Nixon was not a man who was planning on an early release. The next page was a visitors log. Nixon had three visitors during his time inside. His lawyer; his mother, Mona; and, on five different occasions, Arthur Kennedy.

"They *really* knew each other," Rabbit said, more to himself than to Butchie.

"These weren't good guys," Butchie said. "Every time Kennedy visited, Nixon would pick a fight with an inmate, get himself put in the hole for a week or so."

"So whatever Kennedy was bringing him, it was pissing Nixon off," Rabbit said. He clicked to the next file, which were travel records for Kennedy, going back at least three years. "Where'd you get these?" Rabbit asked.

"I don't know what you're talking about."

"Mr. Vasquez, we're on the same side here."

"I don't want to be on your side. I checked you out, Agent Rabkin. You know you don't exist? Nobody with your name in the whole world." It was true. His full name had been changed years ago, when he was still doing military intelligence. "I'm on Hazel's wing," Butchie continued. "If she's riding with you right now, cool, but that don't mean you and me are anywhere close to the same side, let's be real clear on that."

"I'm just trying to figure who's telling us what, Mr. Vasquez," Rabbit said. When was the last time he worked with a crew that he trusted like Hazel trusted Butchie? Not since Afghanistan. FBI wasn't a unit. Not even close. No, if Rabbit wanted a support team, he'd have to build that himself. "You want Hazel safe? I want Hazel safe. Down the line, you need a favor? Maybe I'm a guy who can help you too. Right now, I just need to know where you got these."

Butchie thought on that for a second. "You'd be surprised what thirty-five thousand dollars buys you these days."

Rabbit scrolled through the documents. A flight to Spokane a month ago. Then another flight to Spokane a few months before that. "How many times was Kennedy out there?"

"Looks like it started back when Nixon was in prison. Then it picked up a year ago. But take a look at Kennedy's international travel."

He already was. Spain. Italy. England.

Then twice to Russia. Johannesburg. Libya.

The same places Jack Nash went. Hazel too.

The police car rolled around again, passing Rabbit this time.

Rabbit scrolled through the airline records again, checked the times, the dates. Then he flipped to the records he got from the Yale Library. That was the key. It was finally making sense. Here was their first meeting at Yale, then this was where the foreign travel ended. Libya. After that, it was just Kennedy and Nixon, flying back and forth between Spokane and Connecticut. "They weren't even hiding," Rabbit said. "They were meeting right out in the open. They're probably on camera at Yale."

"So why's a polished guy like Kennedy risking his reputation by even meeting in a library with an ex-con like Nixon?"

"Don't you see?" Rabbit said. "They were looking for something. Then they found it. In fact, Kennedy must've been looking for Nixon for years, or someone like Nixon."

"Says who?"

"Look where Kennedy's international travel stopped."

"*Libya?*" Butchie asked. "What's in Libya—besides dictators, terrorists, and an episode about dragons?"

"Something that should've never been found. Jack Nash's greatest mistake."

80

Connecticut

The Bear is sure. He's sure about how this will end, just as he's sure where Hazel and Ingrid have been heading for the last forty minutes as they drove from Hartford to New Haven.

So The Bear pulls ahead even more and makes a quick exit. He winds through the streets of New Haven for a few minutes, making sure no one is following *him*, then pulls into the parking lot at The Drawing Room, where he's learned Hazel is staying.

Goes inside.

Leaves a package for Hazel.

A gift. A very urgent gift.

Ten minutes later, The Bear is back on the highway, headed toward a warehouse on Water Street. Hazel is resourceful. She found the warehouse where Kennedy collected old secrets.

That's how this all started. Kennedy was hunting for details about his own life, his own hidden past. Then he stumbled onto what happened with Jack Nash in Libya. Kennedy wasn't a bad man. He could've kept it to himself, but when he connected it with Nixon... when he shared the news with Nixon... Lowlifes like Nixon can't help but take advantage. Now it was coming out. The one thing Jack Nash wanted hidden forever.

The Bear parks diagonally across the street from the warehouse. Far across. From what he can see, there's a guard in a small security shed. No one else in the parking lot.

Hazel and that woman—the demon called Ingrid—haven't arrived yet.

Perfect.

He knows how this will end. He'll do his killing in the warehouse, in Benedict Arnold's old home. A nice message. He'll snap Ingrid's neck first. Anything else would be foolish.

The Bear leaves the car. He finds a better hiding spot. Closer to the warehouse.

Then he waits.

81

Washington, DC

Rabbit was still staring at the airline files.

So many flights: Nixon traveling to see Kennedy, Kennedy traveling to see Nixon.

"You think Hazel's dad was at those meetings too?" Butchie asks through the phone.

"The later ones. And clearly the final one," Rabbit said. "If I'm right—if this was a big enough secret to Jack—they must've known Jack would go anywhere to keep it quiet." What struck Rabbit also, however, wasn't just the locations. It was the information itself.

Flights like this, this was all information his boss Moten should have had access to with the click of a mouse. Which meant Moten had chosen *not* to include all of Kennedy's flight records when he gave Rabbit the file.

The police car came back around the block, lights on, hit the siren for just a blip, and pulled even with Rabbit's car. The passenger window rolled down, and the officer motioned for Rabbit to roll down his window too.

"Something I can help you with?" Rabbit asked.

"You can't park here," the officer said, turning down his radio, which was playing *Elliot in the Morning*.

Rabbit held up his government ID. "I'm on business, officer," he said.

The police car rolled away.

"I need to get out of this spot," Rabbit said, mostly to himself.

"No fun getting sweated by the man, is it?" Butchie asked. "Starts making you paranoid after a while. Then one day you find out, government *was* following you. Then that really messes you up, know what I mean?"

"Just listen. There's something else," Rabbit said. "I'm going to the airport. To Connecticut. But you need to tell Hazel: When I first got on this case, they said that the bibles found inside both Nixon and Kennedy, that the pages inside had Benedict Arnold's handwriting on them, meaning they were from his book."

"Okay," Butchie said.

"But I never saw them."

"What're you talking about?"

"I saw reports. But not the actual physical

evidence. Or even photos. It was all happening at light speed." He was talking to himself now, trying to make sense of this. "Moten never showed me the real thing. But why wouldn't Moten show it to me unless..."

"Man," Butchie said, "everything I know I learned from watching Ice-T on *Law & Order*. So if you're expecting me to grasp something here, I'm not exactly grasping it."

"Maybe the reason no one has ever found Benedict Arnold's bible is that it's not actually missing."

"Then what were Nixon, Kennedy, and Hazel's dad looking for?"

"The most valuable thing of all. Each other."

82

Sirte, Libya
1983

J ack and Skip are led out of the palace, across a vast lawn with precise geometric hedges, and into a guesthouse.

Unlike the palace with its massive chandeliers and ornate decor, the house is filled with normal furniture: a leather sofa in the living room, with books and magazines spread out over an ottoman and coffee table. From a back room, Michael Jackson's "Billie Jean" is bleating out. Jack realizes that this house is almost entirely Westernized, right down to the Lego he steps over as they're led down a long hallway, toward the music.

A child lives here.

There's a woman standing at the end of the hall, outside a closed door. She has long brown hair, a razor-sharp nose, and as they get closer, Jack sees that her cheeks are tracked with tears.

She also has a surgical mask dangling around her neck and blue surgical gloves on her hands.

How had Jack gotten here?

Two hundred years ago, when Benedict Arnold was finally revealed as a traitor, he jumped on his horse, went on the run, and left his wife and son behind. Jack couldn't imagine it. Between love and war, you choose love. Always.

Over the next few days, letters were exchanged. Arnold asked for his family to be returned. George Washington agreed, but a deal would have to be made before Arnold could get his "bibles" back.

Of course, there would be a great cost. There was always a rub.

Soon after, a deal was struck, written and preserved in the endpapers of Arnold's old bible. For the rest of the war, Arnold would be true to the British. That never changed. But from there on in, he owed Washington a debt—a debt that would be paid with information.

For a spymaster like Washington, it was an intelligence coup. In the months that followed, Benedict Arnold, to pay back his debt, sent coded information to Washington about impending British attacks—nothing that would turn the tide of war, but information that was used to save hundreds, perhaps thousands of American lives. Was there any other way to explain how a poorly trained group of farmers and fishermen took on the greatest fighting force in the world?

Today, Jack was proof of this. You don't win at war by having the biggest gun, the largest army, or the best missiles. You win by owning the best people. And the ones with the best access.

Naturally, the military could never reveal they'd made a deal with America's greatest enemy. But the benefit was unarguable. It was a detail that would go unmentioned—until World War II, when it was unearthed by a military researcher in the Signal Corps who found Arnold's old books. An actual secret revealed. Sure, the tactics of the operation were changed—everything changes over time—but the idea was back in place. A new unit was formed, always at the ready, looking for opportunities, which they code-named *Benedict Arnold's bibles*.

As Washington himself had proven, when you can find an enemy who's desperate, it isn't just an advantage for the United States. It's an opportunity. And no opportunity is greater than a parent trying to save his sick child.

"I understand you are a man who can help us?" Tariq says, handing gloves and a mask to Jack.

"I am," Jack says.

Tariq opens the door. Jack immediately smells

bleach and ammonia, hears the *woosh-woosh* of an overhead fan.

Jack snaps on the gloves and affixes the mask, then turns to Skip. "I want you to wait right here with this nice man," he says, and meets the eyes of the security guard, a two-hundred-and-fifty-pound mass of a man, bald, with a knife and pistol holstered on his hip, "... and this nice woman." With that, the crying woman looks up, as if she's surprised she's been noticed.

"What is your name?" she asks Skip in heavily accented English. She sniffles once, then wipes her eyes, composing herself.

"Skip," he says. Then, "Nicholas."

"I am Mona." She forces out a smile. "You are a nice boy?"

"I am," Skip says.

"My boy is nice too." She turns to Jack. "You are a doctor?"

I'm a witch doctor, Jack thinks. *I live inside of a magic box. I find ghosts.*

"I'm here to help," Jack says, telling himself that by being here, by helping this boy, he'll be saving American lives. The thing is, he has no idea what's waiting for him in that room.

He kneels down in front of Skip. "Be really good. Understand?" He points over his shoulder. "I'll be right in there. Five minutes."

He kisses Skip on top of his head, then whispers in his ear, "You get scared, scream. Don't stop until you see my face. It's for the camera. You understand? We're playing a game for the camera."

"We're on the show?" Skip asks.

"That's right," Jack says. "Everything you see is make-believe."

83

New Haven, Connecticut
Today

I ngrid, what happened in that room in Libya?"
Hazel asked.

"Does it matter?"

"Of course it matters. What my father did
there—" Hazel cut herself off, made a sharp left,
steered the car toward the warehouse on Water Street. "You said this unit, whatever it was
called, for decades now, they sought out people
with sick kids."

"Our goal was to help those children."

"There was a child in that room, wasn't there?
Did my father kill a child?"

"I told you, it doesn't matter," Ingrid said. "What
matters is someone found out about it."

"What's that supposed t—?"

Hazel's phone started ringing. She saw the number. Butchie. He'd only call if it was time to pull
the emergency parachute.

Hazel picked up the phone, didn't say a word.

"Do you trust Agent Rabkin?" Butchie asked, voice galloping.

"What happened?"

"He called me. He found them. Nixon and Kennedy. He said they knew each other, like they were working together or some shit."

"Working for what?"

"You tell me. He said Kennedy spent years looking for others like himself, looking for each other, for something that happened to them. And then they found it. Something bad that happened with your dad in Libya."

Hazel turned toward Ingrid. She was unreadable as ever but could clearly hear Butchie through the phone.

"They found out what your father did," Ingrid said, still staring straight ahead. "Then they blackmailed him."

"Who you with, girl? The crazy lady?" Butchie asked.

On their right, across from a vacant brick building, was a warehouse, low and gray. According to Hazel's research, though it didn't look like it now, this was the place to be in the 1770s.

"This the property that was Kennedy's?" Ingrid asked.

Hazel nodded. "It's also where Benedict Arnold lived."

"This warehouse?"

"They tore his house down 150 years ago. The question is: Do people know that's the site of his old house? Would Arthur Kennedy know?"

Ingrid lit up her hand-rolled cigarette, inhaled deeply, and blew out a plume of smoke. "You'd need to care. You'd need to want to own it."

She was right. Based on what Butchie was saying, and what Hazel had proof of right here, Arthur Kennedy had a great many *wants*, most important of those being: finding his own past, finding Darren Nixon, and finding out if they were both "pages" in Benedict Arnold's bible.

"You can't park there," a voice shouted. On their left, a security guard approached from a beat-up security shed in the warehouse parking lot. He had a nametag pinned to his chest. It read *Leon*, from a company called *SecureFront*. A rental. The kind of guy who reported, but didn't stop.

"Butchie, let me call you back," Hazel said, hanging up the phone.

"No parking, no loitering," the guard added.

"Sorry about that," Ingrid said, leaning across the car toward Leon. "We have an appointment. Should be on your list. Ingrid and Hazel."

Hazel shot her a look. *List?*

The guard went back to his shed.

"It'll stall him," Ingrid said, reminding Hazel that Ingrid was a professional liar. "He won't care. We'll get in."

"Forget getting in. Tell me what happened in Libya...in that room at the palace...You think that's what Arthur Kennedy found out about?"

"Your father saw the best in people. That was his mistake," Ingrid said. "He wanted to believe that he was changing the world, but he was just uncovering the darkness, including his own. Based on what your friend said, someone else might've uncovered your father's darkness too."

"So Kennedy found Nixon, and what? They took the Libya story to my dad and threatened to go public?"

Ingrid coughed, a deep rattle in her chest. Cancer, maybe. Emphysema? On its way. "Y'know, when Mark Twain finally died, people everywhere thought he'd faked it, because of how many times they claimed he was already dead," Ingrid said. "That's what I thought when I heard about your father. Seems like any minute now, he's just going to pop up somewhere strange and announce it's all been a ruse. Abducted by the agents of the Bilderbergs or something."

"He's gone," Hazel said.

"I know. But it doesn't hurt anybody if I pretend, does it?"

Hazel checked again in the rearview, had that feeling she was still being watched. No one was there. "You think that's why Nixon was killed? That my father murdered him—or hired someone to murder him—because he and Kennedy were blackmailing my dad?"

Ingrid took a final deep drag of her cigarette, threw the nub of it out the window, shrugged. "That's what I would do."

"Ma'am, I don't see you on the list," Security Leon called back, reapproaching the car.

There was a hum in the air, like a river; Water Street backed up to a giant retaining wall that was supposed to block the rush of traffic from nearby I-95.

Two hundred years ago, this was the waterfront, where the aristocracy lived in big Colonial mansions. From this exact spot, you could see all of New Haven Harbor, lined with chestnut trees and bayberry shrubs, all green and yellow.

Today, the street was rutted and pockmarked, weeds growing amid clumps of trash.

"It's okay," Hazel said. "We're just looking at the land. For Mr. Kennedy's estate."

Leon raised a hand up to his mouth in surprise. Another shared evolutionary tell, humans stifling surprise the same way at a warehouse in New Haven as a cave in Rawalpindi.

"Oh, no," Hazel said, "you hadn't heard the news?"

"No," Leon said with real concern in his voice. "Something wrong with Mr. Kennedy? He sick or something?"

"He's met his transition," Ingrid said.

"Oh, *that's so sad*," Leon said. "You family or friends or lawyers or something?"

"Cousins," Ingrid added, "down from Hartford."

"Where'd it happen?"

"Dubai," Hazel said. "Heart attack."

Leon covered his mouth again, shook his head. "Poor guy. He was such a nice man." He took another look at Hazel. "Do we know each other?"

"No," Hazel said. She stared directly into his eyes. Not hiding at all. She let him see her, completely. It was all she could do not to reveal her teeth.

"You look so familiar to me," he said.

"People tell me I have that kind of face."

"I been working for Mr. Kennedy for coming on five years now. Never met any of his family before. Now I get to meet three of his cousins in the last few weeks."

"Our family is very spread out," Ingrid said, jumping in. "Who was it that you met? Amy from Virginia? Short brown hair?"

Leon leaned forward, like he was about to tell a secret. "It was a month ago. You know, the one from the TV. The famous one. Mr. Conspiracy. Surprised the hell out of me when he showed up."

Hazel felt the hair on the back of her neck stand up. She knew she was about to see the monster under the bed all right, and it was going to be a monster she recognized. For her dad to be here, to be meeting with Kennedy and Nixon—here was the final proof that her father was being blackmailed and eventually took revenge.

"You met my father, Jack Nash?" she asked.

"No," Leon said. "The other one."

Other one?

"The younger one. Used to call him Scrappy-Doo," the guard said. "What's his name? Skipper?"

Hazel shook her head, her throat collapsing. All this time, she thought they were blackmailing her father. But what Kennedy and Nixon found…It wasn't a dark secret about her dad. It was a secret about—

"Skip," Hazel said.

"That's him! That's who was here. *Skip.*"

84

Sirte, Libya
1983

Tariq and Jack step into the back bedroom.
There's a boy, maybe four years old, with a tube in his nose, IVs pumping into both arms. He is covered in giant open sores, his face almost unrecognizable as a face, his scalp bare, divots in his skin so deep Jack worries he'll see bone. The skin on the boy's legs and arms is cratered, and a yellow fluid leaks out of the sores, staining the gauze taped around his joints.

Jack can't tell if he's been burned or shot or something worse, though Jack can't imagine what could be worse.

"What happened?" Jack asks.

"Viral infection of some kind," Tariq says. "His sister is already lost."

Jack nods, tries to work out the logistics. Tariq has had a few wives. None of them is the woman crying outside. But this child is clearly his.

"Your government says he can be helped at the CDC. They can start treatment for whatever is devouring him."

"We'll do our best," Jack says, well aware of the rub. To save his son, Tariq gets access to the best medicine in the world. In return, the next time Gaddafi plans to hijack an American plane or bomb another of our buildings, we'll have a heads-up, save hundreds of lives. Maybe even thousands. With the right information, we could maybe even stop a war. Just like Washington did with Benedict Arnold. Just like Jack tried to do with every other young "page" in Arnold's bible in all those other countries.

Everybody wins.

But all Jack is thinking right now is that he needs to get Skip away from this building, away from this country, immediately. Everyone nearby should be wearing hazmat suits. What if it's airborne? These masks won't do anything. Except, of course, no one in the room right now is sick. It's not airborne.

"We need to get him out of here," Jack says. "Bring me Ingrid."

"I do not like her," Tariq says.

"I don't care if you like her."

"She's waiting in the helicopter for you. I entrust my boy to you and you alone, Jack Nash."

The boy's eyes blink open, and Jack can see

him attempting to focus. His sclera are yellow, his pupils tiny dots of black. Whatever is wrong with this boy, it's killing him, quickly. Jack hears the *whoop-whoop-whoop* of a helicopter outside.

"Fine," Jack says, but it's not. Because now he wonders if Ingrid really is in that copter. Wonders what he'll tell Skip. This whole situation, it's a nightmare. This boy. This boy. He must get this boy out while there's still time to save him.

"What's his name?" Jack asks, unhooking the boy from his IVs, from the oxygen.

"Darim," Tariq says.

Darim's eyes are still open and they dart about the room.

As Jack undoes the last IV, he makes a decision that he hopes he won't regret. He reaches down and scoops Darim up into his arms, cradles him against his chest, holds him like he'd hold his own child. Whatever Darim has, if it's communicable, Jack figures someone in America knows how to stop it. Why else would they make this deal in the first place?

"Let's go!" Jack shouts, rushing from the room. Tariq is right behind him. "Skip, follow me! Let's go!"

Jack gets two steps before he realizes no one's running behind him.

"Skip, c'mon!" Jack growls, but as he turns, he

sees that Skip hasn't moved at all. Tariq's holding him by the arm. "What the hell is going on?"

"We trade. The boy stays," Tariq says.

"What'd you say?" Jack asks.

The guard steps in front of Skip, blocks him from leaving.

"Dad, what's going on?"

"Tariq, he isn't part of this," Jack warns.

"He is. He is a part," Tariq says. "I need to make sure I get my son back."

"Dad...?"

"I'm afraid I don't trust your country to do the right thing," Tariq adds. "You get my 'page'; I get yours."

Jack looks down at the boy in his arms, this boy who clutches onto Jack with tiny fingers, Jack able to feel Darim's jagged nails digging into the skin on his shoulder. "Please don't do this. I give you my word. I'm helping Darim."

"Return my son healed," Tariq says, "and your son will be returned, unharmed. This was the agreed-upon condition."

"Agreed? By who?"

"Your country. Your bosses."

Jack wants to drop Darim now, throw him to the ground. But he can't.

"Daddy, what's happening?" Skip screams. "Don't leave me!"

Jack looks over his own shoulder, looking for Ingrid, for a rescue. No one is there.

Mona's crying now too, and then there's the *whoop-whoop-whoop* of the helicopter just outside the window. *This is madness*, Jack thinks. Madness.

Skip crumbles to the ground, sobbing, and Jack doesn't know what to do. Drop the sick boy? Rush the security guard? Be shot here, in this hallway, beside his son? Jack knows only one thing. He's not leaving his boy.

Jack thinks of the knife on his ankle. He is an adventurer. Adventurers always carry a knife. If he could get to that . . .

"Tariq, let's just talk about this like rational—"

"You leave now!" Tariq roars. "You leave now, or I kill your son!"

Darim goes limp in Jack's arms.

Jack's mind keeps scrambling, searching for more options. There is the knife, yes, but Jack is a performer, an entertainer. He isn't a killer.

"*Dad, don't leave me!*" Skip cries.

"I won't leave you! I'm not leaving you!" he calls back. He means it. He can't even see Skip behind the bodyguard. "Tariq, if you touch my son—!"

"LEAVE NOW!" Tariq screams.

"If you want blood, kill me instead!"

"I will! I'll kill you both!"

"Do it then! Take me instead of him!"

"I shall! Your bosses will—"

"*Huuuk.*"

The guard makes a noise, a cry, like an animal caught in a trap, then drops to one knee, then flat onto his stomach.

The guard's face smacks into the floor with a sickening crack, his nose collapsing, a pool of blood spreading out around his face immediately.

There's a tactical knife sticking into the guard's back. The knife that had been holstered on the guard's hip. Someone grabbed it, used it. Someone behind the guard.

"*Skip . . . ?*" Jack asks.

Mona is screaming. The helicopter is still going *whoop-whoop-whoop.*

Skip's face is covered with blood. It sprayed him after he grabbed the knife off the guard's belt and sunk it in.

"H-He was scaring me," Skip says. "I was scared. He said he'd kill you. That he'd kill us both."

"It's okay," Jack says to his son, still cradling Darim. "Everything is going to be fine. It's make-believe. It's just make-believe. Like what we do on the show. It's not real."

Across from them, Tariq seems frozen in place.

"You hear me, son?" Jack says, looking Skip right in the eyes. "It's not real."

Skip nods.

"Take my son's hand," Jack says to Mona, and she does. "We're leaving. Tariq, I give you my word. We'll be back."

But they won't. Because in three months, Tariq will be dead.

Jack cradles Darim with one hand, tugging Skip and Mona with the other as they all run out of the house. The beating rotors of the Chinook helicopter make it impossible to hear anything. Inside the copter, Ingrid is already buckled in.

Seconds later, they're in the air, Sirte disappearing beneath them. The radio engineer hands Jack a headset.

"Jack, can you hear me?" Moten says through the headset. "We'll get Skip back. I promise. I know you're probably confused, but it's politics— we had to do it this way."

"I *have* him," Jack hisses. "You son of a shit, I have him. We're on our way. *All* of us."

Jack takes off the headset and hands it to the radio engineer, gives him a thumbs-up, because everything is fine, it's just fine. He's Jack Nash, after all, the man who solves the greatest mysteries of our time.

He unbuckles his seat belt and slides in beside Skip.

"He won't tell me what happened," Ingrid says.

"He's covered in blood, Jack. What the hell happened?"

Jack ignores her.

Skip is seven years old. What does Jack remember about being seven? What has he retained? He remembers The Story, and when was he told that? Six? Seven? And there it is, right in his head, a man with a Benedict Arnold bible buried in his chest, and Jack sees The Story for what his own father, Cyrus, the great radio entertainer, intended it to be. A primer, a lesson, for this very moment, his father preparing him.

When Jack was a child and first heard The Story, his dad never told him the solution: that when you're faced with the impossible, it's usually because someone's lying, trying to trick you.

Cyrus forced Jack to figure it out himself, as a way to guide him into the adventurous life he loved so much. Cyrus relished his secret identity and the way he could use his public persona to help solve America's problems, the world's problems.

But when Jack had his own kids, he knew better than his father did. The world had changed. Today, it was more brutal, more dangerous than anything in his father's time. World War II had a clear mission, a clear enemy. In Jack's wars, from the sixties and seventies—with Nixon and Vietnam—clarity was an endangered species. No way would Jack throw his kids into that secret life. He swore it.

Indeed, that was the only reason Jack finally decided to tell Skip The Story—and eventually, the solution—a few years ago. He wanted Skip to know the truth, that it was all a trick. For Skip, The Story was no primer. It was a warning. If Skip ever heard The Story, or anything like it, from anyone, he should know he was being lied to. He should know he should walk away.

For that reason, Jack always made sure that Skip's involvement with the show was pure show business. Sure, Skip was a ratings boon, but there were limits. For years, Jack kept Skip far away from his secret.

Now, he'd broken that rule, and they were paying for it. They'd be doing so for the rest of their lives. *God, how could I be so stupid?* For years, Jack thought his father was the naïve one. But it was Jack who was the fool—for thinking he could bring Skip so close to the sidelines and not expect him to wind up on the field.

Right there, Jack swore that Skip would never be on another episode. That was another lie.

"Nicholas," Jack says to Skip, and decides he'll never use that name again, will forbid anyone to utter it. "That was fun, wasn't it? That even looked real. But it wasn't. None of this is."

"It isn't?" Skip says.

"All make-believe," Jack says. He licks his thumb and wipes a speck of blood from Skip's cheek. *His clothes*, Jack thinks, *we'll need to burn them.* "Where did you learn that trick with the knife? How did you know how to do that?"

"Am I in trouble?"

"No, no," Jack says, knowing that the real trouble is just beginning. Jack will be looking over his shoulder for the rest of his life, waiting to see who's coming for his children, coming for him. "You could never be in trouble for make-believe. But tell me, where did you learn that?"

"Mom showed me."

85

That's not— That story's bullshit."

"I wish it were," Ingrid said. They were sitting in the parked car, still staring out at the warehouse. It had a roll-up door that was covered in graffiti and tall enough for an eighteen-wheeler to unload cargo. A simple padlock made it look like there was nothing of value inside, but the row of cameras Hazel spied along the roofline seemed to indicate the opposite.

"It can't be," Hazel insisted. She looked over her shoulder. Leon was back in his shed. No one else was around. "If Skip did that, I'd know about it. It didn't happen. It couldn't happen." Even for Skip to be here a few weeks back, it had to be chance.

But as Hazel Nash knew from her studies in her former life, chance was rarely so easily quantifiable.

It was what had turned her to anthropology in

the first place, what had made her focus her study on the rituals of death and dying. Around the world, entire cultures had developed similar rituals without ever knowing of each other—like the Chinese and Egyptians, who, despite a 6,000-mile gulf of land and water between them, adorned tombs nearly the same way. They even adopted similar views of the afterlife.

Was that coincidence? Or was humanity learning to build coping mechanisms at the same time, the human brain expanding to combat sorrow and longing and confusion, the 150 million people on the planet slowly grasping the same ideas at the same time?

Her brother being in that room in Libya all those years ago, then so recently in Arthur Kennedy's warehouse? That was not simple chance, that was no sudden collective dawning.

That was intention.

As Butchie said, Nixon and Kennedy had been looking for each other. But Skip had been looking too.

"Polosis 5," Ingrid said. "That was the drug they think killed your father, yes?"

"How'd you know?"

"If anything, the Polosis 5 was keeping your father alive." Ingrid reached into the glove compartment, pulled out a bottle of pills, no label on it. "I'm not supposed to bring these inside the hospital," she said, "because Polosis 5 isn't exactly FDA approved." She flipped the top off the bottle, shook a pill out into her mouth, swallowed it dry, then tossed the pill bottle into her purse. "I've been taking it for over thirty years. I imagine your father was too."

"What's it do?"

"In small doses, it counteracts the infectious disease we were exposed to," Ingrid said.

"In Libya."

Ingrid sighed. "You were always the smart one."

"So all this time, it wasn't my father who was being blackmailed, wasn't my father who lured Nixon up to Canada. You think it was Skip. Skip, protecting the one secret that could destroy his life."

"Destroy *all* your lives. If the world heard what your brother did—"

"Skip acted in self-defense!"

"Is that what you think the press would say? You think they'd judge Skip fairly—or would they call him a sociopath? Your father did what any father would do. He protected his son. He buried it and made sure no one heard a word. Think, Hazel. Think what the press would do with that story today. You'd all be destroyed, including your father. Perhaps this is no different than what we did in

Russia, Belfast, and even in Libya, when we rescued those children, the so-called 'pages' in the bible. Something for the greater good."

"This isn't the greater good. Someone died—someone was killed! We're Americans!"

"Then you don't know your history very well," Ingrid said. "If one of Osama bin Laden's top lieutenants had a sick child, and you could help save the child's life in exchange for information that would prevent 9/11, would you walk away from that?"

"You made off-book deals with people trying to kill us. That's . . . that's . . ."

"Treason," Ingrid said.

"Exactly," Hazel said. "That's treason."

"We also saved lives, I can tell you that. Years later, the world watched as the Libyans shot down an American plane. But thanks to the deal we made, there were three other planes, maybe more, that kept flying through the sky." Ingrid's voice was strong, but her hands were starting to shake.

"The ones you brought back here, were they always children?" Hazel asked.

"Sometimes children. A few adults. You're the anthropologist. It shouldn't surprise you that even the worst monsters will go to extraordinary lengths to protect their family."

Hazel looked back at the security shed. Was the

guard still there? She couldn't see from this angle. "So Dad's show, it was all a front? It was just there so you could play secret agent?"

"Hazel, that show fed you. It kept a roof over your head. And the fame it provided your father gave him access to kings, queens, heads of state, and yes, even dictators. Who wouldn't want to have a meal with a worldwide TV star?" She paused. "Even El Chapo let Sean Penn come visit. The great Jack Nash's most precious secret was what he could do once he was invited inside." Hazel again checked the shed. There was still that feeling, of being watched. They needed to get moving.

"Was there ever a bible?" Hazel asked. "An actual bible? Or was that always some ancient code name?"

The old woman made a *tsk*ing sound. "I think so. I hope so. George Washington had to send his messages in some form," she said, taking the tin and rolling paper. Her hands were shaking now, so she dropped them in Hazel's lap. "Be a dear," Ingrid said, "and make me a bit more cancer. No sense putting it off now."

When the cigarette was made, Ingrid lit it, got out of the car, and started limping toward the warehouse.

"Were there others?" Hazel asked, a few steps

behind. "Doing the job, I mean, for the government? Were there others rescuing other children?"

"I don't think they needed anyone else. We were a wretched motley crew."

"My brother wasn't. Not until you dragged him into that hellhole in Libya. Then it turned him into something else."

"You think we wanted that? No one wanted that. But take my word, whatever Skip did to Nixon and Kennedy, they were blackmailers. He did you a favor by murdering them."

Hazel tried to imagine how Skip saw it—more important, how he saw it back then in Libya, what all this looked like to a young boy. What would it *do* to a young boy? And what would it do to him now if the story got out?

"Just keep walking," Ingrid said. When they got to the door, Ingrid took a safety-pin from her purse and within five seconds, the padlock was open. She motioned for Hazel to lift the door. As it rolled up, Ingrid ushered Hazel inside. "Go. Don't look back."

But Hazel couldn't not. She imagined Skip standing where she was standing, imagined him coming to this warehouse owned by Arthur Kennedy. At first, she thought Skip came here because Kennedy found out his greatest secret. But now...was Skip searching for something else?

Hazel stepped inside and looked around. The warehouse was as clean as an operating room. Along the south wall was a Home Depot's worth of tools, each one hung on an individual hook, then shelves of power tools, car batteries, duct tape, plastic tubing, even an engine block.

There were also floor-to-ceiling shelves filled with boxes and wooden crates, complete with a rolling stair-ladder. Hazel was suddenly a little kid at home, sitting between her mother and Skip, watching on TV as the Ark of the Covenant gets stashed away.

In the middle of it all was a car.

Pristine black, the paint so flawless it looked like amethyst. It was old, from the late 1970s, early '80s maybe. Hazel couldn't really tell; cars weren't her thing.

Ingrid let out a little gasp, a sound of honest surprise.

Hazel looked back through the open roll-up door. No sign of Security Leon.

That wasn't a coincidence either. Someone wanted Hazel and Ingrid to be let into this place. Someone wanted them to see the car, the shelves, everything. It was too easy.

"What is this?" Hazel asked.

"A Volga," Ingrid said. She brought the cigarette to her mouth and Hazel could see that her hand was shaking more visibly now, her head had a little tug to the right too, like she wasn't lining everything up.

"It says *Bonra* on the dashboard," Hazel said, peering through the passenger window.

"No," Ingrid said, "that's the Cyrillic alphabet. What they used in the Soviet Union."

There was a noise from outside, by the sidewalk. A man ran by, hood up over his head. His stride was long—six strides and he was gone, around the block. Hazel couldn't see his face, but his body reminded her of something.

When Hazel turned back around, Ingrid was standing in front of the car, her reflection visible in the hood.

"This car," she said to Hazel, and then didn't say anything more for a long time. "I have seen it before."

"When?" Hazel asked.

"With your father."

86

Tell me more about the car," Hazel said.

"I don't know if it's the same car. It must not be," Ingrid said, mesmerized by the Volga. "There are a million cars like this. Of course not. Of course not. But you understand." She tapped her head, lost in some continuum. She took a drag on her cigarette again, then dropped it on the floor, stubbed it out with her toe. Opened the passenger door, sat down, stared out the window, didn't move.

"Ingrid," Hazel said, "I need you to focus."

"We need to torch this place," Ingrid said.

"I'm not burning down this building."

Ingrid opened the glove compartment, pulled out a few papers. The car had been registered to Arthur Kennedy. Not hiding from anyone. Doing everything aboveboard. "Do you have a photo of this Arthur Kennedy?" Ingrid asked.

Hazel took out her phone, pulled up the files she had there, and showed Ingrid the photo on Arthur's driver's license. It was a few years old, but the only other shot she had was of the man decomposing on the streets.

"All this time," Ingrid said quietly, "he was right here. I wish I had known." She expanded the photo. "He never fixed his teeth." She handed the phone back to Hazel. "Look up Dmitry Volkov. See if there is a photo. There is certainly a photo."

Hazel typed *Dmitry Volkov* into Google and thousands of results came up. One of the first was his appearance on Jack's show, when he and Jack injected each other with sodium pentothal, right there on a YouTube video. They were in the Dominican Republic, wearing matching white linen shirts, a breeze working through their hair as they walked along a beach. And then Dmitry is strapped to a chair, just as Hazel had been a few days earlier, and injected.

He answered questions from Jack—*Are you a cosmonaut? Do you know the whereabouts of Jimmy Hoffa?*—then his jaw tipped open, exposing gaps where teeth had been pulled. His eyes fluttered and went white. He was out cold, his body slumped like the dead man—like his son, whom he so closely resembled.

Minus the sun.

Minus the flies.

Minus the bible in his chest.

Dmitry Volkov died in 1986 after a short illness, according to *Pravda*. The caption under the photo of his open casket, translated into English: THE GREAT LION SLEEPS. No surviving children.

"Arthur Kennedy was searching. And he found it," Ingrid said, running her hand along the dash of the car. "His father had a car just like this."

"Is that why, as a boy, Kennedy never got sent back to Russia? The same with Nixon too? Their parents were dead?"

Ingrid nodded. "Their fathers died right after they left, leaving them to grow up in the United States. In Kennedy's case, they probably looked at him to work for the government. Maybe he did, or maybe he was too unstable. He was almost a teenager when we took him. There were a few pages we recruited to our side. In Nixon's case, his mother made the trip with him, but clearly never told him his past. Best to let him forget that awfulness."

"So they didn't even know who they were, didn't know where they were from, did they?" Hazel asked, thinking about her own family tree. And the gaps in it.

Hazel felt someone staring at her back, turned around, and thought she caught a glimpse of her dad standing there. But no. Of course not. There was no one there. Just the street.

Ingrid said something else, but Hazel took off to the other end of the warehouse, where the shelves of boxes and crates were. She opened the first one she saw. Then the next. They were filled with papers.

"Ingrid, these are files. There are files here!" Hazel began to tear open the boxes. Hundreds and hundreds and hundreds of files. She pulled out one. Inside were what looked to be medical records, except they were written in Italian, a language Hazel wasn't exactly fluent in, but she found a few words she recognized: *melanoma...* *infantile...*

There was a body drawing, indicating locations of tumors, two dozen circles across the abdomen of a child. A date: 1999.

She climbed up the stair-ladder. There were boxes already opened on the top shelf, where the ladder rested.

Files from the 1960s, the 1970s.

German, Russian, Eastern European. Here were all the clues that Kennedy figured out. Then he tracked down Nixon, who brought it all to her brother.

Hazel again thought of her family tree. Of her mother, who should've been listed as deceased.

She tore through the box, looking for her mom's maiden name: *Black.*

Nothing.

Looking for a *Claire.*

Nothing.

It wasn't that easy, she recognized.

"What was Kennedy's real name?"

"Anatoli," Ingrid said.

Darren Nixon was Darim Haql. Arthur Kennedy was Anatoli Volkov. In this world she was in, maybe her mother's real name wasn't actually Claire or Black.

She'd need to go through every one of these boxes, examine each paper, attack this problem like the anthropologist she had been. *I am*, Hazel thought. *I am an anthropologist.* Observe. Dig. Collect data. State a hypothesis. Solve it. Determine significance.

I am Hazel-Ann Nash and I am feeling alive.

Hazel came back down the stair-ladder.

Ingrid was still in the Volga, tears running down her face.

"We need to get out of this place," Hazel said. "I need to talk to Skip." And then Hazel was through the roll-up door.

Ingrid, suddenly agile, leapt out of the Volga in a blink, telling Hazel no, telling her come back, telling her she must listen, she must not leave, she must not go to Dubai. But that's not where Hazel was headed just yet.

No, first she wanted to stand in the past.

Here was the sky Benedict Arnold saw: The same sun beat down upon her. *There* was the smell of the sea, buried beneath the exhaust of cars, but the sea is still the sea, the water is the same water. *That* was a blade of grass, pushing up through a crack in the pavement, growing where it shouldn't, because it has grown there for hundreds of years.

Hazel tried to cancel out the sound of traffic. Tried to unsee the retaining wall. Tried to unsee the commuter-train switching station maybe five hundred yards away, and the two men in orange vests doing something on the tracks, one of the men periodically clapping and hooting at the other.

All around was the treason of today. The natural world replaced by screaming machines and men, everything a battle against land or for land. Benedict Arnold a traitor for a speck of dirt.

She closed her eyes. Tried to fill her mind with white noise, so that she just heard her own pulse. The *thump-thump* of her heart.

It was something she used to do in ancient burial grounds and places where trauma had occurred, back when she was still the kind of person who sought those places out.

Her amygdala was ruined, which meant her emotional tuning fork didn't work well anymore. But what persisted was her ability to see the world. The place it was. The place it had been. That's what she was trying to find. A glimpse of what was left, of the residual energy, of what had drawn people to this place. Of what her father had seen. What he felt.

What had brought Skip here, what had happened to him as a boy. It was all she could imagine.

Hazel turned in a slow circle, her arms spread out, let the wind play around her.

Imagined what kind of life Skip had had.

Imagined the secrets he'd kept.

Imagined the shame, the disbelief, the horror.

It was impossible that he'd killed anyone.

Which meant, she now knew, that it was entirely true.

"Tell me something," Hazel said to Ingrid, eyes still closed, though now she more fully understood the desires of those left one step behind, could see them exactly. "What did Benedict Arnold want?"

"The same thing we all want," Ingrid said. "For someone to say they give a damn about us."

"My mother," Hazel said. "Was she part of this?"

Hazel tried to keep herself centered.

Hazel imagined the concentric ripples.

Hazel let time slow down around her.

"Would it change anything?" Ingrid asked.

And then another question hit her.

Why wasn't Ingrid dead?

Why wasn't *I* dead?

So that we would both come here, Hazel thought, and opened her eyes, just in time to see Ingrid scream and for a giant bear of a man to grab the old woman, toss her like a bundle of newspapers onto the pavement, her body skidding across the asphalt back into the warehouse.

A punished grunt escaped from Ingrid.

It was a sound Hazel had heard once before, the last gasp of breath from a dying woman.

Hazel's gaze slid sideways. This bear was now coming for her. Hazel plowed toward him, straight at him, back into the warehouse, the past and the present finally the same thing, as the werewolf was released.

87

Washington, DC

At Reagan National Airport, Rabbit picked up a Starbucks and headed straight for his gate, shoulders wide, letting people see his face. Because Trevor Rabkin wasn't hiding from anyone.

"American Airlines flight 3861 to Hartford is now boarding Zone 1. Zone 1 only," the attendant announced.

For the fourth time in the last ten minutes, he tried Hazel's number. No answer. He tried Moten too. The same. Rabbit had the proof now. Thanks to the files he uncovered at Yale, combined with what Butchie sent, he had all the layers of how Kennedy and Nixon fit together, down to when their blackmail scheme started. He tried Hazel again. Nothing. Better to get to Connecticut and deal with this himself. He was about to shut his phone. Instead, he made a new call. Mallory, his ex-wife, answered.

"What is it, Trev?" she said without a hello.

"Can't I just check in? I wanted to see if everything was okay. If you got the box of toys I sent."

"Yes. Thank you."

"I didn't know if Candace even liked toys anymore," he said, referring to his daughter. "I just figured, well, better to get it to her and let her decide."

"She's four," Mallory said.

"I know, I know," Rabbit said.

"You sound funny. What's wrong?"

An older businessman stepped past him, wearing a suit and a woven straw trilby hat from the 1950s, back when hats had nothing to do with baseball. It looked like something Jack Nash would wear. Or even Moten. Men of a particular taste, men of a particular style.

"I just— Did you ever watch Jack Nash when you were a kid?"

"What, the Bermuda Triangle show? All that?" his ex-wife asked.

"Yeah."

"I remember the one about the Curse of King Tut. That one freaked me out, especially when the exhibit rolled through town. Why?"

"Did you think it was real?"

"Real? No. Of course not."

"Yeah," Rabbit said, "me either." He knew what'd be waiting for him in Connecticut. He had no choice. This was the only way to save Hazel. He started heading for the plane. "Just do me a favor: Tell Candace I love her."

88

New Haven, Connecticut

The first punch Hazel delivered broke The Bear's nose open. It was a right cross, which caught him by surprise. The Bear was expecting a foot stomp followed by an elbow to the gut, the move all humans tend to know.

Instead, she went right for the face, and his nose popped, blood gushing immediately, which is what happens when you've had your nose broken a dozen times over the course of your life. Hit it right, and all of a sudden, you're a bloody mess. The benefit of not having any cartilage there anymore was that The Bear would be fine once the bleeding stopped.

It was an extremely effective tool in a fight, he knew. Maximum show, minimum damage. In The Bear's experience, reasonable people lost the will to fight once they saw blood, provided they weren't intent on killing you or thought you weren't planning on killing them.

As a rule, The Bear tried not to get into fights, because he had a hard time modulating that balance, whether he was being attacked or if he was the attacker. So he had to be methodical, stick to a plan, understand ahead of time what he was and wasn't willing to take, physically.

But still, that punch? It was a fighter's punch.

Muscle memory, The Bear thinks. *Nice.* He had worried that that part of Hazel was gone.

He turns his head and leans into Hazel's second punch, this one connecting with the left side of his head, under his temple, above his ear, which gives The Bear a nice ringing sensation in his head.

A pretty good shot, The Bear thinks. Hazel is stronger than she looks, though already she's wheezing from the exertion, and Ingrid is rushing toward him, screaming, yelling, so The Bear takes one more punch, this one to his kidney.

This makes him actually gasp—it doesn't matter, if someone hits you in the kidney, it hurts—and then he grabs Hazel and tosses her over his shoulder, like a sack of vegetables, and pins her against his body, squeezing her tightly enough that what wind she has left grunts from her.

He does not wish to hurt her. Again.

He will take her to the ground.

He will let her down lightly.

He will protect her head, her precious head, the place with all of the secrets locked away, let her live, give her the chance to leave, but Ingrid? The Bear knows what Ingrid did so recently. She needs to be dispensed with in short order.

To break Ingrid's neck will take half of a second. And then he'll tell Hazel what to make of her, that she is a killer, that what she is made of is lies.

Of course, he also will need to explain to Hazel that she herself is made of lies and contradictions too. That her past and his past have been a tapestry. That what she holds as anger must be released.

It's an effective plan, well thought out, right up until the moment Hazel bites into the soft part of The Bear's neck, under his ear, and rips open his external jugular, and The Bear collapses on top of her, his entire life running from him, beat...beat...beat.

89

azel Nash tastes copper. The werewolf is pleased.

And then she tastes something that reminds her of veal. And then she realizes she is *tasting* something at all, that there is flesh in her mouth, and blood, and the pressing weight of a human on top of her.

She can feel the blunt corner of a shoulder crushing her throat, bristled hair cutting into her cheek. She can't see anything, can't hear anything, can only feel pain, and the warm soak of blood.

His breath on her neck, rasping.

"Help me," he says, his voice in her ear, barely audible, a whisper, a plea, nothing near a threat. What has she done? "Hazel-Ann. Help me."

And then the body is tipped off her.

"Move," Ingrid says, and Hazel sees that Ingrid

has lifted one side of the man up a few inches, giving Hazel enough room to slide out from under his weight.

Hazel rolls away, and Ingrid dumps The Bear back down. He crawls onto all fours, all threes in this case, since he's clutching his pulsing neck with one of his giant fists. He's smart not to stand, because if he stands, he'll be dead in seconds. He'll be dead in minutes if they don't help him, apply pressure to the neck, call 911, get an ambulance here, which will get the cops here, which will get the press here, which will be the end of everyone.

Hazel knows this man.

His face is older now, getting older by the second, as if he's decomposing right before Hazel's eyes.

She tries to remember the two of them. Tries to recall what pushed them together. Tries to recall the feeling of his hand low on her hip—he's the man in the photo, the one in her apartment, the one from the affair—but all she sees in her mind is a young man, an ornate sapphire bracelet, standing in an alley in Tripoli, in the shadow of the Al-Tell Clock Tower, Karl saying that the bracelet was hers and that he'll tell her all about her father, if she could do a favor for him, though this already felt like a favor that would end with blood.

Tripoli. When was that?

"Help me," Karl-with-a-K rasps, dying on the floor of this warehouse.

With his backpack and running clothes, he looks like a German tourist, which she supposes maybe he is.

Ingrid is beside her again now. She's pulled a hammer from the wall and spins it in her hand. Seven decades on the planet, and she's ready to kill, easily.

Hazel takes Ingrid's hand, removes the hammer from it. "No," she says. "We're not doing that anymore."

"Do you know this man?" Ingrid asks.

He meets Hazel's gaze for just a moment, blinks once, doesn't say a word.

"I do," Hazel says.

"He followed us today," Ingrid says. "I assumed he was sent."

"I don't work for anyone," he says. "I pay a debt."

"A debt is a job," Ingrid said.

"Good God," he says, each word an effort, but then, as he sees Hazel, a thin smile creases his face. Hazel hears his words. The words of a man who loved her. "You look beautiful, my werewolf."

90

Hazel grabs a roll of duct tape from the shelves and steps back over to Karl, stares down at him. He's so weak now he couldn't do anything to her but beg. She rips off a length of tape and wraps it around the gaping wound she's left him with.

"If you have something to confess, do it now," she says quietly.

He falls onto his side, then his back, staring up into the lights. He has maybe a minute before he loses consciousness.

"I have been protecting you," Karl says. "I have always been protecting you."

"By killing Darren Nixon and Arthur Kennedy?"

"By killing everyone." He turns his head, faces her. "And keeping you alive."

And then she is in Beirut and Karl is beside her. And then she is in Tehran. And then, as the memories flood, she is in Johannesburg. Belfast. Moscow. Tracking her father's sins, and those he sinned with: tracking the children, the so-called "pages" of the bible who Jack Nash worked with.

The entire world spills out in her mind, and Karl is beside her, behind her, she is flying through the air strapped to his chest, mountains and sky and water, the world tipping, tipping, spinning, spinning, Karl screaming her name, *Hazel-Ann, Hazel-Ann, Hazel-Ann.* No seat belts anywhere. A tangled parachute line. A jump from 6,000 feet into the Russian wilderness, trying to keep from being detected, finding this man who knew her father—finding The Bear! Now she had a concrete lead on what her father had done—on the children who were snuck out of their homes, leaving their families behind. Orphans. When they left with her father, some of them became orphans. And then the rigging is all wrong, and they're spinning, spinning, spinning.

And then Karl cuts the parachute line and there's nothing, just the cold air biting into her skin, 3,000 feet, 2,000 feet, and then Karl gets the reserve chute to deploy, and he's screaming, *Hazel-Ann, curl!*

And she is arching into him, letting him wrap his body around hers as they plummet into the ground, his body breaking her fall. Hazel thinks he's dead. She's out here on Russia's Ratmanov Island, looking for an old KGB agent who knew her father, with a dead man strapped to her back, thinking how will she ever get back, thinking this is the end, thinking she's not doing this shit anymore. It doesn't matter what her dad did. If her mother were alive right now, she'd be a different person; her dad and Skip wouldn't recognize her. It's time to start just being a professor, not some kind of self-destructive death-seeker. If she ever gets off this island, she's going to get a tattoo, something that tells the story of bad decisions survived and a better life lived.

A permanent scar.

And then Karl is saying, "You need to learn to jump on your own," except it's hard to understand him because he's bitten through his lip and blood is pouring from his mouth.

"All those years ago, as I looked to see what my dad had done, *I* was the one who found *you*. But today...was this for my father?" Hazel asks now. "Did you keep me alive for my father? Or for the government?"

"For you," Karl says.

And then he is gone, just stops, no gasping for breath, no last lunge forward. It is just as if he is unplugged, which is how people die, Hazel knows, when their brain stops first, not the heart.

"Did you know him?" Hazel asks Ingrid.

"No," Ingrid says, looking at his face now. His eyes are open, unlike Arthur Kennedy's. Hazel suspects she is lying. Ingrid may not recognize him specifically, but she knows what he is. "I don't know," Ingrid adds. "I don't know anymore."

"Think," Hazel says. "Somehow this man knew my father. I think he worked with him. I think—" And now Hazel is nodding, old memories flooding forward. Her father didn't just *work* with this bear of a man. Her father saved him. As a child. The Bear was young then, one of the so-called "pages" of the bible, a sick child who Jack Nash came to rescue.

"When I went looking for other pages, he was one of the first I found," Hazel adds, staring at The Bear. "He helped me look for others—to see how many orphans my dad's actions created. I traveled around the world with that man. I was intimate with him, Ingrid. And now I just ripped his throat out. Still, that doesn't explain—" She paused. "How did he know about Kennedy?" Hazel demands, though of course she knows the answer. The same way The Bear would've known about Darren Nixon and the threats of blackmail that Nixon made. The same way he would have been expecting her in Dubai when he dumped Kennedy's body. The same way he would know she was here.

Skip.

Or it could be Louis Moten, a man she's never met, but who's apparently been behind the major actions of her family's life since before she was even born.

"I'm just a crazy old woman," Ingrid says. "I'll probably be found wandering the streets tomorrow. And then they'll take me right back to the hospital. And I will stay there, Hazel, until they send someone else to kill me."

Hazel nods, knowing she's right. The only way to bury the stories of the bible would be to bury all those involved with it. For decades, her father's work was kept secret, but now it was all coming out. Whoever hired The Bear, that's why he was here today. To kill Ingrid. To protect Hazel. And to keep the most damaging secrets of all: family secrets.

"Wash the blood off yourself, and then go," Ingrid says. She thinks for a moment. "Take the Volga, leave it at the airport. I'll retrieve it tonight and dispose of it."

"What are you going to do with the body?"

"I will hide it, and then I will burn down the entire block, like we should have done in the first place, two hundred years ago."

91

The Bear hibernates.

"She's gone," Ingrid says, once the Volga has pulled out of the shop and she's closed the garage door, rolled another cigarette for herself.

The Bear sits up.

Feels his neck.

It's a bad wound. But it's not the kind of wound that kills a man. Ingrid knows that. Hazel would too if her memories were back. But no, Hazel's not who she was. Not yet.

The duct tape has done a nice job. An excellent Band-Aid. He'll need to stitch himself, quickly. He'll do that next, after he takes care of the Ingrid problem. Not that she'll be a problem, he can see, as she pulls a nearby chair, sits down, rubs at her face. The things she has seen. The Bear wonders how she has lived so long. It explains why she's ready for this to end.

There will be a scar. He won't be able to be around people for a while. Which is fine. He prefers the absence of people. And besides, to Hazel, he is already dead.

The Bear opens his backpack, removes the hypodermic. Sets it on the ground, a foot from Ingrid. The woman doesn't move.

"Will it hurt?" Ingrid asks.

"No," The Bear says. "Your heart will just stop. But complications happen, as I think you know."

"I should hurt," Ingrid says. "I deserve to hurt."

"I can arrange that for you." He takes a knife from his backpack, sets it between them. It's long and serrated.

Ingrid takes one last puff of her cigarette, then extinguishes it on the palm of her hand, not even wincing. "How would you advise me to do it?"

"Through your stomach," The Bear says. "You won't be able to make it through your breastbone to your heart. If you go for your throat, the pain will be too intense for you to continue. This will be painful, but by the time you feel it, it will be over."

"Why have you waited so long to come for me?"

"I needed Hazel to see what she has seen," he says. "I'm sorry it has to be in this place. If you had been home, I would have murdered you there."

"Why now?"

"For what you did. You didn't even tell Hazel, did you?" The Bear asks.

Ingrid stares down at the ash in her hand. "Who told you?"

"It didn't take much. Simple math, really. This puzzle you and Jack built all these years ago, so many of the pieces were tucked away, forever hidden. Even with the best resources, no one could ever prove anything. But then Arthur Kennedy comes looking, and in only a few weeks, this modest man—who lives so close nearby—suddenly puts all of it together. Such good fortune, don't you think? A minor miracle, really. That is, unless he had some help."

Ingrid shook her head.

"Please don't insult me by denying it," The Bear says. "Kennedy came to see you, didn't he? He came to see you, and you filled him in, pointing him in the right places."

Ingrid still didn't answer.

"What makes no sense to me is: Why? After all these years of silence, why open your mouth?"

Ingrid looks up, looks The Bear straight in the eyes. "We need to answer for what we did."

Now The Bear was the one shaking his head. "You have regrets now, don't you?" he asks.

"Could you let me go? Would anyone even know?"

"I would know," he says. "And then eventually, they would come for me."

"Moten wouldn't have the guts."

"Who?" The Bear asks.

A smile crawls across Ingrid's face. For once, The Bear is confused.

"Agent Moten? Louis Moten? You aren't working for him?"

"No," The Bear says.

"Then who?" Ingrid asks. "Who sent you to do all this, to come after me?"

"I told you, I pay a debt. To interested parties," he says, though he knows now exactly who that party is, that has been made clear, "who would prefer their arrangements remain quiet."

"People like yourself?"

"Like myself, yes."

"Are your parents still alive?" Ingrid asks.

"In a way," he says. His father is driving a taxi now in Bugojno, with a new face, a new name. His mother is long dead, he hopes. Yugoslavia is long gone. Another war to replace it, make it worse. He has not been back to the Balkans. His father would not leave, and anyway, he'd spent half his life tasked with the business of watching, waiting, taking care of these problems with Benedict Arnold's bible.

Some of the so-called "pages"—the ones who

lived here—were recruited by the government, not even knowing why they'd been embraced and promoted. The best kind of sleeper agents were the ones who had no idea they were sleepers, with familial and foreign ties that could one day be exploited. Other pages—the older ones, especially the teenagers, like The Bear when he was rescued—made their own deals, trading favors for a prosperous American life. All these secrets needed to be kept.

Still, every few years, usually when someone died, a few details would leak out. Children would begin to search; parents would make deathbed confessions. That's how Kennedy knew to start digging into his own past; someone sent him an old letter from his father. Whenever it happened, the leaks had to be stopped. This was The Bear's job. This was the price of The Bear's life, the deal he made as one of the first "pages." Another favor given. Another leak plugged.

"When you were younger, what was your affliction?" Ingrid asks.

"Brain tumor," The Bear says. "Benign, it turns out. But I would be dead nevertheless. So I am told."

"What did we get in return?"

"I wasn't privy to that information," The Bear says, "as I was fourteen and dying."

"Insignificant now, I suppose," Ingrid says. "Though know: What we were back then, we aren't like that anymore."

"Nevertheless," The Bear says, "there will always be someone who wants to keep these secrets." He shrugs. "My check has cleared. I do this job. I stay quiet. It is through."

"They could never get you."

"Not now, no," he says. "But one day, I will be your age, and it will be easier. As you can see."

"I made you," Ingrid says. "Twenty years ago, we'd be on different sides of this."

"Twenty years ago," The Bear says, "I would have tortured you for a week before I let you die. Appreciate that I have evolved." He pushes the knife toward her. "Insert it at your belly button and then pull up toward your sternum, if you can."

She stares at the knife for a long time, not picking it up. "When Hazel found you all those years ago, when she went looking for the other children we had 'saved,' that wasn't just good fortune, was it? You found *her*, didn't you?"

For once, The Bear doesn't answer.

"Back then, if you wanted to keep this all quiet, you should've killed her," Ingrid says.

"I almost did."

"But you fell in love with her. Those months you spent together, she thought you were helping her find Jack's secrets. But instead, you were pretending, weren't you? All that time you spent together, traveling the world, you were keeping her off track, trying to keep her from uncovering her dad's sins, from finding all the 'pages' in the bible, including your own page."

"She knew who I was. She knew who her dad was too, though she couldn't prove it back then. It was a hunch for her. A mystery. She said she wanted to help those other children—the other 'pages'—find the truth about their lives. The anthropologist in her saw the one thing we all have in common. That all parents lie to their children."

"All lovers lie to each other too," Ingrid says. "So in that time together, even as you kept her from finding everything we had done, you longed for her."

Again, The Bear doesn't reply.

"I loved him, you know," she adds. "Jack."

"Then you will see him again."

"Do you believe that?"

"I believe that you do," he says. "If you can, do it now. While you have that good thought in your mind. It will ease your passage."

"I can," she says, and takes the knife, gives one deep breath, and then does the job, as she's been trained to do.

It takes Ingrid five minutes to bleed to death

BRAD MELTZER AND TOD GOLDBERG

from the wound, her eyes open the entire time, but she doesn't say another word, doesn't make another noise.

Before he leaves, The Bear—who thinks he might start calling himself Karl again—drops a single chewed straw on the ground next to Ingrid's body, as he was directed.

A sprinkling of Skip Nash's hair, one of his fingernails. It will be more than enough, combined with the straw he left at Ingrid's.

The Bear ponders whether he should kill Ingrid's neighbors.

He puts his hood up, pushes through the back door of the warehouse, inhales, and catches a hint of the Atlantic on the breeze. He thinks maybe he'll find a boat, sail the old spice routes. He relaxes for just a single second, realizes that the next portion of his life is in front of him, and it could be a fine life. He would be rich soon enough, yes, his life could be rich from here on out.

He still won't let the neighbors live.

92

Hazel leaves the Volga idling at the valet station of her hotel, telling the kid who's dressed like a carriage driver to keep it running, that she'll be right back down, that she has a flight to catch and the car is unpredictable, which it is, having stalled on her twice on her way back from Kennedy's warehouse.

She's also worried about her bloody shoes in the backseat. If the valet sees them and there are problems, she doesn't trust this werewolf, isn't sure when it will show up. She has already killed a bear today.

She sprints barefoot through the hotel lobby, up the stairs and down the hall to her room, where she slides her card key into the lock. It lights up green, and she's in.

The door closes behind her, and she allows

herself to breathe, to think, to figure out what her next move is.

Fly to Dubai.

Find Skip.

Tell him it'll be okay, even if it won't.

Tell him she would have done the same thing.

Tell him that she has killed people she doesn't even remember killing.

Tell him that some people deserve to die. Some deaths are good. That you honor the people who love you by protecting them, that if she learned anything looking for Benedict Arnold's bible, it's that, in the end, even her father's treason was to help someone.

Let him sort things out with Agent Rabkin. Maybe there's a way to pretend everything is make-believe again. Maybe Skip promises to stay quiet, promises to keep the government's secret, promises never to go on TV again, never, never, never.

Except, no, Hazel suddenly sees she's in the wrong room, that an error has been made, because there's a woman in her bed: bald, blankets pulled to her neck, oxygen running into her nose, a portable tank next to the bed, eyes closed, skin so pallid it's practically translucent. Hazel thinks that somehow her mother has come back, that she didn't really die, that she's been moved here all along, waiting for Hazel to save her life.

"I'm sorry," Hazel says, starts to back out, not even really thinking now, not even really aware, because who is she talking to?

No, this must be the wrong room, except there's her suitcase in the corner. Stacks of her papers are on the desk—the family trees, the episodes, her random thoughts whittled into her own shorthand.

There is also a bag, with the logo of the Al Qasr hotel on it, sitting on the dresser. A bottle of rum. A bottle of gin. A bucket of ice. A pair of men's loafers.

Hazel looks to her right, sees that the connector to the room next door is open, and standing in the entry is a man, late sixties, in a wrinkled linen suit. A TV plays in the other room.

"Have a seat, Hazel," the man says, points her to the sofa in the corner. "Have a drink with me." He has a subtle twang in his voice, as if he's been slowly cured of being Texan. He also has a gun in his hand—a nine—silencer on the barrel, held gently, not like he's prepared to use it, just like he wants Hazel to take notice of it, though the silencer makes Hazel think that's not exactly right.

"Who are you?" Hazel says.

"Come on, now," Louis Moten says. "You know who I am."

93

I f you were going to shoot me," Hazel says, "you
should go ahead and do it."

Moten regards the gun in his hand like he's
surprised it's there. "Didn't know who was coming
through the door," Moten says, "you or your
brother."

"My brother is off looking for Benedict Arnold's
bible."

"I think we can be honest with each other,"
Moten says. "He's found it." He goes over to the
dresser, pours two inches of rum in a glass, sets it
on the coffee table in front of Hazel, pours three
inches for himself.

"I don't drink," Hazel says.

"Yes you do," Moten says. "You drink, you smoke,
you hunt and track people who might know what
your dad was up to. Maybe even kill one if they
threaten to come after your father. Every now and

then, you dust off some relic and talk smart about it. Even now. You're the werewolf, aren't you?"

He downs his glass. When Hazel doesn't pick hers up, he says, "Suit yourself," and swallows that one too. The reek of alcohol off Moten is palpable, but he doesn't seem drunk.

"I know what my brother did in Libya," Hazel says. "I know what Arthur Kennedy found, and what he brought to Darren Nixon. I know they were blackmailing my dad and Skip—and I know everything Ingrid Ludlow knows. So don't threaten me."

"Ingrid Ludlow is going to be in a padded cell for the rest of her life," Moten says. "Keep that in mind."

"I know what you did all those years ago. I know the bible is just a code name for those sick kids. I know about all the deals you made with our enemies. You saved their sick children, but only if they gave you information. And to keep it all quiet, you grew at least one of them—The Bear—into your own personal assassin."

"I'm just a bureaucrat. Those decisions were above me."

"Bullshit," Hazel says. "In those countries, that's what I was searching for, wasn't it? Did Skip tell me, or did I find it myself? Either way, I realized there was something behind the TV show...I found my dad's old missions. That's what I was looking for."

"Personally, I thought you were looking for ways to kill yourself. But wait until you find out what you've left behind."

"I've left myself behind. I don't worry about that person anymore."

Moten pours himself another inch of rum. Stands at the foot of the bed, touches his wife's foot. She doesn't move. "I've got one last mission if you're interested. Y'know, the family business."

"We're out of that business."

"Skip had two men killed. So don't tell me the shop is closed."

"My brother didn't touch those men."

"No, he hired a monster to do his work. Bringing The Bear in, that's still Skip's doing. You get that, darling, right? Truth comes out, Skip'll be lucky to live through the night. He doesn't know who he's in bed with."

"Skip doesn't need to worry about that monster. I took care of that problem for him."

Moten registers something that looks like honest surprise. "When was that?"

"I can still taste his blood in my mouth."

"Just like your mother," Moten says.

Hazel knows it's bait, something to get her off-track. "I also know about the Polosis 5. No one poisoned my father, did they?" she says. "Just like no one put bibles in Nixon's or Kennedy's chests."

A small grin lights Moten's face.

"That's where you saw an opening, didn't you?" Hazel asked. "Skip hires The Bear, who does the dirty work, but since Nixon and Kennedy were under your watch, now you've got your own opportunity. Once Nixon's dead, you step in and dress him up in that old red coat."

"You've truly got a terrific imagination."

"Don't treat me like my brother. There's a reason why their deaths never made the news, and why Dubai didn't let word get out. It's because you were keeping it quiet; you jumped in and shut Nixon's crime scene down, quickly dressing him up in a Revolutionary coat. Did you steal that coat from my father's house? You knew what that would do. You knew who would come running."

"You."

"And I did. It was the perfect bread crumb, wasn't it—the one way to bring me in and make sure I got involved. Even when Rabbit came to the hospital: You gave him just enough to ensure I'd come sniffing. The only thing I can't figure out is why?"

"And now I'm supposed to reveal it all to you? Grow the hell up, Hazel. When you were a child, your father told you that story for a reason."

"You know nothing about my father. He told me that story so I would leave this life!"

"And did you leave it? Or did you go hunting to see what your dad was up to? Look around, Hazel. Did you walk away from your father's world, or are you standing here with me right now? Whatever timid and safe life your father hoped to scare you into by telling you that story, the story is still a primer. Just as it was when Cyrus told it to your father—and when your father told it to Skip and you, even if he tried to convince himself otherwise. So let me share my own personal belief. If your father was forced to choose, he wasn't letting the family business go to your brother. And neither was I."

"What're you talking about?" Hazel asks.

Moten moves around the bed, rests his hand on his wife's cheek. She stirs. Good. Hazel was worried she was already dead.

"The doctors are done. They won't do anything else for her," Moten says.

"I'm sorry for that." Hazel means those words. It's a memory that will never leave her. She's seen this before, her mother there one day, gone the next.

"You don't have to be," Moten says, staring down at his wife. "There's a treatment being done in North Korea," he explains, and Hazel can hear the utter delusion in his voice, can see that the world is cracking around this man, that Jack's death was just one of many dominos falling at once.

Moten tries to straighten up, and Hazel sees a glimmer of the man he used to be, not this cooked-down version before her. "There is a Gulfstream cleared for international travel in San Francisco. Your friend Butchie can fly you. The North Koreans are excited to have Jack Nash's daughter in their country."

"Do you hear yourself? Your wife is going to die."

"We're all going to die," Moten says. "Take your brother to North Korea. I'm sure he'll be happy to join you on this mission. Keep all of this mess quiet."

It was insane. It had always been insane.

"You dressed that corpse up, you made it happen," Hazel says. "And for what? For this? To keep the program going? To pull one last mission and get your wife treatment? She doesn't want to die in North Korea. Or in this shitty hotel. Let her go. Let everyone go."

"Your father was an opportunist. You'd be smart to learn that. Make the best of a bad situation, darling. Save a life. Maybe four. Maybe even your brother's."

"My name isn't darling," Hazel says. "You call me that one more time, I'm going to break your neck, starting with the little bones first."

Moten smiles. "That's the girl I want working for me. That's the girl who's going to watch my Elizabeth."

"Or what?" Hazel says. "You'll shoot me in front of your wife? Then where would you be?"

Hazel hears the click of the door lock a second before the door opens, enough time to see Rabbit as he enters the hotel room.

Hazel expects Rabbit to pull out his gun, but he just stands there for a moment, staring, like he's trying to make sense of the situation: Hazel at the foot of the bed, Moten on the side of it, Elizabeth between them.

"Sir?" Rabbit asks, barely even getting out the single syllable.

Moten says nothing. He raises his arm, points the gun at Rabbit, and pulls the trigger.

Then Moten turns the gun at Hazel. And fires again.

94

Rabbit's blood sprays the wall, but he doesn't scream. Doesn't even make a noise. He holds his chest, his arm...he's bent over. Hazel can't see where he's hit.

Moten's gun is sliding toward Hazel. His finger squeezes the trigger.

Hazel sees herself moving before she's even in motion.

She pounces toward Moten, sees the barrel of the gun train on her face.

Behind her, she hears a thud as Rabbit crashes backward into the wall.

Moten pulls the trigger. Hazel hears a *click*.

She grabs Moten's forearm, slams the gun up toward his face just as he fires, under his chin.

The slug passes straight up through Moten's chin, and then out the back of his head.

The bullet ricochets, burrowing into the back

wall, missing Hazel's own head by a fraction of an inch as she feels its burst.

She drops Moten's arm, and he slumps like a hand puppet, collapses across the bed, then onto the floor. His wife doesn't move an inch.

Rabbit is across the room in a second, his shoulder bleeding as he pulls Hazel away.

"Hazel, don't touch him!" Rabbit screams, though she can't hear anything he's saying.

He's still yelling, holding Hazel back with his good arm, screaming at her to stay clear. It's the hole in Rabbit's shoulder that finally makes her take a breath. There's barely any blood. Just a black burn mark near his collarbone. If Rabbit's in pain, he still doesn't know it.

"You're hit," she tells him.

Rabbit grips his clavicle like he's swatting a mosquito. Still in motion, he kicks the gun away from Moten's body.

Without a word, he flips Moten over onto his back, starts to apply pressure, mouth-to-mouth, but it's useless. Hazel knows, because she's seen this before too.

"He's dead," Hazel says. There's a hole in the wall where the slug is buried, the wallpaper scorched. "And I should be too. I should be dead."

"You need to get out of here," Rabbit says, now tending to his own wound. He pulls off his tie, twisting it into a quick figure eight, sliding it on like a backpack, to immobilize his broken clavicle.

"Where?"

"You have a plane ticket to Dubai. Use it."

A low moan comes from Moten's wife.

"We need to help this woman," Hazel says. "You can't just leave her here. Plus your shoulder..."

Rabbit dials 911.

"I found Benedict Arnold's bible," Hazel says.

"I don't want to know," Rabbit says, sliding his other arm into the figure eight and pulling tight to straighten his shoulder. "Don't tell me a single thing. Nothing more." His hands are covered in Moten's blood, in his own blood too.

"I ripped out a man's jugular today. And Trevor? The sickening part? I think I used to enjoy it."

"Hazel, whoever you used to be, whatever you've done, that doesn't matter anymore. Okay? Benedict Arnold dies here, like he should've two hundred years ago." There's another moan from Moten's wife. "We need to get this woman to a hospital, so she can die in peace."

"What do we do about Skip?"

"I'm going to guess he's in the wind, Hazel. He knows what he's done. I think you'll be lucky to ever see him again."

Right, Hazel thinks. *I'm so lucky.*

95

Hazel waits until she's finally over international waters—after sitting on the tarmac in New Haven for hours, then being delayed out of New York too—before she digs into her carry-on and pulls out the bag from the Al Qasr that had been left in her room.

Rabbit hadn't seen it, maybe he didn't want to see it, not with Moten's corpse on the floor. She'd been expecting someone to haul her off the flight since the moment she boarded, spent the hours on the tarmac constantly peering out the window, waiting for a tactical team to rush the plane, which would have been a problem, because she wouldn't go quietly. She knows that now.

Complicating matters is that she's in the last row of a 747, the middle seat, jammed between a teenage boy with giant headphones, and a sweating cowboy, white hat and all, who keeps adjusting the AC, not that it ever gets cool.

She puts the bag on her lap, looks inside. There's a folded piece of white paper, her name written on it. She opens it: *Something for your trip —Karl.*

He knew I'd be coming back alone, Hazel thinks.

Inside the bag, there are handfuls of Smarties, Nestlé Crunch bars, and Peanut Butter Cups… and then two ziplock bags, one containing a few clumps of hair, another holding what appeared to be nail clippings, along with a short note written in cursive. Hazel thinks no one writes in cursive anymore, but here she can see the pressure of Karl's hand, feels it on her hip, tries to line up her past with him, tries to figure out how this all happened, how what happened years ago brought her to this very moment. The note says: *All the evidence you'll ever need. All is history.*

Such a precise orchestration, but it still makes no sense. Why would Skip hire someone to frame himself?

A flight attendant comes down the aisle, a piece of paper squeezed between her fingers. She's staring directly at Hazel. Here it comes. She should have packed a parachute. Except, she thinks, it might be hard to find land in the middle of the Atlantic.

"Ma'am?" the attendant says, and Hazel can tell right away that she has that weird tic where every sentence she utters sounds like a question. "I'm sorry? But a gentleman in first class wanted me to give this to you? Is that okay?"

Hazel cranes her head up, but all she sees are the backs of several hundred heads and the darkened cabin lit by the blue glow of their laptops and iPads. She smiles at the attendant and takes the note.

COME TO THE FRONT OF THE CABIN, HAZE. YOU'VE BEEN UPGRADED.

Hazel practically climbs over the teenager, not bothering to wait for him to move. Still, she moves slowly through the cabin with her head down, until she's through the curtains into first class.

There, sitting next to the window, cloaked in the half-light cast by the bulb above him, is her brother.

96

Skip's hair is dyed black and combed forward, so he has bangs.

He's got a growth of beard and is wearing transition glasses, the kind that turn orange, so his eyes look almost alien. With a blue sport coat, red tie, and gray slacks, he looks like a small-town weatherman.

Hazel sits down beside him, tries to collect herself. There are only two other people sitting in first class, both asleep.

"I'm sorry," Skip says. "I told you not to go to Spokane."

"You did," Hazel says. "I didn't listen."

"I knew you'd make it out."

"I didn't know I'd make it out," Hazel says. Skip smiles, but there's not much there, not the luminosity she's used to. "Skip," she starts to say, but he raises a finger to stop her.

"No. Not that name anymore."

"Nicholas," Hazel says, and he nods, "you could have told me. About Libya. You could've told me later, when I was old enough to help you."

"I didn't want to know what was real," he says. "And by the time I figured it out—what I had done that day...what Dad continued doing, helping sick children in exchange for inside information on our enemies—it was too late. They were coming for us. Sure, Kennedy just wanted to know his own past. But once he found Nixon, that was the end. Nixon was a thug, a complete vengeful ghoul. With that crap life he had, when he heard what I did in Libya, all he saw were dollar signs. And he roped Kennedy in too. They started writing me these crazy letters. I thought I could handle it myself, even met with Nixon out in his conspiracy shed. You should've heard what they wanted, the threats they made. They said they'd tell the world I was a killer. I had no choice but to get Dad involved. Everything I did, I did to protect you. To protect us. Our family. They would've ruined us."

"You should've let them," Hazel says. "You'd be in the same position you are right now."

"That's what you'll never understand. You were—" He leans close to Hazel. "You weren't the one on TV. My entire life, all I've ever wanted was to go unnoticed. To disappear. But there was always someone coming, Hazel. I could feel them coming. So if I stayed up all night in a club or a casino, always on camera? No one would come for me, not anyone smart."

Hazel nods once. "Karl was smart."

"Not so smart that he knew who he was working for," Skip says.

"I still don't understand how you could hire him."

Skip smiles at her, something approaching his old smile. "Me? I didn't hire him," Skip says.

"But Moten said—"

"I didn't hire him," Skip says.

Hazel cocks her head. "But if *you* didn't—"

Skip shoots her a look. It's a look she knows. One she's seen before, somewhere. The one thing that every brother and sister share.

Dad? Hazel asks with just a glance.

Skip nods. The one who always fixed their problems, and created them too, even from beyond the grave. Dad.

"He hired Karl to protect us," Skip says. "It's like when we were little. He told us the story with the bible to protect us too. I think he was trying to prepare us for this life."

"No, that's what you always had wrong. However Dad got into this, or even Grandpa got into it with his old radio show, Dad wanted to break the pattern for us. The story was a warning. The only thing he was preparing us for was to walk away and leave this life behind."

"Dad could tell himself whatever he wanted. He knew who we were. Each of us. You got something to leave this life, but I took it as something different."

Hazel considers that, and what Moten had said. Had she really left this life behind? With her brain kicked sideways, those memories were gone. "Tell me the truth . . . These past few years," she finally says, "did I walk away from Dad's world? Or were we both secretly working on the show and its missions?"

"*We?* After what happened in Libya, Dad wouldn't let me near any of those missions, though that didn't stop him from keeping me on the show. And you . . . ? You wouldn't come near the show. Not ever. You hated that life. Dad taught you to run far away from it, and you did. But even so, you found your own danger. There was Butchie and his shipping business. And then, somewhere along the way, you started getting suspicious of the show. You knew Dad was up to something bad. That's what started you searching."

"But what made me so suspicious? Did Moten ever show up and make either of us an offer?"

"Not me, though who knows with you. Either way, deep down, Dad knew what the future held. If

Moten tried to rope us in like they roped him in—
or if Nixon and Kennedy tried to take us all apart
by going public—" Skip cut himself off. "Dad would
do anything to keep us safe. Even if it meant—to
close all the old loops and shut everyone down—
that he had to bring in a Bear. Once Dad hired Karl,
the Nash family secrets could go back to being secrets, and you and I would always have alibis."

"Well, that at least explains *this*," Hazel says.
She opens her carry-on, takes out the bag from the
Al Qasr, sets it between them. "Karl left that for
me in my hotel room. Before I killed him."

Skip looks inside. "You always liked Peanut Butter Cups," he says, and for an instant, he's her
brother again. He pushes the bag back toward her.
"I think I know what else is in there. I saw The
Bear. In Dubai."

"You spoke to him?"

"Not a chance. Dad insisted on no connection.
Told The Bear to stay far away from both of us."

"Is that why all his killings were in Dubai and
Canada?"

"Nothing that was near us, not even in the same
country. Like I said, alibis."

Hazel nods. "That's the reason you went to
Dubai."

"Now you're seeing it. Better to be far away
while everything was going to craptown here.

Also, I thought The Bear was coming right back to the States, though that changed too. He stayed in Dubai for a reason."

"Do we know that reason?"

"If I'm right, what's in that bag is a gift for me too," Skip explains. "Still, the way he was waiting for you in Dubai, part of me thinks he wanted you out there, back into his world. Ever since you tracked him down all those years ago, you've always been The Bear's favorite."

Hazel thinks about this. "So when Dad hired The Bear to protect us…? Did Dad know how The Bear felt about me?"

"Y'mean, did he know The Bear was in love with you? What do *you* think?"

Hazel had no idea. But the more she rolled it around her head, the more she wondered if there was anything her father *didn't* know.

Skip looks out his window, at the blackness of the Atlantic. "I didn't kill Dad," he adds, "you realize that, right?"

"I do," Hazel says. "So that was the one truth: a heart attack?"

"He was quitting the show, quitting his life. He thought it might make them back off, but let's be honest—if I went down for what I did in Libya, they were taking him down with me. Can you imagine the pressure?"

Hazel can't.

"I told him not to go to Moten. I knew Moten would do something to take advantage."

"It was his wife," Hazel says. "He wanted to get her treatment for her cancer. She was practically dead already."

"Dad would've done the same for Mom," Skip says.

They both stay silent. It was true, Hazel recognizes. Dad would have done anything for her, even if it was beyond reason.

"Y'know," Skip says eventually, "it used to take six weeks to sail from England to America? Took the pilgrims sixty-six days to make landfall. And we'll make it in six hours, if you don't count that time on the tarmac. Time isn't the same anymore. I really believe that."

"Redeeming the time," Hazel says, "because the days are evil."

"From an old book, right?"

Hazel nods.

"I should read more old books," Skip says, not for the first time.

"Is it even real?" Hazel asks. "Benedict Arnold's bible?"

"Have we not been having the same conversation?"

"No," Hazel says. "I mean the actual book that

George Washington sent back. Is it real? Is it out there?"

"Dad thought it was, and he was the expert. So I'm going with yes. Maybe it has something good in it. Wouldn't that be nice?"

"It would be," she says.

The flight attendant comes by and asks Hazel if she'd like some champagne, or some warm nuts, or crostini with a salmon pâté. "All of it," Hazel says. "Bring me all of it."

"Two of everything," Skip says.

"Yes," Hazel says, "make it three."

"I thought you couldn't taste anything," Skip says when the flight attendant walks off.

"I think I had a breakthrough today."

Skip grins, then looks at his watch. "We've got three more hours on this flight, and then when we get to London, I'm leaving you. People might be looking for me by then. I mean really looking for me. So that bag there with my hair and nails?" he says, pointing to the bag with The Bear's final gift. "Hold on to that. Every now and then, I'm going to want you to leave a little evidence. Got it?"

"Got it."

"How's your brain doing?"

"It's pretty mucked up."

"Y'know, in the end, you actually figured out who

killed Kennedy. Get it? *Killed Kennedy?* I mean, even Dad never did that."

"I just remembered," Hazel says, "I never found you funny."

There's the kilowatt smile. There's Skip Nash. The flight attendant drops off the nuts and champagne. Hazel has a thousand questions for her brother, because there are a thousand mysteries left to be solved. Who was their mother? Was she even dead? What other damage did Hazel do? What other jobs were done by their father? What mysteries were real? She needs these answered.

But then she realizes she may never see her brother again, so she says, "Tell me what you remember about my first birthday."

97

Havana, Cuba
1975

Season 1, Pilot Episode (1975): "The Instigator"

Jack Nash should be scared to death, but instead he's excited. Life? It's happening now.

He's twenty-nine years old and he's sitting in a hotel bar in Havana, Cuba, the last place on earth, other than maybe East Berlin or Moscow, where an American should want to be.

Last week, he was in New Haven, Connecticut, with Ingrid Ludlow, and it was, he thought then, the sort of thing he could get used to. His show, *The House of Secrets*, wasn't even on the air yet, but already he had the sense that traveling the world with Ingrid, solving a few mysteries along the way, that was not a bad way to spend his time.

Everything seemed...vivid. Yes. That's what he

thought. Everything in sharp focus—the future, the past, right now, all of it.

His father, Cyrus, he'd done a bit of this sort of thing back in the day, working in the Army Signal Corps and as a journalist covering the odd and the unusual, and then on the radio doing the same, before settling in as the host of the "creature feature" Friday nights on Channel 2 in Portland for the last ten years, always wearing a cape or a smoking jacket or a black turtleneck, always staring off vaguely into some middle distance. And really, that's all Jack had been doing in the tiny local news studio in Burbank these last few years—parroting his father's shtick—until the network decided he'd be better off in the field, seeing the world.

"You know one thing you should take a look at," Cyrus had told him a few months before, at the beach house there in Seaside, where Cyrus spent most of his downtime now, most of his uptime too, "is Benedict Arnold's bible."

"Not that," Jack said. Cyrus had been going on about it for years, the fringe mysticism of the Revolutionary War, one of those things Cyrus could expound upon for hours. It was the sort of thing he read about in those crappy mimeographed books he bought from people in their garages, or through the mail, then he'd sit in the backyard, smoking Pall Malls, drinking boilermakers, underlining passages.

"No? Oh, it's quite a mystery," Cyrus said and told him, again, about the legend behind it: that whoever held it could gain great power, that it showed up in the worst places, that it presaged some of the greatest disasters and stopped even more, moving covertly through the hands of the most powerful people on the planet.

"That part is new," Jack said. "The bit about the world leaders and such."

"No? I never mentioned that before?"

"Somehow you failed to," Jack said. They were sitting outside, it was late afternoon, the Pacific at full roar, a storm somewhere out there sending wave after wave to the beach. "How exactly did this transfer take place?" Jack asked, curious to see what conspiracy his father would cook up, and aware too of the way Cyrus's hands were beginning to shake a little.

"Usually," Cyrus said carefully, using The Voice, the same one he employed to scare small children on TV, "inside dead bodies."

"You don't believe that old story," Jack said. It wasn't a question, but already Jack could see that, oh, yes, his father did indeed believe.

"Of course I do," Cyrus said.

"Okay," Jack said, "devil's advocate—if the bible

is such bad luck, why doesn't someone just burn it? All these years, someone should have had that idea by now."

"It's guarded by some of the fiercest creatures alive," Cyrus said. Jack thought his father sounded like he actually had convinced himself of this absurdity. "You come for Benedict Arnold's bible, be prepared to fight a bear."

"Dad, come on," Jack said. "You sound crazy. Like someone on my show. Worse, like someone on *your* show."

"Crazy," Cyrus said, "or exceptionally observant?" Cyrus smiled then, patted Jack on the leg, and told him he'd see one day. Then he changed the subject to how Sirhan Sirhan was likely a government agent.

And yet, here Jack was, in Cuba, by way of Toronto since he couldn't legally get into the country from the United States. Jack was here scouting locations for their very first show, about how in the weeks before JFK was killed, Lee Harvey Oswald tried to get a visa into Cuba. The irony wasn't lost on Jack.

For any American able to get here, it was truly an opportunity.

Last night, Jack checked into the Santiago, an old hotel on the western edge of the city, and was told he'd be met the next day by an attaché from the Canadian embassy who could guide him through the morass of regulations the Cubans had before he'd be able to film.

What Jack notices, however, is that everyone in this hotel bar, other than the employees, is foreign. Russians. French. Germans. Eastern European. He's the only American.

"You must be the guy I'm looking for."

Jack turns at the sounds of English and finds a heavyset man about his age pulling out the chair next to him, plunking himself down. He's wearing a linen suit, white collared shirt, no tie—it's too damn hot for that—and he's got a thin, light brown, leather valise, stamped with the maple leaf emblem of Canada.

"Louis?" Jack says.

"That's right," Louis Moten says. He extends his hand and Jack sees he's got a class ring from Yale, bulky, a little gaudy, but somehow Moten makes it work. He's maybe twenty-seven, but carries himself like he's older, a kind of weary seen-everything-done-everything air.

"What's an Ivy League man from Canada doing in Cuba?" Jack asks.

"Saving the day, seems like," Moten says, then gives Jack a slap on the shoulder, a little harder than Jack was expecting.

"I appreciate your help," Jack says.

"Not a problem," Moten says. "Always happy to help our little brother to the south." He unzips the valise and hands Jack a stack of documents. "I need you to sign those before we go any further."

Jack glances at the papers. They're thick with legalese, but what Jack thinks he's reading is that if anything bad happens to him, Canada isn't to blame. In fact, no one is to blame. His body will be left behind, because technically, he's not here.

"I don't know," Jack says. "This doesn't seem right."

"SOP," Moten says, and when Jack doesn't respond, he says, "Standard Operating Procedure. You weren't in Vietnam?"

"No," Jack says.

"Deferment?"

"Yeah," Jack says. It's not something he likes to talk about; he's pretty sure his father pulled some big strings. Ropes, most likely.

"Aren't you the fortunate son," Moten says.

There's a hint of twang in his voice. More than a hint of derision too. Something doesn't add up. "You don't sound Canadian," Jack says. "Or look Canadian."

"No? What does a Canadian look like?"

"Less linen," Jack says.

"Father's Texan," Moten says. "Spent my

summers there. I come by it honestly." Then, "You drinking?"

"Not yet," Jack says.

"Let's rectify that." Moten waves at the bartender, shouting, *"Dos cervezas,"* and a few seconds later, a waiter drops off two bottles of beer, ice cold. "One good thing about the Communists," Moten says, "they still like to drink." He takes a pen from his pocket. "Sign the papers, Jack, so we can have a good time, all right? Before you betray your government."

Jack Nash is twenty-nine years old. Life is happening all around him. Ingrid is waiting for him fifteen hundred miles away. He can still taste the salt of her sweat. *What the hell.*

*   *   *

Ninety minutes later, Jack's drunk and he and Moten are fast friends, or at least that's what Jack thinks, his head starting to spin a little. They've moved from beer to rum.

"Let me show you something," Moten says. He again opens his valise, and this time comes out with a black-and-white photo that he hands to Jack. "You recognize that person?"

Jack shakes his head.

"This man is staying in your hotel," Moten says.

"In fact, is sitting right there." Moten gestures to his right, to a table with an older man, blond, blue eyed, maybe fifty, his skin as pale as porcelain. Looks East German. He's sitting with a woman in her twenties, wearing a yellow sundress, maybe his daughter.

"I don't know them," Jack says.

Moten taps his index finger on the rum bottle, nearly empty now, so it makes a *pong-pong-pong* noise. "They're dangerous people."

"I'm just here to do this show, get back on a plane, and go home. I'm not looking for trouble."

"That's a good outlook, Jack," Moten says. "You'll go far in this business." He downs a shot of rum, pours himself another, and one for Jack too.

Jack reaches for the shot, then thinks better of it, not liking the way he can't quite focus. He's not much of a drinker, not like this half-Texan, who doesn't seem even slightly buzzed. Then he downs it anyway, because that's what his father Cyrus would do, and if there's one thing he's learned from his father it's that when you're asked to be a man, be a man.

"Attaboy," Moten says.

Jack feels like the world is tipping, like he's already asleep and this is a dream. "Have I been drugged?"

"Little bit," Moten says.

Jack looks around the bar. Everything in his vision leaves streaks of light when he turns his head, like tracers. LSD? Maybe. Everything seems slower, like he's operating inside of a memory.

"Tell me something, Jack. Do your daddy and you ever talk any shop? He ever tell you about the work he did overseas? During Korea? That ever come up?"

"No," Jack says.

"Good. Then he gets to live. Can't have your father telling stories about my father."

"Wait, our fathers knew each other?"

"Signal Corps. They worked together. My dad gave yours orders, though sometimes it might've been the other way around." Moten finishes off the last inch of rum, waves the empty bottle in the air, shouts, *"Por favor, por favor."*

"You're not Canadian, are you?"

"Today? Yes."

Jack tries to stand up, an uneasy proposition, but Moten grabs him by the wrists, yanks him down hard, keeps hold of him. Jack is aware of the man's strength. This guy is nobody's attaché.

"Calm down, Jack," Moten says, his voice hardly above a whisper. "You don't want to make a scene." He applies subtle pressure to Jack's wrists. "You know what's a bad way to die? Severing your radial artery with your own shattered wrist bones. You don't want that, do you, Jack?" Jack shakes his head. "Now I'm going to let go of you. Let's act like gentlemen, all right? Say 'We're gentlemen,' Jack." He squeezes, and pain shoots into Jack's eyes. A pressure point, Jack knows, but it hardly matters. Pain is pain.

"We're gentlemen," Jack says, and Moten lets go of him just as the waiter comes over and drops off more drinks without even looking in Jack's direction. Jack could be naked and bleeding from the eyes and no one would look at him twice, not in this place.

Except the girl in the sundress, who has angled her chair so that Jack can see her in his peripheral vision. She's watching him with no compunction whatsoever. She is beautiful and, Jack can see now, pregnant. Just a bump, barely showing at all.

"I have a job offer for you," Moten says.

"I have a job already. I'm making a TV show."

"I've got a better job for you. One that'll keep your show on the air longer than you ever anticipated. Longer than even my dad kept your dad's show on the air," Moten says. "You wanna get married, Jack? You see that in your future? Big family, bunch of kids?"

"One day," Jack says, and he's not sure why he's answering so candidly, why everything he says is the truth.

"You think that girl over there is pretty?" Louis nods toward the pregnant woman and the East German man.

"She's beautiful," Jack says.

"You think you could spend your life with her? At least three or four years of it?"

"I don't even know her name," Jack says.

"What's your favorite name?"

"Ingrid."

"Then what's your second favorite?"

"Claire."

"Your lucky day," Moten says. "Her name is Claire."

"She's pregnant."

"With a boy. You can give him a name too. Something strong, like William or Thomas."

"Nicholas."

"Perfect. Like the saint." Moten motions with two fingers, and Jack can hear chairs sliding on hardwood. Then the pregnant woman and the East German man are gone.

Moten pours Jack another shot. "Why don't you have a drink, Jack. We need to talk about your future." He pours himself another shot too. "Let me tell you a story I once heard—I think my father heard it from your father, or maybe it was the other way around," he continues. "It's about a dead body with a bible stuffed inside of it. You'll love it. Big mystery."

Epilogue

Los Angeles
Now

H azel Nash decides, at noon on a Sunday, Los Angeles filled with the smell of pumpkin spice lattes, to try jogging for the first time since her accident. She's living at her father's house in Studio City, a life of quiet avoidance.

The disappearance of her brother captivated people for a month. The press hounded her; Skip hadn't been seen since announcing he was going to bring back the TV show. And then his DNA had been found in Ingrid Ludlow's house, and inside an empty warehouse where Ingrid Ludlow's body had been found, after an apparently gruesome suicide, but then it'd been found at the very same time at a hotel in Dubai, where Skip could be seen on a security camera that same day. Skip was being framed, people insisted. How can someone be in two places at once?

It was . . . a mystery. Possibly a vast, wide-ranging conspiracy.

Or just a well-executed distraction.

Even Anderson Cooper had an opinion, had reason to appear in a tight black shirt outside Jack's house for a day, reporting breathlessly for a few hours, until a plane went plunging into the South China Sea and three hundred missing people became far more interesting than one.

And then there was a fire.

And then there was an earthquake.

And then there was an election. People won. People lost. People were angry.

And then Skip Nash was forgotten, pushed to the back end of the Internet, where Hazel sometimes visited him, just to see photos of him, to see people ranting and raving, to see how close they came to the truth, how close they came to knowing The Story.

Very, very far, it turned out.

Hazel laces up her shoes, puts her earbuds in, straightens her headband to keep her hair from rising up on her neck, keep people from seeing her tattoo. She slides a gun—a .32—into her water pack, thinks about it, decides she'd rather have her nine, and hits the road.

She jogs through the neighborhood, crosses over Ventura Boulevard, picks up Laurel Canyon for a few blocks, then over to Coldwater. She has a good sweat going now, her body feeling good. In no time, she's getting that old high, her mind clearing, though that's not always such a great thing, since her mind doesn't have a whole hell of a lot in it, still.

She decides to keep going up Coldwater. It's only a mile from her father's house and she's feeling strong. Up ahead, she spies a little girl playing hopscotch on the sidewalk, who can't be more than five. Hazel thought kids didn't do that anymore, that there was always something better to do than hopscotch, but no, that's what she was doing.

There's a man sitting on the front steps of the house, watching, and as Hazel gets closer, the man stands up, fully alert, and Hazel recognizes the fluidity of his motions before she recognizes his face.

Agent Rabkin steps out into the street and stands between his daughter and Hazel. She hasn't seen him in months. Not since they both got back from the East Coast, after the debriefing, after she promised to contact them if Skip popped up, after she told them she was going to focus on her studies, finish that book she was working on, and her secrets were her secrets, the FBI didn't need to worry about her, no sir.

But in fact, she'd just retreated to Jack's house,

which had its own mysteries, and tried to keep the old habits at bay. Which had worked.

Mostly.

Butchie, he still needed to make a living, see.

"What're you doing here?" Rabbit asks.

"Jogging," Hazel says.

"Right," Rabbit says.

"Is that your daughter?"

Rabbit looks over his shoulder at the little girl. She's not paying any attention to the two of them. "Yep."

"What's her name?"

"Candace."

"She's adorable."

"She looks like her mother, thankfully," Rabbit says. "I get her three days a week, which is good."

"That is good," Hazel says.

They stand there for a few seconds, not talking, just looking at each other. Hazel can't remember ever seeing Rabbit not in a suit. Here, wearing sweatpants and a V-neck fleece, he doesn't look so much like an FBI agent as he does a guy in a Macy's ad in the Sunday *LA Times*.

"Have you heard from your brother?" Rabbit says, finally. Not in an accusing way. Just in . . . a way.

"Can't say that I have," Hazel says, which is true. "Have you?"

"He was spotted in China. I don't think it's him."

"Daddy," Candace calls, "watch me."

"One sec, baby," Rabbit says.

"You should go," Hazel says. "My dad never watched me play hopscotch and look how I turned out. This is a pivotal time in her development."

"Do you eat?" Rabbit says. "You doing that yet?"

"Sometimes," Hazel says. "Taste sort of comes and goes."

"There's a Thai place in Encino that Candace and I like to go to. Exceptionally spicy. We're going to go there for lunch today. If you're interested."

"Like a date?"

"No," Rabbit says, "like three people eating together."

"Two of whom are superspies," Hazel says, and Rabbit actually laughs.

"Y'know, there's been talk," Rabbit begins, "of bringing the show back. An all-new *House of Secrets*."

"That's a dumb idea. Haven't they milked enough of our nostalgia through every old TV show?"

"Agreed. I hate it. But if they did...y'know, they said I could be sort of an unnamed consultant. Maybe work with the host on some special cases. Doing some good. Some actual good."

Hazel stared at him a moment. "That's an even

dumber idea. Like maybe, without getting into hyperbole, the truly worst idea of all time."

"Right. I said the same," Rabbit says, staring down the block at nothing at all. "By the way, you see that story about Moten?"

"I heard you testified. That you're the one who proved he dressed up the bodies in the red coats."

Rabbit didn't say anything. Until: "So. Pick you up in an hour?"

Hazel tries to think of all the reasons why this might be a bad choice. But her total number of friends stands at one—Butchie—and he's been busy looking for a new dog.

"An hour," Hazel agrees. She starts to run off, makes it all the way down to the Stop sign, when Rabbit calls after her. Hazel thinks, *Good. Smart. A werewolf and a rabbit. We shouldn't be near each other.*

"Hey, Hazel?" He jogs down the street to meet up with her. "Just so we're clear, this is a no-gun lunch. So let's leave the pistol at home, okay?"

Hazel flips her hood up, starts to pedal into her run, slowly, slowly, then faster. "I'm not making any promises."